CONFESSIONS OF A LADY-KILLER

George Stade

CONFESSIONS OF A LADY-KILLER

FREDERICK MULLER LIMITED
LONDON

First published in Great Britain 1980
by Frederick Muller Limited, London, NW2 6LE

British Library Cataloguing in Publication Data
Stade, George
    Confessions of a lady-killer
    I. Title
    823'.9'1F   PS3569.T14/
    ISBN 0-584-31057-9

Printed in Great Britain by Biddles Ltd., Guildford,
Surrey

To Dolly, Eva, Kirsten, Nancy

Both the author of the *Notes* and the *Notes* themselves are, of course, fictitious. Nevertheless, such persons as the author of such memoirs not only may, but must, exist in our society, if we take into consideration the circumstances which led to the formation of our society. It was my intention to bring before our reading public, more conspicuously than is usually done, one of the characters of our recent past. He is one of the representatives of a generation that is still with us. In this extract, entitled *Underground,* this person introduces himself and his views and, as it were, tries to explain those causes which have not only led, but also were bound to lead, to his appearance in our midst.

—Dostoevski, "Note" to *Notes from the Underground*

Hell is other people.

—Jean-Paul Sartre

So is heaven.

—Victor Grant

CONFESSIONS
OF A
LADY-KILLER

I

THE following pages are based upon notes taken during and immediately after the events related; upon a very full diary kept up to date by nightly entries; upon high-fidelity tape recordings; upon documents of various kinds; and, above all, upon a disciplined and retentive memory. Everything that follows, in short, is true in the narrow sense of being factual. Should there, after all, be anything not true in *that* sense, it is true in a higher sense, assuming that there is any such higher sense. Let's leave the question of truth alone for a minute. And let's leave alone any question as to whether or not I have interpreted the evidence correctly. It is *my* evidence, after all.

My name is Victor Grant. I am the hero or villain of the narrative to follow, depending on whether you are a feminist or a human being. I will write about myself for a paragraph or two now, because I do not intend to do so later. After a paragraph or two I shall be concerned with what I have done, not with what I am. (Those of you who do not make that distinction, calm yourselves; if I am what I do, one of the things I do do is make that distinction.) But it is important for you to know something in advance about the author and protagonist of the narrative to which presently we shall turn, if you will just curb your impatience. It is precisely because I have nothing to hide that I am going to the trouble of writing this down.

My name, then, is Victor Grant. Until recently I made my living as manager of the Columbia University Bookstore. The job required little from me but an attention to detail (and what, may I ask, is there, anywhere, but detail?) and a watchfulness over the thieving student clerks I had to contend with. The job, in fact, could have been handled more than adequately by someone whose love for books is far less ardent than my own, could only have been handled adequately by such a man. Yes, as you are congratulating yourself on having deduced, the store lost money under my management. But I will bet, if there are any takers, that it is losing money still, in spite of the three new racks of nonbooks on demonology, occult politics, "health" food, feminism, and other follies. In any case, a university bookshop that makes money is not a proper university bookshop. I quit my job at the Columbia Bookstore on Monday, February 18, 1974, one day after my wife deserted me.

I don't think I am going to spend time telling you what kind of person I am, after all. Draw your own conclusions from what I am going to tell you I have done. My wife deserted me on Sunday, February 17, the sixth anniversary of our marriage and the thirty-sixth anniversary of my birth. You may conclude from this coincidence of anniversaries, if that is the way your mind works, that when we said "I do" before a ferret-eyed functionary on an unseasonably warm morning seven years ago she was also offering herself to me as a kind of birthday present. She may have thought so—I may have thought so too. (I don't claim to be the answer to every girlish pipe dream.) But we shall see just how well events have justified that facile conclusion. She was twenty-two when we married and she was twenty-two when we first met the previous fall in German F3001x. We were both taking that course to fulfill the language requirement to-

ward the degree of Bachelor of Science (and I wish I had remained one) from the School of General Studies.

Samantha Woods, for that was her name, was a beginning
freshman and I was a concluding senior. She was taking German F3001x for the first time and I was taking it for the second
time. It is the only course I failed during the six and one-half
years it took me to put myself through college while working
for the Columbia Bookstore. Samantha, on the other hand,
never failed anything, although she graduated with the grade
of "incomplete" in seven courses. I paid the tuition for these
incompletes, as I paid for the courses she completed in lieu of
these, as I paid for all the courses she took during her sophomore, junior, and senior years while I continued to work in the
Columbia Bookstore instead of going to journalism school and
as I continue to pay. The idea was that, unlike me, she would
attend classes full time and graduate in four years rather than
in six and one-half, at the least. It took some persuading (and
some special pleading) for me to get permission to take German
F3002x during the same term that I was taking its prerequisite,
German F3001x, so that I might graduate in February rather
than in June. Just as it took some persuading to convince
Samantha that marriage would not interfere with her pursuit of
an education. Interfere! If she had not married me, she would
surely have dropped out of the race somewhere along the way.
I passed German F3001x (a review of German grammar, which
makes no sense) with a D, but passed its sequel (an introduction
to German literature, which makes at least a foggy kind of
sense) with a C+. On the afternoon of our wedding day, still
unseasonably warm, I dropped by the Dean's Office to pick up
my diploma. Naturally, the assistant dean who shook my hand
did not know that it was my birthday (or that it was my wedding day).

Poor Samantha. She was lured away from me by a consciousness-raising session. Nothing she had ever met in Painesville, Ohio, could have prepared her for Jude (that is, Judith)

Karnofsky. Yes, patient reader, *the* Jude Karnofsky, your favorite science-fiction writer disguised as an anthropologist, prize-
winning authoress of *The Precedence of Women,* itinerant lecturess,
talkshow personality, and cryptolesbian. Before we part forever
I shall feast your celebrity-hungry eyes on choice samples of
quackery even more monstrous in notoriety. We are just getting
started. How many of you knew that the late Jude Karnofsky
was really Mrs. William Austin, wife of my best friend? Very
few, I'll wager. The first class Bill gave as an assistant professor
of English was the first class I took as a college student. He liked
my lean, straightforward prose; I liked him; we soon became
friends. He and his wife-to-be both came up for tenure in 1968.
All during the first days of the student riots their ad hoc committees on promotion met. They were both promoted, he because of merit, she because of blackmail (it was no time to fire
a demogogue-pedagogue just because she had written little and
knew less). They celebrated by copulating on the conference
table in Schermerhorn Hall two hours before the police busted
in (as she often told it—to anyone who would listen). The
following summer he married her—because she was poor, ugly,
Jewish, and aggressive; because he was rich, handsome, WASP,
and deferential; because in a fit of absent-mindedness he had
allowed her to mount him; because she had scruples against
abortion (which scruples she lost, needless to say, three years
later when she became a feminist). She soon began to attend a
consciousness-raising session run by the infamous Erika von
Plaack. And, alas, she soon began to drag along with her an at
first amused and reluctant Samantha Grant, my wife.

While Samantha and Jude sat around listening to horror
stories about husbands who expected their wives to make the
beds, I would visit with Bill and little Tobias. It was his mother,
of course, who imposed that name upon the child. With an
unusual gesture of magnanimity she allowed Bill to select the
middle name. I am not at all ashamed to tell you that I came as
close to tears as I had at any time since puberty when Bill told

me that he had selected the name Victor in honor of the child's godfather, in honor, that is, of me—if I were willing. If I were willing! Something roused itself in my chest and pushed up into my throat so that I could not speak. Don't get the impression that I am a cold or unemotional person just because I know how to keep myself under control. In retrospect I see that those evenings I spent with Bill and Victor Little (as I always think of him in the privacy of my own head) made up the happiest hours of my life. Unless those evenings Victor Little and Victor Big spent alone together were happier still, evenings on which the Austins (or rather, by then, Mr. Austin and Ms. Karnofsky) went to a lecture by someone like Pastor Brevoort (of whom and of whose First Church of Christ, Androgynous you shall hear more), while Samantha sat home studying at the rolltop desk I had ungrudgingly bought for her at a price of two weeks' salary, evenings when two blissful innocents named Victor laughed at *Green Eggs and Ham* (and at even more extravagant fancies by Dr. Grant) until Victor Little fell asleep on his godfather's lap.

Beautiful, olive-skinned Samantha. Her mother is half Italian (the worst half of a thoroughly bad proposition). Her father is an ex-Cockney with a small hard body and a small soft mind. His job, whatever it is, keeps him sitting around boilers and other machines prone to violence, one eye on the gauges. The other eye he keeps on ratty volumes of Shelley and of even less practical utopians, Gnostics and chapel socialists mostly. If he had only had a job that required his undivided attention! Or if he had only had a taste for literature less likely to corrupt his hankering gullibility—pornography, for example. At least then he would not have been so relentless in pressing upon his only daughter the aspirations generated in him by nocturnal lucubrations. I blame him for his daughter's susceptibility to the solemn lunacies of visionary radicalism, for her weak grip on things as they are and must be. And she once had the nerve to say that I reminded her of her father. The alleged resemblance is what first attracted her, so she said. Samantha never knew her own mind, and I admit that I am not an easy person to know, but I can assure you, as I assured her, that my own socialist humanism is impeccably logical. And practical. One Saturday night in early 1972 she came home with her consciousness raised another notch (into Cloud-Cuckoo Land) to announce that she was no longer a pawn in her father's games with the world, she was finally her own woman. Feminism had made her conscious of how much she had been only what he had made her. (Talk about the slow return of the repressed! The taste for quackery she had caught from her father took possession of her forever at the precise moment she thought she had exorcized him.) She had married me, she now knew, because she had loved her father. Now that she was no longer Daddy's girl she no longer needed to be mine. Never mind what I needed.

I listened to this tirade sitting on one of Bill's ancient heirloom chairs, the coffee cup I held in my hand rattling against its saucer. She stood in front of me, her lovely face flushed around the ugly movements her mouth was making. Behind her, on the television screen, George Saunders was bending over to inspect Jack the Ripper's latest victim, who was hidden behind the silhouette of Samantha's waist and hip. (Victor Little was safe in bed.) On my right Bill slumped in another heirloom, his face rehearsing the whole human repertoire of appeasement gestures, his hand inching toward the bottle that three hours earlier had held a full pint of bourbon (his nightly ration). Before his hand got there, before I could put in a word, Samantha looked toward Jude, who then began to lower the boom on poor Bill. The whole time he never dared to move a muscle. He just slumped down further and further, until his spine was parallel with the floor, his hand arrested about three inches from the neck of the bottle; he looked like a man going down for the third time. He was sinking under the weight of Jude's accusations. Just that night apparently, she had become conscious of how he had taken advantage of her revolt against her parents to get her to marry him. He had taken advantage of the fact that he was the direct opposite of her father (a scrappy little Zionist upholsterer). Now that the revolution was accomplished, now that her father had been toppled from the throne in her head, where (she now knew) all her decisive battles had to be fought, she no longer needed the symbol of her first fumbling gestures toward freedom, namely poor Bill.

Yes, gentle reader, I know as well as you what Bill should have done with that bourbon bottle. And I (now) know that the best way to stop the mouth of a beautiful woman from making ugly movements is to stick your fist in it, for my consciousness has been raised too. The spectators are always wiser than the actors—until the houselights come on. Take this opportunity to learn something about yourselves. Confess: are you not, as Bill and I once were, victims of the delusion that a loving husband should use persuasion rather than force?

We were abject, we were apologetic, we were quick to admit that there was something in what our wives had said. (What that something might have been I don't right now recall.) After a while Samantha sat down, and Jude lit a cigarette, and Samantha accepted a drink from me, and Jude sat down, and Bill, that subtle man, began a counterattack in the guise of a capitulation. Since Samantha and Jude were no longer compelled by what they did not know about themselves to accept us, Bill said, they were now free to choose us. Henceforth I would not be prompted to capitalize on my privileged status as Daddy's surrogate and he would not be tempted to profiteer on his favored position as Daddy's antithesis, for is it not true, cunning Bill went on, went on, that a sexist society has cast us all into roles for which we never auditioned? Is it not the lofty mission of Women's Liberation to liberate men as well as women? Is it not precisely what is wrong with men that has wronged women? Is it not in *their* heads that the last battle has to be fought? Can women ever be altogether free until men have been liberated from the fatal myth that men have to be manly, that a manly man is above all one who mistreats women? Choosing to remain married to us would not be a betrayal of their feminism, Bill concluded, but an exercise of it. The sun rose with his demonstration that together we would grow to new and dizzier heights of freedom.

Good old Bill. It had been a masterful performance. God knows what it had cost him, besides a second pint of bourbon. But he had not won over his audience. He had only worn it out. Jude snorted one last time. Samantha said she was too tired to think. We agreed to sleep on it, the men in my apartment, the women in Bill's. Jude said that she couldn't trust me not to use unfair methods of persuasion once Samantha and I were alone (we slept in a double bed). The women would give us their decisions after dinner, which they were going to eat out together. We could eat where we wanted. Bill was refused permission to take his son for the day. I learned later that Jude had dumped him with her ever-ready neighbor, a colleague's wife. I spent most of the morning and afternoon tossing in bed, dreaming alternately of how I had once lapped champagne out of the hollows behind Samantha's clavicles (it was on our first anniversary) and of how with three quick twists I could remove Jude's head from her body. Bill walked down to the Battery and back. After 10:00 P.M. Samantha and Jude tripped in, complacent, smooth, faces flushed with food and drink, brushing off their coats the sparse snow that had begun to fall. They had arrived at a decision. They would stay with us, but only on one condition. As a gesture of goodwill, Bill and I would have to submit to vasectomies.

Now God damn it, I had acquiesced in Samantha's desire to put off having children until she got her degree. I am not a brutal man. Nor am I a devious one. I disdained to employ the techniques of moral blackmail that five years of marriage had made me all too familiar with. Such techniques are inconsistent with my conception of what it takes to be a man. And you feminists and androgynes might just as well stop sneering. On

the delirious evening of her graduation, after I had con-
gratulated her with an expensive desk, a fancy dinner, and even
fancier sex, I suggested that she could now throw away her
birth-control pills. Samantha, with many endearments, beautiful preliminaries to more fancy sex, begged me to be patient just
a little longer. As the circuits of my brain began to pop, once
more I acquiesced. What would you have done? I was sympathetic to her fear of becoming like her mother, dull, self-pitying,
resentful of her husband, a menace to the psychological health
of her children, and now (in her middle age) on the shelf but
off her rocker. Samantha wanted a career of her own. Jude and
some friends were starting a magazine. They had promised
Samantha a job as associate editor. Once the magazine had been
launched and her career afloat, we could have children, as many
as I wanted, a houseful of Victor Littles.

No doubt I am much to blame—for everything. Do you
think I don't know that? I should have asserted my masculine
prerogatives, my rights as a husband. But I loved my wife, or
had you forgotten? This vasectomy business, however, was
another bucket of snails entirely. No sir! I demanded to speak
to Samantha alone. She hesitated (the first break in her complacency), shot a quick look toward Jude, but I dragged her out the
door, down the hall, and up a flight of steps to my apartment.
Nothing doing, I said. In that case she would have to leave, she
said; she had promised Jude. What about the promises she made
to me? I asked. She was no longer the person who had made
those promises, she replied. We argued and argued, back and
forth, and I admit to trying out those techniques of moral blackmail I ordinarily disdain. She wasn't having any of it. I threatened to break her jaw. Nothing a man might do would surprise
her any more, she said. I pleaded, indulgent reader, I pleaded.
She pushed my hand off her knee, my head off her lap, my arms
from around her knees. Some kindly god who does not want the
male of the species to die out saved me just as I was about to
turn on the tears, just as I was about to drop dark hints of an

exemplary suicide. Samantha's contempt would have finished me off there and then, at once and for all time.

My steady-eyed wife looked at me across the ensuing pause as Artemis must have looked at the remains of Acteon. (Am I mistaken, or was there the faintest complication of regret in Samantha's, and her predecessor's, smile?) But some kindly god, a satyr no doubt, came to my aid one last time. (And will someone please tell me just why he has forsaken me?) He guided my attack to the one chink in Samantha's invulnerability. That chink was not her love for me, which is what you are likely to be thinking, but her self-confidence, which was still young and tender. What would happen, I asked, if her writing never developed, if she flopped at editing (Samantha did not know that it is impossible to flop at editing), if the magazine foundered or was never even launched? Did she want to spend her life as some fool's factotum? Might she not one day yearn for a family, for children, for something to give meaning to her life, for some foothold on the future? Diabolical, you say? What about my own foothold on the future? Remember what was at stake. Just in case Samantha had not remembered, I reminded her. She weakened. I pressed home. We compromised. She would continue to live with me, but there would be no more sex (as it turned out, she let me go down on her from time to time during the last thirteen months of our life together).

We slept back to back for the few hours left of that wretched night, the space between us pointed as a sword. Early the next morning we went down to see the Austins, my heart knocking with the mad hope that Jude would be gone. As we arrived, the much imposed-upon (and admirably domesticated) neighbor was leading my godson off to nursery school. He smiled and waved his little wave (hand at eye level, fingers folding and opening). "Daddy's drunk," he said. In celebration? I clawed at the door knob, pushed, remembered to pull, found it locked. Knocked. Samantha reached across me and turned the knob. And there was Jude, standing athwart the living room, all dressed for work. You are very wrong if you think you know what Jude Karnofsky looked like from the picture on the dust jacket of her impossible book. It is, of course, ten years old, and deceptive in other ways as well. For one thing it fails to show her body, no small matter. She was perhaps five feet four inches tall and weighed, at a conservative estimate, one hundred and seventy-five pounds. Imaginary lines drawn on either side of her, from armpit to mid-hip would be straight, except for two convex rolls in the region of what should have been a waist (I am picturing her strapped to a wall and facing a drunken knife-thrower). She carried two saddlebags of fat roughly where a gunslinger totes his pistols. To descend further, Jude's legs were very short, and bowed from buried knee to hypothetical ankle. Whether in motion or at rest, she leaned forward, so that her handbag just about reached the floor. Even to my habituated eyes, she was something to see as she stood there that morning in a brand-new slacks suit (the pants of which would have made no more than pedalpushers for any other woman).

Dirty pool, you say? Unfair to laugh at people because of their appearance? And what makes you think I am laughing? I happen to believe that people earn their bodies as well as their faces. You cannot separate the man (or the woman, especially not the woman) from the body that, so to speak, embodies him (or her). He, or she, *is* his appearance (or hers). His appearance expresses him (and hers, her) and he, or she, (damn this) is an expression of it. I thought we were through with obsolete dualisms. Besides, did I consider it unfair when one day at Jones Beach I had thrown off my shirt and Jude said, "why Victor, you're painfully thin"? No, I just considered the source, which was by no means a model of judicious impartiality, at least not to my way of thinking. And if you believe for one minute that my dislike for her has caused me to deviate from the standard of severe impartiality I have always set myself, answer this: What do you think of her bullying poor Bill into a vasectomy?

For that is what she had done. I could tell merely from the

way Bill sat in his chair, a funny smile on his crumpled face. Oh, that bitch! While she pulled Samantha out to the kitchen, I went to sit beside Bill. We looked at each other and then looked toward opposite corners of the ceiling.

"We worked something out," I said to the southeast corner.

There were angry whispers from the kitchen. "My mother and father went through six marriages and five divorces between them before I was twelve," said Bill to the southwest corner.

I still wonder whether or not I really heard my Samantha's defiant voice saying, "I couldn't do it to him."

"I couldn't do it to him," said Bill, meaning Tobias Victor Austin.

Samantha's voice cut clearly through the whispering: "God damn it, Jude, first my father, then Victor, now you. From now on I make my own decisions."

"A child needs two parents," said Bill.

"Above all, a boy needs a father," I said.

Samantha stormed out of the kitchen, lightning in her eyes, which she flashed once my way, as she blitzed out the door. I could hear her quick, firm steps go across the hall, down the stairs, out onto the street, over to Broadway, into the IRT, up onto the street again, east along Forty-second Street, and uptown to the marble entrance of a building owned by the great publisher for whom she worked as assistant to some ignoramus of a subeditor in three-piece plaids whose reputation she made by doing his job for him and who I am happy to say was fired six months later when the great publishing house was taken over by Amalgamated Disposals, Inc.

There suddenly was Jude, standing in the doorway to the kitchen, a saucer in one hand, a cup held to her lips in the other, her eyes appraising us over the rim. It never occurred to her that I might have wanted some coffee. Satisfied, no doubt, by what she saw, she stepped into the living room, put the cup on the saucer and the saucer on a cabinet (where Bill would have to pick it up), and with the nearest thing to a saunter she could manage on those legs of hers, she left us. She made a little show of closing the door with elaborate care, as though on the dead. Jude teaches her course on gynepology at 9:00 A.M., when students should be getting their much-needed REM sleep, out of sheer cussedness. I went out to the kitchen, taking with me Jude's cup and saucer, placed them in the dishwasher, made a fresh pot of coffee, put it on a tray with two fresh cups and saucers, with spoons, sugar, milk, napkins, and took them into the living room.

"Want some?"

Bill shook his head.

I sat with him, drinking coffee while he drank bourbon, until three hours or so later, he passed out. I carried him to his bed ("painfully thin" Victor had no trouble walking with chubby Bill in his arms), covered him, went back to the living room, took the tray to the kitchen, put the cups, saucers, and spoons in the dishwasher, the milk in the refrigerator, the pot on the stove, the napkins in the garbage bag, and, after a last look around, went to work. Anybody who didn't like my coming in late could lump it.

The months that followed, from January, 1973, until Sunday, Febuary 17, 1974, are not ones I would like to live through again. I suffered sympathetic pains while Bill recuperated from his vasectomy. The publication soon after of his book on the Menippean satire brought some consolation in the form of acclaim from the few scholars and humanists capable of appreciating it. I do not imagine that you have read *An Anatomy of Anatomies* (New York: Columbia University Press, 1973), although it is beyond doubt the best work on the subject. I have copied out its epigraph, from *The Anatomy of Melancholy:*

> . . . this I aimed at, *vel ut lenirum animum scribendo,* to ease my mind by writing; for I had *gravidum cor, foedum caput,* a kind of imposthume in my head, which I was very desir-

ous to be unladen of, and could imagine no fitter evacuation than this. Besides, I might not well refrain, for *ubi dolor, ibi digitus,* one must needs scratch where it itches.

By May, Jude had upstaged Bill with *The Precedence of Women.* Samantha, sponsored by her new friends, began to publish reviews and little confessional articles for the *Village Voice,* the *University Review,* and various organs (if that is the word) of Women's Liberation. She and Jude were soon out five nights a week feminizing. New York, so it seemed, was lousy with scoundrels hot to place their money on the poison-dipped magazine that Jude & Co. were getting ready to fire into the exposed flank of a distracted world. Its name: *Ms. Chief.* Its staff: Erika von Plaack, Editor-in-Chief; Stevie Dickinson (physiologically a woman, but not otherwise), Managing Editor; Jude Karnofsky and Pastor Peter Brevoort, Associate Editors; four creatures named Kate and a cadre of other females, more or less, named Robin, Casey, Tracy, Zazie, Gene, Jess, Joe, and George, for art, poetry, circulation, production, and so forth; and my beautiful exploited Samantha "Woods" [*sic*], Copy Editor. I saw my wife less and less, and when I did see her, she had less and less to say to me. Many nights, after leaving Bill and Victor Little, I went home to practise the magic art of masturbation, and that is one more thing you can lump.

Which brings me to Sunday, February 17, 1974, the day of my birthday and the sixth anniversary of my wedding, neither of which did we celebrate, neither of which did anyone mention, until after supper, when Bill offered me double congratulations. We were in the kitchen, cleaning up; Samantha and Jude were in the living room, back to work at trying to hammer out a position paper on the vexed question of alimony for men (they were against it). Tobias Victor was in bed.

"The flicks?" said Bill.

"What else?" I answered.

"The Devil In Miss Jones?" said Bill.

"And praise be to His Satanic Majesty," I answered.

"Don't forget Ms. Jones," said Bill.

We announced to the women that we were going to the movies, that we were going to see *The Sting,* that if there was a line we would be home late (we had to cover ourselves in case we wanted to see *Miss Jones* twice).

Samantha surprised me by looking up from her documents and rough drafts with a kind of worried frown on her face. And I thought she had stopped caring where I went or what I did. But she did not say anything. Jude surprised me even more by looking up with what was clearly meant to be an encouraging smile. "Have a good time," she said. "No need to hurry," she said. "We've got plenty to do," that double-dyed villain said.

I have never met a woman who really liked going to the movies. Oh, they like to go out. They will go to a movie, or even a ball game, or whatever, just for the sake of going out. But they would rather go out to dinner, to a party, or to the theatre, even to the opera for Christ's sake, where they can be looked at, than look at a movie. For a long time I thought the reason must be that women are so completely out of touch with the real world. They have no need to go to movies, I used to say to myself, because they already live in a world of total fantasy. What need for them to escape things as they are? Reality has never yet caught up to them. That is what I used to think. I now understand that what women lack is not so much a need to escape, as a need for adventure, even imaginary adventure. Has there ever been a woman writer of adventure stories? This deficiency has a genetic cause. It was bred into women during the good old days a million years ago, when men went out on the African plains to hunt while their women stayed at the camp to tend the sacred fire and their happy children. It was of advantage to the species for men to be restless and adventurous, and for women to be placid and domestic. All the achievements of mankind arose from the genetic differences between the sexes, from *sexual dimorphism,* to use a technical term you might want to memorize.

Yes, I know: women seem to have invented agriculture. But look what followed from their pernicious meddling: the Neolithic revolution, and with it the division of labor (other than by sex), the stratification of classes, the invention of slavery, the establishment of priests, police, bureaucrats, and ideologies, the deification of smiling Mother Goddesses of implacable cruelty. The agricultural societies that spread like tumors in the great river valleys of the ancient orient were the most monstrous tyrannies ever to have existed. They introduced overpopulation, urban blight, and a ruling class sprawled in voluptuous ease on the bent shoulders of history's first suffering masses. Oriental despotism is feminine. Compare this Pandora's box to those societies that remained masculine, those great warrier societies that evolved from bands of hunters and pastoral nomads, those societies that produced the heyday of Europe, before it was feminized by Oriental Christianity. They were made up of proud heroes, touchy in their independence, who freely followed the man among them that best deserved their respect, but only so long as he deserved it. They were inspired by Father Gods, casual in their loves and fierce in their vengeance.

My reading is part of me. If you are not interested in the conclusions I have drawn from it, you are not interested in me. I gave up a perfectly good job as a short-order cook to go to college, where I could learn more about books, and to work in a bookstore, where I could get my hands on them. The sex and violence you have been waiting for with unseemly impatience is just a few pages away. *The Devil In Miss Jones,* which Bill and I saw one and one-half times (that is, we saw the superior middle portion twice), has plenty of sex, but no violence, I am happy to say. I dislike cruelty, even to women. I am no sadist —although if I had been one, so observation has taught me, I would have had more success with the ladies. *Miss Jones* is the story (in the unlikely case that you have not seen it) of a rather likeable young woman who commits suicide out of a hopelessness brought on by the absence of men in her life. The devil's agent, a smiling smoothie behind a desk, grants her one wish before consigning her to eternal punishment. Her one wish, like everybody's, is to have her sexual fantasies made flesh. They are, they are. I did not like the ending of the movie. Miss Jones is confined to a cell, the only other occupant of which is a man so crazy he has no interest in sex. She tries desperately to masturbate, but soon learns that she cannot achieve climax on her own. The healthy, masculine paganism that informed the main body of the movie is betrayed by a feminine, moralizing conclusion of vaguely Christian import.

Bill and I walked home from Forty-second Street (we are both great walkers; we average one block per minute), working off steam, pointing out to each other in high glee how neat the fit is between the sexual fantasies of a proper woman and those of a proper man, a resolution forming in my mind. It was time for me to make Samantha a happy woman. It was time for me to do what was best for both of us, no matter what she (mistakenly) thought was best for her, time for me to cease humoring those vagaries of the female will that D.H. Lawrence had so prophetically warned us about.

Bill pushed open the door to his apartment and I followed, a faint smile of aristocratic hauteur on my lips, phrases to match arranging themselves in my head. I had decided to come on like a Renaissance prince, rather than like a Victorian father. The living room was empty. Samantha, my Samantha, and Jude were gone. Upon the wide, empty expanse of the table at which they had been working lay two lonely envelopes. Bill rushed down the hall to his son's room. I picked up the envelope on which was written "To Victor" and stood there holding it, my mind looking off at something in the distance, what it was I don't know.

Poor, pale Bill sleepwalked back into the living room.

"She's taken Toby," he said, and fell into his favorite chair. I frisbeed over to him the envelope with "Bill" scrawled on it.

I still have the note my wife left me when she left me. Here it is:

> Dear Victor,
>
> Please forgive me for doing it this way. I didn't have the courage to tell you face-to-face. You would have made me take your feelings into account, and that's exactly what I can't afford to do. Oh Victor, none of this has anything to do with you, can you understand that? Don't think of me as running away from you, but as running toward myslef [sic]. I've got to have room to find myself in, I've got to find out who I really am. How can I be Mrs. Grant and have an identity of my own? I'm not blaming you. It's just the way things are. Please, don't blame me either. Victor, I loved you and I would love you still if I could love anybody. Right now love is a luxury I will have to do without.
>
> Victor, I want a devorce [sic] not a separation.
>
> And Victor, please understand.
>
> Samantha

An interesting letter. I thought so at the time. Nineteen instances of the first person pronoun (nominative, possessive, reflexive, but mainly accusative) in one hundred and fifty-nine chances (excluding signature and salutation). I do not have to point out to you what kind of self-absorption such numbers reveal. My first name appears in four places (including the salutation), each time as a hypocritical caress. She says "please" three times without once meaning it. Notice her choice of words: doing it, this way, none of this, the way things are, all this, etc. Pronominal evasions, or the equivalent, of what she did not have the courage to face, even in her own words. Never mind her inability to face me. So she was running off to find herslef. When people say they are trying to find themselves I always wonder who is looking for whom. I thought that the way to find yourself was in the eyes of somebody you love, but then I never had the benefit of participation in consciousness-raising klatches—I was still a victim of the sexist delusion that love is a need, rather than a luxury. "Devorce." Some copy editor she was going to make!

I suddenly realized that Bill was looking toward me, his eyes blinking in bewilderment, as thought a fist had materialized out of nowhere to punch him in the nose. I went over to Bill and gently pulled Jude's note out of his limp hand. Naturally I have preserved it, not only for posterity, not only as Exhibit Number One in my dossier on the crimes of Jude Karnofsky, but mainly so that I could read it whenever my hatred needed a recharge (not very often). Men, husbands, fathers, how would you like to return from an innocent outing with a friend to be greeted with this?

February 17, 1974

Bill—

We have taken this opportunity to walk out of your lives and into the future. It is a road open only to those willing to travel without excess baggage. Husbands are obsolete. The social and economic conditions that produced and preserved them no longer obtain. The time is approaching when maleness itself, not merely husbandhood, will be anachronistic, as I feel confident my book has proved to the satisfaction of anyone with an open mind (pp. 604–647).

The future is upon us. We can serve it or we can resist. There are no other options. Those who resist will be swept aside. Those who serve will inherit the earth.

The future is an exacting task-~~master~~ mistress. She brooks no rivals. Once she stood revealed to me I had to choose between serving her and serving you. If I have chosen to serve what will set me free rather than you, my erstwhile lord and master, it is not for the sake of my own happiness. It is to set an example. It is to encourage my sisters to do the same. I expect no acclaim for this. We leave egotism to the men. We have learned that only through selflessness do we find ourselves.

But the time for explanations is past. In any case you have chosen not to understand them. If and when you do, you will have no course but to join us. I shall then be happy to welcome as a comrade whom I must now reject as a husband.

Jude Karnofsky

P.S. I realize how unhappy you will be, and I understand how little men can endure disappointment. I am not heartless, after all. May I suggest that you take your troubles to Pastor Brevoort. He is a worthy clergyperson. He will know how to buck you up.

P.P.S. You will receive shortly my demands for the divorce. Tobias, of course, will live with me. I shall see to it that the feminine side of his nature is properly nourished, that he grows up to be a complete human being, rather than just a man.

With that chilling last sentence my decision to kill Jude Karnofsky became irrevocable. It was her death sentence, you might say.

II

Y ES, my liberal reader, in principle I am as opposed to murder as you are. Did I not say I was a humanist? I agree in principle that one should not take the life of a fellow human being—to assume for a minute that in this case we are dealing with one. I know about golden rules, and categorical imperatives, and treating people as ends rather than means, and all that. You get a pretty good education at the School of General Studies, no matter what those snots at Columbia College may think. But as a practical philosopher and a man of my time I am an ethical relativist as well as a humanist, an ethical relativist because I am a humanist, in fact. No rule of ethics is absolute. Ask yourself this: could you have had any doubt in February, 1974, that the death of Jude Karnofsky would promote the greatest happiness of the greatest number of people? Measure the unhappiness of the monstrous Karnofsky (in being killed) against the happiness of Bill, Victor Little, myself, and Samantha (if she only knew) and tell me on which side the scales dip. I do not even mention the inevitable misery of those women Karnofsky would lead astray if allowed to continue her nefarious recruitments. I do not even mention the heartbreak and tragedy that would litter the wakes of those straying women. Will you tell me, just how did it happen that there are so many females around today with their heads empty of everything but impossible longings and boundless gullibility?

There is a certain solemnity about a proper murder. The solemnity, of course, lies in what the murderer risks, not in what the victim suffers. The victim is only pathetic. His (or her) suffering inspires only sadness. The murderer, if he murders in the proper spirit, is tragic. His risks inspire awe. Tragedy—and surely I am but reminding you of something you already know —emerges out of what heroes do and how they do it, not out of what they (or their victims) suffer. As Aristotle so rightly pointed out, a tragic play is an imitation of an *action*. By now I should not have to tell you that what I had in mind was not to be some sordid eruption of domestic rage or social pathology. Compare what I had in mind with the exasperated husband's impetuous (but oh so satisfying) stifling of his exasperating wife, the pervert's discharge of self-hatred into his victim's body, the random slaughters and mindless bloodshed of political terrorists, Mafia hitmen, drunken drivers, apocalyptic Californians, drug-possessed Zombies, teen-age packrats, zealous cops and superzealous cop-haters, nearsighted hunters, hair-trigger burglars, welching kidnappers, alcoholic fathers, and pill-popping mammas. What I had in mind was not murder at all, but a sacred obligation, sanctioned by the Old Testament and by every other holy writ uncontaminated by Christianity. What I had in mind was revenge, than which nothing is so sweet. Nothing.

If you would use the brains you were born with instead of the pious maxims that were crammed down your throats, you might be able to figure out for yourself what it is that makes revenge so sweet. "Vengeance is mine, saith the lord." Is that so. Well, are we not supposed to emulate Him? Did He not make us in His own image? If you would think a bit, you might be able to figure out why it is that at all times in all places it has been above all the figure of the avenger that captured and captures the popular imagination. Western literature, for instance, begins with the *Iliad*. It is the story of a war that Agamemnon waged for ten years to avenge the abduction of Helen by Paris, that effeminate sot. It is the story of Achilles' killing of Hector (along with a horde of lesser Orientals) in revenge for the death of Patroclus. Western literature continues with the *Odyssey*, the improbable episodes of which an impatient reader races through in his eagerness for the delicious finale. Great Odysseus kills by bow, lance, sword, and bludgeon the one hundred and eight suitors who had committed the unspeakable crime (to the virtuous Greeks) of violating the sanctity of his household. *Prometheus Bound* would be no more than a cautionary tale were it not for the theme of revenge that elevates it into tragedy. The greatest example of Greek tragedy and the only extant trilogy is the *Oresteia,* in which a cycle of revenge is initiated by the unnatural Clytemnestra and concluded by the noble Orestes.

Herodotus, the Father of History, a very sane and experienced man, could only conceive of one motive of sufficient magnitude to account for the Persian Wars, which to him were the greatest events ever to have occurred, events involving the whole world as he knew it. That motive was revenge, revenge begetting revenge and counterrevenge. And what was the offense that begat all this revenge? It was trivial enough: Phoenician sailors had shanghied a few Greek women. One can only applaud the Father of History for the commonsense of his appraisal: "Now as for the carrying off of women, it is the deed, they say, of a rogue; but to make a stir about such as are carried off, argues a man a fool. Men of sense care nothing for such women, since it is plain that without their own consent they would never be forced away." To make a stir over the women would be foolishness; but to neglect avenging the offense would be unthinkable, even if it involved the destruction of empires. I will sum up this apparent (but only apparent) digression by saying that for the Greeks the motive-power behind every great enterprise was revenge. (If you don't believe me, go ahead and check the relevant portions of *Dermaphall's Study Guide to the Greek and Roman Classics,* as I just did—to refresh my memory).

Then came androgynous Socrates, sterile midwife to Oriental Christianity. During the Dark Ages of Christianity revenge fell into disrepute, as did all the other pagan virtues. "Fell into disrepute!" What am I saying? They were stamped down and out, along with the pagans who had them, by the most absolute, the most implacably ferocious and shamelessly self-righteous, the most widespread and long-lived totalitarian regime ever to exist. After the bullying and blackmail, the brainwashing, the witchburning, the unholy crusades, after the slanders, the forgeries, the intrigues, after pagan culture had been razed, uprooted, or rerouted where it was not plagiarized—

I would just as soon not go on with this, if it is all right with you. The subject is too depressing. It is too late to do anything about the Dark Ages, about *those* Dark Ages. One of the things I hate about history is that its villains are beyond the reach of our itching fingers. Can you imagine what it would feel like to get your fingers around the neck of one of those popes? Around Justinian's skinny neck? Around the plump neck of one of those women, some of them wives of pagan philosophers, who infected their addlepated women-friends, their fawning slaves, their uxorious husbands? Infected them with Christianity, that is, as a bisexual nymphomaniac spreads clap. If I could bring back the dead, there are some I would bring back just to kill.

As I said, they are beyond our reach now. Well, never mind, history took its own kind of revenge. The Dark Ages were followed by a more manly era, the Renaissance, the rebirth of pagan learning. The recovery of pagan learning was also the recovery of pagan virtues, among them revenge. ("Virtue" derives from the Latin *vir,* meaning "man.") The evidence is everywhere, if you will just look. But I will only mention one kind of evidence—the popularity of revenge tragedy. Hamlet, the greatest of all dramas, is a tale of revenge. Then there is *Antonio's Revenge, The Revenger's Tragedy, Revenge for Honor, Hoffman, or Revenge for a Father, The Revenge of Bussy D'Ambois, Caesar's Revenge, The Maid's Revenge,* and even *Cupid's Revenge* (not to mention such suggestive titles as *The Woman Hater, The Scourge of Villany,* and *Women, Beware Women*). When I asked Bill if he knew of a choice speech by an avenger, he provided me with these noble and moving lines from *The True Tragedy of Richard III:*

> Methinks their ghosts come gaping for revenge. . . .
> My nephew's blood Revenge, Revenge doth cry,
> The headless peers come pressing for revenge
> And every one cries, Let the tyrant die.
> The sun by day shines hotly for revenge,
> The moon by night eclipseth for revenge,
> The stars are turned to comets for revenge,
> The planets change their courses for revenge,
> The birds sing not but sorrow for revenge,
> The shrieking raven sits crooking for revenge,
> The silly lambs sit bleating for revenge,
> Whole herds of beasts come bellowing for revenge,
> And all, yea, all the world I think
> Cries for Revenge and nothing but Revenge.
> But to conclude, I have deserved revenge.

My sentiments exactly.

The Renaissance, like all good things, came to an end, although its spirit continues to inform every heroic human endeavor, few as they now are. It was followed by a universal failure of nerve. The businessman replaced the aristocrat as the exemplary social type. The businessman's "deal to get the most" replaced the aristocrat's "dare to be the best." And the businessman's wife's favorite form of literature, the novel, replaced tragedy, the soul of which, as we have seen, is revenge. People tell me that the classic novels of the bourgeois era are mostly about young men chasing after money or high social status—or about young women chasing after young men who already have money or high social status. The only obstacle in the way of the triple embrace of boy, girl, and money is some unbelievable villain; it is no doubt significant that he often perpetrates his villainy out of a lust for vengance. It is even more significant that he always loses out in the end. The businessman, like the Christian, believes that virtue pays off, and vice versa.

But on either side of the sluggish bourgeois center there were men and women moved by the noble idea of a life dedicated to vengeance, men moved to live such a life and women moved by such men. On the right there was opera, the main instances of which are tales of revenge set to music that you can only pretend to like. Operas were written, apparently, so that the upper crust of the middle class could wax nostalgic over what it had destroyed. Still, opera would be all right if it were not for the singing (and for the people who go to it). On the left there was popular literature—potboiling plays, crime fiction, adventure stories, boys' books. And in the best of these, what character is it that most agitates our longings, yours and mine? The avenger. I reach back across the years to shake hands with the Count of Monte Cristo.

I am as aware as you that there are models closer at hand. More aware if I may say so; unlike you I have devoted thought and study to the literary (and natural) history of revenge. But I sympathize with your enthusiasm, your desire to participate in the unfolding of my grand theme, your desire to add a grain to the mountain of evidence. You are right: at this very moment the best-attended movies and the best-selling novels are tales in which a man grievously wronged wreaks revenge on those who wronged him. The all-time best-selling American novelist is Mickey Spillane, whose books are invariably tales of revenge (so I am told). His first novel, *I, the Jury* (the avenger's awesome motto), has by itself sold nearly twenty million copies. Its plot was filched from the *Maltese Falcon,* by Dashiell Hammett, who invented the type of mystery based on the adventures of a hard-boiled private eye. In both cases, the detective sets out to avenge the murder of his partner, falls in love with a dame apparently in distress, but discovers that the murderer is murderess, the same fatal dame. A resonant plot indeed! Of course the avenger comes to love his victim! He loves him (or her, especially her) to the extent that he hates him (or her). He loves his victim because his victim allows him to be what he has always wanted to be (without knowing it), what he was born to be; he loves his victim, because her offense was the pretext for him to enact his deepest and dearest desire: to get revenge. I can tell you from first-hand experience that the moment at which the offender's and the avenger's paths cross, the moment at which the offender becomes a victim and the victim of the offense wipes out the offense along with his victim, is a moment toward which the avenger ever after looks back with regret. Not because he regrets what he has done, but because he regrets no longer having anything worth doing to do.

The inventor of the mystery story proper was Edgar Allan Poe. I will assume that you have read "The Cask of Amontillado," in which the avenging hero walls up Fortunato. But I will bet that you have not read "Hop-Frog," in which a King and his seven privy-councillors are tricked into wearing inflammable orang-utang outfits, chained together, hoisted on a chandelier cable, and burnt to a crisp. This spectacular revenge is staged by the court jester, for the avenger is often a figure of fun to those who have wronged him—until that moment when he rights the wrong and shows the world just who it is that is going to laugh last. We laugh with him, of course, as we laugh with Odysseus, with the Count of Monte Cristo, with Sam Spade, Mike Hammer, Destry, Tarzan, Michael Corleone, Paul Newman and Robert Redford (in *The Sting,* but also in their numerous other roles as avengers; if you want to be a star, play the part of an avenger, that's my advice), and all the other bright figures of revenge that color our deepest fantasies. The avenger acts for us. No matter what morality we profess (even to ourselves), our sympathies are with him. Now why should that be? I will tell you.

Consider the working-class machismo that has received such a bad press from the pampered middle-class pets of Women's Liberation. Ask yourself why the working man is so aggressive in his masculinity, why it is that he reacts with such hair-trigger explosiveness to the slightest slight? It is because his masculine pride is all that he has, is all that he is. He has no money, no power, no status. He cannot extend himself by conspicuous displays of expensive learning, or costly real estate, or high-priced women. He cannot buy honor or absorb it from his occupation. He has only what he is, and someone is always trying to take from him the only thing he has. That is why his nose is so sharp to sniff out the faintest odor of belittlement. That is why he is so quick and so violent in his retribution for any act or word that has around it the smallest rough edge of insult. If his belligerence were any less alert, he would soon be ground away to nothing. I am trying to enlarge your understanding. Do you think that just for once you could put yourself in the place of someone who cannot afford to be neurasthenic?

The working man, then, is engaged in a life-and-death struggle to maintain the boundaries of his self against any incursion that would diminish him. Fine. And he has a life-and-death need to reconstitute himself by an act of revenge against whatever offense may chip away at him. So far so good. But that is not all. Before any specific offense whatsoever, the workingman has a motive for revenge. His motive is that everything you have above what he has, you have taken from him. That is how he sees it, at least, and with some justice. Therefore your plumber has a chip on his shoulder the size of your assets. Therefore he overcharges you. And what would you call communism but a philosophy of revenge? Right about now, if you have been following closely, you should be ready to ask what all this has to do with a declassé type like me and a middle-class type like you. Right? Well, that is precisely what I am going to tell you next. Everybody is a working man in relation to the society around him and the cosmos around it. Everybody has a motive for revenge by virtue of the mere fact that he is somebody. Everybody is diminished by age, reduced by circumstances, insulted and injured by the brute refusal of things to comply with his desires. His desires! His life-and-death needs, rather. And what in the last analysis do any of us have but ourselves? Whatever exists in the area between what we need and what we have is a motive for revenge. Whatever stands between where we are and where we want to be is a motive for revenge. Every invidious comparison a man can make between what he aspires to be and what circumstances force him to be is a motive for revenge. Death is a motive for revenge. Disease is a motive for revenge. Every child born damaged is a motive for revenge. The heaviness of matter, the existence of priests, the recalcitrance of women—all these are motives for revenge. Root-canal work, which I have just undergone, is a motive for revenge. I trust I have made myself clear.

Or do you still not see why it is that in those depths beneath our affection for lesser paladins we hug to ourselves the terrible figures of revenge? Well then, listen carefully: the avenger is mankind's only champion against the offenses of existence. He leaps, sword drawn, into the snakepit of cosmic malice. He pits his weight against the wrongs that make the universe wobble. He throws himself into the mangle that we may be whole. Through the avenger mankind defiantly asserts that it exists, and his battlecry echoes down the empty corridors of the world. And I, Victor Grant, avenger, defiantly assert that I have been your hero, whether you know it or not, whether you accept it or not. What I did I did for you.

I will not claim that I worked out a complete philosophy of revenge on the night I decided to kill Jude Karnofsky. Much of that philosophy came to me later—only a few minutes ago, in fact. Let's say, I only *became conscious* of it a few minutes ago. The ideas on the subject of revenge to which I just treated you have always been a part of me (one of the best parts). I was just not conscious of them. My self-knowledge, like yours, was imperfect, and no doubt it is so still. I don't deny it. In any case, it has been a matter of principle with me never to work out a complete philosophy of anything. No complete philosophy can be completely true. Perhaps I will have an opportunity to explain this dark saying later. If I don't, send me a letter. For a whole paragraph now I have been trying to say that what I did on the night my wife left me was to go straight to bed.

Nothing was going through my mind at all. My mind was a blank. At least my memory of what was running through my mind is a blank. And I have no intention of filling in the blanks with surmise. As you may imagine, it would be very easy for me to invent an example of the sort of dream I should have had that night. Instead, I will simply place before you the unusual sight of a man being yanked out of a gap in his own memory by the ringing of a telephone. It was 11:30 in the morning after the nothingness that the night of Sunday, February 17 is always to be. "I'm sick," I said, and hung up.

I took a pee, fixed a cup of coffee, lit a cigarette, and stretched out on the bed with cup and ashtray beside me. Another blank. Near 4:00 P.M. the phone rang again. The Book Store again. I resigned. Doctor's orders. Obscure heart disease. Lots of rest. I put down the phone, placed cup and ashtray beside it, removed the bedspread, the blanket, the sheets, the mattress pad, through all of which the coffee had stained and the cigarette had burned, and turned the mattress over. I put on a clean mattress pad, two sheets, two blankets, we didn't have another spread, and the hell with it, anyhow. I took another pee, lit another cigarette, turned on the gas under the coffee. I believe I ate some cottage cheese and drank some orange juice. I remember chills, flashes of imagery, the coffee boiling over. Another blank.

So it went for an additional four days, during which I must have slept almost ninety hours. More, actually, because I was not really awake those times I got up for a pee, etc. The phone or the doorbell roused me from time to time. I let them ring until whoever was responsible got tired. It had never occurred to me that Samantha might try to get in touch. For some reason—a magical reason, as it now seems—I had come to the conclusion that the next move was up to me. Conclusion is not the word, exactly, because it implies that something led up to it. From the time I first saw those two lonely envelopes on the big table I had simply known that Samantha's decision to leave me was irrevocable until something I did revoked it. Well, "know" is not the exact word that I need either. What's wrong with me? These are obscure matters, and I am determined to be accurate. What came to me was not so much knowledge as a mood, not a thought, but the psychological medium within which thoughts arise. It was a fatality: Samantha was under a spell and only I could break it. Yes, she had been enchanted away from me, and not by a raggle-taggle gypsy-O. The monster who held Samantha in thrall was the Dragon of the Apocalypse herself. Karnofsky had at her disposal all the demonic forces released by the collapse of a civilization, our civilization. I can assure you that one does not attract, gather, and master countermagic of equal potency by a mere snapping of the fingers. Therefore my own demon put me to sleep for five days, while he purified me of alien qualms and foreign aspirations, while he instructed me in the ancient wisdom we all think ourselves so wise in repressing. We got to know each other very well during these rites, my demon and I, very well indeed. At long last. So those five days were not a blank, after all!

My liberation, or re-incubation, so to speak, ended with a crash on Friday evening when Bill got the super to force open the door to my apartment. The crash itself did not wake me. I incorporated it into a short dream involving a tall stack of dirty pots. Nor was I awakened by Bill's shout—"Victor, where are you?" A hoarse voice from the deepest pit of my stomach (there was a definite aftertaste) croaked the reply: "I'm here." And that is what finally woke me up: the sound of my own voice.

"You all right?" said Bill's two heads, the dark-skinned one of which (as I realized in an instant) belonged to the super, who was looking over Bill's shoulder. Was I all right? Let's see. I got up on my elbows and took stock. I had wrestled the two blankets to the floor, but under the sheet I was stiff, sore, weak, naked, cold, and prodigiously erect.

"I will be, by and by," I answered. "And you?"

"I heard from Jude."

As the dark-skinned head swiveled around on Bill's shoulder and floated out the bedroom door behind him, I sat up and waited for the mere thought of Jude Karnofsky to drain the blood out of my erection.

"Samantha's been trying to reach you."

"Tell her that suicide is not my style."

"She wants her desk. She wants her clothes and her books, and that's all she wants. Samantha has her points, you know."

"She can have whatever she wants. All she has to do is come for it. She has her key. Oh, but you two broke the lock coming in, I take it."

"More than the lock, I'm afraid. They said at the Bookstore that you sounded very strange on the phone, and when you didn't answer the door.... I knew the kinds of things that were running through my own mind."

"Let's not bother about the stupid door. I should have known you'd be worried. I should have let you know that I was going to sleep for—what day is it, by the way?"

"Friday. Samantha wants to know when she can send someone over to pick up her stuff."

"Send someone? She doesn't need to send anyone. If you'll

lend me your car I'll take her things over to her myself." (Bill, who liked to go camping, had a station wagon.)

"She wouldn't give me her phone number or address. She won't give them to you either. She doesn't want to see you— yet, she said. She'll call again tomorrow."

"And Jude?"

"Do you want to get something to eat? It's a long story."

Believe it or not, I still had an erection. Bill, whose tact is unfailing, went out of the bedroom as I started to slide sideways from under the sheet, my right leg drawn up and crossed over. You are snorting with impatience, are you? You think these details are trivial, do you? I should think that it was up to me to decide whether or nor my own erections are trivial details. You decide about your erections, assuming you have them.

Bill was in the kitchen pouring himself a shot of gin, the only alcoholic beverage I regularly keep in the house. (Samantha liked a martini before supper. I was not much of a drinker myself. Alcohol used to make me reveal things about myself that people sooner or later used against me. You have to have a good deal more faith in human nature than I had if you are going to drink in quantities when other people are around.) "Don't you want to shave?" he asked.

"No," I said. I didn't want to comb my hair either.

He suggested a Chinese restaurant, not because he likes Chinese food, but because he knew that I did. But I was in the mood for meat, smoking gobbets of rare, bloody meat, thick and fat. We went to the Fatted Calf, an unpretentious place that serves large portions of decent food at reasonable prices. I ordered steak; Bill ordered pork chops. While we waited for the food, Bill drank bourbon and I surreptitiously worked at unhooking my underwear from around a new erection. Bill only started to tell me about Jude's latest outrages when the food arrived. I finished my steak before he had told half of it. I ordered another steak. When Bill pointed with an inquiring look at his second, untouched pork chop, I picked it up by the tail and made it my own in four neat chomps. I ate no bread or potatoes with the second steak, as I had not with the first. I ate Bill's salad and both of mine, sans any dressing but the steak juices I dripped over them. Of course I had no dessert, although I did have a brandy with my coffee. Never before had I eaten a meal like that. Up to then I had been a nibbler, a great eater of fruits, nuts, dairy products, and foods derived from grains, the kinds of food, in short, that my father (who cooked for us after my mother died) never made, and the kind of food I had very little to do with during those years I worked as a short-order cook. The things we do in the process of trying not to do something else!

I did not listen as carefully to Bill as he deserved. I was scanning with my inner ear for the source and content of certain promptings that had so far only announced themselves as a buzz at the back of my mind. I gathered that Jude was not going to ask for alimony. She was against it in principle. Instead she wanted $57,600 or $200 for each of the 288 weeks she had slaved for him as a housewife. She also wanted $50,000 damages for Bill's sexism, which had retarded her growth into full androgynous beinghood. But she would settle for the round sum of $100,000. She wanted the apartment and its contents and was seeking a court order to have Bill locked out. She wanted custody of Tobias Victor. Bill could babysit with him once a week and could take care of him during the summer (presumably so that Jude would be free to travel). She wanted $1000 a month child support, adjusted annually to the cost-of-living index. She wanted the car. She wanted Bill to pay her lawyer's fees. She wanted and she wanted.

Further, Bill had been talking to Martine, his maid, a very nice woman from one of the Caribbean islands. She had gone to work for Jude in order to be near Victor Little. Early that morning she had come to Bill, upset, embarrassed, reluctant at first to talk, her eyes brimming over with tears. Finally that mild and ultrarespectable creature had pleaded with Bill to get his son back by whatever means were necessary, including kidnapping. Jude had taken Victor Little out of his nursery school, a sexist institution that did nothing to prevent girls from being girls and boys from being boys. Jude had ordered Martine to make Victor Little help with the housework. Martine was to teach him how to cook, sew, clean house, wash and iron clothes. For one hour each morning and each afternoon he was allowed to play—with the doll house and accoutrements that Jude had bought him first thing the day after she ran out on Bill. For one hour each evening, during supper (when Jude came home for it), there was a session of catechism in neofeminist dogma. If Victor Little did well, he was allowed to kiss his mother's cheek; if not, she put on a show of being cold and distant. When, the night before, Martine saw Jude unpack three new dresses, little Toby's size, she nearly fainted with horror. She crossed herself and resolved to go to Bill.

You see the problem. I needed an ally, someone to perform a diversionary or holding action. I needed someone to sink teeth into Jude's ample flank until I was ready to move in for the kill. I needed someone to hold her at bay until I could leap for the jugular. I needed something like a dogpack to harry her away from the sacred precincts of Bill's fortune and Victor Little's masculinity, upon which she was swooping down like a wolf on the fold. But only until I was ready to end her depredations forever.

"There is just one thing to do," I said to Bill, who was sitting slumped halfway under the table of our booth, a rumpled half-smile on his face. "Call your mother." Miss Lily, as she preferred people to address her, matriarch, aristocrat, businesswoman, and southern belle, owned big houses and large tracts of land in North Carolina, Maine, Connecticut, Long Island, and Baltimore. She also owned most of a company, located in Virginia, that manufactured swimsuits, which for special buyers she would model over her own still elegant, fifty-year-old contours. (She had married Bill's father at age sixteen.) She had controlling interests in companies that manufactured portable swimming pools and sauna baths and everything needed to equip and maintain them. She was indomitable, unflappable, tireless, and never happier than when engaged in a dozen lawsuits. She was impeccable and she was implacable. She was cool, patient, ingenious, and ferocious. No woman had ever beaten her at anything and no man had ever tried. (All four of her husbands, one current and three discards, still worked for her at Lily-Belle Swimwear, Inc.) Only one person had ever seriously contravened her wishes, and that was Bill, who had married Judith Karnofsky over his mother's silent but unmistakable displeasure. Miss Lily had been displeased, first because she had not selected Jude, and second, because Jude was Jude. She would know how to keep the hands of "the Karnofsky woman" off her oldest son's matri-money and my godson's masculinity, until I could break the arms attached to those hands. Miss Lily's conception of the law was that it had been invented by men for the use of women such as herself. No one had proved her wrong yet.

"My mother . . ." said Bill, sitting up.

"Your mother."

"Jesus!"

"You've got to call your mother."

"There is something diabolical about you, Victor."

"You've got to call your mother. And right away."

Well, Bill hesitated, he wasn't sure, he had to think about it, I had no idea, running to his mother would be bad for his health, it would be a retreat, a regression, he couldn't do it to himself, in fact he couldn't do it to Jude, he couldn't do it to his mother either, it was really too much, I didn't understand, it was all very complicated, Jude and his mother were opposites but they were also equivalents, in their effect on him at least, psychologically speaking it was impossible for him to sic one on the other, his brain would explode, Jesus! Still, it was an idea . . . in a way, but . . .

By then I had paid for dinner and was dragging Bill uptown along Broadway.

"Where are we going," he said.

"To my apartment. So you can call your mother."

"But, I thought we could go to see *Fringe Benefits*. Think of it: *95 percent on the petermeter.*"

With my left hand in my pocket (my right on Bill's arm) I maneuvered the tip of my own one-hundred percent erect peter to where it would be held flat between belly and belt buckle. Passersby were staring at us.

I sat right beside Bill while he called his mother (he forgot to reverse the charges). Miss Lily is a woman of quick understanding. She had only to hear that Jude was asking for a divorce. She did not want to hear any more. She could guess the sordid details, more or less. In any case, she would hear them the next morning at ten, when Bill was to appear at her room in the Plaza Hotel. "You hear?" She would be on the next flight to New York, and if there was no plane conveniently scheduled, she would fly her own. And if there was no opening in the schedules of the New York airports during which she could land, she would drive. One way or the other she would be in the Plaza at ten, and Bill better make sure he was there too. "Yes mother," Bill said. "Yes mother . . . Yes mother."

I am not proud of the way I tried to get rid of Bill that evening. Any other night I would have been happy to sit up with him while he drank himself to sleep. I had done it many times before. And don't be so quick to judge. Whatever vices I have, disloyalty is not one of them. There is such a thing as being disloyal to oneself too, you know. The point is that I had to get free of distractions for a while before I could decide what in me was demanding my loyalty. In any case, I never did ease Bill out. He alluded mournfully to his empty apartment and hinted reproachfully (and unfairly, in my opinion) that I had prevented him from escaping into a companionable fantasy built up on the raw materials of *Fringe Benefits*.

Bill stretched himself out on the couch. Beside him, on the floor, he put a bowl of ice, a pitcher of water, a glass, and the gin, which by and by he just about finished. I sat in the one deep chair, made deeper every month by the collapse of another spring, and wrote an account of the past week's events in a stenographer's pad. I did not realize then that this pad was to become the first volume of my diary, which is now in thirty-nine volumes, if one may speak of a stenographer's pad as a volume. That historic first pad, with its unself-conscious scribble, its dizzying rush in medias res, will be a collector's item, or would have been, had I not willed it, along with the others, to the Columbia Library. You will not be able to read it until I am dead, though. What am I saying? I am dead already, if you are reading these very words, the presence of which before you certifies the lamentable fact they announce.

When Bill fell asleep, glass balanced on his stomach, I put his drink makings away, covered him with the two clean blankets from my bed, got into a sweater and my overcoat (actually a serviceable pile-lined raincoat), for the apartment was getting cold, turned off the lights, sat down and then back in the deepening chair, put my feet up, and tried to cultivate a receptive frame of mind. But all that came to me was first, a vision of a man, naked above the waist, massive of bicep, tricep, and latissimus dorsi, who with a jerk of his wrist shook the scabbard off an army-surplus machete (like the one I have in my closet) and began in the same motion to stride through the heat waves shimmering above the sands between him and an out-of-focus enemy waiting in the distance; and second, sleep.

When I awoke the next morning, sore in the arms, chest, and back, Bill had already gone. I staggered to the bathroom for my first shower in about a week. (Normally, you understand, I am fastidious about my personal hygiene.) I fell asleep and had a quick dream of cutting my way through a swampy jungle. I leaned back against the rough bark of a tree and woke up slumped on the hot and cold water taps, the spray massaging the back of my head. I began to warm up a bit, like a snake in the morning sun, except that the warmth seemed to rise from my interior out to the skin, rather than from an external source. I opened the hot water tap some more. Even now I can recall the feeling of my skin becoming alert and responsive. The heat seeped through me, flushing stiffness away. I stretched, arms up, and then stretched, arms out, until they touched the tiled sides of the shower stall. I opened my hands and pushed until I began to vibrate with the strain. I stretched bending over and stretched twisting to the right and to the left. I opened the hot water tap still more. I breathed in steam and droplets of spray, shuffling my feet in the water on the floor as a fakir might dance on a bed of glowing coals. Then I began to wash, working from the extremities toward the center, lathering and kneading every inch of skin as it rose up to meet my fingers, soaping and stroking the cleft in back and the prominence up front, while time stood still.

I got out of the shower and stood in front of the mirror on the medicine chest. With my hand I wiped away the condensation from the face staring out at me. It looked like the face of someone who looked like someone I knew. It clouded over again. I wiped it clear again: brown eyes, hollow cheeks, a crew-cut beard on a long jaw. The face blurred over once more, and once more I rubbed it into focus. There were flecks of black, yellow, and green in the eyes; thick eyebrows, prominent ridges, the hair washed back and with an irregular part down the middle. The features lost their outlines, grew dim, receded into a haze, but more slowly this time. I pulled them forward by making passes with my hand. The skin was flushed, glistening, the lips swollen.

As very slowly now a thin fog began to come between us, I spread on lather and shaved off strips of beard, until only the mustache was left. The ends of the mustache continued the lines that ran from the wings of the nose to the corners of the mouth, which curved down in the faintest of grim smiles. I rinsed off the remaining lather with a washcloth and then used it to dissipate the mist for good. The face gleamed as though in a medium brighter than air. Its eyes held mine in a cool appraisal. A drop of water ran down across it in a zigzag course. It was a stern face, an inscrutable face, the face of an avenger.

I brought up my arms smartly, fists at the ears, elbows out, and made a muscle, as they say. It is true that I was quite thin, but not painfully so, not by any means. My muscles, although admittedly not very large, were very sharply articulated, as though in an anatomical diagram. The fact of the matter is that a man my height and weight who held himself less tensely would have seemed less thin. (For the record, I was just under six feet tall—five feet, ten and one-half inches, to be exact. And I weighed one hundred thirty-four pounds, as I discovered at Woolworth's that afternoon on a scale I feigned an interest in buying.) It suddenly hit me that my muscles were *always* tense, always drawn up tight. What ignominy! I will bet they never relaxed, even when the rest of me was asleep. What was I afraid of? My muscles, damn it, were not the tumescent coils of a lion ready to charge, but the wrung-out knots of a gazelle rigid in shock!

I let my arms hang down. I slumped. I waggled my wrists to get the blood flowing. I drew in and blew out fifty deep droughts of air, until the mirror steamed over again, until pressure built up in my ears and nebula flashed before my eyes. After a time, the face clear before me again, I began systematically to relax, from the scalp down. One by one areas of face, neck, trunk, and limbs roused themselves into my awareness with a faint tingle, became warm and limber. I went through the process again, from the muscles in the arches of the toes up. This time I held my eyelids closed and my inner eye open. As I went along I threw up ridges of muscles so that they could be located in imaginative space. Then I smoothed them according to their natural contours. Through this procedure, which I have since perfected, the body becomes sentient and supple at the same time. On that memorable morning of Saturday, February 22, 1974, my body began to rise out of unconsciousness like a god from the sea. (Can you beat that? I just now for the first time noticed the date: Washington's birthday! Signs and portents, signs and portents.)

Watching the mirror to see what would happen, I held my arms close in, palms up, and strained, as though curling a heavy barbell. Veins stood out on face and neck. The deltoids humped and the pectorals flattened. The flush deepened. Sweat mixed with the drying shower water. My upper lip began to quiver. I relaxed, as before. Once again I curled the imaginary barbell, this time crouching a bit, tilting my pelvis forward so that I could feel muscles in my calves, thighs, buttocks, and belly tighten, this time observing carefully the position, shape and movement of every visible muscle. I relaxed. I turned over my hands and strained, as though pushing down on the handle of a large box detonator. I stretched my arms up and strained, as though trying to chin myself. I placed the palm of my right hand against the right side of my face and pushed palm and face against each other. I repeated the exercise on the left side. I clasped my hands behind my head, then pushed forward with my hands and backward with my head. I coupled my hands in front of me and pulled them in opposite directions. I put my right foot in my clasped hands as though in a stirrup, then pushed down with my foot and up with my hands. I repeated the exercise with my left foot. I relaxed, and I relaxed again, until I was no longer panting and the mirror was once again clear.

I began now to twist, stretch, and flex whole systems of muscles in a series of segued movements that gradually became rhythmic. As each gesture arrived at its natural point of rest I transformed it into the initial stages of another. A man lifting the ceiling sank into a man doing knee bends who slowly uncoiled into a discus thrower who followed through in slow motion to reach for a fly ball. Gradually the movements separated themselves from recognizable postures. They became first stylized and then abstract, organized according to the shapes and dispositions of the body that formed them, rather than toward an imaginary task. In a few minutes I was panting, slick all over with sweat, and trembly.

The air outside the bathroom was a good twenty degrees cooler. I got into pajamas and my trusty olive-drab army-surplus sweater with the knit-collar. I put a fire under the coffee that had been perked about a week before. While waiting for the coffee to heat I sat at the kitchen table brushing my teeth, feeling very good. The coffee hot, I poured the half cup that was left and lit a cigarette. I took one puff, looked at it, dipped the burning end into the coffee, threw it away, crumpled the remaining cigarettes in their pack (I had smoked Lucky Strikes ever since unfiltered Old Golds became unavailable), threw the pack away, poured the coffee into the sink.

I did not own sneakers. What would I have used them for? But I found a pair of hush puppies (also known as desert boots and fruit boots) in the back of a closet. They were furry with dust fluffs. I had bought them in a fit of sportiness about three years before and had worn them maybe twice since. I also took out a pair of red corduroy trousers with wide wales, flared legs, and a low rise. Samantha, who did not approve of my taste in clothes, had got them for me as a present to go with the hush puppies. Samantha used to say that I only liked two colors: dark grey and light black. As I was putting the corduroys on (over my pajamas), the phone rang. It was Samantha. Wouldn't you know. . . .

"Victor?"

"Whom did you expect?"

"Victor, how are you?"

"Very well, thanks."

"Victor, please."

"Hold on a minute" I went over to the garbage bag and extracted the crumpled pack of Luckies. I pulled out one with as many twists in it as the Watergate case. It did not draw well because of a crack in the paper about two-thirds of the way down. I broke off the smaller piece and lit up again.

"Well, Samantha, what can I do for you?"

"Victor, there are things we have to talk about."

"Is that so?"

"Victor, please don't make things more difficult than they already are."

"Me make things difficult? I wouldn't dream of it. Surely you are thinking of someone else. Oh, I forgot, you don't like men any more. Or have you started going both ways? I understand that Pastor Peter Brevoort—"

The phone slammed in my ear. I put out the cigarette, got my thick olive-drab bad-weather socks, and began to slip the hush puppies over them, when the phone rang again.

"When can I send someone over to pick up my clothes and things?" said Samantha. I held a match to the piece of cigarette I had broken off before, scorching my mustache.

"Your wish is my command."

"Good. This afternoon, then. About three." There was a long pause, which I made a point of not interrupting. "Victor, you shouldn't have said that about me going both ways."

"Why not?"

"It just isn't true, and you know it."

"Prove it by coming back to me."

"That wouldn't prove anything—except that I don't have what it takes to . . . go it on my own. . . . Sex has nothing to do with my leaving you."

"Sex has everything to do with everything."

"Only a man could think that."

"Only a woman could doubt it."

"You are so cocksure about everything."

"Exactly."

"All right, Victor, all right. These people I am with are sure of everything too. I thought, I don't see why we have to be enemies."

"Sure: 'Why can't we still be friends?' "

"You'll be sorry for this," she said, and hung up.

The hush puppies would not go on over the heavy socks. My socks for everyday use, three for a dollar in John's Bargain Stores, were too thin. I had no intention of limping around with blisters for a week. Thus great enterprises are checked by the thickness of a pair of socks. In the bottom drawer of Samantha's dresser, to which a sudden inspiration led me, were two pairs of orlon stretch socks neither too thick nor too thin. Samantha used them for ice skating. (Have I mentioned that for two years, between her release from high school and her escape to New York, she had been an instructor at the Rocking Roller-Ice Rink of Painesville, Ohio?) One pair was pink struggling toward purple. The other pair was a green sinking into yellow. Two of the socks had holes in them, a pink, where the toe should have been, and a green, where the heel should have been. I therefore put on the other two, one pink purple, one green yellow, both without holes. Thus great enterprises lurch forward on the arms of men willing to stare down the raised eyebrows of fashion.

My windbreaker is blue. In white over the left breast area are the schematic drawing of a crown and the word "Columbia." I zipped it on, ran down the stairs, and jogged west, across Broadway, across Riverside Drive, to the walk along the outside of Riverside Park, where I collapsed on a bench. No doubt about it, I was not in very good shape. Managing a bookstore, in case you didn't know, develops not strength of body but orderliness of mind. As I sat puffing and sweating, sore in ankle, knee, and in everything connected with the respiratory apparatus, including my teeth, a girl jogged by. She had on a very professional-looking navy blue sweat suit and very expensive-looking powder blue suede sneakers. I studied her carefully as she went by, thin face effortlessly cleaving the wind. Perhaps you thought I was too proud to learn from a woman. I heaved myself up and started downtown, alternately jogging one block and walking two, until I got to Ninety-sixth Street. Then back uptown. I refused to meet the inquiring look of the big-chested professorial type with tobacco-stained beard who jogged briskly by heading south. The hell with him. His looks were nothing to clear a bloodshot eyeball either.

I stopped on Broadway to buy a few things—white sweat socks, a smoked pork tenderloin (it was on sale), a large tomato (79 cents a pound), and, on impulse, a pepperoni. At home I put the pork in a moderate oven and crawled into bed. When I awoke two hours later, the smoked butt and I were ready for each other. I ate a little more than half of what had begun as four pounds of meat, and with it, a salad of sliced onion, carrot, tomato, and pepperoni. Even in these days, of course, I would not have considered using any dressing but oil and vinegar. For dessert I had three cups of freshly perked coffee and a crumpled Lucky Strike. Another shower, a bowel movement, and I was ready for the afternoon's workout, although I had not yet decided what form it would take.

If I were a literary man, I would pause here to write an excursus on the subject of the transformations that have taken place in the character of my stool, beginning with the memorable bowel movement of February 22, 1974. Men of action do not philosophize—over bowel movements or anything else. It used to be that perhaps three times a week I would strain to produce half a dozen turds something like hazelnut shells in size, hardness, color, and dryness. From the first day of my training period, however, I began to deposit daily and effortlessly a single unbroken length, moist, limber, dark, and thick, but of a penetrating and lingering odor. I began also to perspire, easily and copiously, but only from physical effort. I will not speak of the thin, nervous sweat from my days of suppressed hysteria. My hair, which I did not bother to have cut, became oilier, thicker (in appearance, at least), and to my surprise took on a curl. The pimples disappeared from my buttocks. There were other such changes of equal interest from the scientific point of view, some of which I will mention later, some not. This is not, after all, a tract in cosmetic hygiene. If you don't mind having pimples on your ass, I don't mind either.

I spent the afternoon walking around the city, developing my powers of observation. I would stop before a shop window, run my eye over the contents, turn around, run my mind's eye over the after-image. I practiced trying to make things out at a distance. Was it a boy or was it a girl, that figure in dungarees and fatigue jacket four blocks away? That blur was a cat stalking something along a ledge six stories up. A sparrow landed on a TV antenna. Righties spread tomato sauce on pizza with a counterclockwise movement. Did you know that in the Sixties, right off Broadway, there is a building upon which stands a sizable replica of the Statue of Liberty? A hot chestnut vendor wore a complete glove on his left hand, but on his right the fingers were cut out of the glove halfway down. The ends of his fingers were cracked, shiny, and grimy. The Puerto Rican boy innocently feeding pigeons was actually luring them to where a confederate could snatch one, wring its neck, and stuff it into a green plastic bag. The humped-over man, eyes closed, mumbling, crossing himself forty times, was praying to a fire alarm box. Two lesbians, walking briskly, hand in hand, chatting, smiling, touching heads from time to time, were also sneaking glances out of the corners of their eyes in the hopes that someone was noticing. A little girl dropped purple grapes on passersby from a fourth story window. A prostitute worked her tongue in and out and around her lips at me. Her eyes glittered with hate or from drugs.

Home once again, four hours later, my head buzzing, I sipped on the jigger-ful of gin Bill never got to finish, sliced, fried, and ate what was left of the smoked pork (along with half a head of lettuce), finished the pot of coffee, smoked the last (crumpled) Lucky Strike of my life, poured what I had done and seen that day into my journal, and went to sleep. Thus ended the first day of training for my career as a lady-killer.

III

E VERY detail of the routine
I followed for the next two months or so is worthy of preserva-
tion. Some day I shall write a book on the subject. It would
revolutionize the physical culture industry. I believe I am correct in saying that my approach to the question of how to
promote mental and physical well-being in the human male is
the first truly scientific one. Before you scoff, ask yourself what
other approach is entirely consistent with the science of
ethology. I can tell you in advance that there is none. There is
no other approach that follows the path laid down by our
evolutionary past. There is no other approach based on the fact
that men evolved as hunters and remain hunters still, no matter
how securely they have been tethered by apron strings. And I
discovered it merely by following my demon, alias my inclinations. Of course: one's natural inclinations are always the visible signs of instinctive promptings! Unfortunately, I have no
time to write that book now. You will have to be satisfied with
the sketchiest of outlines. You will get all the detail you could
desire in the account very soon to follow of how I tracked down
Jude Karnofsky and closed in for the kill.

I did not begin with a schedule, I ended with one. And up to the very last day of my training period I would omit, modify, or substitute as the spirit moved me. Regularities made irregular is nature's way, after all. At six o'clock each morning I forsook my bed. Into my jogging clothes, the same as on the first day, except for the pink socks and the pajama underwear. Crosstown and downtown to Central Park, downtown and crosstown to the Reservoir, then once around, jogajog the whole way. Around once again, sprinting ferociously for fifty yards, then walking and panting fifty, then sprinting fifty, then walking fifty, and so on. (Jogging builds endurance; sprinting builds muscle, and under an immense sky the carnivore lopes effortlessly after his prey across a great African plain. When the prey tires, the predator still has enough in him for the final discharging charge.) Then jogajog home, crosstown and uptown to Morningside Drive, uptown and crosstown to my apartment. It is seven o'clock or a few minutes later.

Out of my clothes, into the bathroom, and before the mirror, where each day I labored over the creation of my body— tense, relax, twist, return, stretch, contract, watch and visualize, shaping declivities, rounding prominences, filling in and hollowing out, laying on strip after strip of laminated muscle. A shower around eight, then breakfast: ham, bacon, beef liver, pork chops, sausages, when my budget allowed them; hearts, kidneys, blood pudding, calf's brain, smoked eel, when I could find them; cheese, when there was nothing else; and eggs; and an orange, *not* orange juice; no toast; plenty of coffee, save your tea for foreigners and vegetarians. Back to bed for a well-deserved nap, until ten o'clock, or so.

For the rest of the morning I exercised my mind. I would rather think of my mind as a muscle than as a gas, but you suit yourself. At first I tried merely to recall, not in words but as visual images, the details of things I had once known well, the lay-out of rooms in the house I grew up in on Roosevelt Avenue in Queens, for example. It took me a week before I could spread out across my mind the positions of all the tools on the pine walls of my father's workshop in the cellar of our house. The funny thing is that at first I could not visualize the tools at all, but only the outlines my father had drawn around them. One of the tools kept fading within its outline, no matter how many times my imagination brushed it in. The reason came to me in a flash weeks later while I was trying to figure out what weapon I should use on Jude Karnofsky. The tool in question was my father's thirty-inch Swedish bowsaw. I had removed the blade, strung it with thin steel cable, cocked it with an ingenious device made of a furniture clamp and a car jack, and loaded it with a curtain rod. A formidable crossbow, but when I stepped back to admire it the cable slipped off the jack and sent the curtain rod part way through the wall of our house, three inches into my father's bedroom. I was still trying to pull the rod out when my father came home from work. He locked the saw in the closet under the staircase, where he kept his hunting rifles.

As I was saying, at first I merely tried to recall things I had already once known well, such as the pattern on the linoleum in the kitchen where my father, wearing only his carpenter's overalls with all the loops and pockets, bustled around slamming pots and plates, whistling tunes from Victor Herbert in perfect pitch and with every grace note, goatish tufts of blonde hair hanging from his armpits, his tremendous biceps jumping, as placing on the table two plates heaped with knockwurst, boiled potatoes, and sauerkraut, he said, "try this on for size, she said," and poured me half a glass of beer out of the quart bottle of Ruppert's he would finish with his meal. But after awhile I began to reconstruct things I had never paid much attention to, such as the names and features of my ninth-grade classmates, none of whom was my friend, or the furnishings in the room where for twelve dollars I lost my virginity six feet away from the crib of the prostitute's two-year old daughter, who kept tossing in her sleep. I moved on, finally, to the imaginative construction of situations I had never experienced. I worked out precisely what parts of the body are vulnerable to elbows, claws, and kicking heels when you strangle someone from behind. I visualized in every sharp-edged detail the move- ment of the ice-pick toward the kidney. I visualized all the ways in which that movement might be interrupted or deflected and I visualized all the measures that might be taken to prevent interruption or deflection, and, of course detection.

In addition to these exercises in imaginative construction and projection, I worked to develop my powers of observation and memory. I mastered Dr. Bruno Furst's mnemonic system in ten days. For an exposition of the many improvements I made in that system you will have to wait until I have written the book referred to above. Suffice it to say that after an hour of study I can tell you what is on every page of, for example, a *Playboy* magazine, text and illustration. By the middle of April I had become at least a neophyte in the mysteries of auto- hypnosis. (The best manual for the beginner is Lawrence Sparks, *Self-Hypnosis: A Conditioned-Response Technique,* New York: Grune & Stratton, 1962.) One becomes adept at auto-hypnosis by degrees. I learned, easily enough, how to produce an eyelid catalepsy, how to slow my pulse, how to make one hand cold and the other warm at the same time, how to make my body so rigid that I could stretch out supported only by the back of one chair under my heels and by the back of another under my neck, how to anesthetize my extremities. By the end of two months, I could wriggle my ears, dilate my pupils, depress and flare my nostrils, move my head from side to side like a Balinese dancer. But I could never push myself on to the final degree of adeptness, the evidence for which is that one can produce nega- tive and positive hallucinations. Even against the efforts of my will, my deepest loyalties were to the reality principle.

For lunch I ate some of the cold meat left over from the previous night's dinner, and fruit in season, not enough to slow me down. By mid-March Samantha had gotten into the habit of calling me two or three times a week during her lunch break.

She never asked me how I was doing or what I was doing. She just voided whatever was on her mind into her end of the wire so that it could pour into the ear of Dr. Grant, your friendly dial-a-shrink. "U-hunh," I would say, or "no-kidding," or "What else could you do?" True enough, she would sometimes ask for my advice, but only rhetorically. She never listened when I gave it. Although she would never have said so, even to herself, I had no difficulty in making out that the Misses-in-Chief of *Ms. Chief* were exploiting Samantha. They underpaid and overworked her. They sweet-talked and promised her, but reserved the decision making for themselves; for Samantha they reserved such tasks as typing, filing, making routine calls, and answering routine letters. I would not have commiserated with Samantha even had she given me the opportunity. She was not aware of her own disappointment. She hid it from herself, but not from me, under a forced display of enthusiasm.

By 1:30 I was in the Columbia gym (I had never returned my Columbia I.D.), or in the Teacher's College gym (where the same I.D. was valid), or in the Sixty-third Street YMCA (on a visitor's pass at $4.00 a visit) or in Central Park. I swam or lifted weights or played handball or half-court basketball or touch football. On some days I was reduced to throwing a frisbee. Tennis was too expensive (and too genteel) and squash was too dangerous for beginners, as a kindly exchange student from India remarked when I had almost knocked myself out with the racquet I borrowed from him. I was ejected for incompetence during the first game of basketball I played in Central Park. "Hey man, you been on Mars all your life? Don't you know you got to *dribble* that ball?" said one of the six-foot-six black superstars who monopolize the Central Park game, even in midwinter. I had not been what you would have called a gregarious child exactly. I preferred to play by myself. The other children in the neighborhood seemed to prefer that I play by myself too. How then was I to have become expert in team sports?

A group of Teacher's College students I got in with were

not so choosy as the black superstars, or anyhow more polite. They were not very good athletes either, as I gradually realized. At first I was deceived by their chatter and bustle. From them I learned the rudiments of basketball. From one of them, Irwin Weisskopf, I learned by chance of a Saturday afternoon touch football game in Riverside Park. From one of the Saturday players, Marvin Something, I learned of a Sunday game. The weather was bad, the season over, players scarce, especially players who were willing to spend the afternoon as mute, inglorious linemen. By April I had graduated from the Teacher's College set. I was playing basketball with Columbia College students, handball with white-collar types at the YMCA, and football on Saturday and Sunday mornings with an assortment of stevedores, cops, and moving men in Central Park. It is no crime to be proud of one's achievements, if they are genuine. I am proud of the reputation I established among these rough-and-tumble men as a fearless blocking back and a relentless defensive lineman. One time when I was blocking for the quarterback on a sprintout right, I saw Danny, a 240-pound meat-packer, charging up for the tag. I pivoted sharply on my right foot and shot off my left directly at Danny's chest. The impact straightened him up and sent me flying two yards back. Clarence came over, looked down at me for a minute, reached out a hand to help me up, and said, "You're a regular kamikaze."

"He thinks he's Evel Knievel," said Leon.

I assure you that the laughter this remark brought forth was more affectionate than derisive. Danny put a hand around my bicep, perhaps to save me from toppling over, and said, "You all right, Kniev?"

"Let's play ball," I growled, and the nickname stuck. Kniev is not an elegant nickname, but neither is it entirely without respect.

When late in April one of the captains choosing up sides nodded toward me and said "Kniev" on the fifth round rather than on the eighth and last: when Clarence, Leon, and Terry waited for me after the game to walk uptown with them (the other players seemed all to live in Yorktown or in the Bronx); and when they simply took it for granted that I would stop with them for a couple of beers in a bar on One-hundredth Street and Central Park West (where Terry and I were the only Caucasians), then I understood how Parzival felt when with a curt gesture King Arthur directed him toward a seat at the Round Table.

I sat in that bar for a long time after the other three went home to their wives. I drank beer after beer, although normally two glasses is as much as I can force down. The bartender, who had misheard "Kniev" as "Steve," gave me his view of the Watergate scandal. A short man with hysterical eyes sat down next to me at the bar. "Fred, this is Steve, a friend of Clarence's," said the bartender. Apropos of nothing, Fred suddenly made a long drunken speech about how he had nothing against anybody, even though some white folks were hard to get along with. A woman sat down on the other side of me. "Norma, this is Steve, a friend of Leon's," said the bartender. It took me only a few minutes to realize that I was expected to buy her a drink. While drinking boilermakers at my expense she explained how that faggot bastard, her brother, was bleeding her dry. The bartender, Fred, and I bought each other drinks. The jukebox kept on playing Motown and jazz from the bop era. Two men were loudly arguing the respective merits of Pete Rose and Cleon Jones, who, it was alleged, "couldn't hit a bull's ass with a spade." Three couples at a table behind me kept bursting into laughter over stories they were telling each other about the elaborate and unsuccessful attempts of an absent friend named Alberto to seduce a certain Mavis, whose snatch, one of the men said, was going to rust shut forever if she didn't use it soon. I do not believe I had ever felt more at home with the human species, in spite of the solitary man glowering at me from around the far corner of the bar.

I was giving you an outline of my daily training schedule.

It is not my fault if one thing reminds me of another. That is the way the human mind works. That is the way your mind works, if you are human. Besides, it is by no means certain that the boundaries of things are what they seem to be at the first superficial glance. Ask a philosopher, if you know any. By five o'clock I was usually home for another shower, another nap. By six o'clock I was up again, preparing supper. I am not a gourmet. Save your fancy sauces and your creamed vegetables for men capable of displacing on food the hungers whose proper object is the female body. Notice that there are no female gourmets. How can you displace hungers you don't have? For supper I invariably ate three or four pounds of whatever meat was on sale at the local supermarkets: lamb, pork, beef, or bird, smoked, roast, fried, or deep-fried, but never boiled, never. I am willing to share with you my recipe for salad. Cut a large head of iceberg lettuce in half (unless you have a half a head left from the day before), and the hell with Cesar Chavez. Wrap one of the halves in cellophane and replace in the refrigerator. Cut the other half into chunks about one inch square. Place in a wooden bowl. Add four or five leaves of chicory, or escarole, or romaine, or the like. Add four or five leaves of spinach, or strips of cabbage, or florets of broccoli and cauliflower (if you can afford it). Add one large carrot cut into rings approximately three-eighths of an inch thick. Add a large stalk of celery or two small ones cut the same way. Add a medium-sized onion cut into rings one-quarter inch thick. Add a half dozen slices of cucumber cut the same way. Add one-third of a pepper cut into thin strips. Add one-half dozen cherry tomatoes (they are cheaper). Season with salt, pepper, thyme, oregano, a little vinegar, and lots of olive oil. You may leave out any of these ingredients, or even two, except for the iceberg lettuce and the seasoning. I often did.

I drank about a quart of water with the meal and not much less coffee after it. From the first days on this regime I developed a terrific appetite for hot spices. I began to cut cherry peppers into my salad and to cover my meat with horseradish and barbecue and Trinidad sauces, with pepper I ground myself and with mustard I mixed up fresh for the occasion. This diet, obviously is not for everyone. It is not for women (their metabolism could not take it) or for androgynes (it would blast them apart along their split personalities) or for Orientals (I mean a state of mind or condition of the soul, rather than a accident of birth) or for Christians. While preparing and eating supper I reviewed and fixed in my mind the lessons that might be drawn from the day's adventures up to that time. I continued these meditations for an hour or so afterward. By eight o'clock I was ready to go out on the town.

You are light years from the truth if you believe that I spent my evenings in a pursuit of mere entertainment. Quite the contrary. Will you ever get it into your heads that I am not a frivolous man? The tests and tasks I set myself for the period between 8:00 and 11:00 P.M. were the most demanding of the day. How demanding the rest of my day was you know. Come, see if you can do for a few minutes what I did for three hours or more every night. Try to be something other than what you are. Imagine that you are not gregarious, that you are uneasy at social gatherings, that you have no gift for small talk, that people are usually hostile to you on first acquaintance, that you are more than willing to return their hostility, in spades. Put on the mask of your anti-self, as the poet Wilbur Yates recommended. As I put on a mask, every night—except that your anti-self is my primary one (and my anti-self is your primary one. I give you my permission to think of me as the embodiment of your anti-self; I have suffered worse indignities). All right, then. Remembering that you are no social butterfly, imagine that each night between 8:00 and 11:00 you force yourself to appear at a different place where people gather, at a meeting of the West Side Democrats, for example, or a protest rally or prayer meeting, a PTA meeting, at a theater lobby, a hotel lobby, the lobby of Madison Square Garden, at an amateur theatrical, a concert in the park, at a coffee house, a bottle club, a cafeteria, a jazz club, a pool room (but *not* a bowling alley, not under any circumstances), at a Barnard musicale, a soup kitchen, a publisher's cocktail party (to which Samantha said she was not going), at Dale's Dance Studios (for a free introductory offer), at night court, at the end of the line waiting to see *The Exorcist,* a discotheque, a dance for single but respectable men and women over thirty-five, a hearing on a gay rights bill, at Rockefeller Center, Washington Square, Bethesda Fountain, at Ninety-sixth and Broadway (where junkies hang out), at a topless bar in Hoboken, at bars of all kinds, singles bars, swinging bars, working men's bars, bars catering to journalists, students, hoods, actors, gamblers, hustlers, and even a bar run by and for lesbians, where I was asked to leave.

Oh, I suffered other rebuffs, but not many, fewer than you would think, if you consider the risks of the task I had set myself. That task was nothing less than to disassemble and reassemble my personality into one appropriate for the occasion, whatever it was. I point out by way of admonition that it is no use trying to disassemble your personality unless you have one. Picture me walking down Broadway, with a brisk step and every sense open wide. Crossing, oh, say, Eighty-eighth Street I spot a lit-up storefront four doors in, a couple moving toward the door, a wave of cigarette smoke breaking over them as they open it. I investigate. Paintings on all the walls, forty people standing around talking and drinking out of plastic glasses, a card table, a white cloth, a gallon bottle of wine, a platter of cheese cut into cubes impaled each on its own toothpick, a tower of plastic glasses. It is either the opening of an art gallery, which from the look of things in general will close in a month, or it is the opening of a one-man show, which from the look of the paintings will not do much to keep the gallery open. Even though I have never yet met a painter, nor a painting, nor an admirer of painters or paintings that could hold my interest for two minutes, I walk boldly in.

I keep on the move, cutting a figure eight through the crush, taking in and digesting characteristic gestures, postures, facial expressions, turns of speech, visions of myself trying these on shooting through my head. I avoid the card table, from in back of which a large blonde lady, the hostess I assume, is dispensing wine. She is in a white blouse with long sleeves and a deep cleavage revealing nothing of interest. She has a heart-shaped face (as I bet she tells herself in the mirror) on which the make-up is thick and the smile perfect. She has the kind of teeth that look too good to be real but are, just the same. Some day I'll have to think out this matter of real things that look false. It is not just a question of what real things look false, but to whom and why. How come there are so many people around today for whom everything must be something other than what it is? Why has reality gone soft? She gives everyone who comes over to her for wine a perfect smile and a tilt of her head. But her eyes are restless. They follow everything but the direction of her smile. I can feel them tracking me around the room. How would I go about killing her in front of all these people, if I had a mind to, is what I am thinking.

Simple: walk up to her and empty a gun into her cleavage. In the confusion stride calmly out to a stolen car humming at the curb. Drive over to West End Avenue and up to Ninety-sixth Street. Abandon the car. Into the subway. Out at Times Square. Buy a ticket for *Fringe Benefits* and keep the stub. Sit back and enjoy the movie. I am just as aware as you are that I did not own a gun. Nor did I know how to get one. Do you? And I cannot steal a car because no one ever taught me how to start a car without a key. I am not mechanically inclined and do not pretend to be and do not desire to be (mechanically inclined). And Eighty-eighth, scene of the crime, is a one-way street, a wrong-way street. In this part of the world, at least, even num-bered streets run east. You may have forgotten that I had trained myself to be observant. All right, wise guy, how would you do it?

"I would simply meander over, drink some of her unspeakable wine, bully her in an attentive sort of way, conclude with a request for permission to take her home. The rest, I assure you, will be all too easy."

So says a voice beside me. It is rich and deep, like the voice of God in the movies. I do not flinch, of course. The most delicate of instruments would not detect a millimeter's movement. By that time my self-discipline had become unfailing. Suddenly I feel a terrible longing for a cigarette.

"I beg your pardon," I say.

"She has a fatal weakness for stern-faced types of muscular aspect and working-class origins, such as yourself—if you will permit the characterization."

I bow. This man is no mean observer, either. He unsticks the bottom plastic glass from the stack of four from which he is drinking and hands it to me. He takes out a silver flask and pours me a drink. It is smooth, warming, aromatic, delicious. But what is it? A transcendent brandy of some kind, perhaps, although it doesn't taste like any brandy that ever came my way before. I do not deny that there are people whose experience of brandy is wider than my own.

"Would you happen to have a cigarette?" I say.

He pulls out and springs open a silver case. Both sides are filled with these long, thin, white-filtered, mentholated miseries. "I carry them for my wife," he says. I extract one, even though I know it will taste like liniment. A smoke is a smoke, after all.

"I have a weakness for the audacities of unsponsored ambition myself," he says.

"Seduction was the furthest thing from my mind," I say.

He pulls out another silver case, from which he removes a cigar.

"Surely you exaggerate," he says. He pulls out a silver lighter and offers me the flame.

"Allow me to be dogmatic: seduction is never the furthest

thing from anyone's mind," he says. "Drink up, I have more in my coat, and more in my car, and more at home, and more being made up for me. Why else would a man look at a woman as you were looking at her?"

Believe it or not, this one cigarette is making me dizzy. "I am a student of human nature," I say.

His head is hidden in a cloud of cigar smoke. "And what conclusions have you drawn from your study of the lady in question?"

"She is the wife of a Protestant minister who runs an encounter group. She has had five children and four nervous breakdowns." One of the side-benefits of habitually exposing yourself to danger is that you become lightning-fast on both the in-take and the up-take.

"Bravo," he says. "A well-aimed stab in the dark, if I ever saw one. But a miss, all the same, a miss. She is in fact Muriel Bigalow, first wife of the famous novelist. As everyone knows, she has had four glamorous successors—but no children, and only two breakdowns. During the past fifteen years she has turned down all offers of marriage, not because she hoped Bigalow would return to her, but so that she wouldn't lose his name. I proposed to her once myself. If you will but aim one of those stiff little bows of yours in her direction, she will come over."

"I don't want her to come over."

"Here she comes anyway."

"Would you mind letting me have another one of these cigarettes?"

"Are you a friend of Fiji's?" says Mrs. Bigalow.

Before answering, I bend over the silver lighter, inhale deliberately, and let out a few cubic feet of smoke. "Never met him," I say.

She laughs prettily. She tilts her head. "Fiji is a her, you silly man, not a him."

Well, we'd see about that. Meanwhile, I raise my eyebrows inscrutably, smoke pouring from my nostrils.

"And this is her husband you have been talking to, Allerton Guth, importer, exporter, manufacturer, all-around tycoon, and friend in need." She slips one of her arms through one of his.

"Yes, indeed," he says. But he does not take his hands out of his pockets. He rocks on his toes, his stomach hanging forward. I let them wait as long as it would take to whistle (under one's breath) eight bars of "Mohair Sam," a favorite song of mine that no one plays any more.

"I am Gregory Wallenda," I say, "critic for the *West Side What's New*"

"Ah-ha," he says, "the autodidact as arbiter of taste."

"We believe that the West Side is where it's at," I say.

"Oh-ho," he says, "to Middlemarchians the world is all Middlemarch." (Middlemarch is the name of a self-satisfied provincial community in a novel by George Meredith.)

"We believe that the human and social ingredients of the West Side comprise the recipe of a new planetary culture: urban, funky, polyethnic. We believe that by comparison Los Angeles is no more than a sugarcoated knish." Another of the side-benefits of habitually exposing yourself to danger is that you are pressed into inventiveness.

"And so it is," he says.

"I have come here tonight expressly to see whether the cake is rising," I say.

"Let me introduce you to Fiji," she says. I do not see how I can get out of it.

The paintress is small, an Oriental of some kind, with short hair and a shapely behind encased in what are obviously prefaded dungarees. They are tight enough to reveal the outline of the panties beneath. As she turns to face us, I see an expressionless face and beady eyes, a flat chest. Her hair falls from a topknot of some kind, curves over her cheeks, and closes on her chin like a pair of icetongs. A dyke, obviously. Now why would a decent and intelligent fellow like Guth throw himself to a wolverine such as this? For the same reason that good old Bill married Jude Karnofsky.

I jam a hand into the back of one of hers (it is smooth and rubbery) when we both reach for a cigarette from the case Guth holds open. The truth of the matter is that I had taken my eye off the ball for a moment (a rare lapse, you can take my word for it) to stare at Fiji's companion, to whom no one introduces me. I have just now leaned back to close my eyes, and, yes, I can still see every feature of her Black Irish beauty as clearly as in a technicolor close-up. She is tall, slim, straight, and strong. She is wearing a black dress. She has long, glossy, black hair parted in the center, and she has petal-white legs, arms, and neck. She has green eyes, a few freckles, a face I would gladly kill someone to have my way with. But is she another dyke? Can such horrors be? The very thought makes me droop. What is the use, I think. I mean, what's the use of anything if women who look like that are cesspools of perversion. It is precisely for women who look like that a real man wants to do things. At the bottom of the abyss lies not the death of God but the perversity of women. On the other hand, she may not be a dyke, after all.

I am led to one of Fiji's paintings and placed before it. I would have to close my eyes to avoid seeing it. I can feel the Black Irish beauty behind me and to my right. Spread out below us and in the distance is a city, smoldering and in ruins. It is corrugated by heat waves. The predominating color is a kind of sulphurous yellow. Wisps and tendrils of smoke rise to form a figure slightly above eye level. (Fiji knows something about perspective, at least.) The figure is young and graceful, but whether male or female or both would be hard to say. What may be a penis may also be a coil of smoke; what may be breasts, puffs of flaming gas. The face is green-eyed, cool, aloof, and on the verge of being faintly amused, like that of the Lady in Black, who is not there when I glance over my shoulder.

"The Angelic Androgyne rising from the ashes of industrial civilization," I say. Or, rather, a plump quail waiting for a load of buckshot up its ass.

" 'Fraid so," says Allerton Guth.

"All fear is the fear of a self against itself," says Fiji.

"You know, Allerton, dear, society has forced *all* of us to erect defences against our own, um, true beinghood," says Muriel Bigalow.

"All defenses are defenses of a self against itself," says Fiji.

"Yes, I know, 'deed I do," says Guth. "But I can't help noticing that it is me and my factories going up in all that smoke." And I'll bet he cannot help thinking that it is he and his factories that paid for the paint that depicted the smoke.

"Only if you resist what's got to be, Allerton, only—" says Mrs. Bigalow.

"All resistance is the resistance of a self against itself," says Ms. Fiji.

"All those resistances build up inside us until we want to explode. We *do* explode," says Muriel Bigalow, who no doubt speaks from experience. It is impossible for me to get a word in edgewise. "Don't you agree, Allerton, that apocalypse is a state of mind. And what *are* there but states of mind."

"The turtle without his shell is a phoenix," says Fiji.

"I'll remember that," I say. I do not say that I would rather be a turtle, figuratively speaking, than an angel, literal or figurative, never mind a phoenix. Nor do I say that I would rather be down in the city than up in the clouds. Give me the fire and brimstone every time. The city, as the poet W.W. Auden once said, is the reality principle. I do not even say that if you get rid of your resistances, your defenses, your shell, you also get rid of your character. All defenses are defenses of a self against loss of itself, to coin a Fiji-ism. And if such sentiments are old-fashioned, so be it. I would rather be called a fuddy-duddy than enact in my own personality the Second Law of Thermodynamics. There are many things I could have said if I had not walked into this madhouse to advance my preparations for revenge, rather than to score points in debate. You will just have to keep your mind on the situation as a whole if you want to understand the details. Besides, what is the use of arguing with such people? The only problem is that there are too many of them. You can't kill them all.

I catch a glimpse of my Black Beauty's vigorous back vanishing through the door, the cigarette smoke turbulent behind her exit, a trace of the chill air she lets in reaching all the way to my cheek. It is a chill of the kind I had already gotten to know well by the time I was eighteen. This bitch obviously considered me beneath her notice. Not that I much care. After all, what has she got that Samantha doesn't have? (They are of similar physical types, but this one is taller, has hair a blacker shade of dark and skin a lighter shade of white.) She is probably a lesbian any way. Samantha may have her failings but at least she is not a faggotrix. And if the suspicion that she is ever crosses your mind, don't let me hear about it. Not unless you want a fat lip.

By ten thirty the wine bottles and the gallery are nearly empty. Attached to only one of the paintings is a card with a bit of ribbon dangling from it. On the card is written "SOLD" and in smaller, much smaller, letters, "To Allerton Guth." The painting is a self-portrait. The artist is standing naked before a mirror on the viewer's right, but reaching with her brush toward an easel on the viewer's left. On the easel is a painting of the artist standing naked before a mirror that reflects the artist reaching toward an easel on which there is a painting of the artist standing naked before a mirror. We have therefore two front views (one of the mirror and one on the easel), and duplications of them, and one rear view, at the center of the painting. In my opinion, only the latter is worth looking at. I admit that I almost certainly look for the wrong things when I look at paintings at all, which is not often.

As the gallery empties I hang around, bullying Muriel in an attentive sort of way, as the sagacious Guth advised. (His sagacity must have been on holiday when he married Fiji. But then I have never yet heard of a wise man who was wise in his dealings with women. The stupidest of women is by comparison a genius in her dealings with men. The reason is that the urgency of even a wise man's desire for the women he desires is greater than the power of all the wisdom in the world to control it. No woman has ever experienced that kind of urgency, that kind of desire. Perhaps you think I have not noticed that Muriel is an exception. I will agree that Muriel has not been exactly shrewd in her dealings with men. But she has not been passion's slave either. If women are slaves of passion, the passion is not one for men. Literary types like Dido are the combined pipe dreams and daymares of men stuck with possessive wives or retentive mothers—a pipe dream of getting rid of her and a daymare of the fuss she will make. The passion in question is not for the man, but for having her own way; and the fuss she makes is not a tragedy of love lost, but a soap-opera spectacular of egotism, spite, and blackmail triumphant. One way or another, the woman has the last word. And didn't I read somewhere that Virgil was a queer? These digressions, these *apparent* digressions, are for your sake, not for mine. The information they contain is no news to me, after all. And I can assure you that it is more work to write them out than to read them in.) I am pointing out to Muriel in short, gruff phrases that health lies not in a search for the self but in a discovery of the world outside it, when the last of the sightseers go off home to their television sets. Ms. and Mr. Fiji and Muriel and I straighten up and turn out the lights. At the door Fiji shakes my hand and says that she is looking forward to my review. Guth hands me his card and suggests that I call him some day for lunch. He says that I can put him down for a subscription to the *West Side What's New.* When they leave, Muriel rummages around in her handbag for a key. From the quality of the lock of the door I gather she is not very afraid that the paintings will be stolen. I have not had to request permission to take her home. It was tacitly granted before I was sure that I wanted it.

She suggests we walk, "to get the cobwebs out of our heads." Lead on, I say, although I am not myself aware of any cobwebs. We walk downtown along Broadway, her hand on my arm, gripping the bicep, which I tense from time to time. The pizza joints and hotdog stands and restaurants, mostly Chinese, are still doing business; so are a few drug stores and liquor stores, a Carvel shop, a paperback store, a locksmith, here and there a market, most of the newsstands, and a stray from Greenwich Village run by a couple of earnest nitwits going broke trying to sell handmade wooden bowls, sandals, and backscratchers. Four of the local gay set overtake and pass us, going fast, making sure everybody can hear them filling the air with one-liners from *All About Eve,* which I take it they have just seen for the fifth or sixth time at the New Yorker movie house. They jostle an elderly couple, both of them short and round, she bundled up in her mink, he in his corpulence, survivors, I assume, of the Old West End Avenue set that used to own this turf. Younger men and women, descendants of that set, home late from work or early from play scoot by holding little bags of groceries in their arms, easily in time to mix up their tunafish salad dinners before Johnny Carson begins his monologue. A woman digs in her heels to hold back her husky, which is trying to get at a doberman held back with one hand by a character who is burly and bald and leaning against a car, a toothpick in his mouth, his eyes elsewhere, the hulabaloo of growls and barks beneath his notice. A guy tossing bundles of newspapers out of a truck stops to look Muriel over, spots me watching him, grins. A cluster of Puerto Rican teen-agers swinging uptown in tempo, shouting the lyrics of "Bad, Bad, Leroy Brown," the girls luscious, the boys stringy and tough, force us to detour around them. A police car, the siren yodelling, the flasher spinning off points of red onto all the dark windows and Muriel's teeth, zooms north, zigzag through the traffic. Another zooms by, close behind. Then another. When I follow them over my shoulder, two more are coming downtown. Suddenly there are sirens and flashing red lights everywhere. They all turn West on Eighty-fourth Street. It takes a while for my heart to slow down and my stomach muscles to relax. A couple of prepubescent black boys, with the aspect of purse snatchers, catch my eye and smile, as though they knew something about me. Across the street in front of a hotel that has known better days, a group of old timers, horse players, stand around, looking in their dingy overcoats as though they had stepped out of a photograph taken during the depression. One of the old timers looks like Jimmy Durante. He raises his right hand in a gesture of disgust, then lets it come down to his gray-brown-green fedora, which he lifts. He smooths back his hair with his left hand, a finger of which he then puts to one side of his nose and blasts loose a clam from the other. Distributed among them must be half the fedoras left in America. Under the marquee of a supermarket that had once been a movie house an Oriental gentleman is talking to a Puerto Rican hustler in a silver wig. As we get into the Seventies I note a higher proportion of theatrical types, actors and dancers whose careers do not seem to be prospering. Rough trade slouch against the buildings or into bars. A garbage truck screeches to a halt and two men jump off, but pause with their hands on a trash basket to watch a girl in high boots, hot pants, and hair bleached white, as leaning forward and rigid with anger she gives a piece of her mind to a tall black sport wearing a beige jump suit, a raccoon coat, and a maroon hat wide as an umbrella, his expression a parody of flabbergasted innocence. When we turn east on Seventy-sixth, Muriel, who has not once interrupted herself to look around, is still going on about how much good Transcendental Meditation has done her.

She lives on a block of nursing homes and brownstones just below the Museum of Natural History. Recently planted trees, half of them already dead, line both sides of the street. By this time I have decided that when she asks me up for a

drink, I will refuse. A dirty trick, you say? I should have
stayed away from her if all I meant to do was hurt her feelings? She's lucky it was only her feelings I meant to hurt. And
just what business is it of yours? Would you rather I killed
her? It is enough for me, if not for you, that I maneuvered
myself into a position where I *could* have killed her, if I had
wanted to. You keep forgetting that what I am describing is a
night of preparation for revenge, rather than the thing itself. I
thank you anyhow for the implication that a night in bed
with me would have done her more good than Transcendental
Meditation. But I am not the man for the role of sex therapist
to distracted ladies. There are plenty of ambitious young men
around looking for career opportunities in fields with a rapid
growth potential. Let them do it. Besides, who knows what
kind of legs Muriel was hiding under that long skirt with the
voluminous folds and the dusty hem? I assume as a matter of
course that women who hide their legs have something to
hide.

She turns silent and checks her pace as we approach the
stoop of a renovated brownstone midway in the block. I am
rummaging around furiously inside my head for the right words
with which to turn her down. I am looking for words of a cool
finality, of an unself-conscious arrogance, of an impersonal
rejection to which there can be no appeal. She takes two steps
up the stoop and turns around to face me, so that if I wanted,
I could rest my nose in the sharp angle of blouse at the nadir
of her cleavage. The fact is that I have to lean back and look up
if I want to see her face. I charitably guess that she has arranged
for her position of superiority by instinct rather than by calculation.

"When will I see you again?" she says. Can you imagine!
Where do people get such nerve? What gives her the idea that
any man will want to see her a second time after she has held
out on him the first? I am stupified by her inability to see herself
as others see her (or at least as I see her). Has this dumb broad

got it into her head that she has a scintillating personality? For once, words fail me.

"Aren't you going to invite me up?" It is the best I can manage.

"We've only just met," she says. Why is it that most women only like to go to bed with men they know all too well, whereas most men like best to go to bed with women they hardly know at all?

"So much the better," I say, once again in control.

"Why do we have to rush things?" she says, tilting her head to the left. "We've got time," and she tilts her head to the right.

"No we haven't," I say. "Isn't it about time you became a bit more open to experience? A little longer and that true being-hood of yours will be locked in its defenses forever. You ought to do a bit of Transcendental Meditation on that." I am ashamed of that speech now, but I wasn't then.

"Please, Greg," she says. "Please." Once again I am stupified. I feel the hair on the back of my neck prickle. It comes over me with the force of a revelation that Muriel is afraid. *This forty-year-old-woman is afraid of sex.*

"I'll call, Muriel," I say. "In a day or two." And who knows, maybe I will.

"My number is in the book," she says. "Under Bigalow!" She assumes the unmistakable attitude of a woman who expects to be kissed. I give her a peck.

"Good night, Muriel," I say.

"I'm glad we met," she says.

"I'm glad we met too," I say.

"And Greg?" she says. "Please call."

"In a day or two," I say, and walk off. Well, what can you do? It is still a conquest of sorts.

I trust you have savored this little slice of life from the fatty sweetbreads of New York.

There are other hors d'oeuvres I could spread before you.

For example, one evening when I was standing on Forty-fourth and Broadway scratching my testicles, a reporter from CBS-TV came up and asked me whether I thought President Nixon should be impeached. I said Yes, although I hadn't read a newspaper for a month. A voice behind me said, "And dey should trow away da key." When the reporter, a very handsome woman indeed, walked over to her film crew, the owner of the voice and I lingered, our eyes doing what our hands couldn't. "And to think," he said, "some guys actually get to fuck quiff like that." After she had driven off, my companion and I retired for a beer. He turned out to be a mason tender debating with himself whether he should go home to his wife or return to the construction site, where the regular Friday crap game was in progress. I gathered that he had spent some hours loitering around the site, unwilling either to leave or to open his pay envelope, which his wife insisted on receiving seal intact. "What the fuck," he said finally. "I'm four hours late already. I'll get a load of shit dumped on me no matter what I do. You got a few bucks you'd like to invest?" In a sand pit in Harlem under a building that looked gutted but was merely unfinished I lost thirty dollars and my new friend Chi Chi lost the contents of his pay envelope. I paid out another thirty dollars or so for drinks and two-inch thick pastrami sandwiches (all told we ate at least three a piece) before the bars closed and I tumbled into bed and Chi Chi collapsed on my couch. By 7:30 a hand was shaking me. "Hey Vic, I gotta go. Thanks for everything. We'll have you out for dinner some night. Fawn"—his wife—"is a terrific cook." Well, what did you expect? A parable of vice punished and redeemed by its own passionate excesses? A cautionary tale of blind lust and tragic loss? A sociological fable of mass man and mute dispair? One of life's little ironies? A collapse into brain fever? I ask you to remember that what you are reading is not literature, but life.

I spent one evening at a convention of lady bowlers posing as the inventor of a bowling ball with a liquid center. The single topic of conversation among these short, pudgy ladies wearing team sweatshirts, pants, and white anklets was the dangers of New York, which most of them seemed to be visiting for the first time. One showed me the can of mace in her purse. Another revealed confidentially that she was packing a rod (for which she had a license). None of them, so far as I could tell, had heard of Jude Karnofsky or Erica von Plaack. These women, I decided, were allies. I left early, without even going through the motions of setting one up for an imaginary kill.

I spent another evening buying drinks for a Puerto Rican prostitute named Brunhilda. She went out with only two johns (a shy, thin working man and a teen-ager) during the seven hours I was with her. In my opinion, Brunhilda suffered from an excess of self-respect. As the evening wore on she confided in me that she never had anything to do with pimps or junk, that she wore clean underwear every day, that she was studying to be a dress designer, that she refused to do anything dirty with her johns—if they didn't want to fuck face-to-face and pole-to-hole as God intended, they could go to someone else—that every week she sent half of her earnings home to Puerto Rico, where half of that half went into a bank for Brunhilda and the other half fed her mother and her son.

For my reckless pranks with a printer who had been out of work for eighteen months; for my evening of hot dogs and penny arcades with a seven-year-old boy who had run away from home when his mother and her boyfriend tried to kill him (I finally got him to the house of his father's father, a widower); for my flirtation with a moving woman I picked up a night court (I later beat her at arm wrestling); for my exposure of a charlatan posing as a Professor of Popular Culture at Bronx Community College (and the gratifying sequel in a coffee shop with the student beneficiaries of my triumphant demonstration that comic books, even the pornographic variety, are undercover touts for the tyranny of print); for my impersonation, after a poetry reading at the YWHA, of a minor poet with a major case of narcissism (I won over a pair of dubious, but attractive, schoolmarms when I looked the mournful marm in the eye and improvised these lines:

> It's the body's fluids that count.
> We bleed, sweat, or spout
> whenever we do what we want
> most, or least, to do
> with or without.

Poetry is easy once you have wrestled with prose. I mean to take it up as a hobby when I get more time. Have you ever noticed what suckers women are for poets?); for these and other adventures you will have to consult my diary. Study in particular volumes six, seven, and eight. I sympathize with your appetite for all the details of my training. But you must remember that they no longer have the fascination for me that they have for you. What you are just now having a fantasy about doing, I have done.

On Wednesday, May 29, I got home before midnight, after having spent the evening with a man (and his two silent girl friends) who had once been the star of a TV cook show ("The Garrulous Gourmet"), but who was now dean of a school that taught shy businessman, oppressed housewives, and bad actors how to assert themselves. He was interested in my eating habits and impressed by my controlled self-confidence, so he said. I take it he took me for a kindred spirit. I did not bother to inform him that I was not another con-man, even when he offered me a job at his school. Instead I went home and did my nightly exercises, sixty sit-ups and sixty push-ups. My veins thus blasted clear of the noxious effluvia of New York night life, to which effluvia I am addicted, I sat down with my journal and a glass of brandy. No sooner had I placed myself comfortably in the deep chair, between two sprung springs, when there was a knock at the door. It was Bill, with an unopened quart bottle of bourbon in his hand.

"Bill," I said.

"May I come in," he said.

"Of course," I said.

"Things are coming to a head," he said, sinking onto the couch.

"When they do, pinch it off between forefinger and thumb," I said, getting him a glass, a pitcher of water, and a bowl of icecubes.

"Jesus Christ, Victor," he said, pouring himself a stiff one. "I came up here to get away from men of action—of both sexes. Miss Lily flew in this morning. She's down at the Plaza with her lieutenants on the verge of calling out the National Guard."

"What things are coming to what head?" I said, carefully placing myself in the deep chair.

It took time and patience and an occasional show of impatience, but here are the facts I finally extracted from Bill (the order in which I am giving them to you is not the disorder in which I got them from Bill):

1. For the past two months, in compliance with a court order, Toby had been spending alternate weeks with his mother and his father. This much I already knew.

2. On Friday, May 24, Jude, after picking up Toby, had gone not home to her apartment, but straight to Erika von Plaack's place. This intelligence had been gathered by detectives responsible only to Miss Lily, who had been keeping Jude under surveillance twenty-four hours a day for the past three months.

3. Erika von Plaack lived at 33 Gramercy Park East.

4. Toby had begun to flinch when his mother approached him and to stutter when he spoke to her, but in any case he did not speak to anyone much during those weeks he spent with his mother, except to his invisible dog, Luke. This information came from Martine, who had been fired by Jude and rehired by Bill.

5. On Saturday, Butch, Erika von Plaack's Filipino

houseboy-cum-bodyguard, was seen moving trunks and suit-cases from Jude's apartment to von Plaack's.

6. During the whole time from Friday night until Monday morning neither Jude nor Toby strayed out on the street or near any window. But it was known that they had remained in at 33 Gramercy Park East. And it was known that Jude had left her own apartment upon discovering a bug in her phone. It was known because of the bug on Erika von Plaack's phone, also placed by a specialist responsible only to Miss Lily.

7. At 8:15 on each of the past three mornings Jude had emerged from her new residence and travelled by taxi to the nefarious offices of *Ms. Chief* (which was on the verge of dis-charging its first issue). At 3:58 on Wednesday (Bill and I were talking about ten hours later, early, very early, Thursday morn-ing) Jude emerged from her office and travelled over to Co-lumbia, where she turned in her final grades (B+ for the girls and C for the boys; Jude never gave anyone A's).

8. During the past three days Toby had not been seen unless accompanied by Butch. The two went together on Butch's morning errands, and every afternoon between 1:00 and 3:00 Butch sat by while Toby played in Gramercy Park, riding his tricycle over the dolls his mother had given him. Butch was an internationally recognized master of a number of the Oriental arts of self-defense. On two nights a week he gave classes to friends of La Belle von Plaack.

9. On Friday morning the annual meeting of the Organiza-tion of Social Scientists of America (OSSA) was to open at the Hilton. Jude was to check in at the hotel some time after lunch on Thursday (that is, tomorrow, I mean the day of the morning on which Bill and I were talking). Her plan was to spend the afternoon and evening at premeeting meetings of the Feminist Caucus (of which she was Chairperson) and of the Policy and Program committees (of which she was Vice Chairperson and Secretary-Treasuress, respectively).

10. Jude's schedule for Friday was known: meetings from

10:00 to 12:00; lunch with her angel, that gull of a moneybags who was having his wings clipped and his feathers plucked and his pockets picked by the vultures hatching plots against mankind at the offices of *Ms. Chief*; meetings from 2:00 to 5:00; cocktails at a party thrown by some publisher of anthropology texts from 5:00 to 7:00; dinner with the other editrixes of *Ms. Chief*; participation on an OSSA panel discussion from 9 to 10:30. This information was obtained from the bug on von Plaack's phone, from the OSSA program handout, and from Miss Lily's undercover agent, who was working for *Ms. Chief* as one of the secretaries, all male and as wretched and down-trodden a bunch as had ever disgraced the pants they wore.

11. On Saturday morning at 10:00 the members of OSSA were to gather for a General Assembly. Jude was to be the featured speaker. There was no direct evidence of her subsequent plans. But phrases from three separate phone conversations when put together provided conclusive evidence that Jude had two tickets for a plane scheduled to depart on Saturday afternoon, its destination unknown to Miss Lily's intelligence cadres. Her undercover agent, however, had discovered that Jude was recipient of a grant to do fieldwork for a project entitled "Sexism and Stress: Gender Lag and the Androgynous Ideal on a Frontier Kibbutz." This bit of information had reminded Bill that Jude had a brother named Noah who, after failing as an actor, a folk dancer, and a group therapist, was now a fanatical Kibbutznik. He lived in some parched hamlet that had already been attacked twice by Palestinian guerillas. For the past three weeks Jude had frequently mentioned this brother in conversations attentively listened to and carefully recorded (her tone was affectionate but condescending; affectionate, I take it because he was not much of a man, condescending because he was not quite a woman). Miss Lily's undercover agent had seen letters addressed to brother Noah (but had not been able to get his hands on them).

"So Jude means to take Toby with her to the Kibbutz," I said.

"She means to leave him there, too," he said.

"How do you know that?" I said.

"It's the only way she can keep him from me," he said.

I got up to stretch my legs, and while I was at it, fetched Bill more water and ice. A premonition that I was going to need a clear mind had kept me off the brandy, but I now poured myself an inch or two, or maybe three.

"Can't you get a court order or something, an injunction or whatever?" I said.

"We can't do anything until Friday at 6:00, when Jude is supposed to turn Toby over to me," he said. "Which she will refuse to do, I'm sure of it, and she'll have that Kung Fu Manchu there to make the refusal stick. By then it will be too late for any legal maneuver."

"How about an illegal maneuver?" I said.

"Miss Lily is ready to snatch Toby the minute he sticks his head out the door. Her people are raring to go. There is something about Butch that enrages them. They want to puncture the man as well as the reputation. And of course Miss Lily couldn't care less about any legal consequences. She's willing to hide us out in Virginia or set us up in Switzerland."

"Well, why not, then?" I said.

"Because I don't want to go to Virginia, or Switzerland either," he said. "Because I don't want Toby to see a gang of his father's mother's strong-arm men fighting with his mother's bully boy. Because he might just hurt in the fracas. Because of a hundred things."

"You'll just have to confront Jude at the airport, whether there's a fracas or not," I said.

"Easy to say," he said. "Besides, we don't know exactly when or where Jude is going. She is not booked on any flight to Israel. Miss Lily is checking the passenger lists on flights to Amsterdam, where next week there's a conference on sex roles and social change, and she's checking the flights to Denmark. Miss Lily's mind is made up that Jude is going to put Toby through a sex-change operation before they move on to Israel."

"Jesus," I said. I could see by the expression on his face that Bill had already dismissed his mother's premonition, but that just shows you how much he needed us. How can a man live with a woman for six years and not discover what desperate creatures they are? One of the many ways in which women differ from men is that women do not have inhibitions. With all due respect to Freud, a great man, I very much doubt that women have subconsciouses either. It is an absolute certainty that they do not have superegos. It follows that they are all ego. And there is no check on their egoism from above or below; they are capable of anything. So far as theories of Jude's intentions are concerned, Miss Lily was more likely to come up with something equal to the enormity of the occasion than Bill: As they say, it takes one to know one.

"What are you going to do?" I said.

"I don't know," he said, and fell asleep, his glass resting on his navel but listing dangerously with each breath he took. I carried his glass, his bottle, the pitcher, the bowl, into the kitchen, reheated a mugful of coffee, made myself comfortable in the deep chair. Then I got up, took Bill's shoes off, put his legs up on the couch, made myself comfortable again. Then I got up, put the bedspread over Bill, for May was ending with a chill, made myself comfortable. Then I began to think. Bill did not know what he was going to do, and neither did I, but my duty was clear. My duty was to kill Jude and rescue Toby, for even with Jude dead, von Plaack and Co. were capable of spiriting Toby off to that dangerous kibbutz and that drip Noah.

A funny kind of lassitude settled over me. I kept falling asleep for minutes or seconds at a time. My mind wandered. Images from out of nowhere floated before my inner eye: my head resting on Samantha's navel and then sliding off as the slope of her belly grew steeper with each breath; Miss Lily with an evil smile pointing for the Garrulous Gourmet to look at what she was mixing in a bowl; Toby in a pink bonnet watching with round, solemn eyes from behind the bars of a crib while I tried to push under the bed a protesting prostitute who almost looked familiar. Oh, I was ready to kill Jude, make no mistake about that. Are you kidding? What do you think it is I had been preparing myself for this past three months? Not for a display of my masculine pulchritude in the *Cosmopolitan* centerfold, of that I can assure you. I was ready to kill Jude, but not just yet.

Through months I had evoked a dream of how I would stalk her; how I would spy out every detail of her routine, every habit and haunt; how step by step and day by day I would close in on her; how through ambiguous signs I would let her know but make her doubt she knew that someone was closing in; how in panic and confusion, glancing wildly over her shoulder and into her mirror, she would fall into a trap of her own devising; how as the fatal trap clicked shut she would realize who had baited it and why; how standing in the shadows, a steely-nerved avenger would allow himself a grim little smile. The poet Wilbur Yates has spoken of the attraction for superior men of whatever is most difficult among those things not impossible of achievement. I had dreamed of a murder that would be a kind of poem, something impeccable in form and irresistible in rhythm and inevitable in its conclusion, like the workings of destiny. I had dreamed of an act that would survive its performer, a monument to the immortal spirit of mortal humanity, an inspiration and consolation to future generations of haggard and hagridden men.

I wonder if you will do me the favor of not deceiving yourselves. I have just gone through the trouble of explaining to you why it is that Bill's news had left me in momentary confusion. You have chosen to believe that my reasons are rationalizations. You have chosen to believe that I was afraid. Afraid of what, for God's sake! Afraid of getting caught? I ask you to remember that we are speaking of New York City in the year 1974. Can you possibly think, I mean can you have fallen into the montsrous error of believing for one minute that I had suddenly become squeamish? I will just mention that I have worked as a short-order cook in a hash house run by a Greek. Squeamish! I should think that by this time I was entitled to sympathy, rather than misunderstanding and abuse. Come now, will you not admit that you are after all sympathetic? Will you not admit that you have chosen to misunderstand precisely so that you would not have to face up to your sympathy? Let this be a secret between us. My lips are sealed. If you don't blab, I won't.

Now for your reward: I have a little confession to make. It is possible, just possible, that through a kind of absentmindedness I had allowed some rust to form on the fine edge of my resolve. The labor pains of re-creating myself had turned my gaze inward, like that of an expectant mother. I was absorbed in my own growth, if you know what I mean, and why should you not. Each day I mastered more of myself, and therefore more of the world, not because the self and the world are one, a dangerous and fashionable superstition, but because a mastered body is masterful in relation to its physical environment and a mastered mind is masterful in relation to its human environment. Each day I took in more of the world and took over more of it. Each day the world and I were more taken by each other. I do not have to tell you how sweet all this was to someone who had spent his life up to then gnashing his teeth on sour grapes. Yes, those were good days, the best! Am I boring you? Dear me, my profoundest apologies—and you can use them to wipe the grape juice off your own chin. While I am in a confessional frame of mind, I might just as well tell you that my longing for Samantha, my hatred of Jude, my fears for Toby had been dimmed (but not extinguished) by the bright prospects of my new course. This is not the first time in history that ends have spent themselves in dalliance with the means. Think of human sexuality, for example.

I did not spend the whole night sunk in my chair, eyes fixed on a flotsam of images or on the rise and fall of Bill's belly. I got up, after who knows how long, and looked out the window. The airshaft was all dark, not a light anywhere. No sign of dawn. I made a point of not looking at my watch. I began to wander around the apartment: the small bedroom, once Samantha's study, a square of lighter paint where her desk had stood against the wall; the master bedroom, bare but neat, my own reflection staring at me from the polished window; the kitchen, where I put on a fresh pot of coffee. While waiting for it to perk, I made myself a snack: a slab of leftover pot roast, plenty of salt and pepper, a layer of mayonnaise mixed with horseradish, a layer of cherry peppers cut into strips. I do not remember eating it, although I do remember looking down to find the plate empty. I carried a coffee mug into the bathroom, turned on the light, set the mug on the sink, took off my shirt, looked into the mirror, reached for the mug, saw that it was empty, carried it into the kitchen, filled it, carried it into the bathroom, set it on the sink, looked into the mirror, reached for the mug, drank some coffee, burned my tongue, set the mug on the sink, looked into the mirror, began to flex my muscles. I alternately flexed and sipped until my chest was sweaty and the mug was empty.

I then turned off the light, walked to the bedroom, looked around, walked back to the bathroom, turned on the light, removed two towels from the rack, turned off the light, returned to the bedroom, spread the towels on the lower half of the bed, walked to the kitchen, removed a grapefruit from the refrigerator and an ice pick from the drawer, returned to the bedroom, and stood at the foot of the bed, holding the ice pick in my right hand as one grips a screwdriver, resting the grapefruit in my left hand as one cups the bottom round of a buttock. I remained still for a moment, as my concentration gathered and as my weight shifted forward onto the balls of my feet, and then at the verge of tension and attention threw the grapefruit up and at an angle, my eyes fixed on it as it rose, slowed down, hesitated an inch short of the ceiling, turned downward, gathered speed, and stopped suddenly, about three feet above the bed, where with the classic thrust of a fencer I had impaled it on the ice pick. In eleven attempts I made nine solid hits and one glancing wound to the right, to *my* right that is, but to the grapefruit's left, about where the aorta joins the heart.

I wrapped the remains of the grapefruit in a towel, carried it toward the kitchen, stopped, returned to the bedroom, picked up the ice pick, walked to the kitchen, dumped the grapefruit into the garbage can, placed the ice pick in the sink, removed two cucumbers from the refrigerator, carried them and the towel toward the bedroom, stopped, walked to the living room window, looked out, walked to the bedroom, spread out the towel, placed the cucumbers on it, walked to the closet, opened the door, reached toward the back, knocked over Samantha's umbrella, shoved aside her iceskates, found the machete, removed it from the closet, withdrew it from its sheath, carried it to the foot of the bed, picked up a cucumber, remained still for a moment, resting the cucumber in my left hand as one strokes the nape of a neck, dangling the machete in my right hand as one dangles a machete. I remained still for a moment, until tension and attention gathered to a verge, whereupon I launched the cucumber, rolling it off my fingers so that it spun perpendicular to the ceiling on its course upward and on its fall downward to a point about three feet above the bed, where with the classic swing of an executioner I sliced an inch off its top. With eight forehand cuts I reduced the first cucumber to nine slices, roughly equal in size. With nine backhand cuts (one miss) I reduced the second cucumber to nine slices of varying sizes.

I remained still for a moment. When the splashes and ripples of impulse smoothed themselves out, gathered to a swell, I sprang up with a growl, revolved once in the air, the machete swishing and whirling over my head, and landed smack on the center of the bed, my legs flexed against the spring of the mattress. I slashed left and right, backhand and forehand, grunting and cursing. I hopped straight up and slashed under my feet, whirled around and chopped up the air that had been behind me. I fought in all directions, my footwork precise and economical, advancing with parry and thrust, retreating with jab and feint, dancing lightly off the bed, roaring back up on it, the machete whistling. The air of the room collapsed in shards. The litter was knee high. I stood still, left hand on my hip, knee bent, leaning on the machete, looking down between my feet. I stabbed there once, deliberately and nonchalantly, then leaped to the floor, stood at attention. I flipped the machete up into the air, caught it by the handle, brought it up in a salute, kissed the flat of the blade, slid it home into its sheath.

I remained still for five minutes or so, until the currents of energy reorganized themselves, began to run smoothly. I sat down on my heels, spread my knees, placed the palms of my hands flat on the floor between my feet, leaned forward, uncoiled into a handstand. I slowly sunk downward until my chin touched the floor, then pushed up again. I let my legs tip to the right and raised my left arm from the floor until it formed a ninety-degree angle with my right arm and a one-hundred-and-ten degree angle with the slow arc of my trunk and legs. I reversed my movements until I was standing once more. I remained still for two minutes or so. And now, ladies and gentlemen (and you others, too), for an attempt of a stunt the accomplishment of which would bring you up to your feet in amazement and applause. I had tried it and failed at it twice a day, once upon rising and once upon setting, for a month. I now lay prone on the floor, in the position for push-ups. I placed my right hand behind me, forearm over the belt, my weight distributed on left hand, toes, and chin. I waited while juice and sentience flowed into my left arm and shoulder, which hunched, bunched, as my toes gripped, my thigh and stomach muscles clenched, my chin worked down and in, my rump humped, and then I pressed down and pressed down and kept pressing down until I was all the way up. Nothing to it. A one-handed left-handed push-up is something you might try yourself sometime. Try it at a party, for example, during one of these panicky moments when the gabble runs out and people are looking around for someone to start it up again. Try it that is, if you are willing to make yourself ridiculous just to provide a topic for conversation—unless, of course, you are also willing to put in three months at the kind of training that for me had just come to an end.

I did not whoop my vaunt to the skies, for I was considerate of my sleeping neighbors. Instead I jumped straight up, kicking my legs apart, whipping my arms out, folding sharply at the waist, and touching on either side fingertips to toes. I did this six times. I then straightened up the bedroom and walked once more to the livingroom window. The rosy fingers of dawn were goosing the city into life. A light went on behind the marbled glass of a bathroom window across the airshaft. I shook Bill. "Your mother's calling," I said.

He lay still, except to open his eyes, which he fixed on the ceiling. He sighed. "What evidence is there that you are not a dream?" he said. "A bad dream."

I bent over, slid my arms under him, lifted ("Where are you taking me?"), carried him to the door, set him down. "You need a bath," he said.

"Let me know if there's anything I can do," I said.

"There is nothing you can do," he said, opening the door.

I had no difficulty in checking the impulse to say "Is that so?" Bill meant no disparagement of my abilities. He meant merely that the situation was hopeless. (In Bill the native hue of resolution is often sicklied o'er with the pale cast of thought.) But you and I know better. I knew what to do, and now you know I would do it. And if you see Hamlet, you might tell him from me that his beating himself about the brow was a waste of time. It is no use resolving to be resolute. The will cannot exert pressure upon itself. The unwilling will, that is, cannot will itself into willingness. Can you taste your own tongue? Can you look into your own eyes? Can an itch scratch itself? Resolution is not a choice, but a product. It depends not upon itself, but upon other things. Here is an experiment: Try to will yourself an erection (and keep your hands on the table). Come on now, no one is looking. Well? You are as you were, are you not? Even less so? That's what I thought. Now imagine yourself doing with an erection what you would most like to do with one. This is no time to be timid. The beauty of creatures of fantasy is that you can do with them what you want, they don't mind. Take your time, now. There you go. What did I tell you!

Let's get back to the point of this little demonstration, shall we? If it is not too much to ask. And let us be strictly scientific in the conclusions we draw:

1. The only path from certain conditions to certain others is through a detour.

2. The function of fantasy is to prepare you for facts. (If you insist, I will grant that a fantasy is also a kind of fact, but of a different order, of a very different order, from the hard fact of an erection. This is no time for quibbling.) Now fantasy is to the mind what play is to the body. Therefore I moved from a condition of reluctance through the detour of play to a condition of readiness to kill Judith Leah Karnofsky. (Perhaps you thought all those acrobatics were a kind of displacement activity.) If you are in your mind unwilling to do something, let your mind get your body to do something like what in your mind you are unwilling to do; your body will then get you ready in your mind to do it, and, as Hamlet said, readiness is all. But it took Hamlet four and one-half acts to get ready. Even then, it is only after he has played at words with Osric and played at foils with Laertes that he is ready to tell off the king and to stab his mother.

I'll wager you never expected to find so many solutions to such deep problems in the confessions of a multiple murderer.

I took a shower, and then went to bed, after setting myself for three hours of sleep. And I slept very well, thank you.

IV

I woke up and kipped up out of bed in the same instant. Oh, was I ready. Therefore, I made no plans, which are substitutes for readiness. You can unpack that paradox yourself. I am hot to move on, to recapture in words the stirring events of that day. I will just pause to mention that plans are to events what neurotic symptoms are to impulse and what philosophic systems are to reality. Maladaptatious, all of them, defenses that in fact disarm you, equipment for evading the unpredictables, unknowables, and inexplicables of the events, impulse, and reality that plans, symptoms, and systems are presumed to contain and subdue. Never mind that now, and never mind the clank and stumble of the tripling triplets in the previous sentence. I would rather not take time right now to pull it apart and put it together again more euphoniously. If you think you can do better, go ahead. And you can send your shining jewel of a sentence in to my publisher for him to set in the next edition of this book. I do not remember ever having been grateful to Jude before. Her diabolic plans for Toby would make her rigid in the face of my flexibility, and they were forcing me to act instead of plan.

(Need I tell you that a plan is not the same thing as a plot?)

I had no plan, but I did have a problem: what to wear. My black winter suit and my dark gray winter jacket, my black summer suit and my dark blue summer jacket were tight, unbearably tight, around the shoulders and chest. The pants from my winter suit, which pants I also wore with the dark gray jacket in fall and winter, and the pants from my summer suit, which pants I also wore with my dark blue jacket in spring and summer, were loose, unwearably loose, around the waist. I had no other pants, except the red corduroys, now also loose, not to mention threadbare, and a pair of twelve-dollar, blue gray, imitation-hopsack Levi's Sta-Press, which fit just right. I had been getting by with these last, a windbreaker, a raincoat, and the dark blue jacket, which up until a week or two before had been just wearable. Nor did my shirts fit, for my neck had become a thing of beauty. I looked into my bankbook: $188.73 was all I had in the world. No, wait a minute, I also had eleven dollars and change in my Sta-Press pants pocket. Money was one more thing I had not worried about during the past three months. Nor did I worry about it now. There were always banks to rob, if need be. Nor did I curse the fact that there was no time to work up a disguise. I threw on a tee shirt, the red pants, the hush puppies, the windbreaker, and rushed out the door.

Once outside the door, I immediately spun back around to unlock it, so that I could run into the kitchen for the ice pick. It was not in the drawer! After a spooky moment of near panic —who could have taken it?—I found it in the sink. I shoved it under my belt, but then decided not to risk a perforated intestine. I slipped it into my pants pocket, where it promptly punched a hole. I slipped it into my jacket pocket, where its blade promptly slid through a hole already there. I worked it down my sock, between anklebone and Achilles tendon, but it pricked the side of my heel. Yes, it is possible that I had broken into a sweat. There above the broom closet was our liquor cabinet, never very full and at the moment empty except for a bottle that once held cooking sherry, long evaporated, for Samantha had never yet screwed on a cap or pushed in a cork all the way. I stuck the tip of the pick into the cork, which promptly split. There was no adhesive tape in the medicine cabinet, but there was a box of Band-Aids. I bound the cork with two of them, wrapped the ice pick in a handkerchief, slipped it gingerly into the pocket of my windbreaker, rushed out the door, flew down the stairs, and burst out of the building into a bright spring morning freshened by a breeze that dried the sweat on my face.

I was at the bank five minutes before it opened two minutes late. By 9:16 I had closed out my account after a brief warning to the teller that a fumbling lethargy such as hers was almost always the sign of irreversible syphilitic deterioration of the cerebellum. By 9:48 I was in Barney's at Seventh Avenue and Seventeenth Street, the only store of its kind. In the Ivy-League department I looked over a handsome brown corduroy suit reduced on special to $124.95. When the supercilious salesman made a point of walking off to whisper to the cashier what seemed to be a wise-crack at my expense, I switched the pants of the size 40 suit I had selected with the pants of an otherwise identical suit, size 36. I see no reason for apologies to whoever has bought that brown corduroy suit, size 36. He no doubt had time for major alterations. I did not. And are not most men pear-shaped in these unmanly and unmanning times anyway? For a ten-dollar tip the good-natured Puerto Rican tailor got right down to taking in the waist of the jacket and putting up the cuff of the pants. While he was at it, I picked out an elegant Tattersall shirt with muted brown and tan checks and a button-down collar, a bargain at $14.95. I chose (with misgivings) a snappy, tweedy, brown-and-black, narrow-brimmed Rex Harrison-type hat to serve in lieu of a disguise, for no one had ever once seen me wear a hat, not in the wettest rain or the coldest cold. No one had ever seen me with an umbrella either, and no one ever will, disguise or no disguise. The same goes for rubbers. $19.95 seemed to me a lot to pay for a hat, for any hat, but I had no time to shop around. I decided on a wide, lemon-yellow linen tie, a steal at $4.95, so the salesman said, pointing to the label, the name on which (something like Zucchini), being, so I gathered, the most valuable part of the tie. The raised eyebrows of the salesperson, as I now thought of him, had begun to sink before my frigid and laconic hauteur by the time I let him talk me into buying a pair of cushiony brown, tan, black and yellow argyle socks made of "100% virgin acrylon" going for only $3.98 and a definite improvement in style and comfort over my three-for-a-dollar John's Bargain Store anklets.

I slipped on my new clothes while the salesperson tied the old ones into what turned out to be a very sloppy bundle indeed. He reached over the bundle, false respect and assumed distaste contending for mastery over his features, but I let it dangle from his finger while I counted out exactly $182.28 as deliberately as John D. Rockefeller might have placed one of his famous ten-cent tips under the rim of a saucer.

As you may have gathered, I am not normally very clothes-conscious. But I strolled out of Barney's at 10:40 with a definite sense of well-being, and a girl (who had the look of someone about ready to exchange her scruffy bohemian independence for a husband and a duplex) bestowed on me a long glance of unmistakable admiration. I started toward the subway station on Eighteenth Street, but when a taxi cruised by, the driver looking at me inquisitively, I hailed it, dropping the bundle of old clothes into a trash basket before stepping in past the door held open for me. "To the Hilton," I said, and to hell with the expense. I had five dollars and change in my pocket.

The New York Hilton has nothing that might be called a lobby, exactly, although what a swank hotel is good for, if not to enclose a lobby, is more than I can figure out. Instead, a long, broad corridor cuts straight through the building, from the entrance on Sixth Avenue to halfway toward Seventh, where the hotel ends. I stood just inside the revolving door scanning the visible field before me. I was not so much trying to take in what was there as to see if anything there matched an image I had in my mind. The image I had in my mind was of a short, squat figure with kinky hair and flexed knees, handbag sweeping the floor. Nothing my eye flitted over matched that lurching horror, which to this day stomps through the haunted landscapes of my brain. I therefore looked around slowly and systematically, my attention this time passive and receptive. To my immediate left there was a passage leading to something called the International Promenade, booths and tables arranged around the southeast corner of the building. Along the left side of the central corridor were a row of counters—cashier, reservations, information, and check-in, before which last there was a long line. Beyond these, a sign announced an entrance to Le Grill. Beyond this, another sign announced an entrance to The Old Bourbon Steak House.

To my immediate right was a passage leading to escalators. These, as I later discovered, ascended to nothing more interesting than the first and second mezzanines. On the right or up-town side of the central corridor were a shop selling expensive trinkets, a flowershop, a counter at which you could rent cars or whores or something, banks of elevators, and at the end, a sign announcing an entrance to the Kismet Lounge, for visiting oilmen, no doubt. Before me, on a stand, was a placard: The New York Hilton, so it said, welcomed the Organization of Social Scientists of America. It was members of that august body, I take it, that were standing in line before the check-in counter or hanging around in couples or small groups. They were distinguished by an air of low aspiration, their gabbling faces congealed into the expressions that go with mean calculation and paltry opportunism, whether worn by midwestern dowds, coast-to-coast dudes, or counterculture deadheads in spick-and-span denim. In my by no means considered opinion, higher education was in better shape when professors lived either on unearned income or in genteel poverty, and that was that.

I relaxed, let the air out of my lungs, put on a little obsequious-aggressive smile, looked for a good place to loiter inconspicuously while keeping an eye on the check-in desk. A sudden push from behind sent me flying into a woman who had been standing in front of me and to my right. I caught her by the arms to prevent her from falling and whipped my head around to see whose jaw it was I was about to break. "Out of the doorway, Dummy," said a tall, thin-faced blonde, who did not even look at me as she strode by on high, shiny, black boots. "Why, Greg!" said the woman I had been pushed into and who was now holding me by the sleeves of my jacket. In a panic I whipped my head back to face her, but something I caught out of the corner of my eye on the way made me whip around again: that something was my Samantha's long black hair. And her straight back and her neat waist and her heartbreaking calves.

"Why Greg, I never thought I'd see you again," said the woman who was holding me by my coat sleeves. "And then to have you thrown into my arms by none other than Erika von Plaack—" Samantha was talking to someone on the check-in line. Past her shoulder I could see what looked like the top and one side of a brass scouring pad roughly the size of a bushel basket. Samantha was talking to a blonde fuzzy wuzzy.

"You look marvellous," said the woman who I now realized was Muriel Bigalow, although I had not yet glanced at her. I shuffled left, so that I could watch Samantha off Muriel's right ear.

"How are you, Muriel?" In fact, she looked strange. I bent over to kiss her on the forehead. Samantha bent over to kiss the fuzzy wuzzy on the cheek. Muriel was weary, wary, and a bit wild-eyed, as though someone were winding her hair up on a wringer and she was pretending not to notice.

"You never called," she said.

"But I did: twice. The phone rang and rang, and you never answered," I said, turning the tables neatly. And I had called her, too. I do not remember claiming that my regimen would make you immune to loneliness. Samantha took a step back, almost a curtsy, did an about-face, and began to march toward us, so that I could see her brilliant skin and aloof features, which, however, were not Samantha's. Who was this broad, anyhow, this pseudo-Samantha, and why was she marching right at us?

"You could have been a little more persistent," said Muriel. I sighted on a line running over her right shoulder and over the approaching left shoulder of the pseudo-Samantha to where a fuzzy wuzzy in a flowered, lavender spring coat or cape designed by Omar the Tent-Maker was receiving a key from the check-in clerk. She glanced over our way and I gasped. The face in the middle of that big brass scouring pad was Jude Karnofsky's.

"You follow her up, I'll keep an eye out down here," said a husky male voice behind me. I spun away from Muriel toward the voice, just as she spun away from me to see what I had been staring at. As I completed my spin, one well-built man in a well-made suit was saying "Check" to another well-built in a well-made. Without moving anything else, they turned their heads deliberately and in unison so that they could look at me. They said nothing. Their expressions signified less. I became conscious of Muriel's hand on my shoulder pulling me around to her.

"I can fix you up," she said.

"What?" I said.

"Okay, there she goes," said the husky voice behind me.

"I know that brunette you got such big eyes for," said Muriel.

"What?" I said. Jude, her ridiculous cape swirling around her, was trying to keep up with the bellhop carrying her bag toward the elevators. She was wearing a beige dress and white shoes and white gloves. Believe it or not, even then I felt there was something touching about her attempts to look like a woman.

I felt a light touch at my elbow. "Excuse me," said one of the well-built men, the one in well-made brown. He slid neatly by and moved toward the elevators. The pseudo-Samantha was nearly upon us. "Kathleen," Muriel called to her, but she just marched on by. "Muriel," I said, "I've got to run. Catch up with you later."

I made straight for the elevators, detouring just once to unload a forearm shiver halfway down Erika von Plaack's black-clad back. "Out of the way, woman," I said, as she went flying into a pint-sized Orientaleen of some kind.

A crowd was humped around the elevators. Jude was in the center of it, next to her bellhop. There was a space around her —why, I couldn't say: some obscure phenomenon of group behavior was at work, maybe. The people around her were receiving subliminal messages from her, perhaps. There was an aura of impending death about her, it may be. This is all speculation, of course. I waited at the fringe of the crowd, on the mark to muscle my way through to whatever elevator Jude started for. I was tingling, alert to my toenails, ready for anything. A terrific blow to the back of my left thigh nearly knocked me down. I believe I whimpered. Someone pulled my hat down over my eyes. A hand grabbed me by the back of my jacket collar. A voice hissed in my ear. "Don't fuck with Mother Nature, big boy. Next time I'll twist your head off and jam it up your ass." The hand released me with a forward shove that sent me stumbling. Dimly I heard the near elevator doors opening. I pushed up my hat. In a red haze I saw Jude stepping to the elevator through a lane that had magically cleared for her. The crush drew tight around me and carried me into the elevator, or I would never have made it. I squirmed around to face the doors, which closed just behind the well-built man in the well-made brown suit as he pushed in smiling apologetically.

He looked at me curiously before turning around. Or so it seemed to me. I couldn't see very clearly, because there were tears in my eyes.

And sweat was beginning to run down my brow. Because of the press, I could not raise a hand to wipe my face. In any case, my handkerchief was still in the back pocket of the red corduroy pants, now residing in a trash basket outside Barney's. Nor could I remove my hat, as elevator courtesy required. I suppose I would have left it on anyhow, although I doubted that Jude would recognize me in my new mustache, uncharacteristic clothes, and renovated physique. I could have walked over and bit her on the nose, without her knowing who was doing it. Right then, she could have stuck an umbrella up mine, for all I cared. When the elevator stopped for the first time, I had to restrain myself from stepping out, stepping in the next elevator heading down, getting off at the lobby, and calling out Erika von Plaack, who sooner or later was going to pay for that kick with her blood. Can you imagine the nerve of that bitch? Who was *she* to tell *me* not to fuck with Mother Nature? What was she doing every minute of her unnatural life? I asked myself. Whereas I have always revered nature, the closest thing to a god (not goddess) I have. On the eighteenth floor, the bellhop pushed by with a "Getting out, getting out," Jude a hop-step-hop behind him. The man in brown slipped out right after them, cutting me off. I stumbled forward, my left leg buckling, slammed back the elevator door with my shoulder when it closed on me, then stood still for a few seconds, my heels inside the elevator, my toes outside, adjusted my hat, and strolled nonchalantly out.

Directly in front were two more elevators. To the right, a window. To the left, the elevator alcove continued until it met a corridor at right angles. Jude and the bellhop turned right. I took a step right, to the window. I was not much surprised to find myself standing next to the man in brown. By that time it would not have surprised me to see Pastor Peter Brevoort come crashing through the window in a Superman outfit. We did not look at each other. We looked at an office building made entirely out of glass, so far as I could see, and there was nothing else to see, except maybe three inches of bright blue sky. Someone had put out a Salem on the window sill. The carpet was red. Well-built turned and walked off. I counted to five and did the same, with one exception: he did not limp. Halfway down the right wing of the corridor, which I estimated as roughly three miles in length, were Jude and the bellhop, still moving along. A quarter of the way down, well-made was also moving along. I turned after them, refusing to limp, half relishing the pain. Jude and the bellhop drew up at a door on the left side. The symphony in brown bent over an ice machine on the right side, slid open the door, and proceeded to cool his hands. I walked evenly by his well-clad rump and walked by room 1833 just as the door closed on a piece of lavender cape. I walked on to the end of the corridor. I knocked lightly, not on the door, but on the wall next to Room 1854, where Brown would hear, but not anybody inside. No one answered. I started back. Faintly, through a closed door, I heard a voice behind me say, "Who is it?" Brown was walking toward me. He glanced at the door of Room 1833. It only then dawned on me who, or anyhow what, he was. You were way ahead of me? Fine. You also had less on your mind. Nor had you been kicked in the thigh by that answer to a masochist's prayer. A door opened behind me. I walked up to Brown and said, out of the corner of my mouth, "I'll tell Miss Lily you're on the job." He looked me over, his face without expression, and said, "You do that."

Deceive yourself, if you must, but not at my expense. If you heard a long, drawn-out shuddering sigh of relief, don't look my way. So what if the bright blade of retribution would have to hang suspended over Jude's head for a couple of hours longer? I felt neither relief, nor disappointment. Please get rid of the notion that because I do what you long to do, I feel about doing it as you would need to feel. Not having a plan, as I told you, leaves one ready for anything—except for a kick in the thigh. There is no way of being ready for the treacheries of a von Plaack. If your first outrage is against nature, the rest comes easy. It is tacitly understood among men that there are certain things one does not do. In that understanding lie some of the many advantages women have over men. Imagine yourself playing middle linebacker. Third down, four yards to go. As your opponents, in loud crimson jerseys, break their huddle, you are watching carefully to see how they will line up. They come out in an "I" formation, switch to a slot left. You call a few quick defensive changes accordingly. The opposing linemen get down into their three-point stance. The quarterback crouches, hands under the center, calls "Blue, 44, hut." The slotback goes in motion. An alarm goes off in your brain: it's going to be a draw play. You back up a step. The quarterback, straightening up, lifts a tommygun, and mows you down. As you fall among your teammates strewn on the field, you see their fullback take the hand-off and start his eighty-yard amble to the goal line. Such is the kind of thing that happens when you admit women into the affairs of men. Take it from me, that quarterback was a woman in disguise.

I strode through the lobby, looking neither right nor left. But I did catch a glimpse of von Plaack talking to a man, laughing, poking him playfully in the chest. He seemed to be laughing too, as he rocked on his toes, hands in pockets (where, as I imagined them, his fists clenched and unclenched and clenched, until the knuckles whitened and the skin almost split). Did I, as I pushed briskly through the door onto Sixth Avenue, did I hear a voice calling "Greg, oh Greg, oooooh Greg."

Without hesitation, I turned downtown. Between 1:00 and 3:00, so Bill said, Toby played in Gramercy Park under the watchful eyes of Butchy-Wutchy. It was now 12:20, plenty of time for me to walk thirty blocks and a bit, rescue Toby, restore him to his Dad, remind his Grandma that she could now call off her well-built men in brown and gray, return to the Hilton, kill Jude. Who knows, there might even be enough time for me to break a kneecap or two on the von Plaack. By tomorrow at this time, both Samantha and Toby would be where they belonged, in the arms of the people who loved them. Someday, I mused as I walked along, my stomach rumbling, past the sights and sounds of hotdogs, hamburgers, hot sausages, hero sandwiches, gyro sandwiches, brisket and pastrami sandwiches, fried chicken, barbecue chicken, barbecue spare ribs, curries, knishes, comidas criollas, someday I would tell Samantha and Toby what I had done for them. I would also tell them how, my mouth filling with saliva, instead of buying something to eat, I held on to my last three dollars in case the money was required for the cause of their freedom. My left thigh didn't feel too good, either.

If you have never seen Gramercy Park, you ought to look it over some time. It is a very well-kept spot of money-green off Park Avenue at about Twenty-second Street. I doubt that I have ever earned in a year what it costs to rent for a year an apartment in the houses around it. Within the park were small plots of lawn, flowerbeds, shrubs, some noble trees, a care-taker's hut, a caretaker with a hose, a scattering of old folks on benches, some children, their mammas or nursemaids, a ninety-year-old dandy with straw hat and cane, but no Toby, no Butch, no well-built man in brown or gray, or pink for that matter. Around the park was, and presumably still is, a tall fence of iron spikes, painted black. The west gate, when I tried it, was locked. So was the south gate. To get into the park, apparently, you needed a key. To get a key, apparently, you needed to live in one of the houses bordering the park. The main business of those who *have* is to see that nobody else *gets*.

The east side of the park is the shadiest. Branches on one gnarled old tree with black bark (I can't tell an ash from an elder, although I know lots of other useless things) hang over the fence and sidewalk. I loitered under a bough that somebody was going to have to trim one day soon, leaned against the fence, and let my eyes drift casually over 33 Gramercy Park East. The situation called for a cigarette, but I didn't have one. A lovely four-story pile of brownstone is the von Plaack place. The pictures of it you see in magazines more than do it justice. The time was 1:10 and nothing stirred, except for a white lace curtain writhing behind the open bay window, for there was a fresh breeze blowing. When the sweat on my forehead dried, I crossed over to the chest-high black iron fence around the bit of yard in front of the house.

"Built in 1901 by Henry von Plaack, Merchant and Philanthropist (1850–1950)," so said the engraving on a brass plate under the outward billow of the lace curtains. Henry would be the great-grandfather. Ten years after he died, his son William, Erika's grandfather, died in Africa at age 67, when the impala he had shot turned out not to be dead; it jumped suddenly to its feet, on the way pushing a horn through William's eye socket and out the back of his skull. In February, 1944 Erika was born while her father, another Henry, was dive-bombing Japanese ships. He died in 1955, piloting a jet over Korea. Stephanie von Plaack, Erika's mother, died in 1968, from cancer of the uterus. These facts, if such they really are, have been extracted from an article in a copy of *Newsweek* I carefully preserved for just this occasion. I knew most of it, as I suppose you did, even before Erika von Plaack introduced herself to me with a shove and a kick. And if when the time came, she thought I was going to show her any mercy just because she was an orphan, she was in for a little surprise. Didn't anyone ever tell you that I lost my mother at an earlier age than von Plaack lost hers? Little Victor was only six; big Erika was twenty-four. You have no idea what a difference it would have made, would still make, had my mother only waited a few years longer before dying. How many women have you known who died of a heart attack at age 32?

Still no sign of life. The curtain hung motionless. The garbage had not yet been collected. (In New York, there are some things that even money can't buy.) Three loaded trash cans stood outside the fence, next to the locked gate. In one was a broomstick, a beauty, thick, straight, and hard—high quality goods, obviously, the kind of broomstick I had been looking for when a few weeks back I was possessed by an urge to make a spear. (I knew where to get a chisel that with a little work would do for the business end.) The best way to get from one side of a chest-high fence to the other is as follows: look right and left to make sure no one is coming. Place hands on top of fence. Jump up and push down with your hands until you can lock your elbows. Lock them. With your belly resting on the top near edge of the fence, tip forward, like a seesaw, your body stiff, and reach down with your right hand for a lower grip on the fence. At the exact moment when your feet swing past the perpendicular, push off (make sure to let go of the left hand first), pivot in the air, and land lightly on your feet, knees flexed. I picked up my hat. And still nothing stirred, not a sound to be heard. I extracted the broomstick from the can and pulled it through the fence. If Butch tried any of his jiujitsu on me, I'd crease his skull for him. That is what I said to myself, and I meant it.

The walk was four paces long and about twenty inches wide. The stoop, with its eleven narrow steps, handrail, and landing of black iron, was shaky. On a brass plate under the mailbox was the name ERIKA VON PLAACK in one-inch letters. Below, on a smaller plate, was the name Franklin D. Luala, alias Butch. I lay the broomstick down carefully behind me. I slipped out my wallet to see if a Columbia I.D. would work on the lock as credit cards allegedly work for burglars. (I have never owned a credit card, or wanted to, but I have often wanted to strangle some modish ninnie who kept me waiting on a line while a prettily flustered check-out girl processed his card.) I was sliding my I.D. between lock and jamb (to no effect) when a shadow moved behind the frosted glass of the door. I tip-quick-toed back, tripped on the broomstick, caught myself on the rail, dropped the I.D., picked it up, pushed the broomstick aside on the landing, took the eleven steps in two jumps, the walk in two skips, vaulted the fence, picked up my hat, and strode briskly to the southeast corner of the park, where, my hands on the black iron uprights, I found myself looking directly into the eyes of the old dandy. He shook his cane at me, creaked to his feet, and shuffled off, toward the caretaker.

Butch has a smooth face, bangs, rabbit eyes, and hysterical nostrils. He was wearing sandals (for which I already hated him), beige slacks (flared at the bottom but very tight about the thighs), a mustard-colored body shirt, and a thin necklace made of wampum. He had an enviable physique, but I did not envy it, and still do not. His right hand rested lightly on Toby's shoulder. His left hand held a red wooden toy circus van with yellow wheels. Toby was wearing red overalls, and I hate to admit it, but the two of them made a pretty picture as they came down the steps together, the little boy chattering, the man bending over to listen. Butch unlocked his own gate, crossed the street, unlocked the park gate, sat on a bench under the gnarled old tree, placed the van on the walk, took out lion and giraffe and elephant and clown and ringmaster and trapeze artist, and which of the last three was I?

Halfway across the park, the old dandy was still shuffling in slow motion toward the caretaker, who seemed to be making his rounds, nippers in hand. But the distance between them never lessened, for each time the caretaker would move from one shrub to another, the old man would find himself on walks that no longer led to the caretaker. He would shudder to a stop, revolve in a series of little sidesteps, lurch forward toward another crosswalk. He was scrupulous never to step on the grass. I sauntered across the street, removing cards and pictures from the celluloid holders in my wallet. I emptied a small paper bag from a trash can, ripped the celluloid holders from my wallet, wrapped them in the bag, put the whole business in my jacket pocket. I vaulted the fence, picked up my hat. As I started up the black iron steps, a garbage truck crashed to a halt behind me. I found the broomstick and wedged it into the filigree at the bottom of the handrails, so that it stretched across and about six inches above the next-to-next-to-last (the word is "antepenultimate") step. I walked over to a garbage man as he dropped the last can, and the truck ground off north to the next house. The old dandy seemed finally to be approaching the caretaker.

"Got a match?" I said to the garbageman.

He silently handed me a book of matches through the fence. I struck a match, ripped off the cover, lit it. "Hey, what're ya doing?" he said.

"I am burning the cover of your matchbook," I said, handing him what was left.

"You couldn't just play with yourself, like anybody else," he said.

"That comes next," I said.

He nodded and moved off to his fellows. I extracted the paper bag from my pocket and held one twisted end of it to the burning matchbook cover. When the bag was well lit, I walked over to the bay window, paused to gauge the distance, and with a neat little jumpshot dropped the burning bag between the curtains, now once again fluttering in the breeze. I ran over to the fence, stopped short. I removed my hat and balanced it on the top of the fence, which I then vaulted. I put on my hat and started across the street. His straw hat jerking in all directions, the old dandy was talking to the caretaker, who did not look up from the shrub he was nipping.

"Hey mister," I said to Butch's back. He turned on the bench. "Do you live in that house over there?"

"That is correct," he said.

"Well, it's on fire," I said.

Butch jumped up, came over, peered through the fence at the puffs and wisps of curtain and smoke turning in the bay window. He shot me a keen look and ran for the gate. "Just stay right there," he shouted to Toby.

Before he was three running steps across the street, I had jumped up and gotten a hold on the gnarled black old branch. A button popped off my jacket. I swung up my feet, and my hat fell off. Hanging upside-down like a giant sloth, I moved down along the branch, hand over hand and heel over heel, pausing once to reach down with my left hand to remove the tail of my jacket from the spike on which it had caught. I dropped to the ground just inside the park. Behind me I heard a clatter, a thump, a groan. Butch, I assumed, had tripped on the broomstick and sailed into the door. Good. And may the pain in his big toe teach him that sandals are for women. The caretaker and the old dandy were looking my way.

"Hello Uncle Victor," said Toby. "Look at the circus truck Butch and me got this morning. I'm not supposed to tell Mommy." I gathered the straps of his overalls and the collar of his shirt in my right hand, the seat of his pants in my left. I lifted him over my head easily and pressed until he was at arm's length. Nothing to it, except for the pain that shot through my wounded thigh. I carried him over to the fence, leaned against it with knees and chest. I dipped my hands forward, so that Toby rolled over the spikes, the crossbar digging into my wrists. I released him with my left hand so that his legs swung down to where that same left hand was already through the uprights waiting for a new grip on his pants. I released him with my right hand, moved it back, down, and out between the uprights to catch Toby before he had tipped forward an inch. I lowered him to the ground. "What are we doing?" he said.

I crouched for my jump, then looked back over my shoulder. The caretaker was on the move, the old dandy three steps behind, shaking his cane at me. I jumped, caught hold of the branch, passed over the spikes, one of which ripped the lining in the tail of my jacket, dropped to the ground. I picked up my hat. Would you believe that the button was right underneath it? I put the button in my pocket and the hat on my head. I scooped up Toby and began to run for the southeast corner of the park. Butch was at the window, stomping on something and burning his toes, I hoped. He looked out, saw me, and without a word began to climb over the sill.

"Hey you, stop!" said the caretaker.

"I want my circus," said Toby.

"Slap," said Butch's sandals, some distance behind me, as he landed under the famous bay window.

As I rounded the corner to head for Third Avenue, two things happened: 1) I looked back, saw the caretaker fumbling with a huge key ring inside the park gate, saw Butch on his hands and knees, presumably looking for the key to his house gate; 2) my left leg collapsed under me. I bruised the heel of my left hand, my right knee, and the corduroy over it, but I did not drop Toby. On the corner of Third Avenue and Twenty-first I looked around wildly for a taxi. "Want a cab, mister?" said a voice under my chin. He had been parked right there at the curb all along. I got in and sat back. Butch was a quarter of the way up the block, running pretty well for a man in sandals. Halfway up the block was the caretaker, not making bad time either, especially for someone that bowlegged. The old dandy was taking the corner in a wide curve. "To the Plaza," I told the driver.

Toby, kneeling on the seat, threw his arms around me. The wooden ringmaster he was still holding put a scratch on my neck.

I hugged him back. Is there anything in the world like the smoothness of a child's cheek? "I'll buy you another circus," I said. "Two of them."

"Two thirty-five," said the driver, as we pulled over to the Plaza. To my surprise, my money was still at the bottom of a deep pants pocket—in spite of all the fence-vaulting. Looks like I was another well-built man in a well-made suit. I gave the driver three dollars. I gave the doorman a quarter. You too must have noticed that the people who work hardest for their money are most generous with their tips. My material assets at that moment consisted of four cents and a new suit, slightly damaged.

The door to Miss Lily's suite was opened by a well-built man in a well-made black suit. "Who?" he said, then he saw Toby. He opened the door all the way and gestured with his head for me to enter, his eyes wary. The sitting room looked as though it had been lifted from Versailles. Three men distributed around the edges of the room half-rose from their chairs, heads turned my way. Toby ran to one of them, to Bill, whose mouth was hanging open. Miss Lily, sitting near the center of the room at a little desk with lots of inlay, said coldly, "Have we met?" then, smiling slowly, seductively, said, "Why I do believe it's Victor Grant," making me feel for the moment as though to be Victor Grant were to be Cary Ditto. "And you've got Toby. How enterprising of you. Now here's what I call a true friend. William Austin, you hear what I'm saying? I was beginning to think New York had plain run out of men." But now she didn't sound as though she meant it. Bill grunted.

The phone rang. One of the men I didn't know, the youngest, popped out of his chair, walked over to Miss Lily's desk, picked up the phone. He looked like the kind of chap who wants women to think of him as sensitive. "It's Mrs. Austin," he said. Bill started toward him. Miss Lily stood up.

"Just leave her to me," she said. "I'll take it on the bedroom phone." Bill sat down. "Victor, dear, you will excuse me, won't you?" Miss Lily sailed through a door held open by the eldest of the three men I didn't know. He was tall, slim, smooth, smiling, pin-striped, pewter-haired. Anyone that impeccable had to be covering up something loathsome. My guess was that he had fantasies of waiting in line, a-tremble with anticipation, as one by one the naked boys and girls before him had their hearts ripped out by an Aztec priest.

Mr. Sensitive replaced the phone. Bill made introductions.

The well-built man in black was Barker, head of security for Lily-Belle, Inc. He gave me a nod. The young man who had picked up the phone was Carter (Harvard '68, I would say), Miss Lily's secretary. We shook hands. The man who had held the door was Parker, partner in a firm that handled Miss Lily's legal problems but was otherwise handled by her. "Mr. Grant," he said, and gave me a hand like a silk purse full of caterpillars.

We sat for a while.

"Drink?" said Barker.

"Sure," I said.

"Scotch?" he said.

"Fine," I said. "And has anyone a cigarette?" Barker had a Marlboro and Parker had a Newport. I took a Marlboro.

We sat for a while.

"What have you got there?" said Bill.

"A ringmaster," said Toby, as Miss Lily returned. "Uncle Victor, why did you leave my circus in Gramercy Park? Do you think Uncle Butch will save it for me?"

"In a little while we'll go around the corner to F.O.A. Schwartz and get you a new one," I said.

Miss Lily shot a look at Carter, who jumped up. "And take Toby with you," she said.

"Yes, Miss Lily," he said.

"Toby dear, wouldn't you like to pick out a nice new circus, any one you want?" she said.

"Yes, Miss Lily," he said. I wanted to hug him, but I didn't.

"Maybe I'd better go along," said Barker.

"That won't be necessary." She paused until Toby and Carter had gone out. "The Karnofsky person, I believe, has finally been made to understand her true position. My, that woman has a foul mouth. Not that I expected anything else. As my Daddy used to say, you can't polish a turd."

Bill sighed. He turned to Parker. "What can she do?"

"Legally speaking, many things; she can make considerable trouble for us. But there is no legal way she will get her hands on Toby by Saturday. I'll see to that," said Parker.

"No illegal way either, and I'll see to that," said Barker.

"She won't do anything, except try to get a refund on one of her tickets to Amsterdam. I've already seen to that," said Miss Lily. "Now, Victor Grant, I expect you have quite a story to tell us."

Some people can turn the most trivial incident into an epic merely by relating it. Whereas I am not very good at telling stories, even true ones. It takes a certain kind of person, the kind who depends on the reactions of other people for verification of his own existence. Needless to say, I am not that kind of person. If I had been, I would have faded away long ago. And can you tell me why, when I ask for so little, Samantha had to be taken from me? A sudden longing overwhelmed me, as it overwhelms me now, for the Samantha who during the first years of our marriage used to wait for me to come home from work. I would entertain her with little stories of the day's happenings—and I was as eloquent as a bard, a Homer, an Othello —while she served a sunken quiche or a grayish stew. There was not much skill in Samantha's cooking, but there was plenty of love. Then Jude planted the notion in Samantha's head that I should cook on alternate nights. My uninspired efficiency had a bad effect on Samantha. She lost confidence in her ability to improve on Julia Child. I didn't mind frozen dinners (I gave her forty dollars a week housekeeping money), when they were heated by Samantha, but soon she seemed to lose her appetite for my stories. The rancid spice of the gothic horrors fed her at those consciousness-raising klatches had corrupted her taste. That was something else I was going to ram down Jude Karnofsky's throat.

No one in Miss Lily's suite interrupted me while I gave a laconic account of my day's activities, although Barker grunted and Miss Lily laughed at the spectacle of Butch stomping out a fire with bare toes. True, at one point Miss Lily said, "And that is how you lost a button." I took it out of my pocket and held it up. "Give it here," she said, and fetched a nifty little mother-of-pearl sewing kit She repaired the lining while she was at it, and very neat work it was. Miss Lily is a remarkable woman. It is a myth that men resent being bossed by females. It all depends on which female wants to do the bossing. The point is that she has to be a real female, not a bad imitation of a man. I left out of my account, as not germane, Erika von Plaack's nefarious kick.

Toby and Carter returned with a new circus van. It was bigger than the old one, but I could see that Toby didn't like it as much. We all then had tea and cookies, while my stomach sent messages for something like half a roast boar. I suggested with cunning indirection that Miss Lily could now call off the men who were trailing Jude. Barker put in that they might as well let the four-to-midnight shift finish off, just to see whom Jude was spending her time with. Miss Lily said all right, they might just as well. Bill called Martine, who said she would come. Miss Lily received reports by phone, from the well-built men in brown and gray, I assume. A messenger arrived with summaries of phone calls from and to 33 Gramercy Park East. None of the calls were to the police. Butch had assumed from the beginning the one of Miss Lily's men snatched Toby. Stevie Dickinson swore revenge. Jude pretended not to understand why Toby had been abducted a day before she was due to turn him over to Bill anyhow. Room service arrived with dinner for Toby and Martine. Barker made drinks. Carter didn't drink, but I did, far too much, and I don't even like scotch. Miss Lily said why didn't I just come along with them for dinner, but I refused, and you can chalk up another triumph for the human spirit over base appetite. I was not sulking. When I mentioned an appointment, Miss Lily could have asked me to cancel it. And Bill had not spoken five times all afternoon. You'd think he would have shown a little gratitude. So I left, with a pat on the cheek from Miss Lily.

A respectful nod from the doorman reminded me that I was

fresh out of money. The sixty-block walk home was not very appealing, but I was also fresh out of wings. There was nothing between my belly button and backbone but some fumes of scotch. And there was nothing in my head but misery, which increased with every step I took, as did my headache, the first since twenty years before I had run away from home, the original Migraine Manor. You set out to commit a murder that will be a kind of poem, and none of the rhyme-words fit the meter. It was no use for me to hang around the Hilton until midnight, when Miss Lily's men would leave off trailing Jude. I was too down. Maybe you can go around murdering people when you are depressed, I can't. How was I ever going to recapture that morning's exuberance, its savage glee and inspired ferocity? How can you do anything great unless the world cooperates a little, unless someone, or *something,* gives you a bit of encouragement. Let's face it, I was not being rational.

In the cupboard was a can of mushroom pieces (left over from when Samantha did the cooking) and in the refrigerator two stalks of celery (I always ate the hearts first), and that's all. I trudged down to Bill's neighbor, the one married to a colleague of Jude's, to borrow a half-dozen eggs, and my thigh acted as though Erika von Plaack had her big teeth in it, right up to her receding gums. In the old days there used to be a neighborhood butcher from whom you could buy on credit. If you want to hear some interesting language, you might one day ask the manager at your local supermarket to put four pounds of spareribs on the tab. Mrs. Lindquist is a tall, sturdy, handsome, unsmiling strawberry blonde, a year or two over thirty. She came to the door with a red face, a damp curl of hair hanging over an eye, and flour on her hands. She was so sorry, she said, but she had only one egg left. In fact, she was right in the middle of mixing up some blitz torte for acquaintances of her husband's he had just called up to say he was bringing home from the OSSA conference. The urge to kill her was short, but not easy to resist while it lasted. She asked after Bill, who, it seems, was supposed to have dropped by. I told her that his mother was keeping him on a short leash. She wondered if I would mind telling him to get in touch with her as soon as he could. I said she would probably see him before I did. Suddenly, I had a terrific urge to blitz her from behind while she slid her torte into the oven. I could see myself lifting her patchwork skirt without a word and pulling down her panties, she pretending I wasn't there, the warmth and fragrance rising around us. I saw an invitation forming on her lips, I just knew she was going to ask me in, but she didn't. She had better get back to her cooking, she said, did I want the egg? Before I could answer she had gone after it, returned, and plopped it in my hand. Screw you too, lady, I told her closed door, and what I was holding in my hand was probably a better lay anyhow.

I chopped the celery, sautéed it, added half the mushroom pieces, put the rest in oil and vinegar, beat the egg, mixed in the sautéed celery and mushrooms, poured all this into the pan, folded it over, flipped it, slid it onto a plate, looked it over, added salt and pepper and oregano, looked it over, added thyme and tobasco sauce, looked it over, dumped it into the garbage. I dumped the mushrooms in oil and vinegar into the sink. I called Muriel, but the phone rang and rang until I hung up. I called the Feathered Dragon, but Brunhilda didn't come in on Thursday evenings (when she had her dressmaking classes). There was nothing to see out any of the windows. Henry Kissinger, according to the television set, had pulled off another miracle in the Near East, via a concession from President Assad. Our own president still refused to turn a second batch of tapes over to the Judiciary Committee, which that day had sent him a letter warning that "committee members will be free to consider whether your refusals warrant the drawing of adverse inferences concerning the substance of the materials, and whether your refusals in and of themselves might constitute a ground for impeachment." The committee will be free to consider whether his refusals warrant the drawing of adverse inferences—that's plain speaking for you. The fact is that although Nixon was the opposite of everything I admired in a man, I could sympathize with him. There were times when I also felt that nothing I could do would ever make people like me. The other channels, so far as I could tell, were featuring commercials straight through the evening. I called Chi Chi, but his wife wouldn't say where he was. She kept asking who the hell I was and why I couldn't leave her husband alone. I took a long hot bath, two hours long, and yes, I played with myself, but nothing came of it.

I crawled between the sheets, my head spinning and aching and flashing with broken imagery. I relaxed systematically, from toe to eyeball and down again. I gradually worked the rockets and pinwheels down to a single point of light, then turned it off. I switched on a picture of my left thigh, watched the pain seep out of it, like a thin smoke. I relaxed, let slow waves of blackness roll over me. I switched on my brain, watched the capillaries open, saw the blood flow smoothly, washing out the ache. I relaxed further, retreated further into myself, until I drifted weightlessly in my own weightless body, floating in a cloud. Again and again, I told myself, and got myself to believe, that, after all, I had rescued Toby, my mission was half over, success feeds on success, tomorrow I would kill Jude, Samantha would come home to me. And then? Never mind, what had to be done, I would do. The restlessness drained out of me. I was neither reluctant nor eager, but ready. I still think that *someone* might have made a fuss over me.

I was composed, but wide awake. I began to review the day's events, dispassionately, as though they had occurred to someone else, but the scenes kept dissolving into each other. I let one scene develop according to the logic of the desire, rather than memory. Erika von Plaack strode into my room wearing a ringmaster's outfit, a damp curl of hair hanging over an eye. She smiled, tilting her head, and her teeth were long. She threw back the lavender sheet with a flourish, as Dracula might open his cape. There was flour on her hand. She began to kiss the inside of my thighs, lingering on the left one, and the black and blue turned rosy. She moved slowly upward and took me in her mouth, as gently as though she were trying to swallow a bubble. Her red face rose and fell like a carousel horse on its pole, and at the same time I was behind her, getting ready to blitz her torte. I lifted her patchwork skirt and pulled down her panties. I winked at her rosebud of a rectum and then entered her with my thick, straight, and hard broomstick, high quality goods. I flicked ashes from my cigarette on her spine and balanced my hat on top of it. I took my time. When I came, it was like the eruption of Krakatoa. A man needs a wife to come home to, but the next best thing is self-hypnosis. I slid off into sleep and you might settle into a habit of self-pity.

V

I did not kip up out of bed on Friday morning. I got up deliberately, in stages, and dressed the same way. I was still headachy, but I didn't mind. The armpits of my shirt smelled, but I didn't mind that either. The ache in my head and the smell of my shirt and the emptiness in my belly amused me, in a grim sort of way. So did the stiffness in my thigh, which worked itself out as I walked to the Hilton. Everything amused me in a grim sort of way, including the wooden-faced deadheads marching to their pointless jobs, oblivious of the time bomb ticking by them with a slight limp. My own amusement amused me, but not much. I nodded with satisfaction while through the coffee shop window I watched Jude eat a high-protein breakfast: hamsteak, eggs, black coffee. She left her toast and homefries. Of course, there was no way I could ask the waitress to let me have them instead of throwing them out. America is a wasteful country. That amused me too, in a grim sort of way.

Jude was not eating alone. Her companion looked like one of the original Dead End Kids. Call up to your mind's eye a thin face, a pointed chin, a sullen expression, lank brown hair over one eye, tobacco-stained fingers and lips, high, thin shoulders and fishhook spine, a white shirt (clearly not in its first day of use), sleeves rolled up over a puny bicep. A recurrent American type: just before my mother died, one example of this species, with two sidekicks, had knocked me down and threatened worse, before riding off on my new scooter. My father had not been sympathetic. While I watched, thinking of all this, Jude's companion drank three cups of black coffee and smoked six Luckies, the stubs of which wound up jammed into an otherwise untouched napoleon. The waitress, who looked as though her feet were already hurting, took the napolean away as Jude and her friend got off their stools, leaving a tip of fifteen cents between them. The waitress paused to watch them depart, her face like Mary McCabe's when Father O'Brien exposed himself in the confessional.

If you had asked me, I would have told you that I was beyond the stage where any woman could shock me. I would have been wrong, of course. For that is what Jude's companion turned out to be, a woman (in spite of herself). I gasped as she whipped out of the revolving door, and then I groaned. She heard me, I believe, but her attention was deflected by Jude, who was arrested in mid-stride and then pulled backward when her lavender cape caught in the revolving door. As Jude backed carefully into the coffee shop, I studied her companion. From head to waist she was a scrawny boy. From waist to foot she was a corpulent woman. You know how the fat on some people is firm, shapely even. Well, not on this one. Her buttocks and thighs were all waggle, wobble, and jiggle. Her brown slacks had the aspect of a balloon losing air. They did not conceal any of the turbulence they contained. They revealed all the puckers, tucks, dents, dimples, ripples, and rolls that agitated the surface of the flesh within. When Jude came out, balancing her head-dress and gathering her cape, the other followed. She moved in roundhouse strides, so that the insides of her thighs could flap by each other. Her pants swished. The outsides of her thighs quivered and humped and collapsed. You see what I was up against? You have now been introduced to Stevie Dickinson, Managing Editor of *Ms. Chief.* I was still grim, and I was still amused, but I was also outraged. A body like Stevie Dickinson's is not an accident of nature, but an assault on it.

I loitered around the second mezzanine while Jude and Stevie Dickinson attended a lecture in the Trianon Ballroom. A placard outside the doors announced to the incurious onlooker that Ms. Jody Fishman's theme was "Deconstructing Gender. The Manwomanly Shaman: A Crow for the Future." A sharp pain informed me that I would soon have a deviated septum if I did not stop snorting with derision. My idea was to follow Jude to her room when she went there for a pre-lunch-pee, gain admittance with a ruse, kill her. The applause began at 11:15 and seemed never to end. Neither Jude nor anyone else came out. Was there another exit? Had they all been turned into beetles? I opened a door and stuck my head in. A robust black woman in a white jumpsuit and turban was speaking from the floor—"Crow shamans was too chickenshit to be warriors, that's why they shamans." Right on, Sister! A discussion period was in progress. I scanned the room. Erika von Plaack, sitting in the last row and eight seats to my right, was staring at me. I snapped back my head, slammed the door, and hot-footed it to a spot behind a clump of yammering conventioneers. Von Plaack marched out, looked around, stomped back in. With the merest dip of a knee, I reached down and slipped a nametag off a raincoat lying on the arm of a couch. The doors of the Trianon Ballroom opened. Jude was among the last to come out. She had a hand on an arm of the black woman in white, to whom she was talking nonstop, her face radiating sweetness, sincerity, and concern. Where were Erika von Plaack and Stevie Dickinson?

Jude did not go back to her room. She went straight to the Old Bourbon Steak House, where Allerton Guth, philanthropist, and Fiji, paintress of apocalyptic androgynes, were waiting for her at a table (red walls and rug, and on each red tablecloth a white vase with a single red rose). Well, Jude was not much of a drinker, her kidneys were healthy. My stomach, bladder, and kidneys being empty, I did not need to pee either. I can take what it is necessary to take, but I'll leave it for Christians to inflict needless torture upon themselves. There was no need for me to patrol the corridor, glancing in each time I passed the door of the Old Bourbon Steak House, while Jude gorged herself with oysters, wine, a thick rare steak oozing juice, delicate little asparagus, and an enormous salad. Besides, I was in no mood to run into Muriel Bigalow, never mind Stevie Dickinson and Erika von Plaack. I decided to go for a short stroll. My idea was to come back in time to follow Jude to her room when she went for a post-prandial-pee, gain admittance through a ruse, kill her.

On an impulse I walked into a drug store—the kind that sells everything else. I heisted a pair of rubber gloves (light green), and I pocketed a box of Pine Bros. coughdrops (the candy bars were where the cashier could keep an eye on them). I am not the first man to commit a small crime on his way to righting a great wrong. Think of Cotton Mather filching a flower for his buttonhole from Goody Hooper's garden on his way to a witch-hanging. Think of Lincoln accepting a cigar (to calm his nerves) from a lobbyist on his way to signing the Emancipation Proclamation. I walked outside and downtown a few blocks and pulled up before the Metropole, sucking a coughdrop. The partially opened door was partially blocked by the bouncer. I could still see now this piece, now that, of the topless dancers, but they weren't dancing for me. The bouncer, who was a head taller than me, and twice as wide, who had purple scars and lumps on his forehead, walked over to me, put his left hand on my shoulder, poked me on the chest in tempo with his right forefinger, and recited these immortal lines:

We got tits and we got ass
And they surely a gas.
If you got cash and you got class,
You'll step through the door and buy yourself a glass,
And I don't mean sassafras.
Otherwise, just pass.

"Are we having a meaningful interpersonal communication?" he said.

"That don't rhyme, Frankenstein," I said.

"Yes it do, Fu Manchu," he said.

What we call anger is a signal to consciousness that the body is prepared to do violence. Those dancers and that bouncer were two more reasons for killing Jude, and if the logic escapes you, the odds are that it will not be the first time, or the last. I walked back to the Hilton. The coughdrops may or may not have been giving me stomach cramps, but they certainly weren't preventing them.

For all I could tell Jude was peeing through a catheter into her handbag. From 2:00 until 3:30 she listened to a paper with the intriguing title "Women's Ailments: The Sociodynamics of Psycho-somatic Sexiomatics," delivered in the Mercury Ballroom by Ms. Gaye Smuckler-MacDowell. I read a *New York Post* someone had discarded. The night before, while I had been feasting on air, Nixon had been aboard the *Sequoia* stuffing eleven southern Congressmen with beef tenderloin and lies. This morning one of those Dixie dewlaps had dutifully leaked another one of Nixon's fumbling attempts at blackmail: on some of the tapes were national-security conversations so sensitive that he would rather resign than give them up. Sure. And the Pope would rather give his job to Golda Meir than explain what Cardinal Bacigalupo was doing with the choir boy. From 3:30 until 4:00 Jude sat on a settee in the International Promenade having a whiskey sour with Ms. Gaye Smuckler-MacDowell, who looked very much like Rocky Marciano. I sat four settees behind them, chewing coughdrops and explaining periodically to the waitress that I would order when my (mythical) friend arrived.

From 4:00 to 5:30 Ms. Djuna Katz entertained Jude and a select group of six hundred in the Sutton Ballroom. The title of her speech, a rouser apparently, was "Beyond Man: From Society to Sorority." I sat near the escalator on a folding chair about as comfortable as the bastinado, re-reading the *New York Post.* As papers go, it is not bad to hide behind, but I wouldn't recommend it otherwise. The ads for topless bars, X-rated movies, and massage parlors were disappointing. Among them was an ad featuring a photograph of Jeane Dixon, who, if you called her on the telephone, would tell your horoscope. It has been a matter of principle with me never to look up my sign of the zodiac. Below Jeane Dixon was an announcement of the week's program at the Universalist Church ("where you can be your own person"). Monday: *Libwomen, Libmen* ("a singles rap group"), 7:00–11:00 P.M. Contribution: $3.00. Tuesday: *ESP Forum.* $2.00. Wednesday: *Single Again* ("A rap session for the formerly married of midyears"). $3.00. Thursday: *Gay Woman's Alternative.* $3.00. Friday was once again given over to that perennial favorite *Libwomen, Libmen,* this time until 1:00 A.M., contribution $4.00. Saturday: *Time & Space, Ltd.,* a repertory theater company, to present experimental one-act plays. $2.00. I was glad to see that on Sunday there would be *Church Services* (for "all who believe that religion is wider than any sect and deeper than any set of opinions"), no contribution mentioned. Sure: religion is as wide and as deep as the human appetite for self-delusion. I ask you, and in all sincerity, which is more obscene, the Universalist Church or Linda Lovelace? Which gives you more for your money? Which congregation of self-abusers was more pathetic, those who went for *Libwomen, Libmen* or those who went to *Deep Throat?*

At least I was doing my little bit to arrest the creeping fatty degeneration of the group mind. It is not in my temperament to sit back with a superior smile. Your own superior smiles, at my expense, do no credit to your perspicacity. Here's something to wipe them off with: it is when the group mind grows soft that characters like Hitler and Jesus the Galilean appear. Skeptical pagans and humanist Germans smiled too—at first. And so did emancipated Jews, yes, friends, so did enlightened Jews. . . . This is a serious business. If you are so smart, can you guarantee that there is not right now some wild-eyed charismatic and apocalyptic manwomanly shaman who thinks of Charles Manson as his own John the Baptist? Can you guarantee that he will not find his St. Paul, his Goebbels, his Church, his Reich, his Constantine? "What is truth?" asked Pontius Pilate, that skeptical pagan, a question that I gather is playing around *your* smiling lips. Well, for your own sake, for all our sakes, you had better believe that it is not *beyond man,* that it is not in your horoscopes, that it is not at some ESP forum in some Universalist Church, that it is not among sororities of manwomanly shamans like Djuna Katz and Jude Karnofsky. It is far more likely to reside in the fleshly and workaday throat of Linda Lovelace, which is wider than any church and deeper than any gospel. This paragraph ought to dissipate forever any lingering notion that my career as a murderer was some kind of ego trip.

At 5:30 Jude finally went to her room, but Stevie Dickinson went with her. What for, I don't know. About a half mile down the corridor from Number 1833 was an illuminated exit sign. I leaned against the door to the stairwell and began to re-re-read the *New York Post,* now ragged and lurid under the red light. In the resort and travel section was an ad for a singles weekend at Fanny Sipple's Vegetarian Spa outside Bridgeridge, N.Y. Delicious vegetable dishes! Lectures on plants, pep, and potency! Yoga classes! But nothing was said about Fanny's fanny. Have you ever noticed how pale, lank, and toneless are the cheeks of vegetarians? The cheeks and mouth of human females comprise what ethologists call a sexual releaser. They evolved in imitation of the buttocks as humans gradually assumed an upright posture. Did you know that in the whole of creation only humans have buttocks? Now you know why. Imagine my confusion when I looked up, my mind full of these thoughts, to see Erika von Plaack goose-stepping down the corridor toward me.

I shot through the door and down the stairs, paused on the top step of the flight below. The door I had just fled through opened. Boots clacked on the landing. I was ready to leap down a flight of steps at a single bound. The boots clacked again. The door opened again, then closed. After five minutes or so I crept up the stairs, carefully opened the door, and very carefully peeped out. Only a piece of cheekbone, an eyeball, and a hat-brim would have shown if anybody had been looking. The von Plaack, apparently, was already within Room 1833, which would not remain closed to me forever. But moving down the hall with short, quick steps, her spine and head stiff, her arms unmoving at her side, was Fiji. It was all right with me if she wanted to look like a humanoid, but where was the fun in it? I don't think she saw me. This is slow work. And why should I spare you any of it? When has anyone ever spared me anything?

I walked down to the seventeenth floor and over to the elevator bank. My idea was to wait in the lobby. It didn't look as though I would get Jude alone before her cocktail party. Where was she going to eat? And when would I ever eat again? (I was out of coughdrops.) I was thinking so furiously that I did not notice stepping into an up elevator rather than a down. As the door closed behind me I raised my eyes right into those of Allerton Guth.

"If it isn't Gregory Wallenda, man of the people, stud, stalwart, and critic—and who is so busy formulating acidulous phrases for his column that he has no time to look around at what he's writing about."

Guth did not look entirely sober. His face was red, for one thing. He rocked on his toes. I may have tried to smile. The elevator stopped—on the infernal eighteenth floor. Guth put a hand on the door to hold it open. "And looking very prosperous too," he said. "I take it that the *West Side Whatsis* is flourishing, and why the hell are you not sending it to me?"

"It folded," I said.

"Good," he said. "There are too many words already. Come, have a drink with us. I need an ally. I'm stuck with a bunch of females, except for the Very Reverend Peter Brevoort here, who has one foot in the other camp, if you'll pardon the expression."

No doubt you have seen pictures of him. Perhaps you have seen him debate William Buckley on television, and no pair ever deserved each other more. In case you haven't, Pastor Peter Brevoort, founder of the First Church of Christ, Androgynous, is a burly-plump type who bleaches his hair. What can be seen of him outside of his black suit and shirt, his white collar, is an even mustard yellow, just reward of those who prostrate themselves under sun lamps. From a distance he would look like an overdone duck à l'orange with a butterball where the head should have been and a doily around its neck. He extended his hand. I let him take mine.

"Allerton likes his little joke," said the Pastor. "Please call me Pete." He grabbed me by the bicep with his other hand. "And *do* come with us."

Guth put an arm through mine. Brevoort took my other arm. We marched out the elevator like three musketeers. I heard female voices approaching, the muffled clump of von Plaack's boots on the rug. I dug in my heels, lurched backward, tripped, and sat down on the floor of the elevator, just as the doors closed.

Guth's cry of "deserter" echoed through the elevator shaft after me as I ascended.

There is no need for better evidence of my staying power than that I did not simply go home to sleep forever and dream of pork chops. I got off the elevator about twenty floors up. Imagine the fun if on its way down Jude and company had stepped into the elevator with me. I would have massacred them all on the spot, and these confessions would only be appetizer-sized, instead of a feast. I sat on the window sill and consoled myself with a vision of the elevator doors opening to the lobby, bodies tumbling out to reveal the terrible figure of an avenger, shirtless, panting, dripping blood and sweat. I must have drifted off to sleep, because I suddenly became aware of a hand feeling around inside my jacket.

"Anything you find, you can keep," I said.

"*De nada,*" she said. I kissed in the direction of her pretty young Latin face. I surmised she had been working the badger game, because she was with an associate. He stood over by the elevator, a finger on the button, holding the door open for her getaway. "You got a cigarette?" I said. She held out her pack of Pall Malls. I took two, one for later on. The guy came over, leaned against the window jam, sighed.

"What else do you want?" said the girl.

"I'm hungry," I said.

"Eat me," said the guy. He struck a match and the three of us lit up.

"Between tricks?" I said.

He snorted.

"Why should they pay for it, man, all these bitches giving it away," she said.

"Not all of them," I said.

"No takers," he said. "Nothing worth taking, either."

"You got to remember these people are professors," I said.

"They got pricks, ain't they?" he said.

"Not all of them," I said.

"What's your hustle, man?" she said.

"That ain't a question you ask," he said.

"I'm after somebody that owes me," I said.

"You after his money or his life?" she said.

"Can you lend me a deuce?" I said. He sighed. She just looked down at me (I hadn't gotten up from the window sill).

"We just came out, walked into a exploding stove, man," she said.

"Lucky to get away with our lives," he said.

"How it goes," I said.

He walked over to the elevator and pressed a button. She stuffed the pack of Pall Malls into my handkerchief pocket.

For two hours and some I sat on the window sill and dozed and smoked Pall Malls, my stomach writhing like a poisoned eel. I am not going to tell you my thoughts. First of all, they were not exactly thoughts. Second, you would think I was making a play for sympathy. Have you ever rested your head on the breast of a woman you truly loved, one who was not impatient to roll over and go to sleep, one who was tranquil and serene and strong and round of arm, whose steady heartbeat would rock you back into tempo with the universe? No? Take my word for it, you're missing something. At 8:30 I zoomed down to the International Promenade, leaving my stomach behind somewhere around the fourteenth floor, found a settee with a view of the entrance, and settled behind my trusty *New York Post,* the first few pages of which were now in tatters that fluttered with each passing of the waitress. I explained to her that I would order when my friends came, and she seemed willing to believe that I had some, but she did not bring the bowl of peanuts I suggested might help to pass the time. In the bowl that had been provided for my predecessors were only two and one-half peanuts. I disdained to eat them.

Through the ragged filigree of page 4 I saw Butch limp in. I could not tell whether his toes were bandaged. Ten minutes later Jude and Peter Brevoort walked in, then von Plaack and Guth, then Dickinson and Fiji. I heaved myself up and waggled my head at the waitress ruefully to signify that I had been stood up again. I peeked around the corner into the lobby. Only Butch and von Plaack were visible. He had his head close to hers and was talking in what I gathered was a vehement whisper, his whole body gesturing. Once he stamped his foot. She stood at attention, the out-of-focus gaze of her ice-blue eyes passing over his shoulder and in my direction. On her lips was either a faint smile or a constrained snarl.

For the next hour and one-half I haunted the second mezzanine, keeping an eye on the doors to the Grand Ballroom, inside which the main event of the day was taking place. A thousand grown men and women with expensive educations had gathered to hear a panel discussion on the burning question as to whether or not women were niggers. Jude and Peter Brevoort argued that they were. Onwuchekwa Nasabele, a Nigerian anthropologist, and Mrs. Marcia Danica, a high level executive in a middle-sized corporation, argued that they were not. Who won the argument, I don't know. One thing or another kept me scuttling away from the door through which I was listening—Muriel Bigalow, for instance, one of whose endearing traits is to be at least forty-five minutes late for everything. She was floating along over one of her long, black skirts as though on an air cushion, looking neither right nor left. In my opinion you are better off bashing you head against a wall than lobotomizing yourself with pills. Not everyone will agree with me.

I was five steps beyond them before I realized who it was had just sidled by. I spun around. They spun toward me. It was the novice crooks from whom I had mooched the Pall Malls. They were both wearing nametags (presumably stolen), although a pair less likely to be mistaken for a couple of aspiring assistant professors is hard to imagine. (My own nametag said "Morris Blankman, Wade County Community College.") For one thing, she had the kind of tight-packed, full-bottomed, concave-sided, brawny behind I adore. You don't get a derriere like that if you spend your days sitting on it. He scowled. She gave me what is often referred to as a conspiratorial wink.

Jude spent the next-to-last hour before her appointment with destiny, namely me, at the Rendez-Vous Bar on the second mezzanine of the New York Hilton Hotel drinking praise and

Drambouie poured on and in her by a half-dozen besotted admirers. When she sailed out of the bar, her lavender cape billowing, she was alone. She was all alone, except for her destiny, who thirty paces behind her tread lightly as a pard. I walked into the crowded elevator right behind her, but she was too busy accepting compliments for her bearding of Onwu-chekwa Nasabele to notice retribution closing in. Nor did she notice how as the elevator approached the eighteenth floor everybody fell silent and looked and leaned away from her, and with unmistakable signs of uneasiness. I waited in the elevator alcove until I heard the key turn in her lock, heard the door open and close, heard it open again, most likely to release the fringe of cape it had closed on, heard it close, heard nothing but my own heart beating. I walked inexorably down the corridor toward room 1833.

I raised my hand to knock, hesitated, reached into a back pocket for the rubber gloves, ripped them out of their wrapper, pulled them on, stuffed the wrapper in a pocket, raised my hand to knock. And what, it suddenly occurred to me, was I going to say that would forestall her slamming the door in my face? The light green of the glove on my raised hand tripped a vision combining a memory of something I had seen with a prophecy of something I was about to do. That is how a well-conditioned mind works. I ran down fifteen flights, discarding the glove wrapper on the way, to the Trianon Ballroom. This was no time to get caught in the orbit of one of Jude's satellites. Cleaning persons were vacuuming; cleaning men were emptying ashtrays and disengaging wires. I flew to the Grand Ballroom. One dim work light was on. I sprinted to the long table from behind which the discussants had wrangled. On the center of the table was a portable lectern. On either side of the lectern were light green vases. In the vases were flowers, gladiolus I believe they are called. I rolled them up in pages from the *New York Post,* but the result was unsightly. I carefully ripped a square out of the purple crepe-paper table-cover. I rolled up flowers and *Post* in the purple. The result was not much more sightly, but it would have to do.

I zipped up the first three floors and then dragged myself up the next eight. On the landing above me a male and a female voice were murmuring to each other. They sounded young. Finally the male voice said "Vamos": a door opened and closed; I trudged up five more flights. On the landing of the eighteenth floor I leaned against the wall and puffed. I tried to blot the sweat off my face with the purple paper around the flowers but it was sleazy and unabsorbent. My left thigh felt as though it was inhabited by a Persian fire demon. When the flashes receded and my ears stopped buzzing, I walked over to Room 1833. It was remarkable, even to me, how little I was shaking, after all I had been through. I raised my hand to knock, hesitated, knocked. No answer. I knocked again. A musical voice, very un-Judelike, sang out "Who is it?" Any loverine Jude was expecting would have to make do without sympathy from me. If you hang around with people like Jude, you do not in my opinion fall into the category of innocent bystander. You have accepted the risk of getting yours when she gets hers. Think of Mussolini's girlfriend, who was hung up head down as high as he. "Flowers for Ms. Karnovsky," I trilled back in a melodious *recitativo* of my own. Anything she could do, I could do better.

The lock turned. I moved the flowers in front of my face. The door opened, but not wide. A hand reached out and grabbed the flowers. I did not let go. "Well let's have them," she said. "You've got to sign," I said. "What a bother," she said. "For me, too," I said. The door opened wider. "Where's something to write with?" she said. The door opened wide enough. I pushed in, shoved the flowers at her, slammed the door, leaned back against it, smiled.

"What's this?" she said. I smiled and smiled. "What's going on?" she said. I smiled and smiled and smiled. "Victor?" she said. I smiled and smiled and smiled and smiled. "What the hell do *you* want?" she said.

"You," I said.

We studied each other for a while. Jude was in a pale blue nightgown that you could not quite see through. Over her shoulders was a little frilly jacket to match. On her feet were high-heeled royal blue satin slippers with pale blue pompoms. We spoke at the same time: "You've gained weight," she said. "You've lost weight," I said. We answered in chorus: "About forty pounds," we said. "It's an improvement," she conceded. "You're looking good," I exaggerated.

We studied each other some more. Her eyes were wary, but otherwise there was no expression on her face. There seldom is, or *was,* rather. Jude's method was to mask, rather than to deceive. She did not pretend to be what she was not; she merely hid what she was. Her life-long practice of concealment, become like an instinct, had made her face stiff, immobile. At the moment I was not in a mood to calculate what it had cost her to hide from the world and from herself (until recently) her resentment at having been born in a woman's body. Which resentment was nothing compared to how she felt about men, upon whom a fickle fate had bestowed what no achievement, no vice or virtue, no amount of intelligence, education, character, boldness, determination, sacrifice, fame, riches, or anything else could get for her. Permit me to remark that your sympathy is misplaced. Would it be tragic for a butterfly to envy the frog? Would it be heroic for a lily to surpress its petals and strain to grow acorns? Jude's face was rosy from health and her bedtime wash-up. She was firm, round, and rubbery of forearm, neck, and cleavage.

"Why are you wearing those gloves?" she said.

"A rash," I said.

"I'll put these in water," she said, turning with the flowers. Was she going for a gun? "I'd better call room service for a vase," she said. I remembered the Boston Strangler's surprise at how easily a life could be cut off by a little pressure of the forearm across your victim's throat. Two quick steps and I had my left arm around her neck, but she tucked in her chin before I could get under it. The flowers, their stems locked in the crook of my sleeve, blocked my nose and mouth, poked my eyes. She swung back her elbow and caught me under the rib cage with enough force to life me an inch off the floor. "Woof," I said. She came down on my right big toe with the heel of her triphammer slipper, and I don't care how baby the blue of the pompons. I will remind you that hush puppies do not have reinforced toe-ends. Quite the contrary. I slackened my grip. She ducked and spun to face me, leaving her jacket tangled in my fingers by its frills. The flowers dropped between us. She crouched. I reached for my ice pick.

Where was the ice pick? Alarm signals went off all through me. My mind dashed around wildly, but my body froze on the spot, hands in two empty pockets. "Wait," I started to say, when her left hand shot out like a cobra's head. The three extended middle fingers made mush out of that area under my rib cage already softened by her elbow. I bent over. She came down with a karate chop over my left eyebrow. I back-pedalled, still bent over, one whole side of my face numb. She followed, and in a motion that started somewhere around her pompons, she rammed my chin with the heel of her right hand, her curled-over fingers mashing my upper lip. My teeth clacked shut. I tasted blood and chalk. My head whipped up and back until it thumped against the door. I began to sag. She moved in for the kill. With her body pressed against mine, the fingers of her left hand feeling for my eyes, she cocked her right leg. Dreamily, with resignation, I waited for her knee to smash home between my legs. Up whooshed her thigh—I heard her nightgown rip somewhere; I felt her whole body jerk and contract with the effort—but her knee never reached its destination. Her leg was too short. She tried again, but her leg hadn't grown in the interim.

Out of what heroic depths, out of what archaic reservoir of indomitable masculine resolve, I managed to pull a feeble left hook to her chin I will never know. (The ribbons and lace of her jacket were still caught in my fingers.) She stepped back, a hand to her face.

"You punched me," she said. And will you believe that there was genuine reproach in her voice! How could I do such a thing? She was shocked and she was surprised. She was saddened and her feelings were hurt. She was disillusioned and she was beyond words. That was the message in her attitude. Well, lady, the age of chivalry is long dead, and you helped kill it. Blood from the gash on my brow ran over my eye, down my cheek, through my mustache, and into the corner of my mouth. I wound up and cut loose a good old American roundhouse right. She saw it coming but never moved a muscle on that mournful kisser of hers. Perhaps you will think worse of me for taking something off the punch just before it landed. Both of us were finding it hard to forget that she was a woman. She turned, bowed over, both hands to her face, an emblem of grief. I leaped onto her back.

She staggered forward, tripped on the flowers, tripped again on my hat, stumbled a few steps further, bumped into the bed, flopped on it. My head knocked against hers, right through the blonde frizz. I wrestled with her frantically, the two of us rolling over twice, until I realized that she was not wrestling back. I unwound the full nelson I had on her and unscissored my legs from around her waist. I tipped her back on her back. She was looking at the ceiling with the expression on her face of someone trying to remember something. Her nightgown was in a tight roll around her legs, just above the knees, the flesh plumped up around it, as though she had been fetchingly trussed by a bondage-freak. She had lost only one of her slippers. I mounted her and sat on her stomach, my legs astraddle. I leaned forward to hold her right arm down with my left hand, but the frou-frous of her jacket were still hooked on my fingers. The miserable thing would not shake loose. The grip I got on her wrist was consequently far from ideal. Her left arm was caught underneath her. Blood dripped from my chin onto the freckles between her breasts. "Uncle," she said.

"What next?" she said. The question had occurred to me, too.

"I am about to tell you what is next and why," I said. "Repent, for the wages of sin is death."

"Dear God, what did I ever do to you?" she said. "I always thought you were cute." A coy little smile accompanied this inept and outrageous lie. Cute!

"What did you do to poor Bill?" I said.

"Nothing his mother hadn't done already," she said.

"What were you doing to Toby," I said.

"I was trying to be a mother to him," she said. "And a father too, since no one else wanted the job." She sniffled. "Has that bitch Martine been telling you stories?"

"And Samantha. What did you do to Samantha?" I said.

"Will you let me pull my arm out from under me?" she said. "My shoulder hurts." She pouted and squirmed, but Jude did not have the raw materials to play Marilyn Monroe. "Oooo," she said.

"What did you do to Samantha?" I said. I felt a rage spreading over me like prickly heat.

"Your precious Samantha," she said. "Will you let me move my arm, God damn it. I'm going to faint. Samantha would have left you anyway." She bucked once, twice, three times, at last pulling her arm free. She extended it toward the night table on the right of the bed. She shook her arm as to get the blood flowing. She let it fall, her hand dangling near the knob to the drawer in the table. "It's all pins and needles," she said.

"My precious Samantha would still be my precious Samantha if you hadn't filled her head with your poison and promises," I said.

"You give me too much credit," she said. "And you give her too little. Samantha hasn't what it takes to be a feminist." She bucked. "She has an incorrect view of her independence."

She bucked again. "She will never learn that a woman can only find her self by losing it in sisterhood." She bucked and bucked. Very slowly, oh so slowly, she had been sliding her pointer and index fingers along the drawer until the knob was between them. I noticed for the first time that there was a vase of gladiolus—I think that's what they are called—on the table. A card decorated with hearts lay amid the foliage. "Damn you, get off me!" she said.

"She has too much authentic beinghood, is that what you mean? And if you don't get your hand away from that drawer, I'll bite off your nipples," I said. Do me the favor of calming yourself. I did not mean what I said literally. It does not follow that because I am a murderer, I am also a disgusting pervert of some kind. Besides, my mouth was too sore. I couldn't have bitten through a charlotte russe.

She snatched her hand away from the knob as though it had turned into a Gila monster. "Why do men always have to be so violent?" I shook a drop of blood off my chin. "Why do they always want to steal what they can have for the asking?" She put her hand on my thigh. "Try a little tenderness," she said.

I don't suppose you will ever understand me. I was as hot and itchy with embarassment as with rage. I decided right then that in spite of three grueling months of preparation, in spite of von Plaack's kick and the karate chops and my empty stomach, I could not kill Jude Karnofsky. She was not worthy of my vengeance. I will accept the charge that my conception of revenge was just a hair exalted. But you might ask yourself this: Would Sir Walter Raleigh have fought a duel with his scullery maid? I couldn't even look at her. I was too ashamed for both of us, too flustered and disgusted. To the left of the bed was another of the matched night tables. On the table was an immense basket of gorgeous fruit, probably imported. On top of the fruit was another card, decorated with cupids and flowers. Her hand left my thigh. I reached over picked up a purple plum of the kind my father used to call gorilla balls. Her hand was on the drawer again. I just looked at it. She put the hand on my knee.

"It's just my diaphragm in there," she said.

I bit into the plum with my right eyetooth, the only one anywhere near the front of my mouth that wasn't sore. She finger-walked from the front of my knee to my fly. She pulled down the zipper. She worked her hand past the zipper and through the vent in my underwear. She cupped her hand around my testicles. I didn't know what to do. Would you have known? And no fair peeking into your Emily Post. I sat absolutely still, my eyetooth still in the plum. Then she squeezed with all her might.

Before I knew it, I had pressed the plum past her lips and by her teeth, both parted in a fiendish grin. "Ag," she said. I plopped a second plum in her mouth, now wide open. In that respect they were like her eyes. "Roark," she said. Her hand flopped and thrashed about in my pants like a wounded vulture trapped in a tent. I pushed in an apricot after the plums. She arched her back and lifted me a foot off the bed. She collapsed and bounced back into me with a jolt as I was coming down, then collapsed again, bounced and tried to roll over on a hip. She tossed her head from side to side as if signalling no, no, no, no, no to someone a thousand feet above us. I rammed, crammed, jammed in a nectarine, a tangerine, a pear, narrow end first. I posted forward like a jockey and bore down on the pear with the heel of my hand, my full weight behind it. Her head sank into the pillow, which rose on either side. It pushed her brassy ringlets frontward and over her face, over my hand too. Below my wristbone there was nothing to see but springs and coils and shimmers of hair, except for a strip of forehead red and swollen enough to crack, except for one frantic eye, which I still see sometimes. I turned my head away. I fixed my gaze on the many eyes of a pineapple in her fruit basket, while she twisted, bucked, and heaved, while deep belches erupted inside her and vibrated through my thighs and groin, while she wrenched first one hand, then her other free and tried to reach my face, but failed, her arms being too short, while she clamped her hands around my arm, not as to push it off her face, but as to hang on for dear life, while her bucks and heaves shortened their arcs and quickened their rhythm, while they contracted into the mindless sproings of a highboard just vacated, into a long shudder, an endless shiver, a tremor, then nothing. The unvarnished fact, ladies and gentlemen, is that I had killed Jude Karnofsky.

I may have fallen asleep for a minute or two. A pain in my hand, into which Jude's teeth had sunk, brought my mind back from wherever it had wandered. There was also a cramp in my left thigh, an ache over my right eye, an ague under my ribs, a woe across my mouth, a throb in my right big toe. My testicles hurt all the way up to the adenoids. If Jude had gotten better leverage, a vasectomy wouldn't have made any difference. I stretched my cramped leg to the floor and tried to sit back, but Jude would not let go of my arm. She was surprisingly strong for a dead woman. The lid of her one exposed eye was at half mast. I managed to get my arm loose without breaking any of Jude's fingers, but it wasn't easy. Her arms did not fall back; they remained half-extended, as though she were pulling down the sky with an invisible rope. I was finally free of that wretched little jacket, which now hung in a tangle of tatters from her right hand. I sat back, rubbing my forearm. And then Jude began to sit up. Slowly, steadily, she rose toward me, her hands reaching. If you don't mind I will forego this opportunity to describe her face, but don't think you can imagine it. I was frozen with terror, as you would have been. The touch of her fingers against my cheek at last released some spring. I flew off her stomach, off the bed, and went crashing to the floor, as my left leg gave way under me.

Jude tipped over backwards, her torso weighing more than her legs, which now pointed toward the ceiling at an angle of sixty degrees. I cautiously got to my feet. She did not move. I tried to pull my fly closed, but a piece of skin from her wrist was caught in the zipper. I yanked, and the tab-pull broke off. Yes, my hands were shaking. What is so surprising about that? Without looking at her, I slid the pillow from under her head and put it over her face. Her legs dropped to the bed and her arms folded themselves across her breast. A nipple peeped through the seductive disarray of jacket rags. The fact is that for the first time Jude seemed, well, let us say beautiful. She was by no means slender, but given her ample flesh, there was something particularly moving in the dramatic tuck of her waist, the new neatness of her ankles and knees. I suppose Butch gets the credit for all that. Her thighs and calves swelled with those curves that are the source of our idea of beauty, that filled the first men with a hollow ache and will torment the last man until his last minute of misogyny and love. Her skin was white and smooth. She looked like a piece of statuary carved by a master. Then her sphincter muttered and gurgled. There was a smell.

I sat by the vanity table looking at her, until out of the corner of my eye I caught a glimpse of my own face in the mirror. It was no match for hers, to be sure, but it was still something to make your heart skip a beat. Except for a crooked rill of drying blood, it was purple. Not much sweat had come off my face onto the crepe paper, but a good deal of coloring had come off the paper onto my face. My left incisor was broken off in a straight line one third of the way up. My upper lip was roughly the size, shape, and color of a mango. A long drop of coagulated blood hung from my chin. Neither, by the way, was my hair combed.

Before the bathroom mirror I washed the purple off my face and hands. I washed the blood off my face and lapel. I washed the blood off Jude's freckled chest. (Her hands were cool and dry.) I put a wad of toilet paper on the gash in my brow, but the blood seeped through. There were no Band-Aids or the like anywhere, but in the dresser I found a half-slip and a tampon, or whatever you call them. In her pocketbook I found a little curved scissor, and, incidentally, almost four hundred dollars, which I pocketed. I cut the packing out of the tampon and bound it over my eye with a strip of slip, and how's that for a touch of dash. I cleaned the sink, cut tampon, slip, and washcloth into little pieces, and flushed them down the john.

I replaced the scissors. One of Jude's slippers was in my hat. I picked it up to put back on her foot. Her toes were round and plump, unlike mine, which look like Brazil nuts with the shells still on. One long highlight ran from the top of her thigh over her shin and instep to the space between her first two toes. My hat covered most of the bandage, but only if I gave it a rakish tilt that was not actually my style. I gathered the flowers (Yes, I was right about the kind; there is a picture of them in the *American Heritage Dictionary;* the plural is "gladioli."), flushed the stray leaves and petals, flushed away my green rubber gloves. I walked to the door, turned, looked everything over, walked to the bed, and sat down, one hand around the flowers, the other around Jude's ankle. (It was cool on top and warm underneath, where the blood had collected.)

Jude's body was purer, but also more mysterious, than her personality, which had left it. Her flesh was bright, but somehow hard to see, as though veiled in its own translucence. And its lines were classic, yet subtle. The eye followed them easily, but could not come to their end. Her flesh, how shall I put this, her flesh had a confident look, the look of something restored to itself, freed from motives not its own, yes, freed from aberration and artifice. I do not believe this is all in my head. Jude's body looked complacent, self-possessed, self-absorbed, too knowledgeable to speak, that's the point, confiding in its silence, but without any anxiety to be understood, talking only to itself, but expressive of everything. The bow-shaped muscles separating her thighs from her trunk were on the verge of a smile, or were they. Was I seeing things? No, I was not.

The simple truth is that there was no longer anything accidental about Jude. There was no longer anything personal and social about her, and therefore nothing stupid or cranky or trivial. She had become entirely human when she became entirely her body, at the same moment, to be precise, when she began to rot. Jude had become all of us, so far as we are human. Do you see what I mean? I mean that only in our mortal flesh is humankind one. Only in our humanity, as distinct from our personality or sociability, do we have dignity, and god damn it, you might forget about the sound and concentrate on the sense. I am trying to tell you something important. Only the flesh is sane. Every human body at rest recapitulates the natural history of our species. It is wise with the millions of years of tragedy and farce that shaped it. That long perspective rules it like a sense of proportion. Until, that is, it is overcome by mental obsession, or social oppression, or by death.

A great emotion surged through me; which one I can't say, but it wasn't necrophilia. I moved my hand under her calf to feel the weight of her flesh, which was heroic and doomed. My eyes stung. All right, yes, it was as much the female as the human in her that was getting to me. Has an ironic fate marked me as the last human being to love the woman in women, and not something else? I will have you remember who it was that restored Jude's femininity to her. I was a murderer? Very well. But I was also an exorcist. I cannot say how long I sat there looking at Jude. It suddenly came to me that I was teetering forward in a doze. Strong emotion is as tiring as strenuous activity, in case you have never had any. The wild idea that I could make Jude's death look like a suicide flew by from somewhere. On an impulse I leaned forward and opened the drawer to the night table. Sure enough, there was a nasty little automatic, made of shiny stainless steel, except for the plastic grips.

I closed the drawer and wiped off my fingerprints with the bedspread. I walked resolutely to the door, gripped the knob through my jacket, hesitated, did not look back, opened the door, walked out. I was hampered in my journey down the stairs by the condition of my thigh, my toe, my testicles. I was limping in three different rhythms. Had she been there, Martha Graham might have learned something. On the eleventh floor I paused to quench the pain with a bit of self-hypnosis, but I had trouble bringing on the necessary pitch of concentration. I continued down, and paid no attention to those unequal and undulating stairs, that swaying banister, the tilt and loom of the walls. On the landing of the mezzanine floor were my old friends, the Hispanic hustlers.

"Ai Dios!" she said, and crossed herself.

"Your fly's open," he said.

I presented the gladioli to her. She took them, her mouth open a little. She offered me a cigarette. I took three.

I will spare you a description of my walk home through the ruins of Amsterdam Avenue. I wouldn't want to cause you unnecessary pain. I pulled up before the Feathered Dragon, which showed the only light in an otherwise empty building. Through the window I could see Brunhilda sitting alone at the bar. She did not see me. I lurched on home like a Triffid, and if anyone I knew saw me, I didn't see him.

Samantha was not there to greet and congratulate me, not there to make a fuss over me, nor was anyone else. I called the Feathered Dragon and asked for Brunhilda. Samantha has no one to blame but herself. A wife who will not minister to her husband has no complaint if he turns elsewhere. The same goes for a husband who does not minister to his wife, I have never denied it. Let her turn elsewhere too, if she likes. You won't hear me complain. It is a rule of mine to be scrupulously fair, to accept, without flinching, a tit for every one of my tats. You have never yet heard me defend the double standard, and you never will. The point is that the latter case, that of the neglectful husband, did not apply to our marriage, mine and Samantha's. It did not apply. Brunhilda agreed to spend what was left of the night with me. There is a take-out barbecue on Broadway a few blocks uptown from the Feathered Dragon. It stays open until 4:00 A.M. I asked her to make a stop there, to buy three pounds of spareribs, two pounds of fried shrimp, two barbecued chickens, two loaves of French bread, two packs of Luckies, a quart of cole slaw, lots of pickles, to hop in a taxi and fly to my waiting arms.

I lay on the couch, my left leg twitching and jerking in a way that reminded me of Jude. The phone rang and my heart stopped. It was Chi Chi, of all people. The crap game was over, he was four hundred dollars richer, and he never forgot a buddy who staked him when he was down. I declined a kind invitation to visit at his expense an afterhours club where the women were choice. Brunhilda breezed in, took one look at me, shook her head, pulled me into the kitchen, put the big bag of food on the table, sat me down under the light. She unwound the piece of half-slip with a titch-titch, but the hunk of tampon was stuck. "Que cosa!" she said.

Without having to ask where anything was, Brunhilda walked from room to room collecting this here and that there, slamming drawers and cabinet doors. I began to gobble spareribs and shrimp. She soaked loose the piece of tampon with warm soapy water. She washed my face, my ears too, going easy over the lip, slapping me once on the cheek so that I would stop chewing for a second. She shaved the eyebrow. She disinfected the shaved area and her fingers with brandy. She spread on some false eyelash goo to make the area sticky. With her left hand she pinched the lips of the wound closed. With her right hand she stuck thin little strips of adhesive tape crisscross along the wound, first pulling one tight on a downward diagonal and then pulling the next tight on an upward diagonal, until she had in effect stitched the wound together, and without a motion wasted. And all the while she went on about what fools men were, what children, what devils, their tantrums and violence, their restlessness and greed, how God put them on earth as a trial to women, how all they knew was to pull things apart for women to put together, how they could fly to the moon but couldn't keep two feet on the ground and expected some woman to patch them together when they fell on their heads. She made a pad out of gauze and put it over the tape-stitchery. I wrapped my arms around her waist and snuggled the healthy side of my face up against her breast, but didn't stop chewing. She let out a sigh, gave me an impatient little pat on the back of my head, disengaged, and went off to replace the remnants of her first-aid gear.

I suddenly jumped to my feet, ran to the bathroom, got down on my knees before the toilet bowl, and threw up. It all came out pretty easily, being so close to the surface. "You finished?" said Brunhilda. She helped me up, sat me on the ledge of the tub, handed me the mouthwash, which burned something awful. She scrubbed the bowl and turned on the bath water. Then she began to undress me. She threw me a quick, mock-indignant smile with her young eyes when she saw the busted fly zipper. She washed me all over, scolding and clucking at the size of my toe, the green and yellow of my thigh, the maroon welt under my ribs. She even managed somehow to shampoo my hair without getting a drop of water on the embroidery over my eye. Then she wrapped me in Samantha's terrycloth robe, which my spendthrift wife couldn't be bothered to cart away.

Careful to chew only on my molars, admonished continually to slow down, rinsing frequently with beer, I ate a chicken, the rest of the spareribs and shrimp, a pound of cole slaw, and a loaf of bread. Brunhilda nibbled daintily on a wing and filled my ear about her son, his brilliance and mischief, what good reports the nuns wrote of his schoolwork; about her own progress at the school of needle trades, how an instructor had plagiarized one of her patterns and sold it to a dress manufacturer; about her mother, who needed a set of teeth; about. . . . I must have fallen asleep in mid-chew. When I awoke, there was still a piece of bread in my mouth, and Brunhilda was leading me by the hand. We were in the bedroom. She pulled back the covers, de-robed me, poured me into bed. Then she began to undress: large breasts, short waist, derriere a soupçon flat, legs a touch thin, beige skin a shade blotchy, but more than the sum of her parts: comfortable, poised, certain of her worth, sure of her welcome, a tropical queen at home with her consort. I mumbled that I had been punched in the balls. She caught the hint. Lie back and relax, she said; leave everything to her. So that's what I did.

VI

THE latest scientific wisdom is that we dream every night. You can't prove it by me. Science would be all right if it were not for the scientists, who are mostly a bunch of superstitious old women. (The reason, I believe, is that too much mathematics softens the brain. Its devotees assume that the reality behind reality is (1) orderly, (2) ideal, (3) awesome, (4) coincidental with products of the human mind, for example—numbers. Theosophists, Rosicrucians, and other witlings assume the same. I bet anything there are more church-goers among mathematicians than among historians, for example, or among short-order cooks, for instance, both of whom know that reality is an exploding stove. They know that reality is (1) disorderly, (2) material, (3) obvious but unpredictable—Mother Nature, after all, is a woman (4) incidental to anything a human may think of it. And is not feminism a kind of religion? Personalities aside, that is why I oppose it, as all humanists must.) I woke up suddenly, my mind a blank. I looked at the clock: 9:30; I looked over my shoulder at the bed: empty. I had forgotten to pay Brunhilda, nor, it seems, had she remembered to ask. I drew no flattering conclusions. I thought

of checking my wallet, but reconsidered the thought as un-
worthy. I slid off to sleep, my inner eye on a young Puerto Rican
beauty stretched out before me. Leave everything to me, she
said and put a pillow over her face.

"Hey hombre," a voice said. "Wake up." It was Brunhilda,
with containers of coffee and juice and some limp Danish. I
looked at the clock: 9:50. At about that time, worried friends
were knocking on the door of Number 1833, a room at the New
York Hilton occupied by Judith Karnofsky, noted anthropologist, author, editor, and feminist, who was due at 10:00 A.M. to
adress a General Session of the Organization of Social Scientists
of America. I refuse to accept the blame for their disappointment. Why couldn't they have stayed in bed, nursing their
hangovers, like any other conventioneers? If the truth be
known, I had done them a favor. Every falsehood that enters
your ear leaves a residue like wax to clog or irritate the brain.
Brunhilda, who was lying next to me on top of the covers,
licked Danish off her fingers, reached into her pocketbook, and
presented me with receipts for the food and the taxi. Those two
receipts are just about the only documents relating to these
confessions that I have not preserved. The total was something
under thirty-five dollars. I gave her five twenties.

"I owe you seventeen dollars and thirty-eight cents" (or
some such figure), she said and opened a pretty little beaded
purse that she had obviously made herself.

"A tip," I said. There was a particular pleasure in giving to
Brunhilda, a whore, money that had belonged to Jude, a harpy
who had never once tried to please a man for either love or
money, never mind fear of getting struck by a bolt of lightning.

"A tip?" she said. "For me?" She smiled demurely, which
is not something you often see Brunhilda do. She reached over
and rumpled my hair. Correct me if I am wrong, but had it not
been twenty-eight years since someone last rumpled my hair?
She made a coy little smile, which is something else you do not
often see Brunhilda do. She turned on a hip, finger-walked from

my knee toward my crotch, and whispered in my ear: "Want to go round one more time?"

Her breath against my ear gave me goose pimples. There was a shriveling sensation down below. How was I going to get out of this without hurting Brunhilda's feelings? But why did I want to get out of it? I tore the rim off a Danish with my right eye tooth and held the rest up to Brunhilda so that she could bite into the prune filling, the best part, which she did. I began to sweat. I think I must have been a little feverish.

"I don't feel so good," I said.

"Pobrecito," she said. "Lie back and relax. Leave—"

I sat up with a jerk. "Thursday," I said. "I'll call you Thursday."

"Hokay querido," she said, getting up briskly, straightening her dress, picking up her handbag.

"Would you do one last favor?"

"Sure."

I asked her to stop at Daitch's Supermarket, not because it is any good, but because there is nothing better as close. I asked her to buy groceries, mostly salad-makings and honest meat, whatever was on sale, as much as she could get for forty dollars, which I gave her. One of the teen-age thugs Daitch kept around for the purpose could deliver.

"No rice?" she said.

"No rice."

"Bread?"

"No bread."

"Beans?"

"Uh-unh."

"Potatoes?"

"Nix."

"Noodles?"

"Never."

"Platinos?"

"Absolutely not."

"You got to eat *something* besides meat and grass." Here she gave me a lecture about how I would get worms, how I would get a wind like a barber's cat, how my feet would swell, how I had to make the meat stretch, how I had to make better use of my money (she apparently considered the fifty-dollar fee for her services a sound investment, and she was right.) All this was music to my ears. Samantha never scolded me about anything, no matter how many opportunities I gave her. Brunhilda is too sensible a woman to have mentioned cholesterol. She has enough of the old, comfortable superstitions not to need the irksome, modern ones. When, two hours later, the groceries arrived, there was a five-pound sack of rice and two packages of dried kidney beans. (I told the delivery boy to leave the cartons in the hall. From behind the door, which I had opened no more than three inches, I handed him a dollar tip, much as Jude had reached for the bunch of flowers.)

I whiled away the afternoon until the six o'clock news doing nothing in particular, eating the rest of the chicken and later eating about four pounds of a crusty and succulent roast pork shoulder, sipping beer, dozing, watching an absurd television program in which male athletes competed against female (the women were given handicaps), reading in a very good book by Norman Cohn entitled *The Pursuit of the Millennium: Revolutionary Millenarians and Mystical Anarchists of the Middle Ages,* many of whom are still with us. (Says Cohn: "Some of the great ladies who turned to Catharism were clearly moved by emotional conflicts such as nowadays would have led them to theosophy or maybe to psychoanalysis"—or feminism.) I would have listened to a news program on the radio, but Samantha had taken it. When I protested, she said, "I left you the TV, didn't I?" True enough, but for the reason that the moving persons who carted away her stuff had found the set a bit too heavy for them. That's how I explain it. (Let a woman become the weight-lifting champion of the world first; then I just might reconsider my attitude toward Women's Liberation.) No, I take that back. She took the radio because the television was more valuable. There is nothing petty or vindictive about my Samantha. How can you think I would have gone through so much trouble to get her back if she had been just another castrating bitch? It doesn't make sense. I kept waiting for her to call, but she didn't. Neither did Bill. Was there no one who cared enough for my feelings to call and break the terrible news of Jude's death? After all, I had been a close friend of long standing.

The only communication of any sort I received was from the mailman. He buzzed and, when I buzzed back, shouted into our ancient intercom that he had a package for me. I told him I was sick, would he please bring the package up. The fact that it was illegal for postal workers to accept tips never stopped him from accepting the ten dollars I put in the mailbox every Christmas Eve. From behind the door I reached out for the package. "This is the worst time of year for colds," he said to the closing door. "Myself, I always wear a sweater under my uniform," he said. The package was of a size to hold a folded pair of suspenders, say, or a banana. It was from Barney's. Never had I worn suspenders, any more than I would wear a tutu. The damned thing was tough to open. I dropped it twice and broke a fingernail, too. Inside, there was excelsior, then a layer of tissue paper, then another layer, then my ice pick. I have always believed that an occasional rush of blood to the brain is good for you. It flushes out the capillaries. Just make sure you have something nearby in case you need to sit down suddenly. Wrapped around the ice pick and held to it by a rubber band, was a note from Charles Poswhistle, Gentleman's Fittier: "You dropped this."

The anchorperson smiled and introduced herself as Belinda Eberhard. She explained that she was pinch-hitting for the vacationing regular, whose name, as I recall, was something like Beowulf. She recited the headlines of the stories to follow. The first of the headlines was this: "Woman's Liberationist Judith Karnofsky Found Murdered in Mid-Town Hotel." There was a barrage of commercials, then the story. The nude body of the controversial feminist and best-selling author was found at 9:30 this morning by Erika von Plaack, associate and friend of the deceased. (We were treated to some badly-lit footage of the door to Room 1833). Death was by asphyxiation. The coroner found no evidence of sexual assault (footage of men carrying a stretcher, a canvas sheet decently draped over the haunted old female hills and dales). Investigators found no evidence of forced entry (footage of hard cases hanging around the door to Room 1833). The victim may have known her assailant, but police were not ruling out the possibility that he gained admittance through a ruse. Robbery was a possible motive, but certain features of the case suggested that the perpetrator was deranged. Deputy Inspector La Paloma was quoted as saying that he and his men were investigating a number of promising leads (footage of a short, neat man with soulful eyes talking to a reporter from another network: "We have every confidence of an early solution to this heeness crime"). A young Hispanic couple, described by police as a prostitute and her pimp, who allegedly and unsuccessfully had tried to extort money from a guest, was wanted for questioning. Listeners with information should call such-and-such a number, which faded from the screen as the anchorperson promised a live interview with Erika von Plaack later in the show.

I decided to wait out the rest of the news for the interview with Erotica von P. Yesterday the Supreme Court had decided to decide whether or not Nixon had to give Jaworski another sixty-four tapes, as though it were not already perfectly clear that the White House was a behavioral sink. The President's lawyers, Buzzard and St. Crow, were confident that the Court would arrive at a just decision and that justice was on their side. So Inspector La Paloma was confident of an early solution, was he? So the perpetrator was deranged, was he? And how about the perpetratee? The real question was whether I would turn myself in to save the girl with the Pall Malls and her boyfriend. Well, if I were in their place and they were in mine, would they turn themselves in to save me? I know, I know: that's not the point. A woman with amazing teeth and lots of blonde hair swirled it around in slow motion to show the wondrous properties of Walla Walla Balsam Shampoo. The screen blinked. Two more striking blondes were seated facing each other across a little round coffee table. A close-up of the table, on which lay a magazine. It was a prepublication copy of the first issue of *Ms. Chief.* On the cover was a cartoon in Fiji's inimitable style. It depicted Erika von Plaack in feathered headdress and war paint giving a hot-foot to Uncle Sam. The camera stepped back. One of the blondes was the reporter admiration for whom had first brought Chi Chi and me together. Her name was Helen Flesh, and she had a new hairdo. The other was the incendiary von Plaack.

On a cue from Ms. Flesh, the "Queen Bee of American Feminism" (according to *New York Magazine*) delivered an eloquent panegyric to her fallen comrade, but failed to move me. On a second cue she went on to describe in a harsh, bitter voice how she began to worry when Jude, who was never late, failed to appear for breakfast. She knocked on the door to Jude's room, but got no answer. A reluctant chamberperson finally let her in. She saw Jude reposing on the bed and assumed that she had put the pillow over her face to shut out the morning cacaphony you could hear everywhere through the jerry-built walls of that wretched hotel. Then von Plaack removed the pillow. She knew immediately that Jude was dead.

FLESH: She was suffocated with the pillow?

VON PLAACK: The police have asked me not to divulge any details.

FLESH: Who do you think did this terrible thing?

VON PLAACK: Some grunting hog of a male chauvinist, some impotent pip-squeak who can't get his rocks off any other way, some mama's-boy trying to cut the apron strings, some warty toad who will croak on his own poison if I don't get to him first, some maggot, some slug, some dung beetle, some *man.*

FLESH: I see.

VON PLAACK: Whoever he is, he is as good as dead.

FLESH: Did I hear you say something about getting to him first? Do you mean to take matters into your own hands?

VON PLAACK: [*Pauses; smiles; sits back; pulls out a long cigarette holder; stuffs in a cigarette; lights it; inhales; allows the smoke to flow out over her lip and into her nostrils*] Just a bit of wishful thinking, dear, and please don't put words into my mouth. Naturally, I'd like to get my hands on him. But I wouldn't dream of breaking the law, even though it was invented by men, for men, and at the expense of women. For women, that is, who are women, rather than tricked-up dolls for men to play with.

FLESH: [*icicles hanging from her words*] Let's leave that for another time, shall we.

VON PLAACK: Anything you wish, love.

FLESH: I take it, then, that you do not believe Trude Karnofsky was killed by a chance injuder—I mean trance inchewder!

VON PLAACK: You said it.

FLESH: You do not believe she was killed by the postitute and her primp?

VON PLAACK: Nor by the pristitute and her pomp.

FLESH: [*drinks water*] You believe that she knew her assailant?

VON PLAACK: That's right?

FLESH: Do you have anyone particular in mind?

VON PLAACK: No comment.

My television set has certain incorrigible peculiarities: the only colors on Channel Five are various shades of pink, lavender, and purple; the image on Channel Four looks as though painted on a sheet of agitated rubber. Neither the Ten O'Clock News on the first nor the Eleven O'Clock News on the second told me anything I didn't know, except that OSSA had threatened to hold its next convention in Minneapolis, that Pastor Peter Brevoort had the knack of blubbering at will before a camera, that Stevie Dickinson vowed revenge and didn't care who knew it. I stayed up late in the company of Norman Cohn and his apocepileptics, hoping for a call. And I woke up late the next morning, still hoping.

I could feel healing juices from the chuck steak I had for breakfast and from the leg of lamb I had for dinner doing wonders for my wounds, nor had Brunhilda forgotten the mint jelly. (In a natural state herbivores grow meat for carnivores to eat. The carnivores thrive to weed out herbivores least fit to survive. The herbivore that feeds a carnivore, it follows, is working toward the improvement of his species. Metaphysically speaking, carnivores are male.) I killed some time by opening a pile of bills. Seems I owed $400 more than I owned. I read around in a one-volume abridgement of *The Golden Bough,* by Sir James George Frazer, a very wise man, who, however, makes the mistake of assuming that religion is an advance over magic, that science is an advance over religion, and that heroes are no longer lured to their deaths by smiling temptresses. I admired the communist haunches of some gymnasts who were displaying them for television audiences. I couldn't stand it any longer. Finally, I called Muriel. She did not sound well.

BIGALOW: Hello.

GRANT: Hello, Muriel.

BIGALOW: Hello?

GRANT: Gregory Wallenda here.

BIGALOW: Hello?

GRANT: It's Greg.

BIGALOW: Hello-alowalowalowalow . . .

GRANT: Muriel, I—

BIGALOW: Alowalowalow.

GRANT: Sorry I missed you, but—

BIGALOW: A. Low. Down. Dirty. Rat.

GRANT: Me?

BIGALOW: Where were you when I needed you?

GRANT: When? When?

BIGALOW: [*pauses*] I'm trying to remember. . . .

GRANT: Well, see, I got in this fight. It was this big, black guy with purple scars on his forehead. And will you believe that he recited poetry? His own, I believe.

BIGALOW: I'm woozy and tired and I can't sleep and I've taken too many pills and I can't take any more cause I don't want to die.

GRANT: Have you tried a hot bath? Where the hell is that big-shot ex-husband of yours?

BIGALOW: [airily] Maybe I'll change my mind. Who knows?

GRANT: Now don't talk like that. I'll call Allerton Guth. I'd come over myself, but—

BIGALOW: [sharply] Is Erika von Plaack there with you?

GRANT: [moves his lips soundlessly]

BIGALOW: You still there?

GRANT: But that's craz—I mean, why—

BIGALOW: [teasingly] She asked for you.

GRANT: Now damn it, that's—

BIGALOW: She said, "How about introducing me to the Corduroy Kid? I got a feeling we're two of a kind." That's what she said. Verbatim.

GRANT: Now listen, Muriel. Remember she pushed me into you. Well, I pushed her back.

BIGALOW: Bravo! Two of a kind, that's just what she said. Obviously, you scratched her where she itches.

GRANT: Then she snuck up and kicked me when I wasn't looking.

BIGALOW: And you kicked her back. You really know how to turn a girl on.

GRANT: Well, she turns me off.

BIGALOW: She asked for your name.

GRANT: [aside] I can't take much more of this. [in a croak] Did you tell her?

BIGALOW: I don't know your name.

GRANT: Sure you do. I'm—

BIGALOW: The Corduroy Kid.

GRANT: The reason I called, Muriel, is to inquire—

BIGALOW: [*sings*]   Look out Kid

It's something you did

I don't know when

But you're doing it again.

GRANT: I want to write an article about—

BIGALOW: Beware the frumious bandersnatch, Kid. She'll come in the night and steal your body.

GRANT: I understand you knew—

BIGALOW: [*sings*] I ain't got no bod-y.

GRANT: Hey Muriel, will you stop? *Please.*

BIGALOW: Maid Bagalow is laid low and doesn't know where to find it.

GRANT: "It?"

BIGALOW: How can you give what you don't have?

GRANT: You can't. I mean, you don't have to. I called to ask about Jude Karnofsky. I understand you knew her. I thought I'd write an article—

BIGALOW: [*sings*]   Pore Jude is daid

A candle lights his haid

GRANT: "His?"

BIGALOW: I'm glad she's dead. I wish somebody would kill them all, your girlfriend Erika, Stevie, Casey, Stacey, Tracy, Samantha, the whole rat's nest. Even Fiji.

GRANT: I've heard that Samantha—

BIGALOW: Men have no idea how women like that try to humiliate women like me. [*cries*]

GRANT: God, Muriel, I'm so sorry. Is there anything I can do?

BIGALOW: Does your prick reach your ass?

GRANT: What?

BIGALOW: Then go fuck yourself.

She hung up. What did I ever do to her? If any of you have discovered how to keep a woman on an even keel, I wish you'd let me in on it. The sad fact is that there is no way. I'd put up with anything, even feminism, if it would only keep them happy. In fact, I did put up with it, for over a year. Happy! I'd gladly settle for an interlude of sanity every now and then. Is that too much to ask? The handle of my phone, whatever you call it, was all sweaty. The damn thing rang the instant I put it down. I sat there looking at it while it rang, not wanting to pick it up, but I did. The voice at the other end was Bill's, more or less.

AUSTIN: The memorial service is on Thursday.

GRANT: I may be out of town.

AUSTIN: The funeral's on Tuesday, but that's just for the immediate family.

GRANT: How are you holding up, Bill? You sound a little remote. I'm awfully sorry—

AUSTIN: No you're not.

GRANT: Just what do you mean by that?

AUSTIN: You hated Jude.

GRANT: Didn't *you?*

AUSTIN: Only sometimes. I also loved her—sometimes.

GRANT: It's you I was about to offer my sympathy to, not her.

AUSTIN: The police seem to consider me a suspect.

GRANT: *(long pause).*

AUSTIN: Victor?

GRANT: It never occurred to me—

AUSTIN: I can produce an alibi if it comes to that.

GRANT: Phew!

AUSTIN: I was with a woman.

GRANT: Well, will the police believe her? They might think—

AUSTIN: Her husband walked in on us.

GRANT: Oh, no.

AUSTIN: We were calmly talking it over about the time Jude was killed.

GRANT: How do you get yourself in these fixes? On the other hand, if she corroborates—

AUSTIN: I suppose I'll have to marry her some day.

GRANT: Now wait a minute. You just got rid of one wife.

AUSTIN: I beg your pardon.

GRANT: What about Toby?

AUSTIN: Somehow I've never been able to get along without a woman. Before Jude—

GRANT: What about Toby?

AUSTIN: What about him?

GRANT: Does he know about his mother's death? Has he met his new mother-to-be?

AUSTIN: I've got an appointment with his therapist for tomorrow. She'll know what I should tell him. In fact I'm hoping she'll take on the job herself.

GRANT: His therapist!

AUSTIN: A wonderful woman: wise, cultivated, sad-eyed, Viennese, ill-fitting refugee bridgework showing lots of stainless steel, a genuine accent, cigarette ashes all down the front of her blouse. They don't make them like that any more.

GRANT: A therapist!

AUSTIN: You're repeating yourself again. What's wrong with you today?

GRANT: Toby doesn't need a shrink—anymore than Jude needs her horoscope read.

AUSTIN: What suddenly made you such an expert in child-rearing? *(pauses)* What was that you said?

GRANT: Jude's killer has already given him all the therapy he needs.

AUSTIN: Didn't you once tell me that your own mother's death—?

GRANT: There are mothers and then there are mothers.

AUSTIN: Toby's developed a bit of a stutter. If you ask him a direct question, he gives the answer to his invisible dog, Luke. He has extreme phobic reactions to pigeons. He's hyper—

GRANT: *(splutters)* Extreme phobic reactions—! Now you listen to me, Bill. You send that woman back to her husband. You

send Ms. Anna Freud there to a good dentist. Martine is all the
woman Toby needs right now. And you spend every moment
of your summer vacation with him. You eat all your meals with
him and stay sober until he falls asleep. And if he can't sleep
you hold him on your lap so that he can lay his head against
your chest and feel your heart beat. You watch his diet and
wash his ears and wipe his behind. Take him every place you
go. Involve him in everything you do. Explain things. Show him
how things work. Let him watch you shave. Show him how to
make a bed, how to cook simple, wholesome foods, like steaks,
chops, roasts—

AUSTIN: I don't know how to cook. I'm not very good at
making beds, either.

GRANT: Learn together. I don't mean spoil him. I don't mean
you should act like some guilt-ridden ex-husband making the
most of his visitation rights. I mean you should provide some
continuity and stability to his life. I mean that you should make
sure there is something in his life he can take for granted, that
something being you. I mean simply that you should *be there*. I
mean, in short, that you should act like a father. There were
some experiments with monkeys—

AUSTIN: I don't think "that woman" will go back to her
husband.

GRANT: Did you hear me?

AUSTIN: Yes, and a very pretty speech it was, too. I agree
with every word of it. In theory. But you seem to have forgotten
that *my* mother *didn't* die. It's not self-evident to me that parents
are the people best fitted to bring up their children. Besides,
Toby frightens me, the responsibility, I don't know how to
handle him, we get on each other's nerves. Besides . . . it's either
"that woman" or my mother. You follow me?

GRANT: Do I happen to know this answer to a widower's
prayers?

AUSTIN: Well, you'd find out soon enough anyway. It's Ursula Lindquist.

GRANT: But she already has three children. And she always seemed, how shall I say, she always seemed so *married*.

AUSTIN: It's her husband, in fact, who's going to deliver the eulogy for Jude this Thursday.

GRANT: Kaspar Lindquist! I wouldn't have believed he could open that draw-string mouth of his enough to—

AUSTIN: He's a compromise candidate: a professional anthropologist, a professor at Columbia, a feminist fellow-traveller. He's written an article to prove that the high suicide rate in Sweden is a product of sexism. The odd thing is that in his own home he's something of a tyrant.

GRANT: Come away from this, Bill. These lives are too disorderly. You don't want to saddle Toby with another disgruntled woman. You don't want to throw him among a crowd of sibling rivals. Let's go away this summer, just the three of us: you, me, and him. I'll teach you both how to cook and make beds. Together, we can—And oh, I forgot. There's reason to believe that Samantha's coming back. She—

AUSTIN: And after this summer? Motherhood is unto death, for better or for worse. You willing to take that on? Are you proposing to me? For Samantha too? I'm glad she's coming back, but frankly, Victor, I never noticed that your own domestic life was some kind of pastoral symphony either. I have to plan, not for two months, but for the next fifteen years. Remember that continuity you spoke of? No, Ursula will be all right. She's just disgruntled, if that's the word, for the moment, not constitutionally. And her children are the only brothers and sisters Toby is ever likely to have.

GRANT: Promise me you won't do anything irrevocable until—

AUSTIN: It's not a matter of doing anything. It's what's happening, irrevocably. Why don't you take Toby out for a day? Take him to the zoo. Teach him the rudiments of one of those sports you've become so good at.

GRANT: I have to go out of town.

AUSTIN: There you are. Jude had her faults, but whoever killed her wasn't doing Toby any favors. I sometimes wonder if my mother . . . Give me a call when you get back.

GRANT: Wait, hey Bill, we didn't settle—

As I put down the phone, it occurred to me that the father I had described was my own. Why then had I hated him so? He had taken me everywhere he went all right, but I never wanted to be with him. He tried to teach me things, but I never wanted to learn. I always hoped he would cut himself shaving. I provoked him until he shouted and threatened. But he never did hit me. (My mother did, once, around the time my father was getting wounded in the Battle of the Bulge.) I made things difficult for the women he occasionally brought home for dinner. I was snotty to his crew when they tried to cheer me up, tried to explain things to me, tried to turn me into a mascot. Strong, good-natured, imprudent men all, and over the sound of their hammering and sawing, around and between the studs and rafters of the house they were building, cutting through the dust and debris, flowed the clear sound of my father whistling tunes from *One Touch of Venus* (in which movie Ava Gardner, who looked then much as Samantha looks now, was beautiful enough to occlude the brain).

The phone rang. I went to the closet and got out my corduroy suit and the hat. The phone kept ringing. I got my new shirt out of the hamper and my new tie off the rack, while the phone rang. I rolled the pants around the shirt and tie, and rolled the hat in the jacket. The phone rang and rang. I fetched some cord, pants under one arm, jacket under the other, and stood looking down a at the phone, which continued to ring. Yes, I picked it up. Go ahead and laugh. And laugh some more at a thought that came to me: Hecate had decreed that through all eternity, as a punishment for killing Jude, I would pick up this phone to stop it from ringing, only to hear news that got worse and worse. And all along I would knew that the last caller was to be Jude, whose words were difficult to make out, her mouth being full of. . . . There was an unseemly, and perhaps unhealthy, excitement in Samantha's voice.

WOODS: Did you see Erika on TV?

GRANT: I've been sitting here all by myself waiting for you to call.

WOODS: Isn't she something?

GRANT: We've got lots to talk about.

WOODS: Didn't it make you shiver?

GRANT: Well, yes, in fact, it did.

WOODS: I feel sorry for whoever killed Jude. That is—

GRANT: So do I.

WOODS: I mean, I don't really.

GRANT: Think of him holed up somewhere, hunted, lonely, wifeless.

WOODS: Who do you think did it?

GRANT: Some man. Von Plink is right about that. Any man.

WOODS: Of course some man did it. But which, what kind?

GRANT: A grunting hog, a pip-squeak, a mama's boy, a toad, a maggot, a slug—

WOODS: Very funny.

GRANT: Samantha, let's talk about us.

WOODS: Stevie is convinced that Bill did it.

GRANT: That freak, that fishhook, that centaur, that inverted semicolon, that totem pole, that quasi-moto, that pseudobod, that androgymess andropodge, that—

WOODS: Stevie is a friend of mine.

GRANT: So is Bill!

WOODS: I *tried* to tell her Bill couldn't do a thing like that . . . but she wouldn't listen. I've never seen a person actually hiss and spit before. Erika tried to calm her down.

GRANT: So von Plank, at least, doesn't blame poor Bill.

WOODS: Well, yes, I think she does, actually. Anyway, she asked me if I knew whether he had a corduroy suit. But otherwise she didn't say much, now that I think of it. She was sort of preoccupied, reserved . . . maybe 'cause she knows I'm a friend of Bill's. She was, you know, like trying to draw the rest of us out. She asked me about you.

GRANT: That goose-stepping brown skirt, that blonde beastress, that—

WOODS: Don't start again. Besides, Erika is half Dutch.

GRANT: Surely you didn't tell her anything!

WOODS: I gather that she saw someone at the convention who . . . I just don't know. Apparently you don't look anything like him.

GRANT: Who the hell *did* he look like?

WOODS: She didn't say.

GRANT: The rest of you she was trying to draw out, who are they, I mean you?

WOODS: Some of the girls from *Ms. Chief,* people you don't know, Fiji, Robin, Kate, Tracy, oh, and Erika's secretary, Franklin Luala, though we all call him Butch. We all met at Erika's place. We had to decide what to do about Jude's murder.

GRANT: What did you decide?

WOODS: To hold up distribution of the first issue until we can get a black border printed on the cover. It's the least we could do.

GRANT: That's not what I meant, dammit.

WOODS: Well, Butch was pretty excited. He nearly came to blows with Stevie. He has this way of putting himself in a trance? It seems Jude's spirit told him that Miss Lily had hired a hit-man. He wants to go after the guy who snatched Toby. Erika forbid him to do anything until she gives the word.

GRANT: She wants to read her Ouija Board first?

WOODS: Fiji—she's the art director?—she doesn't say much, and then she speaks in these parables, but if I understood her right, she thinks her husband has something to do with it. He's a millionaire named Allerton Guth.

GRANT: Sounds like he should have knocked Fiji off first.

WOODS: Robin thinks it's just some anonymous psychopath

who crawled out of a sewer. New York is full of them, you know.

GRANT: I know.

WOODS: And then Kate was just saying that the murderer might be some Aunt Tillie who felt, you know, threatened by Jude, when Erika got a hysterical phone call from a woman named Muriel Bigalow. She was screaming so loud we could all hear her. She kept raving about Erika stealing her body and about the Corduroy Kid having his prick up his ass.

GRANT: Not by preference.

WOODS: What?

GRANT: Did von Plunk return this Muriel's body to her?

WOODS: The funny thing is that Erika seemed really shaken. She turned white as a sheet. Then she and Fiji rushed out. That's what broke up our meeting. Erika just called back a minute ago to tell us that the instant they got Muriel to St. Luke's she went all over catatonic. What a day. . . .

GRANT: You sound to me like you're enjoying it. Clearly it beats staying home with dull, ordinary old me. I haven't had brain fever or spoken to a ghost in weeks. Nor do I hiss and spit much.

WOODS: Victor, that's not fair. I'm the one who always has to call you. You never call me.

GRANT: But you won't give me your phone number!

WOODS: That's not the point.

GRANT: How about the good Pastor Brevoort? Has the Holy Spirit granted him a vision of the culprit?

WOODS: Pete was really broken up by Jude's death. He and she were supposed to fly to Amsterdam right after Jude's lecture. They were going to attend this conference on sex roles and social change?

GRANT: So she never meant to take Toby.

WOODS: Whatever gave you that idea?

GRANT: So who does Brevoort think killed Jude?

WOODS: Erika says he sobbed something about a protegé of

his, a young man with a history of jealous rages. Pete wanted to call off his trip, but Erika convinced him that Jude would have wanted him to carry on. Erika says this protegé hasn't got the balls to beat his meat. The things she says. . . .

GRANT: I take it, then, that none of your crew has it in for the girl with the Pall—I mean, the pistitute and her promp. Damn it, I mean—

WOODS: The police expect to apprehend them any minute.

GRANT: How do you know that!

WOODS: One of Erika's best friends is a policewoman on the case. She's gorgeous! Tall, stern, raven-haired, beautiful skin—and she's the youngest woman ever to become a detective on the New York force. She told Erika that she was going to make Spam out of those Spics when she gets at them, and you can bet that she will.

GRANT: Why would they want to kill Jude, for the love of God?

WOODS: Why would anyone want to kill Jude?

GRANT: Some day I'll tell you. Meanwhile, Superwoman there must have *some* pretence of a motive.

WOODS: The theory is that Jude pays the girl to come up to her room. After awhile, when they're both undressed, the girl's partner starts banging on the door. The girl lets him in. Then they either try to rob Jude or they threaten to expose her if she doesn't come across with money. Jude resists (Butch has been teaching us some keen ways to disable would-be rapists). They kill her.

GRANT: How? I mean, with what?

WOODS: Outside of the police, only Bill and Erika know, and she won't tell us.

GRANT: So Jude finally came out of the closet. . . .

WOODS: I'll thank you not to speak of my friends in that way.

GRANT: But you said—

WOODS: Jude never had sex with a woman. I know that for

a fact. And anyway, why shouldn't she, if she wanted to?

GRANT: As long as she didn't want to have sex with you. *(waits for an answer)* Samantha? *(waits)* Samantha, speak to me.

WOODS: If I had given in to her, she might still be alive. Did you ever think of that?

GRANT: If she were still alive, you might some day give in to her. Did you ever think of that?

WOODS: Would it have been so horrible, after all? It seems such a little thing. What would it have mattered?

GRANT: It wasn't such a little thing when I—

WOODS: Jude was like, you know, timid to do it the first time with these women here, they seem so experienced. And Erika kept egging her on to practice what she preached. Erika can be a demon sometimes. And Pete kept saying that heterosex was only half of it, that she wasn't a homophobe, was she? And that there was only one road to perfect personhood, but you had to go both ways on it.

GRANT: And you, do they say these things to you?

WOODS: Jude was in such a turmoil. I'd never heard her weep or plead before. And I kept saying I couldn't, I'd have to think about it. She called me some awful names. I called her other names back.

GRANT: Have to think about it!

WOODS: Now she's dead.

GRANT: Don't tell me you feel guilty about Jude's death too!

WOODS: "Too"?

GRANT: Now Samantha, you listen to me—

WOODS: What's that whistle every time you say my name?

GRANT: What whistle? Samantha, will you—

WOODS: That whistle. It's those awful cigarettes you smoke.

GRANT: Funny. . . . I never noticed before. . . . It's a tooth I broke off in a fight. You should have seen this big black stud I tangled with.

WOODS: Oh, Victor, you're not becoming a common rowdy, are you? Bill told Jude that you weren't working, that you've been gambling and hanging around in bars with roughnecks.

GRANT: You'll be happy to hear this: it will make you proud of me: I've finally managed to give up smoking.

WOODS: Anyhow, it's nice to hear you say my name. Everybody around here calls me Sam.

GRANT: Remember how you used to say the smell got in your hair? Oh Samantha, come home, please come home to me. Come away from those people. Their lives are too violent and disorderly. *(pause)* I just had an experience of deja vu. . . . I can hire a U-Haul and have you moved, desk and all, in a couple of hours.

WOODS: A couple of hours ago Erika said practically the same thing.

GRANT: She had an experience of—?

WOODS: She wants Stevie and Robin and me to move in with her.

GRANT: So that you can practice what you preach? Samantha, don't do this. Beware the frumious—

WOODS: Everybody's always telling me what to do. She says Butch will be able to protect us, that we can work on the magazine together, help each other with our writing, that after working together, we can play together. Pete's moving in when he returns from Amsterdam. He and Erika are cousins, you know. She's been dangling a promotion before me. I just know I won't get it unless I move in with her.

GRANT: I'm going to get von Plaack. I'm going to tie her up in a cave. The first day, I'll cut her toes and fingers off. The second day I'll cut her nose and ears off; the third day, her lips and eyelids; the fourth, I'll pull out her tongue and eyes; the fifth day, I'll peel the skin off her breasts; the sixth day—

WOODS: That's disgusting. Talk about violence! If I didn't think you still had some consideration for me, I'd wonder if it wasn't you that killed Jude.

GRANT: Come home to me. I love you—which is more than any of your new friends can say.

woods: I don't want to be loved, I want to be promoted. And I still haven't found myself. I'll call again Thursday, or maybe I'll see you at the memorial service.

grant: Wait, not Thursday, I'll be—

It was beginning to look as though my work were not done. Who would have thought that a simple murder would have so many consequences? And I can't say I liked the looks of any one of them. If you want to expose the motive parts holding together a group of people just murder one of them. I felt like the kid who smashed his radio with a hammer to liberate the orchestra of little people playing inside: sparks, smoke, dust, broken connections, a dead mouse. (That kid was me.) Now I had to clean up the mess without getting burned on a hot wire. Well, I didn't want to. Hadn't I done enough? It was discouraging. I had fought the dragon and won, but where was my reward? Where was my princess? Where were the cheering crowds? Where was that sun-lit kingdom awarded to me by its citizens grateful for the health and order I had restored? Why couldn't you rely on people to do what was expected of them?

I tied up my suit in two compact bundles. I peeked out the door. No one in the hall, left or right. The door to the incinerator chute is in a closet, which also contains a sink. I scurried in. Smoke was seeping past the little chute door. My building, including the incinerator, was built before American know-how accomplished the miracle of producing more garbage than goods. To keep up, the super has to fire the furnace twice on weekdays and once on Sundays. I opened the chute, letting out a cloud of smoke, and stuffed in first my corduroy pants, which were rolled around the Tattersall shirt and the yellow tie, and then the jacket, which was rolled around the sexy-Rexy hat. Large gains are won by those who know how to withstand small losses. Still, that was a nice suit. I have never been able to find another just like it. And the last time I tried to switch the pants (which were too large) that went with a size 40 jacket (which fit) for the pants (which fit) that went with a size 36 jacket (which was too small), I got caught. I saw no reason to burn my new socks.

I fetched the high-priced scissors Samantha bought once to save money. Her idea was to economize by cutting my hair for me. After one attempt, she decided that the price of my haircuts was one expense we would have to leave room for in our narrow budget. I never let out one word of complaint, myself. I didn't mind my head looking like a terrace garden so long as Samantha had done the terracing. I positioned myself before the three-sided mirror on our old oak dresser and began to cut, especially along the sideburns, on the back of the neck, and around the ears, areas left exposed by the hat. Cutting your own hair is no easy matter. You might try it yourself next time you plan to stay out of sight for a few weeks. But it is only one of many skills I had picked up during the previous three months. I finished up with a pair of clippers priced twice as high as the scissors. Believe it or not, there is a wave to my hair, which up to then I had suppressed, more or less. In the bathroom, I wet-combed my hair straight back, eliminating the part, and then placed fingers on my scalp, as though about to give myself a massage. I scrabbled my hair around. The result was a roguish mess of curls.

I cut some of the droop out of my moustache and clipped the rest of it short. I shaved my three-day's growth of beard down to a piece of elegance around the muzzle. The border on either side continued the line from nostril through curve of moustache to edge of jaw. A central stripe under the lip broadened at its base to include the ball of chin and then swept back and up on both sides to meet the corners of the mouth. I shaved under the jaw to just short of the chin, for who wants to itch every time he looks down to check whether there is gravy on his tie. (My facial hair, like my pubic hair, grows thick and black. The hair on my head and armpits is brown. The scant hair on my chest is brown, black, red, and grey.) I suppose I should admit that the exposed skin under my mouth was shaped something like a plump set of buttocks, as seen from behind. But it is not anything you would ordinarily notice. The general result of my barbering, in fact, was to make me look less like a Bulgarian bandit and more like a machiavellian advisor to a dissolute prince. The contribution of my broken tooth to the air of disreputable dash was considerable. The black eye, which was anything but black, somehow jarred, but it wasn't permanent, after all. In any case, there was not much chance of anybody picking me out of a line-up as the Corduroy Kid.

Now that I looked like a man of policy (rather than a man of action), I began to think like one. Normally, I am not so plastic, you understand. Normally I can resist the influence of even my own appearance. I would not say I was rattled. Nor would it be correct to say that my self-confidence had been shaken. Even less was I suffering from "ontological insecurity." (Note to younger readers: this phrase, once much thrown about, but surely obsolete by the time you read this, was coined by a psychotherapist who believed that insanity was good for you. He argued that schizophrenics, whom he nonetheless admired, got that way because their parents did not give in to their every whim. Such deprivation gave them an insecure sense of self. The term was picked up by lazy men to explain why they could not accomplish anything and by stupid women to explain why they were not in the running for the Nobel Prize in physics. Their patriarchal parents, you see, stomped out the fires of their yearning for calculus.) The question of self-confidence scarcely arises. I thought of myself as a man who can do what has to be done. I am still that kind of man. But how can a man who thinks of himself as a man who can do what has to be done do it when he doesn't know what has to be done?

Up to the moment of Jude's timely demise, I knew what had to be done, and did it. The consequences were not those I had every reason to expect. That wasn't my fault. But I allowed myself to be disappointed. I even allowed myself to be resentful. Let's get everything out into the open. My reaction was childish, soft, and if I may say so, uncharacteristic. If controlled rage had been my most effective emotional condition before, it was now to be unrestrained calm. What good would it do me, would it do Samantha, Toby, Bill, if I were to run around knocking off von Plaack, van Dickinson, ffon Brevoort, Le Butch, Les Stacy, Tracy, Casey, La-las Kate and Robin? You'd think I was developing a taste for murder. Nothing could be further from the truth. Once is enough for a man with essentially healthy impulses. For one thing, murder is wearying— unless you are a professional hit-man, who never feels anything, and prefers it that way; or unless you are a psychopath, who seldom feels anything, but can't stand it, and has to commit murder to prove to himself that he is still alive. (All right, maybe there is something to the notion of ontological insecurity.) I began instead to calculate. I began to weigh alternatives. I now know that it is useless to weigh things for which there is no scale. I now know better than to calculate equations in which all the terms are x (which is the way of things outside mathematics), but I didn't then. What I did know was that a man of policy is above all a man who knows when to do nothing. Having accomplished Hamlet's task and survived, I would now accomplish Prince Hal's.

I needed a place to lie low in, until things blew over a bit, until, at least, the visible wounds of my struggle with Jude Karnofsky were no longer so visible. I wanted to be somewhere else if the police came snooping around for leads from the Austins' friends. I also needed some money. And I needed a weapon—just in case. After all, I could not count on there always being a basket of fruit within reach. That fabulous an optimist I had never been, even before my mother died. Stevie Dickinson was just capable of trying to make good her threats on Bill's life. If I was going to protect him I needed more than a couple of purple plums, assuming they were available, or a compromised ice pick. Surely you cannot believe that I was afraid of a face-to-face encounter with Butch. But suppose he snuck up behind me on sneaky sandalled feet? I was not a beneficiary of his lessons in the art of maiming people with your bare hands. (Not that they had done Jude much good.) And when Erika von Plaack came after the Corduroy Kid, I expected her to be carrying a bazooka—at least. What I needed, then, was some firepower of my own. I naturally assumed that all stevedores and construction workers have underworld connections, or at least, aspirations: I called Chi Chi.

QUATRONE: Yeah.

GRANT: It's Victor.

QUATRONE: H'ya doin, ole Buddy.

GRANT: I got a problem.

QUATRONE: How much you need?

GRANT: It's not that kind of problem.

QUATRONE: You should've come with me the other night. They got this fat bimbo, who, believe it or not—

GRANT: It's not that kind of problem either.

QUATRONE: Whatever you do, don't marry her, whoever she is.

GRANT: I need a gat.

QUATRONE: A what?

GRANT: A rod.

QUATRONE: This connection . . .

GRANT: A heater, a roscoe, a piece.

QUATRONE: You mean a handgun?

GRANT: Exactly.

QUATRONE: They're not hard to come by, if you ain't too particular.

GRANT: Can you get me one?

QUATRONE: What I'm trying to say is most of what you see on the street ain't too reliable. And you don't want anything with a history.

GRANT: What do you advise?

QUATRONE: What do you want it for?

GRANT: [hesitates]

QUATRONE: I don't want to know *exactly* what you want it for.

GRANT: For your own protection, you understand.

QUATRONE: I unnerstand. I mean the workman is only as good as his tools, is all. You want to put some fear into a guy, you can get along with this tool. You want to hold up a crap game, you better use that one. You want to go bear hunting, you got think big.

GRANT: I never thought of that.

QUATRONE: Well, you got to.

GRANT: I want it for defense.

QUATRONE: You want a big caliber, then. Lots of stopping power, forget hitting him between the eyes at 100 yards. You gonna carry it with you?

GRANT: Well, yes.

QUATRONE: O.K., we try for an automatic or a snubnose. Shoulder holster?

GRANT: And ammunition. When can you get it?

QUATRONE: Hold on, now. Are we talking business?

GRANT: I didn't mean you should do it for nothing.

QUATRONE: It's gonna cost you maybe two, two-fifty, three, depending. I get another fifty for my trouble.

GRANT: It's a deal. I'm really grateful—

QUATRONE: Relax. Just leave everything to me. No more business?

GRANT: No more.

QUATRONE: Good. When you coming over to eat? Fawn don't like most of my friends, but she's got to go for you. I can fix you up with her sister Laurel. She's another gourmet cook. You like stuffed eggplant?

GRANT: I never tried it, but I'm—

QUATRONE: We can try out the hardware at my brother-in-law's shooting range. His name is Glenn, for Christ's sake.

GRANT: You see, I don't want too many people—

QUATRONE: You don't have to worry. He's a scumbag, but I

never let on. Some day it may be useful to know a bull who ain't your enemy.

GRANT: A detective!

QUATRONE: Through and through. The Chinaglia's are all what you might call pillars of the community. The other brother—Clark is his name (the old lady was ashamed of being Italian)—he's a priest. He's a pain in the ass too.

GRANT: Look, thanks a lot, Chi, but—

QUATRONE: As I was saying, you don't have to worry about meeting Glenn. He's working overtime on that case of the dyke who got a mouthful over at the Hilton. He says half the force is on the case.

GRANT: Got a mouthful! What do you mean? There was nothing in the news about—

QUATRONE: Well, I ain't supposed to say. They always hold something back, so if some crackpot confesses. . . .

GRANT: What are there—five murders a day in New York? How come all the fuss about this one?

QUATRONE: She was a big noise, you know. Whoever nabs the guy that put it to her is in line for a promotion. And then, there are all these women's groups raising hell.

GRANT: I suppose they expect to catch the perpetrator any minute.

QUATRONE: Glenn ain't so sure. One team of detectives led by a gung-ho snooper named Haggerty is going after those dopey Spics. Did you hear what happened? They tried to work the badger game on this honcho from New Mexico. An unrepentant bachelor, he calls himself. Well, he pulls out this six-gun a yard long and sticks it up the cat's nose. Then he tells the chick to give him a blow-job or he cleans out her boyfriend's sinuses with a bullet. So she gives him a blow-job. Then he sends them packing with a boot in the ass apiece. Glenn says he wears these pointy cowboy boots, size 14, about.

GRANT: Why didn't Glenn run the son of a bitch in for sodomy?

QUATRONE: He was laughing too hard, I guess.

GRANT: I hope they both get away.

QUATRONE: I'm with you there. If they killed that ball-buster Karnofsky they ought to get a medal. Besides, Glenn don't think they had anything to do with it. Another team's looking into the husband. That's a matter of course. Glenn's working with a team that's checking out everybody who was registered at the Hilton. Seems Judy-doody there had some fuzz under her fingernails that turned out to be corduroy. And she had a bruise on the edge of her right hand. The word is she was fooling with that Oriental self-defense horse shit. So Glenn is looking for a guy with a corduroy jacket and a damaged head.

GRANT: Look Chi, about that gun. Don't pick up anything yet. Just see what's available, sort of. I mean, if it's not too much troub—

QUATRONE: No trouble. I already got an idea what's available. For one thing, Glenn's got a .45 ain't doing nothing. The former owner is dead, and he stole it to begin with. If you don't want to come out here, I can bring it by your place some night after work. Say, don't you live on the same block as—

GRANT: Same house.

QUATRONE: No shit.

GRANT: I knew her slightly.

QUATRONE: No shit.

GRANT: Her husband too.

QUATRONE: Why would a guy want to marry a cunt ain't got no use for men?

GRANT: He didn't know, I guess.

QUATRONE: That's something you always know.

GRANT: Love is blind, they say.

QUATRONE: He's gotta be queer.

GRANT: He wouldn't be the first man to be deceived by a woman. If a woman wants to pretend feelings she doesn't have, she's got the equipment for it. Everything's hidden. Whereas a man—

QUATRONE: Don't remind me. You think he did it?

GRANT: I know he didn't.

QUATRONE: Hey, you oughta talk to Glenn.

GRANT: Let's not anybody talk to Glenn, O.K.? Not yet.

QUATRONE: You got to make up your mind, Vic.

GRANT: I'll call you Thursday. I have to leave town for a few days.

QUATRONE: Whatever you say, ole Buddy.

GRANT: Thursday.

QUATRONE: I'll be talking to ya.

As usual, what was easy as sin for everybody else was going to be difficult as virtue for me. If you believed the gun-control nuts, picking up a handgun in New York was like picking up crablice in Mexico. All you had to do was stand on a corner. Sooner or later someone who was carrying would walk up and ask you to name a price. Even my father, as I recall, used to have two or three pistols stashed among the rifles in his closet under the staircase. I thought of calling Brunhilda, but if you think I wanted one more Puerto Rican on my conscience you still don't know me very well, although I am becoming resigned to that. What did Chi Chi care? He hadn't been given Pall Malls by that girl when he most needed them. Glenn Chinaglia and that blow-hard cowboy (may his Birchite bones hone the beaks of desert vultures)—they could afford to laugh. They hadn't been pulled out of the Slough of Despond by a conspiratorial wink from one of her laughing eyes. They hadn't been inspired by her tight-packed, full-bottomed, concave-sided brawny behind. I would have been in a stew of anxiety anyhow, even if I were not indirectly responsible (through no fault of my own) for the danger she was in. Must I say it again? I killed Jude Karnofsky not because I hate women, but because I love them. I'll bet that poor girl would have gotten me a gun, if I had asked her.

"Going to the country, Baby I can't take you." I suddenly heard myself singing that phrase from a blues lyric. It hit me that it had been running through the back of my mind all the while I was talking to Chi Chi. Well, well: it was about time that my demon began to speak to me again. Upon Jude's death, no doubt, it had assumed that its services were no longer needed. Now we both knew better. I was ready to listen, but I had to hear more. Going to the country certainly beat hiding out in a turkish bath, for example, not that I had seriously considered anything so desperate. It also beat riding the subways or fighting off vermin in a flop house. Why these improbable visions of myself abandoned in the lower depths had popped into my mind I can't say. Besides, I needed a retreat that would not sound like a hide-out if I ever had to account for my where-abouts. Picture me explaining to Inspector LaPaloma or Glenn Chinaglia or Wonder Woman what I had been doing for three nights in a turkish bath. Going to the country, but where? It was fifteen years since I had been further away from New York City than Hoboken. I settled myself comfortably among the sprung springs of the armchair. I closed my eyes and relaxed. Going to the country, Baby I can't take you. What followed?

Pictures began to form in my head. Survivors creep out from the smoldering rubble. They are dusty, gaunt, ragged, and haggard. Their eyes gleam in blackened faces. They draw themselves up, pause, look my way. Their arms hang at their sides.

Going to the country, Baby I can't take you.

The air between us is corrugated by heat waves. The sky behind them is a kind of sulphurous yellow streaked with ragged clouds of black and grey. Wisps and tendrils of smoke rise all about us from broken blocks of concrete and twisted iron rods.

Going to the country, Baby I can't take you.

They turn their faces to look at a figure standing on top of a scorched hill. Her shoulders are broad and bare. Her hair is black and long. She is wearing what appears to be a white gown or toga. There must be a wind on the hill, because her toga is pressed flat against her right side, but on her left it ripples and flaps. She is shouting something, but I can't make out the words, although I can hear her voice. Behind her is the blackened skeleton of a tree. She tilts back her head, raises her arms, and extends them, as though to embrace the sky. She is pointing at me with the melodramatic stance of a fencer. Her face is green-eyed, cool, aloof, and on the verge of a derisive smile.

Going to make my get-away, yeah,

They turn their faces toward me. They begin to walk, following their faces, their bodies rigid, their arms stiffly at their sides. In the distance behind them mountains rise like a series of worn granite steps, each farther level less distinguishable from the haze through which. . . . The sunlit farthest peak floats above the haze in technicolor blue. In a clearing among the pines, a hale old man sits on a rock. His left hand rests on a large black dog couchant beside him. On his right a younger man leans back on his elbows, his legs spread. He is naked from the waist up, except for crossed bandoleers. A cigarette hangs from his lips. He squints one eye against its smoke. The two men and the dog look downslope into the roiling clouds before them, as though they expected someone to step out from it momentarily.

Going back to find the lost clue.

In the back of the closet, behind an iceskate, under Samantha's umbrella and my machete, lay the shoebox I was looking for. I pulled it out. The cord around it was secured with one of Samantha's impossible knots, about the size of a golf ball. How many times had I worked myself into a rage trying to undo one of them but succeeding only in tightening the knot, fraying the cord, soaking the whole business with sweat? And how many times had Samantha seen what was up, taken the package or whatever it was from me, pulled a bobby pin from behind an ear, picked once or twice, opened the knot, returned the package, pecked me on the forehead? Of such things are marriages made. I was not ready then, nor am I now, nor will I ever be, to forgive Jude Karnofsky, who cut through the Gordian knot of my marriage, although she died for it. I sliced through the cord around the shoebox with my machete. Samantha's notes to me were tied with a pink ribbon. My letters to her were tied with a blue ribbon, and why hadn't she taken them with her? My father's Christmas cards to us, still in their envelopes, were tied with a green ribbon. There was no need for me to cut it. The return address was plainly visible: Pinetop, Vandernut Stage, Tannerton, N.Y. 12078.

I was in no mood to rake through the brown and falling leaves of our six-year-old phone book. Half the pages were wholly or partially missing anyhow. I had called and Samantha had written for a new one, but all we ever got for our trouble were promises, promises. So I called information. The phone rang nine times, until someone at the other end finally picked it up—and then put it down again without answering. I called again. A thick, slow Southern voice answered. I could make out the words "help you" half sunk in molasses. I asked for the number of Greyhound Bus Lines. She gave me a number. I dialed it. A voice answered in what I took to be Chinese, although it may have been Japanese, for all I know, or Balinese, for that matter, or Shang-ri-lan, for all I care. I hung up without answering, my knowledge of Oriental languages being lamentably meager. I called information again, and asked for the number of Greyhound Bus Lines again, and got a new number, nothing like the first, from a voice with a friendly Jamaican accent. I dialed. A metallic voice answered: "The number you have dialed, 549-2000, is not in service in area code 212. Please check the number and dial again. This is a—" I hung up. I called information once more, asked for the number of Greyhound Bus Lines once more, and got a number, different from the other two. The voice was genteel, but unsure of its r's: "diwectowy assistance," it had said. I dialed. After fifteen rings, a snotty, supercilious, swishy voice said "Greyhound." I asked when buses left for Tannerton, New York. "This line is for Boston service only," he said, and hung up. I dialed again. After twenty-one rings, someone picked up the phone. I could hear her speaking, but not into the receiver: ". . . said to Sadie, if Marvin wanted to join the JDL, why couldn't he ask his mother first?" I could not make out the reply. "If this character is such a noble Marxist, why does he want to leave Russia?" said the first voice. Then she spoke into the receiver. "Boston service," she said. "Can you tell me what number I should dial to inquire about Greyhound service to Tannerton, New York?" I said. "No," she said, and hung up. I called information, for a change. I explained carefully that I wanted one of the Greyhound Bus Lines numbers. I wanted specifically the number of a desk that could inform me about service to cities in New York State. "Let's see," said the cheerful midwestern voice. "Boston service only, no, Philadelphia service only, no Washington service only, no, here, try Nationwide service, 594-2000." I hung up and then dialed 594-2000. A metallic voice answered. "Please stay on the line. In a few minutes your call will be automatically relayed to the first available operator," and she went on about Greyhound service from lower Manhattan and Upper Bronx and Middle Queens, and then said the message would not be repeated. So I stayed on the line, for about five minutes, until the line went dead. I dialed 549-2000. A voice answered in Chinese. I hung up and dialed 594-2000. A metallic voice answered. "Please stay on—" I hung up. This was getting interesting. I called information. "Directory assistance, please," said a voice that was Indian, or Pakistani, or Egyptian, or some other kind of Arab. I asked for the number of the Greyhound Baggage Claim desk. "Sure thing," he said. "Is it Package Arrival Information you are wanting or is it General Shipping Information?" he said. "General shipping," I said. "You betcha," he said, and gave me a number. I dialed it. After one ring, a rough voice of the kind I knew I could talk to said "Hold on." Then he shouted away from the receiver. "You get those packages sorted in

thirty seconds or you'll be prying them out of your asshole."
Then he spoke into the receiver. "What can I do for you?" he
said. I explained that I was having difficulty getting through to
Greyhound information. Those people upstairs, he said, were
too busy cultivating their hemorrhoids to do anything else. I
vigorously expressed my assent to this observation. Could he
tell me anything about service to Tannerton, New York? Greyhound ain't got service to Tannerton, he said. What I wanted
was the Trailways Bus System. I asked whether he had the
number handy. Sorry, Pal, he said, someone had stolen his
phone book. Thanks friend, I said. Don't mention it, he said. I
dialed information. The phone was actually getting hot. I expected it to start smoking any minute. "Directory assistance.
May I help you?" said a voice that was a remarkable imitation
of Marilyn Monroe's. "You sure can, baby," I said, "but I'll
settle for the number of the Trailways Bus System." "It's little
enough," she said and gave me the number. I dialed it. "Trailways Bus System. At your service," said a voice that was only
a fair imitation of Bugs Bunny's. Would he be so kind as to tell
me, I asked, the schedule of departures for Tannerton, New
York. "You want Adirondack Trailways," he said. "You got
their number?" I said, but he had hung up. I called information.
The phone rang thirty-two times until someone at the other end
picked it up—and then put it down again without answering.
To give the phone and myself time to cool off I pulled out my
directory. It shed bits and flakes of brittle brown paper. All the
entries between ADEL ROOTSTEIN USA INC to ADOREE MADAME HAND
LAUNDRY were missing. I stood up and walked once around the
chair. I sat down, thought for a minute, then picked my way to
the back of the book, and there it was: "Trailways-Adirondack,
Tickets—Schedules & Information . . . 947-3500." I dialed. A
voice answered in Chinese. I slammed down the phone, which
tinkled with hypocritical self-pity. I jumped to my feet. I sank
back into the chair, checked the number, and dialed, looking
alternately from book to phone for each digit. The line was

busy. I placed down the receiver carefully, as you would kiss a scorpion. It tinkled, then whirred once deep in its throat. I walked twice around the chair, sat down, dialed again. The phone rang forty-eight times without anybody answering, so I placed down the receiver, gently, as you would pet an unfriendly Doberman. "Rowr. Fizz," it said. I stood up, shadowboxed for a minute or two, sat down, dialed again. The line was busy. I stood up, walked around the chair, stopped, crouched, jumped twice, each time touching my fingers to my toes on either side, sat down, dialed again. There was a single ring, then nothing, so I replaced the receiver, cautiously, as you would set down an anvil on a glass-topped table. "Ruhr. Ing," it said. I stood up, walked to the bathroom, turned on the light, placed myself before the mirror, exercised my facial muscles, turned off the light, walked back to the chair, sat down, dialed again. After a dozen rings there was a click, then more rings, this time a tone higher. A rich, musical contralto said, "Operator 248. What number have you been calling?" I told her. There was another click and a metallic voice broke in: "The number you have dialed, 947-3500, has been changed to 840-2500. Please make a note of it." I ignored her well-meant suggestion, and I would have ignored it even if there had been pencil and paper handy. At that time my memory was just about infallible. I placed down the receiver, fighting contrary impulses, as you would reach into a hole under a rock. "Grerr. Sizz. Pop," it said. I stood up, extended my hands downward in front of me, clasped them, jumped over them, unclasped them, sat down. I dialed 480-250, then slammed down the receiver. It rang once, low and slow, like a record running down. I picked it up, listened to the tone, which sounded hoarse and tired, dialed 840-2500, very deliberately, as a drunk might pluck cactus spines out of his nose. "Adirondack Trailways," said a voice, faint, whispery, with a gargle in it, but suspiciously familiar. "If you would be so kind, I should be grateful for information as to when your buses depart tomorrow for Natternun, New Tork,"

I said. He said something I couldn't make out. "You'll have to speak louder," I said: "We are poorly connected." A muffled baritone rumble wow-wowed something. I thought I made out the words "not" and then "coming through." "What?" I said. "[unintelligible] with you," he may have said. "I can't make you out," I said. Absolute silence. "Hello," I said: "Hello, hello, hello." "No need to shout," he said. "I'm right here. At your service, whenever you need me, twenty-four hours a day." His words came through loud, clear and pure, as though he were standing beside me. I suddenly realized who he sounded like. He sounded as I sound to myself—which may not, of course, be how I sound to others. I went all over goose flesh. "Who are you?" I said. "Wouldn't you like to know," he said. "All right, wise guy," I said; "just tell me when the buses leave for Tannerton." "To Natternun we have five departures daily," he said. "The first is at—" pops, crackles, whirrs, a tink, sparks under the dial face, a creepy movement in the receiver, as though something were crawling through it. I held the infernal thing at arm's length, so I could watch the sparks shoot through the holes. When it became quiet I held it gingerly to my ear. Not a sound. I jiggled the plunger. Quieter still. I held the receiver before me, so I could look at the scorch marks around the holes. I let my hand fall by my side, the receiver with it. I just stood there for a full minute. Then I smashed the receiver into its cradle as you would hammer a stake into a vampire. I stood still for another minute, looking at the thing. Then I grabbed the whole business with two hands, yanked it free from the wall, whirled around three times, and let it fly. The base stopped abruptly, in mid-air, about six inches from the wall, for in whirling around I had wrapped myself in the wire. But the receiver flew off the cradle and into the framed print of a silly painting entitled "Peaceable Kingdom" that Samantha had put up. Base, receiver, print, and frame fell to the floor amid a shower of glass, plaster, and paint. The phone let out one whimpering ting.

I let the chair have a straight left to the head, then a right upper cut to the paunch, then a left feint followed by a looping right over its guard, two quick left hooks, a right cross, a bolo punch with the left, a flurry, until the chair slowly tipped over on its back. I let it lie and walked to the bathroom. I washed my face with cold water and then sat on the edge of the tub, sucking a skinned knuckle, until my heart slowed down. I walked back into the living room and looked down at the phone, its entrails hanging out. Among the debris was what appeared to be a steel pill, about the size of a nickel, but thicker. Little springy wires were attached to it. I picked it up. "I see," I said, for never before had I held in my hand an electronic surveillance device, vulgarly known as a bug.

If I know you, in my place you would have asked yourself fearfully who had planted the bug and why. You would have agitated yourself in an attempt to remember whether you had said anything incriminating. I did nothing of the sort. I swept and picked up the pieces of glass, plaster, paint, print, frame, phone. I went into the kitchen to make myself a little bedtime snack, for I had suddenly become very hungry. I removed a pork loin from the refrigerator and with my machete reduced it to six chops. I put the chops on a wire rack, the rack in a pan, the pan in the oven, set at 450 degrees. In a small bowl I mixed up some barbecue sauce (tomato, soy, and Trinidad hot sauce, oregano, sage, salt, pepper, cayenne pepper, cumin, garlic powder, grated onion, vinegar, olive oil, powdered mustard, a pinch of brown sugar, three pinches of chili powder). I then sat at the table and began to write up the day's events, too many of which consisted of nothing but words, if you want to know how I feel about it. I wrote quickly, in a kind of trance, careful not to think about any case that could be drawn up against me by whoever had been eavesdropping on all those words. After a half hour, I turned the oven down to 300 degrees and painted the tops of the chops with sauce. For the next hour, I set aside my writing every fifteen minutes to turn the chops over and paint them with sauce. I then ate the chops with two glasses of ice water and three stalks of celery. I could tell that I had made the chops hot enough, because when I finished eating the roof of my mouth hung down in shreds.

VII

I am only human, you know. For some reason my internal alarm clock failed me, and I didn't wake up until well after 9:00. Within ten minutes I was jumping down the stoop on my way to the IRT—and wasn't that Stevie Dickinson's monstrous posterior lagging after whoever it was ducked into a hallway across the street. If so, she was wearing a leather jacket of the kind I had once owned myself. By the time I had crossed over to look, the hallway was empty. Within ten minutes I was on the Seventh Avenue Local heading downtown. Then I made the mistake of getting off at Ninety-sixth for the express. By the time it came, the local had no doubt gone to the end of the line and was on its way back again. I know people who would have been flattered, but I was in no mood for the liberties that someone's hand began to take with my behind. When the train stopped at Seventy-second, I revolved half a circle; but the men all looked equally guilty. It never occurred to me that the culprit might be a woman. Why not? I just can't get used to the idea that the goal of feminism is to make women imitate the worst in men. All the way from Seventy-second to Times Square, the same hand (presumably) took liberties with my privates. I can't say I enjoyed it, but such petty irritations, which arise inevitably out of the circumstances of post-Neolithic civilization, are nothing that a grown man would want to make a fuss about. You should have heard Jude on the subject, however. As though anyone were likely to grope her, except by mistake.

To get from Times Square to Port Authority you follow, as instructed, the yellow signs. These take you downstairs and up; they take you around hairpin turns that spill into steep ramps going down, along dangerous overpasses, through a series of quick turns right and left, through an echoing tunnel, into a long, narrow passageway, its walls lined with ruined posters announcing the arrival of plays long ago gone forever, past a turnstile, up an elevator, into a brightly lit promenade. The glass-enclosed Adirondack Trailways ticket area was beyond the information booth, to the left. Something was wrong with the overhead fluorescent lights. Many of them were out; the others flickered. Is there no part of advanced industrial civilization still in good repair? At first I thought all the ticket windows were deserted, but I was wrong. Behind the middle window of the seven was a man on a high stool. One of his shoulders seemed withered, tucked up and in. There was a scar on his neck, from under his ear straight down into his collar. I restrained my impulse to reach through the bars and twist his nose off when I realized that what had seemed like a fanfare of belches was actually a question.

"What?" I said.

"You're late," he said, or so I understood him to say.

"That so?" I said. He didn't say anything. "Well, when's the next bus?"

"Where do you want to go?" he said.

"To see my father." It was a dumb thing to say, but I was not entirely awake, or something.

"You're doing the right thing," he said.

"How do you know?" I said.

"You're getting to that age," he said.

"Well, then, let's have a ticket," I said.

"Think I can read your mind?" he said.

"To Tannerton," I said.

"Nothing surprises me anymore," he said.

As it turned out, the next bus would not leave until 12:01. That gave me two hours to kill. It cost me another token to get back to Times Square, where I had noticed the word SALE across the window of a little wedge-shaped store specializing in denim clothes. I picked up a snazzy pair of light blue brushed denim pants and a jacket that almost matched. At the last minute I weakened and bought myself a kind of cowboy hat, also of light blue denim, with a red and white band that looked as though it had been cut from a tinker's neckerchief. I wore it tilted forward, and it covered Brunhilda's handiwork pretty well.

Up in the air, and a very nice day it was, I walked east to Herman's, which sells sporting goods, not for athletes, but for tennis players, golfers, bowlers, skiers, and such-like, people who spend their summer holidays at Southampton and spend their winter weekends looking out through picture windows at machine-made ski slopes. Sure, and it's for this they get their divorces. I can understand a man wanting to be free to come and go as he will, and I can understand a married man looking to get laid—that's the way men are—but you don't have to discard your wife and desert your children, thus adding to the world's already ample supply of neurotics. Come and go as you will, so long as you come home too; get laid if you want, so long as you keep quiet about it. A good wife puts up with masculine vagaries, just because they are masculine, and if they are truly masculine you can count on her being a good wife—but she doesn't like to be humiliated. What you show the world when you show off your bimbo is not your masculinity, but your doubts about it. This is good advice, even if I didn't follow it myself. But I intended to, once I got my Samantha back. The rugby-type jersey with broad horizontal stripes, white and red, suited me very well, I thought. Three pairs of sweat socks and a pair of blue suede sneakers cost me over thirty bucks. I was preening before a mirror, turning this way and that, when an immense longing for Samantha came over me. I sagged at the knees and leaned back against the wall. What is the good of any attainment—good looks, style, bravery, character—if you can't see it reflected in the eyes of an admiring woman, yours alone? For some people mirrors are enough, but not for me.

I spent a long time looking over the hunting knives, but decided against buying one. Even a half-competent policeman, assuming there are any, would be able to trace such a knife back from the scene of the crime to the man in blue denim who bought it. A block further east, in Marboro's Book Store, I prowled around the tables of remainders looking for something to read on the bus. I had about given up, when in the back of the store, on a table heaped with paperbacks, I found a stained, bent, and dishonored copy of a thick book entitled *Extraordinary Popular Delusions and the Madness of Crowds.* Across the front someone had scribbled "59¢" in black crayon—about twelve pages per penny. Three blocks west, at Kaufman's Army and Navy Store, I bought a surplus musette bag, into which I stuffed the Sta-Press pants, the sweat shirt, and the hush puppies I had been wearing, the extra sweat socks, *Popular Delusions.* I had lunch on Eighth Avenue, in a workingman's bar, where the rye whiskey is cheap and the sandwiches thick. I had two brisket of beef sandwiches, with lots of horse radish, pickled green tomatoes and cherry peppers on the side.

As it turned out, I needn't have hurried. Only two people were at the gate before me, so I was not going to have any trouble finding a seat by a window, and besides, the bus only arrived three minutes before departure time. I got on the empty bus with a half-dozen others, and took a seat in the first row, on the right (as you look forward), opposite the driver, so I could also look out through the windshield. It takes so many words to say the simplest thing! Wouldn't you know it: the fat woman who puffed her way aboard at the last minute had to sit right next to, and partially on, me. She knew how to keep herself occupied, I'll say that for her. For one thing, she read the *Daily News,* which she held spread out before her, cutting off half my field of vision. She finished it about the time we arrived in Albany, one hundred fifty miles and three hours later. For another, she ate. Complacently, deliberately, steadily, implacably, she transferred a variety of crunchy things from a bottomless paper bag to her mouth, from bag to mouth, from bag to mouth.

I enjoyed the first part of the journey, along Route 9W, while there were at least gas stations to look at. After that we drove through great country, but you couldn't see much of it. I suppose the Thruway is a very safe road, if you don't fall asleep from boredom. I soon began to long for a billboard, an ash heap, anything—the scene of a crash, wrecked cars, and shattered bodies. Well, that's the way the human mind, the kind I happen to have, works. That's what happens to people when you deprive their senses of nourishment. People then begin to imagine horrors, to long for them. When you walk into a dark room it is not golden babies playing on a sunlit meadow you think you see out of the corner of your eye. Nor is it the winking thighs of a ballerina. No, what you think you see is some horror, with salivating chops. If there is nothing to see out there, you begin to see what is in here. If you can't feed on reality, you feed on yourself. When reality stops pressing up against you, you begin to seep out into it. You contaminate it. Nature is interesting; human nature is interesting; and so are the products of the interactions between them. These three categories, in fact, contain all the interesting things in the world. But the denatured nature of the landscaping around the thruway is a soporific. It is no less than a negation of both humanity and nature. I woke up with a start near Kingston when the bus slowed up to go around the burst-open carcass of a deer. *Extraor-*

dinary Popular Delusions and the Madness of Crowds pleased me right
from its Preface, the next-to-last (or penultimate) paragraph of
which I shall quote entire:

> Religious manias have been purposely excluded as in-
> compatible with the limits prescribed to the present work;
> —a mere list of them would alone be sufficient to occupy
> a volume.

Five passengers got out at Albany, including the fat lady.
There remained, then, two other passengers, me, and the driver.
Just before we took off three new passengers got on. With my
seatmate's departure, the outside of my thigh, the one she had
been sitting on, suddenly felt cold. I was not surprised to see
that she had left the *Daily News* behind for someone to get it
back into a readable condition, for no woman has yet learned
how to read a newspaper without shuffling and rumpling the
pages. I suppose feminism will change all that. I don't know
how you feel, but I shall regret the time when women are no
longer endearingly scatterbrained. The front-page headline was
certainly a breath-stopper. The bus driver must have heard the
rattle in my throat, for I caught his eye in the rearview mirror
when I looked up. He probably also saw me bang my head
against the window—which is how I responded to the first
paragraph of the news story that began under the headline and
to one side of a large photograph of the severely beautiful
Detective Kathleen Haggerty. Here is what the headline said:

KARNOFSKY
KILLER KILLED

The story continued on page three. According to spokes-
men for the police, Detective Haggerty, who would not speak
to reporters, had been working undercover and overtime on the
Karnofsky case. Acting upon a tip from an informant, she
located Rosita and Gilbert Nieves, who were cousins, at a mid-
town bar. The police had reason to believe that the Nieves

cousins were the couple, described by witnesses as a prostitute and her pimp, who were seen in the Hilton Hotel at the time of Karnofsky's death. Detective Haggerty won the confidence of the couple with some rounds of drinks. She allowed them to believe that she was a prostitute who had just conned a tourist out of his money. Pretending to be under the influence of alcohol, she engaged the Nieveses in conversation until such time as she was convinced that they were indeed the duo whose movements she had been tracing. When Gilbert Nieves began to appear suspicious, Detective Haggerty drew her sidearm and identified herself as a policeperson. Upon her announcement that both the Nieves were wanted by the police for questioning in connection with the Karnofsky killing, Gilbert lunged for her. Witnesses say that at the same time he shouted "Rosy, beat it!" At some point in time while the two were grappling, Detective Haggerty's gun discharged. Police would not say, and witnesses were not sure, whether the shooting of Nieves was intentional or accidental. In any case, he was hit twice in the lower abdomen. Rosita Nieves made her escape and is still at large. Gilbert died on the operating table. His only words before losing consciousness were "We didn't do it" and a string of obscenities. The bartender told this reporter that he also heard the word "zipper."

There were two other pictures of Kathleen Haggerty on page three. The first, at the head of a brief account of her meteoric career, was taken on the day of her graduation from the Police Academy. Her uniform was spiffy, but her face was unsmiling, her hair was short. The second was taken outside the bar in which Gilbert Nieves had been shot. She was standing hipshot, in velvet hotpants, high boots, and a short jacket of what I took to be silver fox, of the kind my father brought my mother when he got out of the army. Under this jacket, I surmised, she wore a shoulder holster, and in the shoulder holster, a gun. If she was wearing anything else, you could not see it. Her left hand, by her side, was sunk into the curls of a wig, as though she were about to hold up a severed head. Her own black hair was tousled, like a mane. She was glaring straight ahead into the camera, and her expression was decidedly unfriendly. It's just not fair. Why should a woman like that have such shapely, plump, juicy-looking thighs? The kind you long to sink your teeth in, right up to the gums. Her features seemed familiar, perhaps only because they were so classic. I already knew everything contained in a re-cap article on the bottom of the page, except for the fact that *Ms-Chief* was due to hit the news stands on Thursday. Who cared about that? I had other things to occupy me.

Three passengers got off at Schenectady. Two got on. Sure, I could have turned myself in. Sure, my doing so might save Rosy of the Supernal Behind from assassination by Haggerty. It might, but then again it might not. Committing one murder to cover another is not all that unusual, you know. Surely Rosita had enough sense to turn herself in, and with someone present, family, a lawyer, the press. Even a Haggerty would hesitate to shoot her in front of the television cameras. What then? Would the D.A. press charges? Would a grand jury indict? Would a jury of twelve convict? On what evidence? Even if the police framed her, it would be at least a year before she was sentenced—and then there was the appeals process, if her court-appointed lawyer knew anything about how to make a name for himself. I had plenty of time to turn myself in, if it came to that. I could perhaps save sweet Rosy O'Nieves some inconvenience, some months in jail, but the way she was going, she would soon enough have to get used to doing time anyhow. You decide: Was my life a fair exchange for her convenience? And if I went up the river, who was going to protect Bill, or Samantha, or Toby? I convinced myself that the police would ultimately settle for the lesser charges of prostitution and resisting arrest—of which, you might just remember, she was guilty. I am as aware as you that the police are capable of rigging a suicide. Every other week you read how someone on Riker's

Island was supposed to have hanged himself with a shoelace. And I too shudder at the thought of laughing-eyed Rosita at the mercy of all those yardbird dykes. But she was just going to have to take her chances. That's what I was doing. And on top of that, I had to live with my guilt over involving her, whatever her fate, never mind the fate of poor Gilbert, for whom, I remind you, there was no longer anything I could do. Haven't you Christians been saying all along that the torments of conscience are a thousand times worse than the afflictions of the flesh? No, it was clear that I could not allow myself the luxury of a clean conscience. I had too many responsibilities.

Two passengers got off at Amsterdam. Well, I had talked myself into going on (don't always be so sure that you know more about me than I know myself), but what I wanted to do was to find that little Girl with the Pall Malls and put two comforting arms around her. Together we would wait for Haggerty to appear. Together we would show Haggerty what kind of exploding stove she had walked into. Together we would dump Haggerty's corpse on von Plaack's doorstep. But this line of thought was unmanly. Pipe dreams are all right for women and poets, but not for men, who have to make their way in the world as it actually is. Wishful thinking disequips you for the daily struggle that brings home our daily bread. And if you find it too much for your delicate sensibilities to live with regret, with remorse, with guilt, you ought to join a monastery, or get yourself a sex-change operation. That's what we have wives for, to be our consciences. Another passenger got off at Jacksville.

The outskirts of Jacksville and Tannerton overlap. "Last stop," said the driver, as the bus halted at a five-cornered intersection, obviously the center of the town, and I jumped off. Then I jumped on again to retrieve my musette bag from the overhead rack. As I reached up for my bag, I scanned the empty bus. Empty! What was it doing empty? Explain that one, if you can, just explain that. Now, dammit, besides myself and the driver, seven people got on in New York. Five got off at Albany, three got on, leaving five. Three got off at at Schenectady, two got on, leaving four. Two got off at Amsterdam, leaving two. One got off at Jacksville, leaving one. Well, where was he? Or where was she? For I had kept tally only of the grand totals, not of the subtotals of each sex, a serious oversight, obviously. I did not walk down the aisle to see if anyone was hiding behind a seat. Uncertainty is a necessary condition of human existence. Why should I humiliate myself in a vain effort to banish it? Already the driver was looking at me with a thoughtful expression on his face.

On four streets the stores began to peter out about a hundred yards away from the intersection. On North Main Street they straggled on for maybe three hundred yards and around a slow turn. On one of the five corners was a cop, looking over the traffic, from time to time throwing a switch in a metal box that controlled the red light, for it was nearly five o'clock in Tannerton, and people were starting home to their spouses and children, as were millions of other people, from Baffin Island to Miami Beach, from Montauk Point to South Bend. In a world without feminists I would have been among them. I asked the cop how to get to Vandernut Stage, to a place called Pinetop. Three passersby stopped to look and listen.

"What do you want to go there for?" he said, squinting. All along one side of his face and neck was a purple birthmark. He was very tall and thin. Except for the teen-age girls, in fact, almost everybody I had seen was either thin or fat, some very fat. The teen-age girls were just right. A pair of them joined the spectators.

"What's it to you?" I said.

"Ain't no massage parlors up thataway," he said. He looked around with a grin at the circle of interested Tannerton citizens. A fat woman of about twenty-five, who so far as I could see had only one tooth, laughed.

"Is there a taxi?" I said.

"Just left for Jacksville," said the cop. He spoke fast, with some kind of local inflection, so there was always a hiatus before I could figure out what he had said.

"Could I walk it?" I said.

"You got legs, ain't you?" said the cop. The same toothless woman laughed.

"It's about sixteen miles," said a short, thin, oldish man, the look of outrage on his face most likely permanent. I took him for a druggist.

"Seventeen," said the cop.

"Sixteen," said the druggist.

"Patch, someday someone's gonna feed you to the chickens," said a voice behind me. The speaker was a boy of sixteen, maybe. His neck was long and strong. One ear stuck out from his head at about an eighty-degree angle. His right arm was snug around the shoulders of a pretty, dark-haired, very short girl.

"Hoot's fixing to tow a wreck up to Floyd's," he said.

"This gentleman wouldn't want to be seen with Hoot," said the cop. Someone snickered.

"How do I find him?" I said.

The druggist pointed. "Come on," said the boy; "I'll introduce you."

Under the words "HOOT'S GARAGE," painted in black enamel by a shaky hand, were the words "Proptr. Traer Van Houten Gheynst," painted likewise. The owner of the name and proprietor of the garage was in size and shape something like a cross between a rhinocerous and a snowman, except that his face and hands were reddish purple. The brownish red hair on his round head was cropped short. He was bending from the waist, his long and equally wide back and his short legs absolutely straight, to lift up with one hand the intact rear of an otherwise demolished car. Admittedly, the car was not a large one. He was not bent much, for his immense chest and belly would have gotten in the way. With his other hand he was affixing a hook to something under the car. The hook was attached to a chain attached to a winch attached to his wrecker. The boy went over to him. The girl stayed with me, her eyes on the ground. I couldn't hear the boy speaking, and I couldn't make out Hoot's words (as he dropped the car and slowly cranked himself erect, swivelling his head and blinking hugely), but when his lips moved—and they didn't move much—a kind of soft buzz, a sort of low static, filled the air.

"Yeah, he'll take you as far as Floyd's," said the boy as he walked over.

"What's Floyd's?" I said.

"Floyd runs a junkyard about five miles from your father's place," he said.

"How do you know that?" I said.

"I been there," he said.

"No, I mean, how do you know he's, that I'm—," I said.

"He said he expected you'd be along any time now," he said.

"I see," I said. I took out three dollars. "Could I buy you two, er, an ice cream soda or a boilermaker or something."

"No you can't," he said. "I owe your father a favor or two."

"Your father wants Charlie to work for him," said the girl. I saw for the first time that her front teeth were spotted with cavities.

"Doing what," I said.

"I got a way with machines," said the boy.

"Charlie's an orphan," said the girl.

Hoot talked without a break all the way to Floyd's, filling the cab of his wrecker with alcohol fumes. I couldn't make out much of what he said because like the cop he spoke without separating his words, and anyway the words came out of his ruined larynx in a low, rapid, raspy rumble. I couldn't read his lips because they hardly moved. In any case, the sound of his voice did not seem to issue from his lips, but from all around me. Nor was the sound of his voice easily distinguishable from all the others that vibrated through my head. The wrecker rattled, clattered, growled, and murmured amazingly. A mile or two out of town, the road began to go up and up. Each time he changed gear, and that was often (how many gears does one of those things have, anyhow?), the grinding whine of the motor went a pitch higher and a few hundred decibels louder. In the lurch and lull between the seventh and eighth gears, as I reached for the door handle in a sudden vision of us careening backwards down the mountain, I made out the words, "Don't look like any son of Ivan's." Ivan is my father's given name. He was born, you see, shortly after the Russian Revolution.

We passed a house or an unpaved road curving into the woods every half-mile or so. Trees flickered by on either side. The windshield was so dusty and bespotted there was no seeing through it, except for wavering streaks and patches of gray and gray green. I must have fallen asleep watching the splats of insects fill in the spaces between the mud spots. I came out of it when Hoot swung into a driveway. He opened his door, stepped down, slammed the door, and stomped off. I stepped out myself, a little drunk, slightly dizzy, and somewhat shivery, for it was cold. Ahead of me, to the left, was a shack, nicely finished in tarpaper. On my right, a corrugated iron fence ran along the road for seventy yards or so and then turned in. The driveway cut between the shack and the start of the fence, dipped along a downslope, then rose to where I could see two garages that looked as though they had once been stables. I could hear Hoot's voice like a slow buzz saw. In a moment he came out of the first garage, followed by a man and a boy, the three of them splashing through and around mud, tail pipes, inner tubes, broken glass, assorted nuts, bolts, and gears. The man had bow legs and a beer belly. The boy looked like Charlie. "Faith," the man shouted. A woman popped her head out of a shack window, looked at Hoot, looked at me, withdrew, slammed down the window. By the time the three males got to where I was standing, she had come out the door, slammed it, and started toward us, a six-pack of beer in one hand. We waited in silence until she arrived, handed the beer over to the man, clopped back to the house, slammed the door behind her. Then the man handed the rest of us each a can of beer and took one himself, all the while keeping his eyes on me. You couldn't tell anything from his poker face, but I supposed he disapproved of my beard and clothes, at least, but I was too old to start worrying about what hillbillies thought of me. The boy handed us each a Camel and took one himself. We all squatted, puffed, drank.

"First today," said Hoot. The man belched.

"First what?" said the boy.

"You could tell your father I came across a portable forge he might be able to use," said the man.

"I'll do that," I said. I was shivering steadily.

The man nodded, rose, turned, started toward the garages, threw his beer can at a drum, which he missed. Hoot also missed. He took a full can with him into the wrecker and drove off after the man. The boy drop-kicked his can end-over-end into the drum, took my musette bag, and walked over to the shack, against which rested a motorcycle. He strapped on my bag and forward-passed me a helmet. I lateralled my can into the drum. The helmet smelled of perfume. I never got a chance to offer Hoot a tip.

If you have never taken a ride over mountain roads on the back of a motorcycle, I recommend it next time you are trying to think up a form of self-punishment a little out of the ordinary. Make sure your driver is a seventeen-year-old daredevil who steers with one hand while he drinks beer with the other, who takes hairpin turns at sixty miles an hour. Make sure that you have a denim cowboy hat to clutch to your breast with one hand so that you only have one left over to hang on with. Make sure you are wearing thin cotton clothes so that you can feel the full glory of the clean, thin, frigid mountain air. A denim suit will do it. We stopped suddenly, from seventy miles an hour to

zero in about twenty yards, which we traversed neither for-
wards nor sideways, but somewhere in-between. I tried to get
up, but I was stiff with cold. The expression frozen onto my face
must have been that of a man who just realizes he has stepped
not into an elevator, but into the empty shaft. The boy was too
tactful to let on. He helped me off and handed me my bag.

"Can I buy you a tank of gas?" I said.

"Naw, me and my father, we owe Ivan a couple," he said.

"You going to work for him too?" I said.

"I guess you know Charlie," he said.

"Just met him," I said.

"Lucky Ivan was down to Hoot's when Charlie passed
out," he said. "Hoot was getting set to pour water on him. Ole
Ivan really roused them at the hospital. Paid for the mastoid
operation, too. Raised hell when he heard Charlie'd been going
around for a month with an ear ache and nobody did nothing."

I flapped my hat at the cloud of insects that had gathered
around our heads.

"Them is black flies," he said. "You'll get used to them by
the time they're getting ready to leave, come mid-June."

"I don't expect to stay that long," I said.

"I never could understand why anybody'd want to live in
New York," he said. "It ain't safe." And he roared off, his front
wheel two feet off the ground.

The blacktop driveway curved slowly, continuously, end-
lessly, to the right, through a forest of gloomy old pine trees.
Their tops were out of sight, but I could feel them, as a kind of
weight. It was dark in there (cold and damp, too), but I could
see that the ground had been picked clean of deadfall, cleared
of brush, raked free of needles. There were cracked and scrofu-
lous rocks, clumps of fern, patches of moss and of a creeping
springy plant with shiny dark green little leaves. Something
rustled. A big bird (hawk? owl? pterodactyl?) sailed from one
tree to another. Just about the time I had walked what I cal-
culated to be a full circle, the forest ended, abruptly. In one

stride I had moved from deep shadow to bright sunlight, the last of it. The sun was getting ready to set behind a house on a rise about sixty or seventy yards in front of me. Or was it a group of houses, of different sizes and shapes, stuck together, all made of pine logs that glowed goldenly in the sun?

On one side, there was a round tower, three stories high, with a peaked roof sporting a pennant; on the other, a square, squat tower, with slot windows. Between them, as I could now see, was a dozen or so units, square or oblong, of one, two, or three stories, one of them an A-frame, each with its own chimney, their silhouettes complicated by balconies, porches, sun decks, dormers, outside staircases, ramps, and railings. The effect was not of a jumble, but of an organization that would not quite declare itself, or that kept shifting. Immediately to my right, half in the woods, was a large three-walled shed, also made of logs. Inside or in front of it were a pickup truck, a jeep, a couple of cars, farm machinery. Beyond it was an apple orchard and next to that a small field, recently plowed, tilting up away from me and past the house. The field and the orchard were bordered on the far side by big old trees, along which ran a brook of some size, judging by the footbridge. Beyond the bridge was a log cabin, then more pine forest. On my left were a chicken coop, a small barn, both made of logs, a fenced-in pasture running up and over a hill, broken up by a few trees, many rocks, a cow, a creek, a half-dozen horses, chickens. A shot sounded faintly from beyond the house. I took a few steps toward it, heard a sound of sawing, turned sharply to my left, and there was my father, who had been hidden from view by a wedge of pine trees. He hadn't changed much.

He was a little thinner and he moved a little slower than I remembered, and it was hard to tell how much of his hair was blond and how much white. There was still a tuft of it growing out right above his forehead, about where a horn would be. I watched him split and saw for a while. I felt some of my old hate for the ease and economy of his movements, for I had been a clumsy boy, a clumsy man, too, if the truth be known. What I used to hate above all was his patience, especially his patience with me ("Easy does it," he'd say). Or maybe what I hated most were his attempts to encourage me ("Now you're getting it," he'd say as I frantically bent another nail.) In between saws and chops I could hear that he was whistling "Yesterday," a Beatles tune. He stooped, picked up an armful of wood, placed it neatly on a stack, turned, saw me, rested a hand on the stack, said, "It's you."

"It's me," I said.

"Well, well," he said.

"Well, well, well," I said.

"Welcome home," he said. If we had been Italians, we could have thrown our arms around each other's necks, but we weren't, so we didn't. Another shot sounded from behind the house.

"That's Melody," he said. "My girlfriend, shooting varmints."

"What for," I said.

Thus began our first conversation in over twenty years, not what you would call an auspicious beginning. It was not easy for me to forgive my father. For what? For being my father. For my need of his help. For his willingness to give it. For killing my mother. We talked for a couple of hours, he as usual doing most of the talking, while it darkened around us, while the black flies went off to spawn and die (a new generation is born each morning), while we worked a two-man saw now and then to keep warm ("Don't push, just pull," he would say. "Now you're getting it"). Seems my father had grown rich, by my standards, since I ran away from home. Even before then, the Ancient Order of Hibernians had talked him into buying from them a lodge and thirty-five acres of choice Huntington land, on which they had danced, drunk, fought, and played soccer; and a widow with a hankering for Florida coaxed him into buying from her an overgrown golf course in Northport. His credit was good, and in those days he was an instinctive optimist; unlike other men in his situation, he never for a minute feared a return of the Depression. Besides, he had nothing to lose. He designed and built a house on a gorgeous half-acre of oak and mountain laurel. He sold it for $70,000, a lot of money in those days. Half-acre by half-acre, he designed, built, and landscaped himself out of debt and into prosperity. He designed and built some high class restaurants in Greenlawn. He built Carvel stands along the North Shore of Suffolk County; he acquired county contracts and kicked back what he had to, until his toes ached, but he soon gave up that kind of work, there was no fun in it, he was not, after all, particularly trying to make money, he was just trying to keep busy. Remember, he said, he had no wife to entertain, no children at home to worry about. The money just came.

"Why didn't you find yourself a wife?" I said.

"I already been married," he said. "I already done my duty to mankind," he said. "Your mother was a saint," he said.

In 1965 he began quietly to unpack his holdings, piece by piece, his interests in shopping centers, in warehouses, in lumber yards, and at considerable profit. He didn't like the looks of the economy. He didn't like the kinds of contracts he was getting. He didn't like the looks of our involvement in Vietnam. Long Island was turning into a suburban slum around enclaves of the very rich, no place for ordinary decent folks. He had a premonition of disaster, which grew. In 1968 he had a heart attack, and why hadn't he told me?

"Samantha knew," he said.

"You know Samantha!" I said.

"She's called me at least once a month since you were engaged," he said. "And we'd have lunch whenever I came into the City on business."

"Behind my back," I said.

"Samantha values my advice," he said.

"How about my advice!" I said.

"She seems to feel you don't understand her, and she's probably right," he said.

"Did you understand Mama?" I said.

"Your mother was a saint," he said.

"Well, dammit, why the hell didn't Samantha tell me about your heart attack?" I said.

"I wouldn't let her," he said. "I didn't want you to come home until you had your own inner reasons."

"You know about our separation?" I said.

"That's not all I know," he said.

There was another shot from behind the house. In 1969, my father continued, he took the repair of his heart into his own calloused hands and moved north for good, moved onto these 350 acres of woodland and overgrown pasture and orchard given to him in partial payment of a debt by a bankrupt tycoon, who told his other creditors they could squat for theirs. Just for the exercise, he built an addition to the log cabin, which was already in three sections, the oldest dating from the turn of the century. Just to have something to do, he built another, then a couple or three more a year. (He and his men could now put up the shell of a cabin in a week.) Just to keep his mind off the way the country was coming apart, he began to restore the orchard, to clear the pastures. This work did him good. He recovered some of his usual equanimity. A plan came to him: he would make Pinetop self-sufficient, a fortress against the coming days of rage and devastation. Just to keep his money working, he bought into a lumber yard, a quarry, a well-digging outfit, a logging outfit, a sawmill or two. Just to help out some of his new friends who were in financial difficulties, like most of the people in these parts, he took over a firm that sold ready-measured logs for cabins. Just because he liked the style of the company's president, who stopped on her way to Maine for a quick glance at the area's prospects, he acquired the local franchise for Lily-Belle swimming pools and prefabricated saunas. None of these businesses meant anything to him. Making money, it seems, becomes a habit, not that he was making much. The point was to prevent the erosion of his original stake. With taxes and inflation the way they were, you understand—and, all right, he wanted something ready for me to move into when the time came. Besides, the inevitable political and economic collapse might come in stages, rather than all at once, think of ancient Rome . . .

"I know Miss Lily," I said.

"Of course," he said. "A fine woman."

Just before the sun went down, a tractor growled out of the woods, going too fast. It swerved by us, coming far too close, so that the logs it was dragging skidded right up to our toes, and stopped, abruptly. The driver vaulted out of the tractor and unhooked the chains from the logs. He was not very tall, and he did not have much of a waist, but he was as broad and deep of chest as you can comfortably get. His biceps were tight against his fitted western-style denim shirt. His thighs thrust his jeans forward and his calves thrust them back, so that his legs in silhouette were like an S. His brawny back and buttocks swooped or curled into the melodramatic tuck of his waist. He was wearing a cowboy hat and fancy boots, both sort of battered. A cigarillo stuck out from between white, strong-looking teeth, between two of which, nevertheless, I caught a glint of gold.

"Maybe you two remember each other," said my father. How could I forget? I still had a scar where, when he was nine and I was fourteen, Bengt Olson busted open my head with a bottle of Mission Orange Soda, and for no better reason than that I had set free the rabbit he trapped. You may not believe that there were still rabbits in Flushing in those balmy days between the first and second World Fairs, but such is the remarkable fact.

"Looks like folks still can't resist beating up on you," he said.

"But they don't get away with it any more," I said.

"Shake," said my father.

Shaking hands with Bengt Olson is like reaching into a bag of walnuts. I noticed that the top two-thirds of the ring finger on his right hand was missing—which reminded me that he was a lefty, for when a finger is missing from the right hand, it is usually the left that is responsible.

"I always wanted you two to be like brothers," said my father.

"People around here call me Bang," said Bengt-Bang.

"That so?" I said.

Bang and I smoked cigarillos and my father a corncob pipe while the two of them squatted and talked over chores ripe for the doing.

"Those sucklings gotta have their cubes cropped," said Bang.

"Wednesday," said my father.

"Give Victor here a chance to see whether he's cut out for country living," said Bang.

"Don't worry about Victor," said my father.

"I ain't," said Bang, who then vaulted into the tractor, waved, and roared off, leaving a miasma of exhaust behind him.

"Bang's a good boy," said my father, although he seems to have been the first to notice it. At least the judges who on two occasions sent Bang away thought differently. But he had been on his good behavior since my father took him along on the migration to Pinetop, except for the time he shot a man. Miraculously the bullet hit nothing of importance on its way through this clown's chest. Bang's story, and my father believed it, was that this hollow man was trying to steal a deer. Bang lung-shot a good-looking six-pointer, so his story went; it ran a few hundred yards and dropped; when Bang came up, there was a certain headstrong logger, well-known for inflicting damage on bar-room furniture, dressing out the deer. Words were exchanged. The logger levelled his rifle at Bang, who then quick-drew the six-shooter he always carried with him on the hunt. My father convinced the victim it would be worth his while to swear that he had shot himself while looking over Bang's gun. No one but the police believed him, and that's how Bang got his nickname.

Along with Bang on the exodus to Pinetop came his father, his mother, a spinster aunt, and two illegitimate children, to which a third had since been added. At this piece of information I may have sniffed my disapproval, although, like you, I was beginning to feel something like envy for Bang. Apparently he would hardly look at a respectable woman and wouldn't look at the other kind for very long, either. Every time my father introduced him to some nice girl, Bang would scandalize her with a piece of buffoonery, like the time at a dance he slipped a cucumber into his B.V.D.'s. He had looped a string around one end of the cucumber, run it up over his belt and down to his ankle, where he tied it. Every time he took a long step, the cucumber jerked up and out. (When Bang danced, and it wasn't often, he danced snug up against his partner, and long steps were the only kind he took.) After escorting the dazed girl back to his table, he pulled out the cucumber, sliced it up with his jack knife, and ate it.

"Why, he's never grown up," I said.

"It ain't his fault," said my father.

Bang's brother, Bertil, whom my father had sent through college and who lived with his family in Tannerton, was head accountant, overseer, and trouble-shooter wherever Grant money was working. I remembered him as a solemn seven-year-old in short pants and glasses, whose favorite occupation was snitching on Bang. The latter was honcho at Pinetop, and good at his work, so my father said. The trouble was that Bertil wouldn't work with his hands and Bang couldn't work with his head. What's more, they couldn't stand each other. It took a better man than either of them to get the best of them both. And here my father gave me a significant glance.

"Don't look at me," I said, when a teeth-rattling clangor broke out from the house.

"Supper's on," said my father.

Melody turned out to be a well-put-together blonde of thirty with a hairdo. Veal in wine sauce and asparagus do not in my opinion constitute a meal, but Melody subscribed to the common superstition that lean meat and light meals were indicated for people with heart trouble. As I learned later, she worked in a nursing home, where, no doubt, light meals were the rule, but not for medical reasons. Most Saturdays after work she drove up to Pinetop, stayed over on Sunday and on Monday (her day off), then drove home after supper. She would have moved in for good, if my father had allowed it. It was not that she loved him particularly, or even that she was after his money, but that, believe it or not, he represented to her a step up the social ladder; for Melody's ruling passion was to erase the stigma of being the daughter of a man with an aversion to regular employment. But my father never kept company with any woman for over a year—not because he saw much difference among them, but so as not to ruin their chances for marriage with someone else. "Sure," I said. He could fool the local yokels if he wanted, but once you got to know these benevolent dictators a bit, you learned that behind Ivan the Good there is always an Ivan the Terrible. Look, he said: no woman had ever lost through her association with him. He had spent a fortune on dancing lessons for one of them. It wasn't his fault she had no sense of rhythm. He had opened a beauty shop for another. He told her and told her that she shouldn't marry her chief operator, but she couldn't get it into her head that pansies were not that way because they had missed out on the love of a real woman. Did I expect him to live like a monk? To a healthy man women were not a luxury, but a necessity. Remember, he said, my mother was a saint. It was not something he was ever likely to forget. Did I want a stepmother? To the sons, you know, all stepmothers are wicked.

Melody said very little all through supper. She kept shooting sharp, suspicious looks from my father to me, as though we had been plotting against her. At one point she announced to my father, with some kind of challenge in her voice, that if he were to look in the freezer, he would find a squirrel and a woodchuck she had shot, dressed out, skinned, quartered, and packaged. If he wanted to eat overgrown rats, when he could afford filet mignon, it was all right with her, although cutting off their heads and touching the squirrel's claws made her sick to her stomach, no matter how many times her own father had made her do it. And he would have to clean the guns himself, the .22 Marlin (for the squirrel) and the .222 Remington (which knocked over the woodchuck at 50 yards), she hadn't had the time. My father praised her on cue, told her how when the cities were choked with corpses, she would know how to survive, helped her with the dishes, walked her to her car.

I was honored by a visit from my father's vassals, unmistakably come to pay their respects to the heir apparent, namely me. Arne Olson, carpenter, Bang's father, was still pretty much like a plank of knotty pine. He shook my hand without a word, for he was not a man to waste anything. His wife, Astrid, hadn't changed much either. But rake handles never do turn into butterflies, so far as I know. His sister Kristal, sixty, plump, cheerful, and not all there, blushed and said, *"Välkommen hem, Kära du,"* for she often forgot her English, little of it as there was. These three shared a cabin with Ylva, Ebba, and Svea, Bang's three daughters, who courtsied and handed me a bottle of homemade blackberry brandy, with a ribbon around it. Another one of the cabins across the brook was shared by Jack Longhenry and Hank Littlejohn. Jack was bald and Hank was not wearing his false teeth. These two lifelong bachelors had mischievous eyes and immense hands. They gave me a letter knife made from an antler, the handle lovingly carved into the shape of a voluptuous naked woman, also with a ribbon around it. Bang, who occupied a third cabin, gave me nothing but a raised eyebrow and a satirical grin.

My father and I sat up before a slow fire in a room, above the entrance to which was a brass plaque that said "Library," as though you might otherwise think it was the first butler's second gazebo. He had gotten into the habit of spending two or three hours there every night, reading I suppose. Half the shelves were empty. On the others were complete editions of Victorian novels, Harvard Classics, and other venerable bores, from Virgil on, many books on farm husbandry, game cookery, soil chemistry, home medicine, blacksmithing, handloading, spinning, weaving, tanning, and woodcraft. There was also, surprisingly, a good collection of children's books, including *Green Eggs and Ham,* and a fancy edition of Burton's *Arabian Nights.* And there was a shelf of the ancient philosophers and historians, another of Americana. My father asked me if some time when I had a minute or two I would write him out a list of the thousand best books ever written. I said that I didn't know too much about serious literature between Homer and Ryder Haggard, but that with the help of a learned friend (Bill), I would do what I could. When, months later, I put the question to Samantha, she immediately replied "Emily Dickinson's *Complete Poetry,* in three volumes." Not being much of a poetry reader, especially when the poetry is written by New England spinsters with a yen for minsters, I had to take her word for it. Did you know that homemade blackberry brandy goes down slick as ice cream?

My father's harangue, being half-baked, was a little harder to digest. But that's the way it is with autodidacts. (The word means "self-taught.") And I'll ask you to remember that I have a Bachelor of Arts degree from Columbia University. Nothing on any diploma says anything about the School of General Studies, if that's what you want to know, and if the Columbia College brats don't like it, they can take their fathers' money off to Vassar. A society, said my father, is like a ball of yeasty dough in a fine mesh bag. The dough is mankind. The yeast, which makes the dough active and gaseous and straining against the mesh, stands for the passions of the human heart. The crisscross strings of the bag represent all that holds a society together: institutions, laws, understandings, habits, sentiments. Some of these are conscious, some not, just as some of the strings are visible, some sunk in the dough. No one invented the bag. It was implicit in the dough from the beginning. In fact, it *is* dough, spun out and hardened. The dough excreted the bag as a spider excretes its web. Sooner or later, every such network of inhibitions begins to show signs of wear. A strand snaps here, another unravels here, a whole row runs there. At first, the dough spins out patchwork with a kind of shy enthusiasm, happy, you might say, to expend some of the energy that kept it churning. But spokes begin to pop all over. The dough thrashes about like a sack full of cats. In an attempt to contain itself, it spurts out filaments of its own substance in all directions. The bag has lost its symmetry. It no longer looks like the system of latitudinal and longitudinal lines on a map of the globe. It looks more like a much frayed, ripped, and mended body stocking, eleven sizes too small for the circus Fat Lady with hiccoughs and a twitch who is wearing it. When the rate of breakage exceeds the rate of repair, the dough gives up, humps sullen, quivering, as a laboratory rat that has been frequently shocked and seldom rewarded soon ceases to jump. The energy once discharged in the excretion of restraints is converted into inner turbulence. The dough throbs and quakes. Finally, it boils through the gaps in the network. It erupts in the form of private madness and mass panic, religious quackery and political terrorism, hedonism and asceticism, pointless chicanery among the great, haphazard violence among the little, general demoralization, sexual perversion, breakdown of the family, mistreatment of children, disrespect for fathers. The final outcome is anarchy and revolution and civil war, or conquest from without. It has happened many times before and it is happening here, now . . .

"You sleepy?" said my father.

"Mumph. What? No. Sleepy? Not a bit," I said.

"I am describing to you the world you live in," he said. "You have to understand it, if you want to deal with it; otherwise, it will deal with you." I was not awake enough to argue, but in my opinion, you do not need to understand a shuttlecock to swat it.

In America, he said, the dough has been hyperactive from the beginning, the bag haphazardly patched together from remnants and synthetics. From the beginning American character has been an unstable mix of two dispositions, each made more volatile by the presence of the other. These are the prophetic and the pragmatic. A classic instance of the prophetic American would be Jonathan Edwards. A classic instance of the pragmatic American would be Benjamin Franklin. In the middle of the second half of the twentieth century, a would-be Ben Franklin becomes a Richard Nixon. Jonathan Edwards degenerates to Charles Manson. Richard Nixon and Charles Manson are our representative men. We created them; they polarize each other. Nothing can prevent the forces they exemplify from tearing us apart.

"I guess you better go to bed," said my father.

I may not have been as sleepy as my father thought. My theory is that people predict what they desire. People who predict a universal cataclysm lust for it. My lusts are different. All I wanted was my Samantha back.

The room above the library ("Bedroom," said the plaque) was warm from the fieldstone chimney that rose from the fireplace below. There was also a cast-iron stove packed with paper and kindling ready for the match. Although laid out as a bedroom for two, it was furnished with many of the things I had left behind me when I walked out of our home on Roosevelt Avenue for good. There was my radio, my books by Edgar Rice Burroughs, thirty-nine of them, *Dracula*, the complete tales of Poe, the bedspread knitted by my mother, the desk built by my father, the crossbow constructed by me. There was even, in a sneaker-box at the back of the closet, my pornographic cards and photos, cartoons and pamphlets—far more difficult and risky to collect during the dark days of the early fifties than the butterflies and stamps that satisfied ordinary boys. Instead of reading *Popular Delusions,* I spent a nostalgic half-hour looking these over before I put out the light.

Just for the fun of it, pretend there was something to my father's exposition: Would you describe me as prophetic or pragmatic?

VIII

AT 6:30 A.M., when New York ladies of the night are snuggling into the arms of their fancy men, my father woke me by tickling my foot, which is how he used to do it twenty years before. Bang joined us for breakfast. I ate more of the homemade sausages and he ate more of the homemade bread and cheese, but I'll bet I ate more altogether. The coffee, I assume, came from a store. Bang's chore for the morning was to show me around. Mine was to go with him. My father's was to make the rounds of his businesses, which would just about run themselves, he said, if only those chronic bankrupts he had for partners would be satisfied to sit on their thumbs. He was going to have to build them a golf course, buy them lessons too. That's how smart companies got their executives out of the way.

"This here's a woodworking shop," said Bang, holding open the door of a log shed, inside of which was Arne Olson humped over some yellow birch that he was twisting into a chair. "This here is a metal shop,"—and this here is a bee hive, and this here is a sugarbush, where you make maple syrup, and this here is a cider press, where you press cider, and this here is a smoke house, where you smoke, and this here in the side of a hill is an earth cellar, which stays pretty near fifty degrees all year around, and which was well stocked with sauerkraut and canned tomatoes and root vegetables and pickled meat and pickled pickles and which could serve as an air-raid shelter, if the time came. "Seen enough?" said Bang, when Floyd arrived with the forge.

"I'll prowl around on my own," I said.

Yep, just as I had thought: those *were* three army surplus machetes hanging next to the broken scythe in the barn. I buckled on the one with the least mold on its sheath and belt, every man his own security blanket. The machete only broke the back of a straw I threw into the air, so I took it to the metal shop and put a very pretty hollow-ground edge on it. A clogged and rusty file on the earth floor behind the lathe gave me an idea. No reason why the bounty of Pinetop should not include an untraceable knife. But in my fear of someone walking in on me, I worked too fast. The file burnt my fingers, dropped, chipped. I stuck it into the floor, tang end first, and pounded it out of sight. I started again with a new file; my father could afford it. I worked slowly, grinding, dipping the file in a bucket of water, grinding, dipping, grinding, until I snapped out of the trance. I had ground too much off one side. As much off the other side would leave me with something good for flipping flapjacks, maybe, but not for fending off a maddened feminist. I pounded it into the floor. I put a new grinding wheel on the lathe, for I had worn the old one down to its nub. I could not find another ten-inch file, so I settled for a twelve-incher. On the back of a piece of sand paper I traced the outline of the file. Then I drew in a homely, but serviceable design: five-inch handle, seven-inch blade, double edged for two inches from the point; 1 1/8 inches wide; 3/8 of an inch think. Then I got back to my grinding, which requires more concentration than you would think.

"What are you playing at," said Bang from the doorway.

"I needed a manicure," I said, at the same time adroitly slipping the file up my sleeve.

"Think you can manage your own lunch?" he said.

"I can manage yours too, if you'd like," I said.

"Better not risk it," he said. "I got work to do."

I did not fuss over lunch. I just pried the pigs' knuckles out of a mason jar, smeared them with hot mustard, crunched them down, for I was in a hurry to get back to my grinding. I rushed over to the metal shop, flung open the door, and stopped short. There was Bang, with his shirt off, working out with a big, old axle, in lieu of a barbell. Oh, all right, yes, he was stronger than me, and what of it? When he saw me, he slowly lowered the axle and slowly straightened up. He was reddened from exertion, so I could not tell for sure, but I do believe he was blushing. Poor Bang: no doubt he wanted the world to believe that all those muscles came from ferocious thoughts.

"What are you playing at?" I said. "Is this the work you had to do? I won't disturb you, then," and I tiptoed off.

In the wood shop, now empty, I found a piece of yellow birch about the right size, peeled it, and began to whittle a handle for my knife. I also began to understand why craftsmen always have a smug and self-satisfied air about them. At two o'clock my father interrupted me to announce that he was home and that he was going to take a nap. By three o'clock I was back in the metal shop grinding away; around four o'clock, for the sake of variety, I hacked out a fingerguard from a piece of an old brass lock. Near five o'clock my father interrupted me to ask if I wanted to help him cut firewood, something he did every day to keep his aorta unclogged. Just after six, Bang came by with a rifle, for I had asked him if he would teach me how to shoot straight.

"Woodchucks are feeding," he said.

"I wouldn't want to kill anything," I said.

"Then stay away from guns," he said. "Killing's what

they're for." Maybe you can think of an answer to that one; I couldn't.

"This here is a Weatherby Mark V bolt action rifle," he said. "These here are .22-250 Remington cartridges, as good as you can get, if its varmints you're after." Whether I was after them or they were after me was a question. "The 55 grain slug leaves the muzzle at a velocity of 3810 feet per second, carrying 1770 foot pounds of energy, unless you handload and heat them up, which I don't do with these. You can rely on it up to 300 yards." What I was interested in was something you could rely on up to 30 inches, but I didn't say anything. "This here is a 3x-9x Leopold Vari-X AO Scope. Here, hold it like this, about three inches from your eye, and turn this till the reticle comes in sharp."

"What's the reticle?" I said.

"The cross hairs," he said. "Okay. You work the bolt like this. No, since you're right-handed, you work it like this. You load up like this. You release the safety like this. Now you're ready to shoot."

"This your gun?" I said.

"Your father's," he said. "This particular model doesn't come in a .22-250 for lefties. My own varminter is a Savage 99C lever action, a shade less accurate, but a lot more convenient. Here, let me make sure its sighted in."

He sat on the ground, legs spread, and braced his elbows on the inside of his knees. "See that tree, there, in the corner of the field?" he said. "See the the chickens under it, pecking horseshit?"

"Wait," I said. "What are you going to do?"

"That big Red way on the right is eighty, oh ninety, yards away," he said.

"Bang, don't," I said. He took his time aiming, then fired. The blast would have made me wince anyhow, even if I had not seen the chicken's head disappear in a splatter of stuff I could not make out, thank God. The chicken jumped straight up, its wings flapping, scrambled a few steps, fell forward, rolled over, kicking, flapping, and spurting loops of blood, thrashed onto its feet, lunged sideways, landed on its neck, tumbled, flapped this way and that, for a long time, while we walked toward it.

"You didn't have to kill that chicken," I said.

"Lot easier on the chicken if you kill it before you pluck it," he said. "Gotta eat, don't you? If you don't kill what you eat, someone else has to do it."

He picked up the chicken (its feet still quivering), and cleaned it with three strokes of his jack knife and a yank, though I did not look very closely. "Never cared too much for giblets," he said.

We sneaked along a stone fence bordering the beyond pasture, staying low, Bang scattering glances around like Chinchingook, or whatever his name is. "There," said Bang.

"Where?" I said.

"Right there," he said. "On the fence, damn it! No, on *that* fence, crossing into this one. There."

"I don't see it," I said.

"Here, prop your elbows here, and run your scope along the top of the fence," he said. I did, twice, and saw a lot of stones, but nothing else. On the third run I noticed what at first looked like a distant megalith on a pile of ruins. It was a woodchuck all right, standing on its hind legs, leaning forward a little, paws at its sides; it now looked like a suspicious old farmer's wife, apron still on, listening to a tale of woe from a tramp.

"She's a hundred twenty-five yards away, or there abouts," he said. "Your point of aim is two hundred. Aim at her belly button and you ought to hit her under the breastbone." I did not, of course, know where a woodchuck's navel was, but I knew where Erika von Plaack's was, assuming she was built like other women. For the fun of it, I tricked out the little farmer's wife in boots, leather skirt, silver fox, and a blonde wig. "Okay," Bang said. "Get the butt snug against your shoulder. Left forearm straight up and down. Release the safety. Take a breath. Hold it. Squeeze." I squoze, squeezed rather, and nothing happened.

"You got your finger on the trigger guard," said Bang.

"Oh," I said, and moved my finger. The gun went off. Somewhere across the field the bullet ricocheted off something, howling like a banshee.

"Singe your eyebrows, did you?" said Bang.

"I have just decided that firearms are not my *métier*, " I said. "You got a boomerang I can practice with?"

"You ain't a quitter, are you?" he said. "What would your father say? Anybody tell me Ivan's son is a quittér, I'd flatten him."

I was surprised to see that the woodchuck had not moved a hair, except for the smirk on its face. I took a long aim, holding my shot for when the cross hairs wavered back to the wood-chuck's midsection. It stood still, daring me. I fired again, again, again. "Why doesn't the dopey thing make its getaway?" I said.

"You got her charmed," he said. "That sometimes happens."

He gave me ten cartridges, five for the gun and five for my pocket. My orders were to slide over the fence and crawl toward the woodchuck on elbow, belly, and knees, shooting once every ten yards till I scored. It seemed unlikely that the stupid beast would stay put for this barrage, but my knowledge of wood-chuck psychology was limited, nor have I since labored to make up the deficiency. So I squirmed ahead, shooting every ten yards, but nothing else happened, except that I got a layer of cold mud over the front of my denim jacket and pants and my rugby-style shirt, and except that once the nervy beast flicked an ear. Naturally, I became furious at it. "Die!" I'd say as I shot. "Don't go for your hole, Erika baby," I'd say as I crawled. "Your demon lover is on his way." I was just raising the rifle for my tenth shot, from about twenty-five yards away, gritting my teeth, cursing, saying "Die, die, die," when I felt a tap on my shoulder. You can imagine my surprise. It was Bang, who obviously had not been crawling.

"Might be a case of instant *rigor mortis,*" he whispered. "Just to be sure, I'll circle around and come up on her from behind the fence. Stay put for three minutes, then walk slowly right at her. Better take out your machete in case she goes for your throat. They'll do that when they're cornered." He was the expert, after all, so I did what he said, rifle in the left hand, machete at ready in the right. The woodchuck never moved until I was close enough to reach out and tickle it with the machete, when it leaped. I yelped, put up an arm to protect my eyes, back-pedalled, hit a rock, sat down in a puddle of mud. The gun went off, but I hardly noticed. When nothing happened, I peeped over my arm, and there was the woodchuck, a foot away from my face. "No," I said, and dropped back, flat out in the soup, resigned to the fact that any second a rabid rodent would be chewing and clawing through my arm to my eyes. Again nothing happened, so I peeped out again. The woodchuck was still a foot from my face, obviously falling toward me in slow motion. But it never landed, so I took another peep. There it was, miraculously suspended in the air a foot from my face, its paws reaching for me, as Jude's hands had reached. I did not pass out, I insist on that, but I did let my head drop back and my arms flop out to either side, rifle and machete still in my hands, and I closed my eyes. I cautiously opened them. Then I saw a spot of blood under the woodchuck's shoulder. Then I saw it had a long, thin, rigid tail, not a tail, but a stick. Then I saw that the far end of the stick was in a hand, a left hand. Then I saw Bang's face, grinning diabolically. Then I saw it all. Bang had shot the woodchuck earlier in the day, impaled it on a stick, and propped the stick against the back of the fence.

"Peek-a-boo," he said.

"Is he dead?" said another voice.

"Just resting," said a third.

Bang withdrew the woodchuck, and I rose after it, as though our noses had been attached by an invisible string. Beyond the woodchuck and behind Bang were what for an instant I took to be the busts of Jack Longhenry and Hank Littlejohn perched on the fence. They climbed over.

"Just like Lazarus," said Jack Longhenry.

"Lazarus didn't have no machete," said Hank Littlejohn.

They grabbed me each under an arm and lifted.

"Look at that," said Jack Longhenry. "He's camouflaged on both sides."

"Good thing, too," said Hank Littlejohn. "Nothing gets a woodchuck madder than someone wearing baby blue."

"That so?" said Jack Longhenry.

"Scientific fact," said Hank Littlejohn.

Bang was inspecting the woodchuck, turning it on the stick, as though to see whether it had cooked evenly. "Fourteen shots and fourteen misses," he said. "At least you're consistent."

"Then who nicked its ear?" I said.

"What?" he said. "Nicked, huh, huh, huh. Well, I'll be, heh, heh, heh. You're right, ha, ha, ha. Nicked, ho, ho, hoo, its, hah, hah, hah, ear, hoo, ho, ha, HAH, HAH, HOO, HOO, HOOO, its EEEEAR." He grew red in the face, he shed tears, he leaned back against the fence and slid down until his rump touched the ground, too weak from laughter to stand, I suppose. One end of the stick went into the soft ground. At the other end the woodchuck hung like an ensign.

"Hee, hee, hee," said Jack Longhenry.

"Hee, hee, hee," said Hank Littlejohn.

I failed to see what was so funny. Besides, although I agreed with Melody that a woodchuck was just another kind of rat, the thought of Bang impaling it made me queasy, and if you think the woodchuck's prior death makes any difference, you have no more imagination than Bang. All sympathy for one's fellow beings starts with an imagination.

I about-faced and stalked off. After a half-dozen steps, on an impulse out of the blue, I whirled and released the machete with a neat side-arm flick of the wrist. It moved through the air like an overhead fan slipped from its moorings. It put a space between the woodchuck's head and its shoulders easy as a toff doffs his derby, nor did it pause to say "How do?" That shut them up. I about-faced again and strode off.

Thus it is that a normally tender-hearted man is goaded into bloody-mindedness. I couldn't help it: a titter escaped me: you should have seen how Bang jumped when the woodchuck's head plopped into the crown of his Stetson.

My father was hustling around the kitchen, setting the table, whistling a Beatle tune (called "Norwegian Pine," or something like that). "Venison stew," he said when I lifted the lid of the dutch oven to see what smelled so good. "I knew you'd take to working on the land," he said, looking me over. "You'll find a clean work suit in my dresser. The master bedroom, right above us," and he pointed toward the ceiling.

The shirt fit, but the pants were a size too large. The stew was perfect: big chunks of venison, tender squares of slab bacon, whole small carrots, onions and turnips, sparse cubes of parsnip, lots of pepper. This evidence of my father's class made me proud. It pleased me, I mean, that he had not padded out the stew with potatoes or vulgarized it with wine. What pleased him was that everything except the pepper was right off his land. I was only able to sneak a glance at the *Tannerton Times,* all eight pages of it, before I was lead into the Library, a captive audience of one. (Chuck Colson had pleaded guilty to obstruction of justice, as well he might; Rosita Nieves was still at large; the Reverend Walter F. Schide, Pastor of the Gilder Bible Church, said that it was not the children attending Christian schools who were being sheltered from reality, but the others: "The teaching of evolution shelters students from the real answers about the origins of the universe"; the Millville-Smuggleton Lawn Ornament Gang had burgled a plaster duck).

What we call reality, said my father, is not found, but made, and not by poets. It was not designed by anybody, God, man, or woman. It was not built on any plan. It is a by-product of the things we do together. It is the sense of things we have in common by virtue of the things we do in common. It comes into being at the same time and in the same way as the institutions, laws, understandings, sentiments that constitute society. This commonsense reality is the only reality that counts for much. If you are not insane, the degree of reality of a thing depends on the number of people you come across who act as though they believe in it. It does not depend on the number of people who think they believe in it, or on the number of people who are aware that they think they believe in it. Very little of what goes for reality is made up of anything so definite as a belief or an idea. Most of it is more like a network of tacit assumptions, of unconscious expectations, of felt dispositions to do this or that. It is what we take for granted. It is the shadow cast on the dough by the mesh bag that contains it.

Now what happens, he said, refilling our glasses, when the strings go pop?

"Women become feminists," I said.

"Feminism, . . ." he said. "Feminism, . . ." and he lifted a finger, the look on his face that of a sage on the verge of a sneeze. He shrugged. "A tempest in a teapot."

"It shipwrecked my marriage," I said.

"A landlubber was at the helm," he said. "Feminism has nothing to do with Samantha's leaving you. You lack a sense of proportion on the subject. Samantha told me how hysterical you used to get."

"I did not," I said.

"Women are always feminists. That is one of the things you still have to learn."

"Was Mom a feminist?" I said.

"Your mother was a saint," he said.

"She never had a chance to be anything else," I said.

"Well, you may have a point about feminism," he said. He could afford to be judicious. His wife was not in the hands of fiends with designs on her body and soul. At least, I trust not. He raised a finger again. "Normally, the innate feminism of women is contained by the mesh bag—which, you understand, is only a metaphor for the institutions, laws—"

"You don't say," I said.

"A state of mind may be personal, private, or public," he said. "Normally the inbred feminism of women is personal and secret, and therefore mad, by definition. Sometimes it expresses itself privately, that is, domestically; only their husbands and children are exposed to it. But when things fall asunder, it goes public. It erupts into politics. It comes out of the closet, so to speak. The reason is—"

"Yeah, I know," I said: "the strings are unstrung."

"The reason is that neither men nor women believe in womanliness. No one knows what it is, even. It no longer has its place in a network of secure definitions we take for granted. When men no longer value what women do, women no longer want to do it. They become feminists."

"What is to be done?" I said.

"There is nothing to be done," he said. "But you might try sympathy."

"Why encourage them?" I said.

"Then neither assist, nor resist," he said. "Just act like a man. Act like a man anyhow, but maybe while you are at it you'll polarize the females around you into womanliness. Samantha—"

"Are you insinuating—?"

"Feminism will pass," he said. "All things do. Of course nothing will ever be the same again. But then nothing ever is. Things won't change much, however. In the long run they never do."

"In the short run?" I said.

"Stay out of their way," he said.

"Is that what you're doing here?" I said. "Staying out of the way?"

"What I am trying to do here is rehabilitate reality." And on that strong line he got to his feet and marched to the kitchen, from which I could hear doors slamming. I was in no mood to take the blame for his being in a snit. Stay out of their way, he said. I expect you to answer this question honestly: who had gotten in whose way first: me in their's or they in mine? My father came back from the kitchen mumbling about how he could have sworn there was a jar of pig's knuckles in the refrigerator. In one hand he had a plate of cold meatballs and sausages, in the other, a plate of cheese and limpa cut in wedges.

"What's in these meatballs?" I said.

"Black bear and pork," he said. "Now you listen to me."

"That's what I've been doing," I said.

"And you might stop answering me like a snotty thirteen-year-old," he said.

"Dad, the world is not coming to an end," I said. Black bear or not, the meatballs were delicious. Where did he learn to put ginger in them? "One of the things wrong with the world is that so many people are predicting its demise. You've got the sickness you think you're trying to cure."

"Do you deny? . . ." he said, waving a finger. "Under the best of circumstances there is a madman bottled up inside each of us. The pressure of times like these pops his cork. He becomes the presiding genius of the times. There are always Charles Mansons. It is only in times like these that he finds followers. There are always Richard Nixons. It is only in times like these that he becomes president. There are always murderous impulses. It is only in times like these that everybody feels free to act upon them."

I choked on a meatball. My father pounded my back, but he kept on talking, never mind that I was helpless to answer.

"Do you deny," he said, "that there are no longer common-sense notions of sane and insane, right and wrong, true and false? Do you deny that people no longer know what to believe about anything? Do you deny that people no longer know what to expect from anyone or what is expected from them? Everybody is gullible and full of doubt, nihilistic, and self-righteous, self-assertive and ill at ease. Nobody knows what the appropriate behavior is, no matter what the occasion. Nobody knows how to do anything. People don't know how to make anything or how to use what they've got. They don't know what to eat or how to cook it. They don't know what to wear or where to live or how to furnish their playpens. They don't know whether to have kids or how to raise them. They don't know how to court their women or whether to marry them. They don't know how to entertain themselves or each other. They don't know how to keep themselves clean and healthy. They don't know what health is. They don't know how to mourn their dead, damn them. What do you think of the fact that the fastest growing academic discipline is the social pseudo-science of thanatology? They don't know all the things that every illiterate peasant or stone age grub-eater knows without ever having to think about it. They don't even know how to *fuck*—without reading a book on the subject. There's a how-to-do-it book on everything from how to bamboozle your boss to how to wipe your ass, and they're all wrong. They have to be. You can't learn how to live from a book. You have to learn from example. No, what you just called "the world" is precisely the reality we put together in common, and nobody believes in it anymore. That world, and there ain't no other, *is* coming to an end."

I suppose my father learned how to put a diatribe together from his readings in the ancient writers. They put a high value on rhetoric, I understand. For a reconstructed carpenter, he was pretty fluent. I was impressed, but not convinced. Reality had never been a problem to me; nor is it now. If you can touch it, it's there; if not, it's in your mind. That is as good a fiction to live by as any other. I had a tough time falling asleep, not because I felt the bed collapsing under me, but because every time I closed my eyes I saw that woodchuck hanging over my face. The woodchuck that kept me awake was only in my mind, but whoever said that a thing in the mind has no effect on the rest of you? Not me. Ever have a wet dream?

I would have gotten up early if anyone had bothered to wake me. I put on the green work clothes, the pants hanging down in back as though someone had amputated my rump. And I put on my poor battered, muddy, hushpups. I did not strap on the empty machete case, it being my policy to leave symbolic gestures to those incapable of any other kind, assuming there is another kind. After a breakfast of scrambled eggs and four little trout from the freezer, I walked out into a solid wall of black flies, for it is a peculiarity of theirs to prefer muggy, overcast weather. My father and Bang were splitting stones and dripping sweat and swatting flies. They would start with a stone about the size of a bass drum and whack it along a seam with a twenty-pound hammer, until finally, after many whacks, it opened like a hungry clam. There were perhaps a dozen slabs of stone six or eight inches thick strewn around them, a pile of bags of cement to one side, and next to the cement an area (big enough to play half-court basketball on) that had been cleared, desodded, and levelled. I guessed right away that they were going to lay the stones for a patio, but I will leave it to you to guess what they could possibly want one for.

"Need any help?" I said.

"We're about to break for lunch," said my father.

"I just ate," I said. "It so happens that I neglected to bring an alarm clock with me."

"Well, join us for coffee," he said.

"I had some," I said.

"Have some more," he said.

"I'll join you after your nap, maybe," I said.

"Going hunting?" said Bang. I was tempted to point out that the man he shot was still walking around, whereas my game was dead and by now buried, but avengers learn how to do without these easy triumphs along the way. Silence, secrecy, and cunning—wasn't that Joyce Kilmer's motto?

In the metal shop I cut the tang off the file, ruining two hacksaw blades in the process. I then ground and filed and emory-papered an eighth of an inch off each edge of the bottom five inches of the file, the tang-to-be of the knife as distinct from the tang-that-was of the file, although to speak of file and knife is in the one case anachronistic and in the other premature. I slipped only once, and not very far, but enough to grind smooth the prints on three fingers of my right hand. I then filed the piece of brass I had hacked out of a lock into an elegant and elongated teardrop, and without accident, for you cannot call a blister an accident. Then I drilled overlapping holes in the center of the teardrop, along the long axis, until I had room enough to fit in a small file for squaring out a slot. The drills, which kept breaking, must have been cheap, but I had still wrecked enough tools to pay for one of the daggers lifted from Agamemnon's tomb. We will not speak of the price of Band-Aids. When the slot was as snug on the tang as a noose on a witch (the humane English used to hang, rather than burn, their witches), I epoxied the guard in place. I glued it, that is to say, around the tang and up against the bottom of the blade, which was, of course, a quarter of an inch wider than the tang. You really should be able to follow this. It's perfectly clear to me. Maybe you ought to look up the word "tang." I then glued two brass washers I made (for shock absorption and for looks) around the tang and to the underside of the guard. I would have made a third washer, but I ran out of small drills. I then glued the two halves of the birch handle on either side of the tang and up against the lowest washer, and if you cannot follow this, how do you make out your income tax? I will not insult either of us by drawing you a picture. If words are not enough, nothing is. By my rough calculation, a word is worth a thousand pictures. That is why painters are so neurotic. With four small clamps still a-clamping (two a-squeeze on guard, washers, and handle halves, so that their little molecules would bond, and two keeping the handle halves intimate with the tang between them), I drilled three holes through the handle of what we are almost ready to call a knife. Finally, I tapped in three lock rivets, and by the holy sweat of Hephaestus, I had me a prophylactic against feminists as potent as a cross is against vampires. A test jab of only moderate force put an inch and a quarter of the point into a pine log. What law is it that decrees a knife must go in easier than it comes out?

I smuggled knife and clamps, some sandpaper and emory paper, some steel wool and a file up to my room, for there were still finishing touches to be put on; there are always finishing touches still to be put on. I was just stuffing it all into the musette bag, when there was a knock on the door. "Up and at 'em," said my father. "We're going to make sopranos out of some pigs." Mutilating baby pigs is not my notion of how to spend an afternoon, but being a dutiful son (from time to time), I went along.

Bang was waiting outside with a pan of boiled leftover seed potatoes and buttermilk in his right hand and an evil pair of shears in his left. One blade was straight and the other was hooked, like a finger that summons. This second blade is the one I did not like the looks of. Around the pig pen, in which you could have fit two tennis courts, was a split rail fence, for decoration I assume. Inside this fence, attached to its two lower rungs, was another of heavy woven wire, the bottom of which was sunk in the ground, for pigs, like other prisoners of war, have a propensity to dig tunnels. In the center of the pen was something like an overgrown dog house, made of logs, for a change. To one side was a roof on four log posts, for shade. Under this was a trough, now empty. Here and there were old tires and bowling balls for the pigs to exercise their noses on. My father had opened and diverted a spring so that it ran diagonally through the pen. It crossed a shallow pool with a concrete bottom, for the pigs to wallow in. Pigs don't sweat, you see. (Why don't you just try yourself to re-write the next-to-last, or penultimate, sentence, so as to avoid the rhyme, but without using more words. I'll bet you can't. At least I managed to tuck "shallow" and "wallow" away in positions of light stress.)

"Hogs usually have litters of eight—twice a year if you let them," said my father in the tone he used for lecturing at me. It would have been interesting to eavesdrop on a conversation between him and Jude Karnofsky, but that was no longer possible, not in this world. Maybe I could get Butch to call her spirit back for a panel discussion with my father on futurology. "What we got here," he said nodding to a heap of little fellows shouldering each other to get at their mother's teats ("Rumpff," she said), "is five males and three females. We are going to castrate three of the males, for eating, and keep two, for breeding." ("Wheenk," said a tyke as he was dislodged from a teat.) "This is our first try at raising our own from birth. Up to now we'd buy us a shoat in spring and slaughter it come late fall, about two hundred-fifty pounds' worth." ("Week, week," said the tyke, burrowing for a place.) "All we got left from last year's is a jar of pickled knuckles around somewhere. It's not really economical to breed your own, not with the kind of winters we get up here, certainly not on a small scale, but we want to find out how it's done against the time when we got no choice." (The sow lifted her head, looked at us, said "Howruff," dropped her head.) "The time may be coming when you can't just go and pick out a plump weaner anytime you feel like it, and the only way to learn how to do something is to do it." The sow, apropos of nothing, suddenly scrabbled ponderously to her feet, trampling her young in the process. "Squee. Squeeeii," they said.

"Come with me and be my love," said Bang, and he gave the sow a slap on the rump that made dust fly. ("Ronk," she said) "Don't be coy, now. Here's something to make your little heart go pit-a-pat. Guaranteed to do wonders for your complexion, too." And she followed Bang, or rather the pan, which he held an inch ahead of her nose, up the gradual slope of the wooden ramp and into her boudoir. There was a sound of abandoned slurps and contented grunts, and Bang ducked out, in his hands a hammer and two boards, which he quickly nailed across the doorway. The piglets milled on the ramp behind him, trying to get in. The sow's nose appeared between two boards with a snuff and a ruuuunnnk. "That ought to keep you home where you belong," he said, and patted her on the nose.

"Maybe you ought to put on a crosspiece," said my father.

Bang gripped a board and pulled. "These'll hold her," he said. "Be good, now," he said to the sow, turned, squatted, picked up a suckling, lifted the tail, looked under, said, "Pass, sister," and let her squeeze in under a board. He picked up another, looked, said, "You, sir, are wanted for questioning," and handed him to my father. He selected two more males, tucked them under his arms like footballs, and carried them over to the fence, where on a stump was a roll of cotton, a peanut butter jar, a bottle of alcohol, and a tube of salve. He pulled out a length of clothesline, tied one end of it around one sucker, looped it through the fence, tied the other end around the other. "Squeewink," it said. "There, there," said Bang. "Soon all your little worries will be over. The big ones, too, for that matter. Before you even have them."

While Bang poured alcohol into the jar, my father flipped his piglet on its back, two of its feet tight in each hand. He pressed its hind legs up against its chest. Bang dipped a wad of cotton into the alcohol and swabbed its white, scared-looking thighs. All three little pigs were still, but a groinnk from the house had an unmistakable note of suspicion in it. Bang got out his pocket knife and opened the small blade. "Prepare yourself," he said. "I am about to improve your morals." I could feel my scrotum shrink and my anus crimp. He dunked the blade into the alcohol. "This will hurt me more than you," he said. With two heat strokes he made a short, straight cut high up on the inside of each thigh. The testicles popped out like a couple of seedless grapes. There was hardly any blood. The pig lay as though under a spell. Bang slid his right hand under the testicles until they rested in his palm. He carefully lifted them to expose two cords, like sprouts on lima beans. They passed between Bang's index finger and the stub of what had been his ring finger and thence into the pig, right up to its heart and head. At least, that's how mine are planted. How about yours? With his left hand Bang swirled the cutting end of the shears in the alcohol. He hooked the curved blade around the cords without touching them. He carefully closed the straight blade as far as he could without doing any damage. Bang has a remarkably steady hand. Then he clenched his fist. I would not have believed that so tender a vessel could hold so terrifying a noise. Signals fired and pulsed through me in all directions. The victim's tethered brothers began to squeal in sympathy. "WAAAGHSQUNK," said the sow. "OoEEEUNNKK."

"Good God in Heaven," said Bang. "Next time we leave this job to the vet." He squeezed salve into the wounds, and my father released the castrato, who bucked off, fell down trying to bite its ham, got up, ran a few steps, tried to bite, fell, got up, ran, tried to bite, fell, got up, shook itself, jogged to the trough, looked in. The sow still let out bellow after bellow of such a raucus, snoring roar you thought it had either to burst its throat or strangle. "Quick," said Bang, "hand me another before our brains turn to soup." My father pulled the slipknot on the line around one of the sucklings and flipped it on its back. Bang swabbed its thighs, and there was a sharp crack, crack of boards breaking. We all looked up.

The sow roared down the ramp like an avalanche. It overran its feet and plowed up three yards of the good earth with its nose and knees. It exploded onto all fours, scattering mud and froth from its chops. It charged off, in the wrong direction, wheeled in a skid, and charged again, straight at us. My father put a hand and a foot on the fence, changed his mind, and ran off. I hopped nimbly in the opposite direction. Bang stood still, facing the sow full on, pocket knife in hand. "Holy Mother of God," he said, and in one motion dropped his knife, turned, and hurtled the fence, the sow snapping clack, clack at his thighs.

It crashed into the fence and bounced off, right onto the last tethered suckling. It scrambled to its feet and charged, following its nose, but it so happened that the nose was pointed at my father, who was half-way onto the roof of the pig house. The sow chomped on his foot and began to shake it something awful. "Let go," he said. Instead, it got onto its haunches for leverage, forefeet in the air, and pulled on the foot with short jerks that whipped my father's whole body around. He lost his hold on the peak, slid, jammed his forearms and elbows into the drainpipe. The sow pulled up the slack, until my father hung on a line from roof to pig like a flying buttress. "Help," he said. Bang got there before me, a fence rail in his hands. The pig ignored the whacks he gave it on ribs and shoulder, but got on with its shaking, until Bang split its ear. Then it turned on him, and my father did a belly whopper on the turf. "Umph," he said. "Whoa," said Bang.

Bang back-pedaled with such speed and control I wondered whether he had spent a season playing cornerback somewhere. All the while he fenced with that dexterous snout, like a St. George whose lance had been bewitched into a stick. He splashed backwards through the wallow, caught one of his cowboy heels on its farther rim, and went flying onto his back in a patch of mud. Even while in the air, he had never stopped jabbing at the pig. Even as he hit the ground he jabbed, but the thrust went awry, and the sow mounted him, belly to belly. Bang screamed as the sow's jaws closed on his face.

But by that time I had a two-hand grip on her tail, which was rough and gritty. I braced my heels against the same rim of the wallow that had tripped Bang, leaned back, and heaved mightily, if I say so myself. My sudden fear that her tail would part from her rump was a bit presumptuous, that much I admit.

She glanced at me over her shoulder and turned back to Bang, whose hands were clenched on her ears. I took a turn of her tail around my fist and heaved, putting all I had into it, down to the hair on my toes. The shirt split down my back and a joint popped in her tail. She curled to her left, trying to get at me. Bang wriggled free. I took a circle step to the right, careful to clear the wallow edge, leaning my weight away from hers. Bang crawled and then ran in a crouch for the fence.

The sow curled to the left and I circled to the right. She curled some more and I circled with her, quickening the pace and tightening my arc. Around we went, faster and faster, like the Protopopoffs doing a Death Spiral before a packed stadium and to the strains of Tchaikovsky. The scene beyond the sow became a blur of horizontal streaks. Centrifugal force straightened her out, lifted her feet off the ground, while still I whirled her, once, twice, and let go. She landed six feet away on her chin, with a "Wurf-unk." She landed, that is, with her nose again pointed directly at my father, believe it or not, who was limping across our field of vision, from left to right, heading for the fence. The sow charged him. Dizzy as I was, I looped to the right, as ages before I had led interference for Terry on an end run. With impeccable timing I pivoted sharply on my right foot and shot off my left. I met her in mid-air, shoulder to shoulder and cheek to cheek. The impact did not, as I thought, shake my toenails loose, but it was enough to knock her flying onto her side, and I wish Danny the meat packer had been there to see it. The sow rolled, scrambled to her feet, charged, in the wrong direction, wheeled in a skid, found me, charged. I took off for the fence.

When the fire and brimstone from her nostrils scorched the seat of my pants, I curved abruptly to the right. She whooshed by, on a tangent to my course. She braked, skidded, tipped over, scrambled to her feet, charged. Again, when she was a stride from decorating my haunch as with two pairs of pinking shears, I tightened my curve, and she pounded by. And so it went, for six passes, me loping in an irregular spiral, she charging by on tangents. On the sixth pass, she braked, fell down, heaved to her feet, turned, looked at me, sighed, went down on her belly, hind end first, and rested her chin on the ground, her sides heaving. We looked at each other for two minutes, maybe longer. Then I strode over, and no spectator would have been able to detect hesitation in my step. I slid my hand under her jowl and lifted her head. I scratched her chin, all the while looking into her eyes. "Nuff," she said. I bent over and placed a kiss smack on her low brow.

Then I straightened and turned, my back to her, my face to the fence. I pressed my ankles and knees together and I plumped out my buttocks. I arched my back and I raised my arms up and out.

"Bravo," said my father, clapping his hands.

"Olé," said Bang, clapping.

"Olé," said Jack Longhenry.

"Olé who?" said Hank Littlejohn, but he was clapping. Now where had they come from?

The four of them were sitting on the fence. Blood dripped from my father's mangled work shoe and oozed from the perforations on either side of Bang's jaw. On the ground beneath them, one of the piglets, a female no doubt, was nibbling on a testicle.

While my father and Bang dressed each other's wounds, I sneaked a quick look through the *Tannerton Times,* which Arne Olson had brought back from an errand to town. On the front page was a picture of Jeb Stuart Magruder entering prison. A panel of experts re-affirmed that the eighteen-and-a-half minute erasure could not have been made via the foot pedal, as Rose Mary Woods had argued. At least sixteen members of the House Judiciary Committee had received campaign donations from the dairy cooperatives. Rosita Nieves was still at large. A source in Puerto Rican Harlem had informed this reporter that the word on the streets was she had fled south to the Barrio.

Kathleen Haggerty apparently was using up some of the many vacation days she had accumulated, pending further investigation into the circumstances of Gilbert Nieves's death. Deputy Inspector La Paloma insisted that no charges had been lodged against her and that she had not been suspended. Under the heading 666 WORLD GOVERNMENT COMING SOON, the Gilder Bible Church ("the friendly, fundamental church") invited us to See and Hear Alarming Facts on screen, to listen to a Startling Message from Rev. Ungar Rich, a 25-year student of Bible prophecy. JESUS IS COMING SOON. Sunday, June 9, at 10:30 A.M. See slides from a recent trip to Israel. There was a small picture of Rev. Rich pointing to the license plate on an Israeli bus. The number was 666-174. The Millville-Smuggleton Lawn Ornament Gang had struck again. Last night they substituted a dead cat for the plaster frog on Mrs. Louise Westover's bird bath. When Officer "Patch" Giesing attempted to remove the cat from the stick on which it had been propped, a small fireword of the kind known as a party-popper went off. The dead cat had been booby-trapped.

A rabbit, so I discovered, was roasting in the oven. It is not beneath my dignity to cook. You have to eat to live, you know. You might remember that next time you are inclined to feel superior to the people who prepare your food or who in general maintain your wretched existence so that you can diddle it away in an office. It is people like you who make it so hard for women who want to be women. Think how you would feel if the dopes you worked for looked down on you for the work you do for them. They probably do, anyway. It is people like you, not men like me, who are driving the Muriel Bigalows crazy. Has it ever occurred to you how many more lives are preserved each day by housewives than by brain surgeons? There was a grumble of distant thunder. I basted the rabbit with bacon fat and turned up the oven, for though I had never eaten rabbit, my intuition told me the crustier the better. By the time my father hobbled in, enough bandage on his foot for two medium-sized mummies, I had a dutch oven full of my patented spicy tomato sauce a-simmer, and I do not see why I should give you the recipe.

"My, that's good," he said, emptying the stein of beer I had poured him, and how many New Yorkers realize that Ruppert's beer is still extant? A clap of thunder rattled the dishware.

A cauldron of potato dumplings was working by this time. Bang sidled in, clean clothes on his body and a sheepish grin on his face, not to mention four rows of those little round Band-Aids. One row on each side went from chin to cheekbone, the other from chin to corner of the jaw. The whole lower half of his face was yellow with iodine. He stood my trusty machete in the corner and handed me a paper bag. On the bag were the words "Price Chopper." Under those words was a picture of an axe cutting through a coin and into the woman's head stamped thereupon. "Here," he said, "now you can throw away those fruit boots." I put out the salad, mostly of home-grown black-seeded Simpson lettuce, and I put out a steaming dish of brake greens that Astrid Olson had left for us. Then I spread the dumplings on a platter, placed the rabbit couchant on top of them, and ladled sauce over the whole. If I tell you how good it looked, smelled, and tasted, you might be tempted to put aside these memoirs in a vain attempt to fix yourself some lapin à la Grant. Take my advice, stick with the book. The chances are that you need spiritual nourishment more than the other kind. The thunder was terrific, lightning outside, and the lights inside dimmed. First came gusts of wind, then the deluge.

When my father had oohed and Bang had ahed (over the food, not the storm) I opened the bag. Inside were a pair of cowboy boots, engraved or inlaid or tooled or whatever you call it in three different colors of leather. The design was elaborate, but I made out a longhorn bull, a lot of pines and vines, some of which turned out to be snakes, and a flower.

"Those bastards in Wyoming took half a year to make them," said Bang, his mouth full, "and then they came a size too long and size too narrow, but they look about right for you."

They fit very well, indeed, snug, supportive, and yielding as the right woman's arms. The leather was thick but flexible. I did a brief mambo, the last dance anybody had bothered to teach me. I hopped to the left and clicked my heels, hopped to the right and clicked them again.

"To Victor, Subduer of Sows," said Bang, raising his stein.

"To Victor the Victor," said my father, clinking his stein against Bang's.

"To the sow," I said, "a worthy opponent and a graceful loser."

After dinner Bang joined us in "The Den," so-called, I suppose, because of all the wild animals that occupied it. Perched on shelves were a stuffed fox, a fisher, a bobcat, a wolverine, and a mink, all local. Spread over the back of a leather coach was a bearskin, also local. Stretched out on the wall over the fireplace was a wolfhide that Bang had brought back from his travels. On the other walls were old six-shooters and lever action rifles, knives and tomahawks, but no scalps. While we drank beer and smoked and fed the fire, my father told us of the catastrophes recorded by ancient historians. Bang was a skillful storyteller, of the droll and rueful variety. There was evidence of deliberate art in the tall tales he told us of the five years he had spent out West doing this and that, begetting his first bastard, for instance, to provide a home for whom he had come back East. I left them limp from laughter with my ribald accounts of the antics of certain feminist agitators. None of us were very sober by the time my father got up to fetch the skewers of raccoon shish kebob he had marinating. Bang heaved to his feet, on which he was not very steady, and said, "Now don't go away."

He returned with a guitar, the kind you've got to play yourself, not the kind you plug in. "Here's a little song I want to try out on you," he said, as my father came in with the skewers. I do not see why it should have surprised me that Bang was musical, but it did, and he was. I am all for the arts, but I usually find it hard to like the people who produce them. Bang was also a man of numerous voices, as it turned out. He sang the woman's part in a voice like Billie Holiday's and the man's part in a voice out of the black South, gin and strain moving around in it like gravel. "Wrote it just last night," he said, strumming some chords that were ironic about their own melancholy. When it came, the song seemed derived in tempo and accent from "Lady Sings the Blues." I remember very well hearing the news of Billie Holiday's death. I see no reason why I should not tell you this, I've told you so much else: I also remember having had a fantasy of rescuing her in the nick of time. I brought her to a deserted cabin in the woods, nursed her, fed her wholesome food, got her to exercise, cured her bad habits, accompanied her on the piano, which, however, I do not know how to play. I had a similar fantasy when Marilyn Monroe died. The deaths of Janis Joplin and Mama Cass did not stir my imagination, for one was queer and the other was fat. "I call it 'Blues Moving Out,'" Bang said, hitting a dark and dirty sequence of notes tumbling down over each other. While my father and I roasted the shish kebob in the fireplace, Bang performed, and it beat *Der Rosenkavalier,* which Samantha once dragged me to see, a thousand times over.

THE WOMAN: Come lie down by me baby
Put your head where it belongs
Wrap yourself around me baby
Hug me all the day long
Forget about the rent baby
Forget about rights and wrongs.

THE MAN: Got no time to lie around baby
Bed ain't where I belong
Got no time for love baby
No time for right or wrong

Got to keep moving baby
Got to blow my own horn.

THE WOMAN: I woke up this morning
Felt awful cold in bed
Didn't go to work this morning
Had a queer pain in my head
Didn't see the sun this morning
Just thinking about what you said.

THE MAN: I woke up this morning
Felt sunshine in my head
Didn't go to work this morning
Left that work, left this bed
Come tomorrow morning
Doing something else instead.

THE WOMAN: Let me tell you about women
They go up, they go down
I'm just a stay-at-home woman
But I been around
A man who got no time for women
He haunts the dirty end of town.

THE MAN: Let me tell you about women
They go up, and sometimes down
A man who got no time for women
He always got them around
A man who spends his time with women
He wears his feet the wrong way round.

THE WOMAN: I ain't going to hold you
You'll be back some day
I ain't going to tell you
All I got to say
I'm just going to tell you
It's no better any other way.

THE MAN: I'm just going to tell you
There ain't no more to say
I'm just going to tell you
I won't be back this way
I'm just going to tell you
You can't love the blues away.

"Amen," said my father, and he handed Bang a skewer.

We ate in silence for awhile. " 'Horn' and 'belong' don't rhyme," I said.

"Close enough for jazz," Bang said. We ate some more. The radishes from Astrid's garden had an honest bite to them, but Kristal's bread gave me the hiccoughs.

"Maybe that's the point," said my father.

"There ain't no point," Bang said.

We chewed on that one a bit. "Some things just don't rhyme," I said.

"Amen," said my father.

"Bang, how come you never got married," I said, for alcohol makes me indiscreet. "Most men take a stab at it, one time or another."

"Guess I never had the courage," he said.

"To marry or not to marry," I said. "It's a question as to which takes more courage."

"Either way it don't rhyme," said my father.

"Amen," Bang said and I said, pretty much in unison.

We walked Bang part-way to his cabin, my father limping, not so much to display our manners as for the pleasure of peeing under the stars, for the storm had passed and the sky was clear. I must say that beery-eyed as I was, the stars were very impressive. A cool breeze blew through the split back of my shirt.

"Can you lend me some money?" I said. I had just about resolved to go home without asking, but the events of the day had softened me. Besides, it was too dark for either of us to see the other's face. No matter how bright the stars, they do not illuminate much.

"Name your price," he said.

"Well—," I said.

"Don't be bashful," he said.

If that's the attitude he was going to take, dammit, I decided to make it easy for him to refuse me. "A thousand dollars," I said.

"A thousand it is," he said. "It's all going to you anyway. Except the people already living here get their cabins, board, and a bit, for the rest of their lives. I'm relying on you to do right by them." A meteor or something streaked across the sky, from nowhere to nowhere.

"You're assuming—," I said.

"You settle your affairs in New York and move to Pinetop," he said. "We need you here and you need something to do worth doing. New York's finished. Leave it to the grave-robbers."

"What about Samantha?" I said, or perhaps the right word is "wailed."

"What's the matter?" he said.

"Nothing," I said.

"Are you crying?" he said.

"No," I said.

"There, there," he said. "We need Samantha too. And we need more children, male children."

"She doesn't need us," I said, and I hate people who snivel. Sometimes I hate myself, but not often. "She doesn't want children, and she doesn't want me, and she doesn't want to be a frontierswoman. She wants a career."

"She wants to do something worth doing," he said, "because Samantha's made out of the right stuff. Ain't nothing more worth doing than what we're doing up here."

"You tell her that," I said.

"I did," he said.

"What did she say?" I said.

"That she wanted a career," he said.

"Some day," I said. "Some day she'll say that and I won't be able to restrain myself."

"Those dingbats she's hanging out with have already begun to knock each other off," he said. "At least I hope it was a dingbat," and he gave me one of his significant blue-eyed looks.

"It was a dingbat, all right," I said.

At eleven the next morning, the door to my room kicked open with a bang; I rolled over and reached into my musette bag for the knife, and I did not have to think about doing it, either, never mind how deep in sleep I had been. It was only Kristal, who looks nothing at all like Erica von Plaack. She blushed and smiled and nodded.

"Tid till at vakna latmask," she said. Folded neatly on her outstretched arms were my denim pants and jacket, my rugby-style shirt, the work pants and work shirt. *"Här har du dät,"* she said, placing the clothes on the foot of the bed. It was nice of Kristal to do my laundry, but I was annoyed just the same, not so much at Kristal for having snuck into my room to get them as at myself. She could have slit my throat and I would have slept right through it. When I die, I want to know what is happening. I have been saving up one last tremendous curse at existence, and I do not want it to go to waste, even if I have to deliver it silently, for it is hard to deliver an audible curse when your throat is slit. My knife, by the way, was not in the musette bag.

"Tack tack," I said, which is about as much Swedish as I remember from all the hours I spent with the Olsons, waiting for my father to come home from work.

"Varsa god," she said. From behind her skirts came Ylva, carrying a mug of coffee, and Ebba, carrying a plate of *bullar* (a kind of coffee cake), and Svea, holding up a little tray, on which were piled six hundred dollars and a check for another four hundred.

"Tack, tack," I said.

Kristal unfolded the work shirt and held it so I could see how she had sewn up the split back.

"Tack, tack," I said.

She held up the work pants so I could see how she had taken in the waist and seat.

"Tack, tack," I said.

"Bengt väntar," she said.

"Tack, tack," I said. The four of them filed out. I washed, packed, dressed and all the rest, in a hurry, and you cannot blame Kristal for not realizing that you must never, never starch brushed denim pants, even less a brushed denim jacket. I hustled down to the kitchen, where Bang was waiting with a mug of coffee and a cigarillo. On the table was my knife, transformed utterly.

"Ever been soul-kissed by a sow?" he said. "It's something that stays with you. Since I couldn't sleep, and I didn't think you'd mind, I lifted the knife from your bag. I got myself sober working on it." There were fewer colors around his jaw than there had been around my eye, but his colors were more unusual.

On the way to town, after we whizzed by the apparitions of Jack Longhenry and Hank Littlejohn lurking in the shadows of the woods by the driveway—and why do people who live in the country drive so fast?—I played with the knife, while Bang explained what he had done to it. First he had removed my birch scales, put a taper onto the tang and a thread on the end of it. He ground a pretty little convex dip in the clip and a counterbalancing swoop on the belly. He chopped out a choil, scooped out a fuller, and slimmed down the swage. He put a reverse curve in the quillon and squared off the ricasso. Heat to cherry red, and quench the glow, then heat to pigeon blue, and cool it slow, for a temper true. He alternated leather spacers with the two I had made of brass. He slid on the full round walnut handle, with finger grooves, that he had made out of an old piece of rifle stock. He followed with leather and brass spacers to match the first series. Onto the butt end of the tang he screwed a pommel worked out of a solid brass knob, and by Jesus, those handle parts were as tight as a matador's asshole. This here heavy pommel, in Bang's opinion, balanced the knife perfectly. See how it handles? It took him almost as much time to buff and polish as to do everything else, but that there satin finish, he thought, and I agreed, turned a mere tool into a work of art.

"My father see this?" I said.

"He went to the hospital," Bang said.

"The hospital!" I said.

"Seems I didn't do too good a job sewing up his foot," he said.

"You sewed up his foot!" I said.

"We got surgical gut and needles and all that stuff," he said.

"What did you use for anesthetic?" I said.

"That's one thing we don't got," he said.

"Neither of you has a lick of common sense, either. You're like children," I said, making a short, backhand slash with the knife.

"It was his idea," said Bang.

The 12:15 bus was waiting at one of the five corners, but did not look as though it would wait for long. The driver slammed shut the luggage compartment and started for the door. "Hey Lewis, hang on a minute," said Bang, and then to make sure Lewis hung on, Bang parked his pickup diagonally across the path of the bus. "You got to buy your ticket in there," Bang said to me; "the driver ain't allowed to sell them."

"Bang, you going to give me grief today?" said Lewis.

"That's up to you," said Bang.

I had already taken a step into the stationery store when I noticed the tall, thin cop leaning in a slouch against its window. He was looking me over with what he must have thought was a killing sneer. I bought a ticket and a *Tannerton Times* and a *Ms. Chief,* hot off the presses, and an all-day sucker which I gave to the cop as I walked out.

"New York is all over snags," said Bang. "Don't get yourself hooked on one. We got enough to do up here, so you don't have to go around brooding and pitying yourself. We got us a windmill and a waterwheel to build this summer. That kind of work makes the time go fast."

"We'll see," I said.

"Listen to what I say, Vic," he said. "I notice more than people think."

"I got some unfinished business to take care of," I said.

"Give me a call if you need help finishing it," he said.

"Why don't you two kiss each other good-bye and let me get out of here?" said Lewis.

Bang and I shook hands, and he pulled forward, out of the way. As I stepped up into the bus, I heard him address the cop. "Hey Patch, what's this I hear about you and a dead cat?"

"I guess you mistook a porcupine for your teddy bear," said the cop. Some woman laughed, the door closed, the bus lurched into motion, and I nearly fell into the lap of an elderly sourpuss.

I cannot say that I had enjoyed my stay at Pinetop while I was actually there, but I did in retrospect. Do not rush to the conclusion that I therefore intended to return. If you are an American, New York is the reality principle, although Philadelphia, I understand, comes close.

IX

L AST February, so it seems, the Watergate grand jury named our president as an unindicted co-conspirator. Jaworski had seen to it that he remained unindicted. Whether Jaworski was indicted for tampering with a grand jury the *Tannerton Times* did not say. According to Stevie Dickinson, Kathleen Haggerty was taken off the Karnofsky case because the Neanderthals who ran the N.Y.P.D. were afraid she would solve it. Deputy Inspector Manuel La Paloma denied the charge. There was interesting news from California. Thirteen transsexual inmates of the Vacaville facility are being given female hormones and the majority are supplied with brassieres. Bruce Seeger, a spokesman for the State Department of Corrections, said that the transsexual prisoners are not allowed to wear skirts, however. He added that "It is established as the ethically and morally proper thing to do to assist people in their change to whatever their sexual identity seems to be." There was nothing new from the Gilder Bible Church. The Millville-Smuggleton Lawn Ornament Gang last night deposited Mrs. Westover's plaster frog in a watering trough owned by Willard Chance, whose farm was off Felton Drive outside the village of Climax Hill, and who demolished the frog with a blast from his twelve gauge shotgun.

The black border on my first issue of *Ms. Chief,* sure to become a collector's item, was not so black that you couldn't see through it. Erika the Indian's naked foot, as Fiji drew it, was high-arched and sexy. Was I seeing things, or did the Uncle Sam to whom she was giving a hot foot look something like me? I skipped the "Inaugural Editorial," by Chief von Plaack, the main point of which seemed to be that competing feminist journals had discredited themselves by unconscious identification with the aggressor. They aped the scholarly solemnities of men or wore the gloss of well-kept mistresses. Nor did I linger over "Gay Blades," the first installment of what was promised as a regular column by Pastor Peter Brevoort, who called for a united front of oppressed minorities, such as women, gays, our Black brothers and sisters in God, and Hungarians. Nor did I read much of an article entitled "Feminism and Free Air," by Jude Karnofsky. Pollution, it seems, is caused by the activities of men. Men pollute nature because they hate it. They hate nature because they identify it with women. They hate women because they identify all women with their mothers. They hate their mothers because their mothers would not let them drop turds wherever they pleased. It is also for these reasons that sooner or later men will drop nuclear bombs all over the place, if women do not stop them. In a postsexist society men will be equally responsible for childrearing. Grown men will thence hate other men as much as they hate women, thus promoting equality. And they will no longer bomb and pollute nature, for they will identify it with their fathers, with men, with themselves. Nor did I tarry to savor the flavor of a tidbit by Stevie Dickinson entitled "The Bottom Line," the meat of which could be boiled down to these irrefragable propositions:

1) Women are oppressed.

2) It is men who oppress them.

3) Men will not cease to oppress women voluntarily.

4) Women must therefore force men to cut it out.

5) The only question that remains is one of tactics. Stevie herself was clearly in favor of open warfare. Only on the antepenultimate page of the magazine, at the bottom of the first paragraph of "Fem-Con-Notes," which was to be a regular feature, did I find the initials "S.W.," alias my poor Samantha. Her paragraph was a strictly objective account of a conference on the question of pay for housewives. Everyone at the conference agreed that housewives should be paid, but nothing, apparently, was said about who would pay them. It tugged at my heart to see that Samantha had still not learned the distinction between "that" and "which."

I looked up to find myself in the Port Authority terminal. In an outrageously expensive toy shop I bought Toby a very well-made addition to his circus van: a hemispherical cage, six slouching, crouching, jumping, snarling, pawing, yawning tigers; a tiger-tamer whose arms, legs, and head moved; his pretty assistant; and all the accoutrements. I would have loved a toy like that myself when I was Toby's age, and not just then. But my godfather was Arne Olson, who never bought toys for anyone. In a Hoffritz store I got myself a Washita medium honing stone and an Arkansas hard stone, both overpriced.

I had forgotten about Jude's memorial service. When upon my knock, Bill opened his door, there was a surprise or two in store for me. Over his shoulder I could see what looked like a convention of crows. There were a lot of people, and all of them were wearing black. They all stopped talking and turned to look at me. There was Parker (the lawyer) polishing his smile. There was Carter (the secretary), looking superior but still anxious to please. There was Jude's mother, big, soft, bewildered, and probably drugged. There was her father, red-faced and beaky, moving his head around in short, furious jerks, like a tormented rooster. There was brother Noah, who looked as though he had been living on locusts and wild honey. There was someone I did not know, who could only have been a rabbi. There was Kaspar

Linquist (Bill's new girlfriend's husband), looking dry, and Ursula (his wife), looking wet. There was Martine, looking harried. There was Toby, who ran over to me and wrapped his arms around my leg. And there, on the table, on the table upon which our wives had left Bill and me those two fatal letters of farewell, on this long, polished insignificant table, rested a basket of fruit. It was identical to the basket of fruit from which I had served Jude her last supper. Attached to it was a card decorated with cupids and flowers. I could not read what was written on it. But I could feel, from beyond the card, from across the room, the pressure of Miss Lily's X-ray eyes upon me.

"Nice boots you're wearing," said Bill.

"I'll bet Uncle Victor has a present for me," said Toby, patting his invisible dog Luke.

"I'd better try to catch you later," I said to Bill. It was a pleasure to hug Toby, and he was already tearing at the wrapping around his toy as I backed out the door throwing apologetic nods around the room.

I was interested to see that someone had fixed my telephone. I picked it up, and sure enough, there was the dial tone. While I was at it, I called Chi Chi Quatrone to tell him that I did not want to buy a gun after all. He said that his brother-in-law had no time anyway—he was too busy with the Karnofsky case. Glen and half his team had been taken off the investigation into registrants at the Hilton. They were now working with the team assigned to Karnofsky's personal background, including her family (and Glen said you'd have to meet this Noah before you'd believe him), her friends, and friends of the family, which last category, I supposed, included me. Any hot leads? I asked. No hot ones, and all too many lukewarm ones. Noah has a bug up his ass about Aunt Jemima there, Chi Chi said. Martine! I said. That's the one, he said. How about the Nieves cousins? I said. They're out of it, he said.

Some day I would like to get good news that was not mixed with bad. I started off a pot of chili and got to work opening mail, writing checks and a deposit slip, until a knock at the door interrupted me. If you think it is hard to conceal an icepick on your person, you should try a twelve-inch knife. I slipped the knife and the hand that was holding it into a manila envelope and went to the door. I boldly threw it open, ready for anything, except Miss Lily.

"Victor, you look different every time I see you," she said. "How do you do it?" I believe I mumbled something about her own infinite variety.

"May I come in," she said, looking pointedly down at the inch of knife that had sliced its way through the envelope.

"How is dear Ivan and his colorful assistant?" she said. Miss Lily, when she sits, sits very straight, on the edge of the chair, knees and ankles together, balls of her feet pressed against the floor, as though to maintain a quarter inch of space between her nouveau-patrician behind and her perch.

"I do not remember mentioning that I was going to see him," I said.

"It was one of my men that fixed your phone," she said.

"I trust you will convey to him my appreciation," I said. "Would a gratuity be appropriate?"

"It was also one of my men who tapped it," she said.

"I see," I said. I must have looked odd gnashing my teeth that way. You are in a position to appreciate what it cost me not to try out my new knife. I put it on the table. "Will you excuse me? I have something cooking." I drained the kidney beans Brunhilda had insisted on buying, poured them in with the browned meat and onions, added tomato sauce, vinegar, and many spices, all the while cursing southern ladies and Alexander Graham Bell.

In Miss Lily's lap were two cassettes and in her hands was my knife. "The hand that made this was country-smart," she said.

"Four hands, actually," I said.

"I find it just a weany bit back-heavy for a fighting knife," she said, holding it as you would to core out someone's navel.

"The knife was made, perhaps, for a stronger arm than yours," I said. "The craftsman, perhaps, but aesthetics before utility."

"That is always a mistake," she said. "I am the only one who has listened to these tapes," and she tapped them with the knife.

"Ah," I said.

"You ought to put them in a safe place," she said. "An unfriendly ear might draw conclusions." She passed me the cassettes with her left hand, for her right hand held onto the knife. "You have my word that there are no duplicates." Miss Lily was notorious for being as good as her word.

"I am obliged to you," I said.

"Yes, you are," she said.

"Aha!" I said.

She studied my face. Then she smiled broadly and gave me a playful pat on the cheek with the flat of the blade. I refused to flinch.

"You saw, of course, that vulgar basket of fruit," she said.

"It made my teeth itch," I said.

"You know, of course, that there was one like it in Judith's room," she said.

"How could I possibly know that?" I said.

She leaned back in the chair. "Victor, Victor," she said. She stuck the point of the knife into the wooden arm of the chair, admittedly an old one, and rested her hand on the pommel. "I also give you my word that nothing we say will go beyond this room. It was 'swept' by one of my men not three hours ago."

"Whatever happened to the notion that a man's home is his castle?" I said.

"The original basket of fruit was sent by Stephanie, alias Stevie, Dickinson, who always makes me think of a slug hooked for bait."

"And the second basket? I said.

"The shop girl could not tell whether the voice on the phone was that of a man or a woman," she said.

"That could be Stevie Dickinson, all right, but it could also be a lot of people, nowadays. Half of the popular songs you hear—" I said.

"There was no return address on the envelope that arrived one day later with money to pay for the fruit," she said. "It had been dropped into a mailbox not two blocks away from the offices of that absurd magazine. One feels dirty merely talking about these sordid people." She gripped the handle of the knife and pushed it forward, as though putting a stickshift into reverse.

"I can appreciate what a trial all this has been for you," I said.

"Would you like to hear what was written on the card?" she said.

"I am not sure I would," I said.

She pointed with the knife as though the words were in the air between us:

"Here is your card
Fear death by earth, air, fire, or water.
One must be so careful these days.
                                    —Madame Sosostris."

"Who is Madame Sosostris?" I said.

"According to William, she was a bisexual fortuneteller," she said.

"Why are you telling me all this?" I said.

"That spayed polecat means to murder my son," she said.

"That is certainly possible," I said. "But is it not the case that only the police, the victim's family, and Erica von Plaack know, er, um, how Jude's death was implemented? And, of course, the murderer."

"Low as they are on the evolutionary scale, these creatures have been known to communicate with each other," she said.

"Surely you have the resources to protect Bill from any attempt on his life," I said.

"That little man in charge of the case was very polite," she said. "But he made it clear that if any of my men were reported in the vicinity of von Plaack, et al., they would be clapped in jail on a charge of conspiracy to commit criminal something or other. He has chosen to be officious about my means of gathering intelligence. I am not worried about his silly charges. But I am worried about the hiatus between the time my men are removed from their posts by him and the time new men are put back by me."

"The solution, then—" I said.

"William is being tiresome about my attempts to provide him with a bodyguard," she said. "He says that if he sees just one more of my men loitering around, he will pack up his household and emigrate to Stockholm, Sweden."

"Maybe that would be best," I said.

"No, it would not," she said. "And what makes you believe that spavined mink would not follow him abroad? Did I tell you that she was observed prowling around the lobby of William's house, *this* house," and she pointed to the floor with the knife. "There have been phone calls, with heavy breathing."

"No, I don't suppose Bill would emigrate to Old Virginny," I said. "You could move in with him. You'd be more than a match for—"

"You seem to forget that I am under suspicion," she said.

"Under suspicion!" I said. "Who suspects you?"

"Well, I do believe William does, for one," she said.

"Poor Miss Lily," I said.

"I am a mother," she said. "Naturally my own son's mistrustfulness pains me. But it does not affect my maternal instincts. He has already wasted much of his life in childish attempts to prevent me from helping him. I must be careful not to push him out of my reach. He needs me, all the more because he thinks otherwise. And now, Victor, he needs *you*." She leaned forward to lay the blade of the knife on my knee.

"Maybe I could talk him into coming with me to Pinetop, at least for the summer. Once Samantha—" I said.

"William's latest folly has announced that she *will not* be rusticated," she said. "I gather that all these years she has been saving herself up to live high on the hog."

"Maybe *I* could move in with him," I said.

"I think it best, Victor dear, that you stay as much out of sight as possible," she said. "Don't you?"

"I don't like this," I said.

"Do we understand each other?" she said.

"Understanding is not assent," I said.

"I thought you cared about Toby," she said.

"Now wait a minute," I said.

"She may not want to leave witnesses," she said. "She may have decided, correctly, I might add, that the life of his son is worth more to William than his own. Once, under the influence of too much bourbon, William said that I would only get my hands on Toby over his dead body. It would be ironic if—"

"Would you like a bowl of chili?" I said.

She paused to study my face again. "If you have chopped raw onions to put on it," she said.

"You can chop the onions while I make some pan bread," I said. She phoned down to Bill's apartment and told Carter to bring up four bottles of beer, and make sure they're good and cold, hear?

"This knife is sharp, but it could be sharper," she said, slicing through an onion.

"Yes, ma'am," I said.

"The way you do is to clamp the stone to your workbench so you can hold the knife with two hands," she said. "You've got to lean down hard on it."

"Yes, ma'am," I said.

We clinked glasses of beer and she took a ladylike dab of chili on the end of her fork. She tasted it with a faraway look in her eyes. Then she dug in. "Victor, you're a genius," she said.

"I'd be interested to know how Bill feels about all this," I said.

"My, what a foolish girl Samantha must be," she said. "Did you ever make chili for her?"

"Does he share your fears for his life?" I said.

"When you finish your business up here, and it had ought to be soon, you come South," she said. "You'll be a great success. I'll see to it."

"Is he taking precautions?" I said. "Just in case, I mean. I could lend him my knife, I guess . . . .."

"We are as short on real men back home as anywhere else," she said. "But at least we still remember what they look like. We know how to reward them, too."

"Well?" I said.

She put down her fork and she cut us each another piece of bread. If there had been black-eyed peas, I have no doubt she would have eaten them off that knife. She wiped at her plate with a piece of bread and put it in her mouth. She sat back and studied my face some more.

"William is not like you and me," she said. "He has a morbid conscience. He has convinced himself that he is somehow responsible for Judith's death. I do not believe he could explain, even to himself, what led him to this superstition. But it has sapped his will, which was never robust to begin with, except when it came to thwarting me. In many ways William takes after his father."

I walked her to the door. She turned in the doorway to face me. She flipped the knife up so that it revolved three times in the air before coming down into her hand, pommel-end first. "See for yourself," she said. "Bill will be alone tomorrow. The Linquist woman is off to visit her father for a few days, and she's taking Toby with her. Her father, I understand, is a big baby who lords it over his women. I'm flying South tonight, but I'll be back some time this weekend, to tie up any loose ends,

hear?" She flipped the knife, watched it go up, said "I'm counting on you," and walked out. I caught the knife handily.

Miss Lily could have saved her advice. One of the many
things my father had insisted on teaching me was how to
sharpen a knife, never mind that I might want to do something
else, such as lie on my back in the doghouse and dream of
Sheena the Jungle Queen. (We had a doghouse, but no dog,
because my mother was "allergic" to animals, all animals.) I had
just gotten out a shirt cardboard for the final superfine hone
when Samantha called. She was nice enough to say that she was
sorry not to have seen me at the memorial service, which went
off all right, she guessed, although the rabbi couldn't have
known anything about Jude. His description of her as wife,
mother, obedient servant of God, shining example of Jewish
womanhood in a dark time, left too much out. Erika nearly
burst a blood vessel trying to hold in a laugh. Kaspar Linquist
was sort of creepy. He kept referring to Jude as a fallen hero,
a Viking, and he called up before his listeners' eyes a vision of
her feasting in Valhalla. I was sorry not to have seen her
(Samantha), I said, but I could think of a single remedy for our
separate sorrows. She was especially sorry, she said, because my
father, to whom she had just been talking, said that I had very
much changed, very much for the better. I said that her paragraph in Ms. Chief was admirably lucid, but she grew impatient
when I tried to explain to her the difference between "that" and
"which." She was so nervous, she said: she could smell blood
in the air. Kathleen Haggerty had just come back from a vacation in Puerto Rico looking like the cat that swallowed the
canary. Did I think she was as beautiful as everyone said? I said
that Kathleen was to Samantha as Lena the Hyena was to Daisy
Mae. Don't be a dope, she said. Come home to me, I said; come
home and I would shield her from all the world's violent
females. As for that, she said, she had worked out a compromise
with Erika. She would move in with Stevie for their mutual
protection until Erika had finished remodelling her mansion to

accommodate them all. Don't, I said. She had received a twenty-five-dollar-a-week raise, she said (Don't, I said), but she had counted on a new title—Associate, or at least Assistant, Editor—and she hadn't gotten it. Don't, I said. Everything was set, she said, for her to move in this coming Monday. She would have moved in earlier, but Stevie had something mysterious she had to get done first. For the sake of her soul, and moreover, her body, I said, don't. Once she had moved in with Stevie, she said, I would be allowed to visit her. What's the matter? she said. I thought you would be pleased, she said. "I thought you were so dying to see me," she said. I was, I said. I am, I said. I just caught a whiff of that blood in the air, I said.

The doorbell rang. Damn it, I said. She wished I wouldn't curse, she said. She heard enough bad language every day at *Ms. Chief* to last her a life time. Someone's at the door, I said. Oh, she said. I let Brunhilda in, with a finger at my lips, signifying silence. She extended a middle finger, signifying that I should stuff it. Who was it? said Samantha. A friend, I said. Brunhilda blew in my other ear, the one not covered by the receiver. I must have been rattled, because I could have sworn I felt the breath go right through my head and into the telephone. What kind of friend? said Samantha. A friend in need, I said. Brunhilda unzipped my fly and pulled out the contents. At this time of night? said Samantha. I haven't been able to tell night from day since my wife left me, I said. Brunhilda began to wind the telephone cord around my stiffening transmitter. Victor, she said, was I being unfaithful to her with another woman in her own home? Would she rather I was unfaithful to her with another man? I said. Brunhilda squeezed oil on the head of my trussed member and began to hone it on the Arkansas hard stone. Well, was I? Samantha said. No matter what I said, I said, she would never be sure until she came home, where she could keep an eye on me. Samantha hung up.

I placed down the receiver and tried to stand up, but being tethered, managed only a crouch. I raised the knife high over my head and then brought it down full force, like a whim of Yahweh's, to Brunhilda's breast. At the last possible moment, however, I twisted my wrist and stayed my hand, so that she suffered no more than a light tap with the pommel. "Ai," she said. I am ashamed to say that I laughed at the stricken look on her face.

While Brunhilda worked away at removing the dressing from over my eye, I pulled down her panties and rested my ravening right hand on the pillow of her behind, to assuage it. Against the cushion of the breast I had pretended to stab, I leaned the undamaged side of my unquiet head, to quieten it. The theme of her monologue, which passed literally over my head, was a paradox: a family is a cross not to be borne, but without a family you were nothing. Her own family was a colony of vampires, they were draining her dry, and she gave me instances, but how could she turn her back on them? Only someone who had already gone over to the devil—. She wasn't by any chance related to Gilbert and Rosita Nieves? I mumbled, for I was drowsy, for half of my mouth was covered by the wired bodice of her dress. That was not an easy question to answer, she said.

Their mothers were the infamous Nieves sisters, dead in a suicide pact, no relation to Brunhilda. Gilbert was raised by the saintly sister of a common-law wife of that no-good stepson of the martyred wife of Brunhilda's mother's worthless brother-in-law. Rosita was raised by a TV repairman, whose wife put on airs, no relations. But if she, Brunhilda, was related to Gil, and it was more than she could figure out, she was related to Rosy, for if you were related to someone, you were unavoidably related to that someone's cousin. Therefore Brunhilda had chipped in fifty bucks when money was collected for getting Rosy out of the country. All for nothing, she said. Why all for nothing? I said. On Tuesday, Rosy, against instructions, had slipped away from her hide-out, presumably to buy mangoes, for which she had a craving, and had never come back. Brunhilda doubted that the body would ever be found. Ai, I said. Don't be such a baby, said Brunhilda; the eye was as good as new. The scar would only make me more interesting, she said. You'll be glad to hear that my toe, my thigh, my ribs, were also as good as new, if still off-color. My testicles were likewise fine, thank you. The lump on my lower lip, in front of the broken tooth, has turned out to be permanent. Ai-yi-yi.

I would have been satisfied with a quickie, but I did not want to offend Brunhilda, who took it for granted she was on call for the night, there being no limit to the concupiscence of men. I would not, if I were you, jump to the conclusion that I doubted the temper of my mettle. Never doubt the temper of your mettle and you'll never have reason to doubt it—that's my motto. I was going to need my wits about me, come morning, not that I mean to imply that sexual intercourse scatters your wits, not as I practice it, but then I have never experienced the intriguing perversion of having my mind blown. I would have to sniff out an answer to the question of whether Stevie was in fact preparing to murder Bill. Why be so scrupulous? you ask. It's a fault of mine, I admit it. I agree that there were already sufficient grounds for terminating her miserable existence. But I did not see it as my mission in life to purge all the world's evil. You are asking too much of me, although I am grateful for the compliment. Let other people purge those who are doing evil to them. I was having enough trouble trying to purge those who were doing evil to me. Poor Rosita. Well, Kathleen Haggerty would just have to wait her turn. So I concluded, and it is not the first time that a mistaken conclusion was reasoned out of unimpeachable premises.

I have figured out why bank clerks keep you waiting before they take your money. The operative psychology is that of the glutton who says, "No, I couldn't," before with a sigh of reluctance he snatches up the last piece of cake. I re-opened my checking account, realized that the checks I had written the night before were no good, tore them up, wrote new ones, rented a safe deposit box, deposited therein two cassettes and forty-some incriminating spiral notebooks, converted a fiver into a roll of dimes, stopped at a stationery store for a roll of tape to repair the envelopes in which I had placed the invalid checks, mailed them, dropped my new boots off at the cobbler's (a millionaire, I surmise) for him to replace the high, treacherous, leather heels with low, trustworthy, rubber ones, dodged traffic and the unleashed breasts of summer-session students, got to Butler Library, in which there were telephone booths that no one but the FBI would want to tap, and they could tap away all they wanted, for all I cared, for (1) I had not yet committed a federal crime and (2) feminist organizations were probably on the list of subversives, as well they might be, and therefore candidates for disruption, by whatever means, including my own. Maybe I had committed a federal crime, after all. A tricky lawyer, I suppose, might argue that I had deprived Jude Karnofsky of her civil rights.

I first called Bill, who planned to skip lunch, but not dinner, which he would like to eat with me, if I didn't have some barroom brawl planned for the night, and it was good to hear some of the old warmth back in his voice. He did not feel like going out; would I mind fetching some ready-made grub we could eat in his apartment? Leave everything to me, I said. I then dialed *Ms. Chief* and again got the right number on the first try, which left me with forty-eight dimes. The answering voice was that of a wry and weary young man. I introduced myself as Vladimir Tepish, of the *West Side Hammer*. I was doing a piece on the first issue of *Ms. Chief;* were any of the editors available to answer questions? Most of them were over at Erika's place, he said. They were going to spend the whole day brainstorming. The idea was to precipitate some wowsers for re-doing the joint. The idea behind the idea (and here he lowered his voice) was to outdo the *Playboy* mansion. Maybe, he said, I could get myself invited to the party they were having that night; everybody who was anybody in publishing would be there. Would he be there? I said. He was not anybody, he said; he was not so much *in* publishing, as beneath it. So everybody who was anybody at *Ms. Chief* was out? I said. Well, he said, Tracy, Stevie, and, oh yes, Sam had come in for the morning, but they were just getting ready to leave. And how about him, I said. Secretaries and gal fridays (all of whom were men) worked 480 minutes a day, every day, and they damn well made the coffee, too. He wasn't the kind of person I expected to be hired there, I said. He knew what I meant, he said; but where's the fun in buggering someone who liked it?

The cabbie asked if I minded his not turning on the meter, and I said No. I asked if he minded my paying him in dimes, and he said Yes. I gave him his tip in dimes, six of them, whether he minded or not. I assumed a nonchalant position in a doorway opposite 444 Park Avenue South, from which the lunch-hour crowd was pouring, but I saw no one who looked like a refugee from the Amboy Dukes grafted onto a pair of loosely-packed duffle bags. I was just counting out seven dimes for a pack of cigarettes, when through the store window I saw dropsical thighs flip, flap, flopping and a skinny arm hooked around Samantha's. I threw down some more dimes (too many), grabbed the cigarettes, and tripped on the way out, just in time to get a clear view of the ponderous smeerp Stevie Dickinson planted on my wife's cheek. Samantha's head recoiled as though she had been hit by a line drive. She disengaged, smiling nervously, said something to which her masterful companion only nodded, and walked uptown with her precise and emphatic step, a sufficient reason in itself for nay normal man to fall hopelessly in love with her. I forced myself to follow Stevie Dickinson, who suddenly heaved a right and hoisted herself into a bus, which—wouldn't you know it?—closed its doors behind her and blasted off, as though it had been waiting just for her.

Nobody without a lot of time on his hands takes a bus in New York City (by which I mean Manhattan), but then by my standards Stevie Dickinson was a member of the leisure class. Certainly the exchange value of her labor was nil. For the ten blocks down to Twenty-third Street a brisk stride would have kept me neck-and-neck with the bus, were it not for all the people cluttering up the sidewalk. Then the traffic, vehicular but not pedestrian, thinned, and I had to sprint full-out to Fourteenth Street, where Stevie Dickinson got off. I do not believe that I actually knocked anybody down. And if I did, there was ample compensation for him in the dimes that kept bouncing from my pocket, so there is no need for me to apologize here. Stevie walked, if that is the word, two blocks downtown along Broadway and into a cafeteria. I sauntered by and then I sauntered by again, but I could not see her through my own reflection in the window. I strolled in, just in case she was trying to make a get-away through the ladies' room window, though I do not see what I could have done about it. I stood behind her for a few seconds, where she was slouched over a table, and I had to exert the full force of my iron will against an impulse to push her face down into her plate. On this plate were mashed potatoes, Spanish rice, and cheezed-over macaroni, which explains a lot—to me, anyhow. There were also on her tray a side dish of bread pudding and three cups of black coffee. While sipping a glass of cranberry juice, I watched her drink all of the coffee and eat some of the potatoes, a little of the rice, less of the macaroni, and none of the pudding, into which she stuck four cigarette butts, nor did she once look up from the manuscript she was defacing with a blue pencil.

I'll say this for Stevie: she had tact enough not to impose herself on a neighborhood in which her mere presence would depress property values. If you were to walk along West Third Street in the general direction of Portugal, you would sooner or later (depending on where you started) come to Broadway. If you were to cross Broadway, still heading toward Portugal, you would find, to your surprise, that you were no longer on West Third Street, but on Great Jones Street. If, pursuing your vision of a cheap vacation, you were to continue for another fifty paces, past an office building owned by the Traders Trust Co. (a contradiction in terms), you would come to 3½ Great Jones Street, into which Stevie Dickinson heaved her lard. From across the street I watched the second floor. I did not need to watch the ground floor, because Neros Hero's [*sic*] occupied the whole of it. Stevie Dickinson had just eaten, remember. Besides, Neros Hero's had its own entrance. I did not need to watch the third floor, because there was none. The point I am trying to make is that for me to watch any floor but the second would have been a waste of time. No light went on and nothing visible stirred behind any of its four windows. In the foyer were two mail boxes, one for Stevie Dickinson and one for Ermaño— Artiste [*sic*]. I deduced from this, for in those days I still believed in deductions, that the second floor was divided into two apartments. In silent blue suede sneakers I tiptoed up the stairs, at the top of which I made a second deduction. Because the word "Ermaño" was artistically splashed in pink paint across the door on the right, I recklessly assumed that Stevie Dickinson was holed up behind the door on the left. Between the door on the left and the door on the right, was another, that opened (with a creak) to a watercloset.

A stencil across the door informed anybody who was interested that Neros Hero's was open from five in the morning until six in the evening, this not being a neighborhood in which people lingered after dark. At long communal tables on either side of a central aisle, working stiffs ate their foot-long sandwiches. If by chance you catch the eye of a man such as these, you nod and look elsewhere, unless you are also looking for trouble. I could see why Stevie Dickinson preferred to eat farther away from home, nor do I mean that anyone here would have whistled or sucked his teeth at her. In these declining United States, the last besieged outpost against feminism is manned by manly men who move around heavy objects for their living. Feminists know that they cannot convince, convert, confuse, or confound the men who carry the world on their backs. All private pathologies aside, that knowledge is the undercurrent of feminist hysteria and desperation. The working classes, god bless them, are a stumbling block to all utopians, right, left, or beyond the pale.

> I'll give you one—O
> Red fly the banners—O
> What is your one—O?
> One is workers' unity
> And ever more shall be so.

Dripping gravy from a steak and onion hero, I walked east on Great Jones, south on Lafayette, west on Bond, north on Broadway, back to Great Jones, my mouth full of beef fat and gristle, both of which I like. Northeast Distributors; Great Jones Clayworks; a severe-looking woman in tight pants, frizzy hair, and saucer-sized sunglasses sticking up posters for a troupe of African dancers with naked breasts; four guys sitting on a tailgate solemnly eating sandwiches and watching her; John J. Nutt, Export, & Son; M.A. Hassan, Importer (of dirty pictures?); Air Compressors Exchanged, Repaired, Rented, Bought, Sold; a skulking cat; a man in shorts riding a bicycle and wearing a gas mask; Serving Soho-Noho, Freddy and his Van, moves furniture, art, etc.; Karadajian Leather Goods; Gordo Traders; Great Ball Truckers; warehouses and office buildings; a dead cat; Jogging Machines; Buttonholes: Flags and Banners; Ronald Nuter, Ltd.; men unloading trucks or pushing dollies; secretaries, their behinds fat or flat. Behind 3½ Great Jones street was a vacant lot, scattered bricks and ailanthus trees. Behind the vacant lot was the building that had adjoined the building whose removal had vacated the lot. It had no back windows. No windows anywhere looked out on the back windows of 3½ Great Jones Street. Through a space between two buildings on Bond Street I saw that an ailanthus tree shielded the world from whatever abominations affrighted the huddled shadows of Stevie Dickinson's apartment.

I walked the six miles home in the manner of Muriel Bigalow, oblivious to the action around me, for I was thinking furiously. The paradox of thought is that it removes you from the world it is supposed to help you understand. But I have proof that the mind continues to take things in even while playing with itself. I returned to the world, and therefore to myself, before a foot-long commando knife in a display case in an Army and Navy store. I bought not the knife, for I already had one something like it, but a fatigue cap and a good-sized tool box. Nearer home, I bought carpenter's tools, some in this store, some in that, including a sturdy little pry bar and some heavy-duty chisels. If I could not pose as a carpenter, being the son of one, I might just as well give up this game of impersonation altogether. Nearer still to home, I stopped for my reheeled boots, for eight pork chops, cut from the shoulder, where the meat is fat and rich; a jar of honey; salad makings; a canister of baking powder; a quart of bourbon; two cold bottles of rosé. I bought rosé because I do not know anything about wine. In fact, I do not want to know anything about wine. I consider it a virtue not to know anything about wine. I dropped off at my apartment everything but the eats and drinks, which I carried down to Bill's. He was wearing only a ludicrous and baggy pair of underwear shorts, loafers, and black socks, with garters, for Bill's calves were thin.

"You're early," he said.

"You got company?" I said.

"I'm emulating you," he said.

"Congratulations," I said. "You're the first. But—"

"Of many, let us hope," he said.

"I've never even seen a pair of shorts like that," I said. "As for garters—"

"The future of mankind depends on it," he said.

"You mean—" I said.

"I want to know every detail of how you did it," he said.

"It's a long story," I said.

"I have just now done four push-ups," he said. A few days ago I could only do two and a half. You do how many?"

"I've never tried more than a hundred at a time," I said.

"Tell me everything," he said. "I want to be made over again."

"To begin with," I said, "you've got to think of yourself as a hammer, rather than an anvil. It's not a question of *being made*, but of *making*—"

"Good, good," he said; "that's just what I want to hear. Together we will set out on the great adventure of forging a new self for me."

While I honied the chops and mixed the biscuit batter, Bill talked nonstop, like a miser of words determined to blow his stash. He was fantastical and he was funny, all the more so for the mock-shy way in which he drawled out his words. Except for a slight feverishness, this was Bill as I first knew him, my first friend. How many of you, with all your promiscuity, can truthfully say that your friendship was accepted, nay embraced, by the first person to whom you offered it? Jude's death, he said, had driven him into melancholy adust, Hamlet's disease, dark and deeper than which is no sea dingle. Perpend: in the soul's subterranean grots, the wish is taken as father to fact, and judged accordingly. If you wish someone's death, but do not admit it to yourself, and that person dies, the unadmitted wish turns to unwot guilt, which surfaces as depression. Bah, I said.

Wait, he said: his depression made him yearn for drink; his guilt kept him from drinking. He punished himself by remaining dry. His dryness increased his depression, which increased his yearning for a drink. (Here I took the chef's knife from him, for I did not want bits of finger in my salad.) He apologized for the grumpiness, now gone forever, of last Sunday's phone call, but that was the first time since his sophomore year in college that he had gone forty-eight hours without a drink. On late Tuesday afternoon (around the time I was decapitating a wood-chuck), as he was driving home from Jude's funeral in a rented limousine, his mother sitting beside him, something happened.

His half-focussed eyes came to rest on a girl in a light blue sweat suit who was jogging effortlessly along the footpath by Belt Parkway, her blonde curls unfurled, her clear features cleaving the wind. Suddenly the setting sun seemed to pour its gold into him, rather than over the horizon. He tingled all over. A weight fell from his shoulders, scales from his eyes. He felt like a man who had accommodated himself to a life sentence of hard labor, suddenly reprieved. Was it no more than the body's recovery from a twenty-year round of hangover follow-ing upon besottedness following upon hangover? He thought not. The experience was momentous, if internal. Miss Lily had not an inkling, even when he told her to go back to Virginia and stay there. Ursula had no clue, even when he told her that he could not in decency think of remarrying for a year, if then, and should he choose to spend July in the country with his friend Victor she would have to accommodate herself. That same Tuesday, having set his house in order, he felt surcharged with energy, but did not know what to do with himself. He looked at his naked body in a mirror and did not like what he saw. He waved his arms and hopped on one foot. In all his library of six thousand books there was nothing that told you how to forge a new outer man to fit around the born-again inner one. A remarkable omission, but it inspired him. A life-giving sense of purpose rushed into space vacated by the deadening weight that had fallen from him earlier.

He would write a book. He would do for the body's health what Robert Burton had done for the mind's sickness. He would write a Menippean meditation, a dizzy carnival of words, a satire and a celebration, a compendious conflation of all the world's learning, lore, disputation, and delusion about the sub-ject, whether alchemical, anatomical, artistic, or astrological;

whether gastronomical, geometrical, gerontological, or Granto-
logical; whether histological, historical, or hysterical; whether
paleolithic, phenomonological, political, or pragmatical;
whether teratological, theological, tropological, zymological, or
pseudo-polypanprotodeuterologological. How, for example,
did body-builders go about building their bodies before the
invention of mirrors? He had already filed 300 note cards. His
book would be a ten year's labor of love, and written to last
forever. While it was a-writing, he and I would test theory with
practise. What did I say?

For roughly seven seconds I did not say anything, and
sometimes I wish there were a God, just so I could ask Somebody to forgive me. There being no God, you can see, dear
readers, why it is I need you—though not as much as you need
me. What I then proceeded to do, my friends, was to get Bill
drunk. This calls for a celebration, I said, and uncorked a bottle
of rosé. After what he had just told me? he said. Precisely
because of what he told me, I said, pouring two glassfuls. Look,
he said, what he needed me for was to push him onward. He
was perfectly capable of sliding backward on his own. He was
no longer the slave of his appetites, I said, but their master, and
mastery does not exist unless it is exercised. That's a point, he
said, as I handed him a glass. He could exercise his mastery and
thus make it grow, I said, as he had been exercising his muscles
to make them grow, by drinking one glass of wine, but only
one. If I said so, he said. We clinked glasses. By eight o'clock
Bill had passed out in his favorite chair.

Bill and I were different from each other in this respect:
when he drank too much, he passed out, but never got sick;
whereas when I drink too much, I get sick, much as I would
prefer to pass out. In four hours or so, when Bill woke up, I
intended to be sitting beside him with a pot of coffee ready, and
who is to say that I had not been sitting beside him the whole
time? I would tell him that I had allowed him to get drunk as
a lesson. Bill was far too trusting, of his friends and of himself.

I had heard the theory that manipulation is inconsistent with friendship, even if the manipulation is for the friend's sake, but I ignored it. You are not going to tell me, are you, that my creepy crawling (as Manson's Family described it) into Stevie Dickinson's apartment was not for Bill's sake, but for the sake of some obscure itch of my own?

It took me only ten minutes to straighten up (Bill had eaten two chops and six biscuits; I had eaten two biscuits and six chops), and to dump the trash, including three empty bottles, down the incinerator chute. I tucked Bill's paisley robe around him, not because he looked cold, but because he looked so defenseless wearing nothing but those ridiculous shorts with the design of green apples and the hair curling out of the fly. I pushed in the lock-release button, tested the outside knob, closed the door, opened it, looked again to where the crown of Bill's head showed over the back of the chair, closed the door, sneakered to my apartment. With a razor blade I undid Kristal's stitches in the work pants. I folded pants, work shirt, and fatigue cap over the tools in the tool box. On top of these I lay a comb, a mirror, and a stub of eyebrow pencil Samantha had left behind. I changed into tee shirt, Sta-Press pants, hush puppies, and sweatshirt. I then placed the tool box into the musette bag, which I slung over a shoulder, as though it were one of those pocketbooks men have suddenly taken to wearing. I went out the door, locked it, stood thinking for a moment, unlocked the door, went back in, fetched my knife (just in case) from where it gleamed dully at the back of the closet, next to my machete. I put the knife in one of Samantha's pink purple skating socks (the one with the hole in it), the sock in the tool box, the tool box in the musette bag, which I slung over my shoulder, and out the door I went, sweating, pausing on each floor to make sure no one was about, onto the street, hugging the shadows, over to Morningside Park, where even the cops did not venture after dark, downtown and crosstown to One-hundred-tenth Street and Manhattan Avenue, into Central

Park, where even the muggers were afraid to venture after dark, downtown and crosstown to Ninety-sixth Street and Fifth Avenue, east to the Lexington Avenue Subway, on which there was not likely to be anyone I knew, down to Union Square, where only junkies and the ghosts of soapbox orators ventured after dark, downtown along Broadway, where stray pedestrians walked quickly and looked over their shoulders, onto Great Jones Street, where there was no sign of life, except for a man rolling a vacuum cleaner about the size and shape of an oil drum out of the Trader's Trust building and into his van, except for the lights in Stevie Dickinson's windows.

I walked around the block to Bond Street and ducked into the space between two buildings, one of which was a warehouse, its elevator shaft marked (as a warning to impetuous firemen) with red bulbs, one behind the window on each landing. In the back alley, by the depraved light of these bulbs, using Samantha's pencil, I enlarged and darkened my eyebrows, darkened my mustache and beard. I parted my hair in the middle and slicked it down (with spit), so that it would show under the fatigue cap, which looked good on me, although I no longer looked like me, although it was a browner shade of green than the work suit. I did not bother to remove my Sta-Press slacks, but pulled the work pants on right over them. I did remove my sweatshirt before putting on the work shirt. I left comb, mirror, eyebrow pencil, and sweatshirt in the musette bag, which I hid under a mattress someone had (I assume) discarded, for if the mattress were still in use, the user would find it lumpier than usual, but not by much.

The van, the man, the vacuum cleaner were gone from Great Jones Street, but light still issued from Stevie Dickinson's windows, as did a sound of hammering. She, like Erica von Plaack, was having her lair redecorated, I reasoned, for in those days I still believed in reasoning. I hush puppied up the steps. The hammering stopped, abruptly. I had just put my ear to the door when it opened.

"What the fuck do you want?" said Stevie Dickinson. There was sawdust on the arms of her dingy white shirt and on the thighs of her white carpenter's pants, which thighs looked like a pair of tackling dummies stuffed with hair rollers. Up close like this, I could see that what I had thought was a faint mustache was in fact a tobacco stain. Her front teeth were gray brown; her gums were red and puffy.

"Gotta leak?" I said, with the smallest of nods toward the john.

"You a fucking wise guy?" she said.

"I'm a plumber," I said.

"What leak?" she said.

"Downstairs," I said. "Right over the veal and peppers. Thinned out the gravy."

"Who the fuck are you?" she said, squinting.

"Nothing wrong there," I said, with a large nod toward the john. "And Mr. Ermaño doesn't answer."

"He summers in Tunisia, buggering Arabs," she said.

I swear on the memory of my mother, whom, you will remember, my father rightly described as a saint, that all I wanted was to get out of there. Since the john was in the hall, I assumed there was no plumbing in her apartment, for in those days I had not yet broken the habit of forming assumptions. I was just about to say, "Well, I'll have to hunt up the super for a key to Nero's," but Stevie Dickinson beat me to it.

"Let's get it over with," she said, holding the door open for me.

X

$\mathbb{T}$HERE was a stink of cats. And there were the stinking cats themselves, long-haired, red-haired brutes, three of them, with baleful eyes. There were long-haired dust-fluffies, like dead mice, humped around the unevenly worn floor, for Stevie Dickinson's apartment was a converted loft, although the conversion was far from complete. The walls, ceiling, and floor had been painted a dirty white. Partitioning off the far right corner of the room was a screen (Art Deco nudes, long bodies and small breasts), behind which Stevie no doubt dressed, so as not to break the mirrors. Or maybe it was for the cats to drop their stink behind, in privacy. There was also a lot of unfinished carpentry: shutters, shelves, a kitchen counter, a windowseat, and in the far left corner, amid a clutter of sawdust and planks and tools and nails, a loft bed.

Next to the bed was a so-far unpainted pine dresser, good for maybe three weeks of careful use. On the dresser was a lamp, white base and red shade, price tag still attached. Over the lamp was a cross, from which the Palestine prototype of Charles Manson drooped. From behind the crucified rabble-rouser, three palm leaves sprouted, like feathers in His cap.

Next to the dresser was an as yet unvarnished pine chair (give it two weeks), upon which lay a chenille bed spread, red tufts on a white background, still in its plastic sheath. Curtains to match adorned the window next to the chair. Next to the window was a print of Venus hanging ten on a clam shell, her face much like Samantha's, her body very different, as I well knew, and as Stevie Dickinson was dying to find out, if she didn't know already, and that's a another reason I sometimes wish there were a God, to devise and administer tortures worthy of the crime, for when it comes to devising and administering tortures, mortals cannot hope to compete with God, try as they may.

"That's a man-sized job you've taken on," I said.

"How the fuck would you know?" she said.

Whatever made this pathetic creature botched in God's image think Samantha liked chenille? What makes you think I could afford the luxury of pitying her? Remember whose wife all this chintz was supposed to seduce. What possessed me to think I would find evidence of her intentions towards Bill strewn around her apartment? I must have been crazy. If anywhere, those intentions were clogging the drains of her brain, which you couldn't get me to plumb on a dare, not with a Roto-Rooter and a money-back guarantee.

"I'd better see if there's a blockage under there," I said, pointing to the cabinet under the sink.

"Keep your grimy fucking paws off the counter," she said, and rolled her thighs past each other toward the loft bed.

I squatted before the cabinet, opened it, pushed aside the box of kitty litter, and opened my tool box, in which there was no pipe wrench, for carpenters do not as a matter of course lug pipe wrenches around with them. I clanked the tools around for a minute and then turned to shout across the room that the leak or stoppage or whatever must be somewhere else, after which I meant to beat it, before I caught something.

But Stevie Dickinson was not across the room. She was

standing over me, her arm raised high above her head, like some Old Testament lunatic with bad news for blasphemers. At the end of her arm, three miles away, was her hand, and in her hand was a hammer, already on the down-swing. I moved my head sideways, like a Balinese dancer, so that the hammer caught me on a trapezius, rather than between the eyes. The hammer bounced off my trapezius, which was thick and strong, and out of her hand, which was thin and weak, no matter how fell. My left arm went numb. In my right hand was the knife, how it got there I will never know. It was still in Samantha's sock, except for an inch that had worked through the toe-hole. The point was pricking the skin on her size 11 neck, and how it got there she will never know, for she was watching the hammer, which had still not hit the ground by the time I was up and making a dimple where she would have had an Adam's apple, if the Father of her God of the Palms there hadn't played one of His ghastly jokes on her.

"Take it easy," she said, and that is what I said too, but she was already saying "it" when I said "Take," so that the last word was mine.

"What do you want?" she said.

"Don't you mean what the fuck do I want?" I said. I could tell that my left arm would not be paralyzed forever. It had begun to tingle.

"I have around sixty dollars in my wallet," she said, and she pointed somewhere behind her.

"Good for you," I said. I could now slowly open and close my left hand.

"I have an obstruction in my vagina," she said.

"You can do better than that," I said. I could feel my trapezius swelling. At the current rate, in a minute it would be kissing my ear lobe. My left elbow was now responding to orders from above, but not entirely as directed.

"I can do something else for you," she said.

A drop of blood ran down her neck from under the point

of the knife. I pulled back a few inches. She mistook the movement for a signal and dropped to her knees. I mistook her movement for the onset of an attack and thrust like a fencer. She never even saw the knife split the air over her head. Before I could poise for another strike, she was unbuckling my belt and unzipping my fly.

"Leave everything to me," she said.

I was too flabbergasted to say anything. She pulled down the work pants, only to expose the Sta-Press slacks.

"What the fuck is this?" she said.

She undid my Sta-Press pants and pulled them down. She pulled down my John's Bargain Store briefs. Then she took my joint in her mouth. I let her, because the fact is that I did not know quite how to stop her. All right, smart aleck, what the fuck would you have done?

You'll be interested to know what I felt. I wish I knew. It was not only disgust, and not only at her. It was not only embarrassment, and not only for myself. It certainly was not pleasure. For one thing, her mouth was cold. There is no doubt that she was good at what she was doing. Her skill must have been instinctive, for it is unlikely that she had much practice. What a waste! you say. I agree; but for nature to be bountiful, she must also be wasteful. Why not just relax and enjoy myself? you say. You must never have met Stevie Dickinson. I grabbed her by the hair, as you would hold a severed head, except that my fingers were not yet functioning well enough to have borne the weight. I tucked the point of my knife under her chin. I looked around, as though for a witness to the fact that I had not intended this.

My eyes came to rest on a poster, a blown-up photo of a mob of feminists at a demonstration. In the foreground a beautiful young woman with black hair parted down the middle held a placard. It read MAKE WAR, NOT LOVE. Next to the poster was a wardrobe with a full-length mirror set in the door. Gooseflesh I had experienced, but never before had I actually felt the hair on the nape of my neck stand on end. You might argue that all women are beautiful when they do what Stevie Dickinson was doing, although I would not myself. As I saw her in the mirror, she had suddenly become pretty, if your tastes run to fifteen-year-old boys. Because that is what she looked like, a pretty boy, rather than a woman, beautiful or otherwise, but not exactly, for I was seeing double, first this, then that, then this and that simultaneously. Perception is never pure. You always see what you know or think you know as well as what you see. I knew what I knew, but I was not sure what I saw. What I saw gave me the creeps. I may have moaned, but not for the reason Stevie Dickinson may have thought. With a jerk of the wrist I shook the sock off the knife, and switched it to my left hand, for an unobstructed view. It has been many times observed that revulsion and fascination go together.

A swollen, crooked vein ran down from under her hair to the right side of her nose. Her closed lids were hidden in plum-colored shadows. Long eyelashes glinted where they curved off her cheek. A faint flush illuminated her skin, a faint sheen. Highlights ran along the clean line of her jaw, the whorls of her ear. Pastel shadows washed the shallow of her cheek. They tinted the fine down there copper, then pink, then red, then purple, as she moved. A skein of hair fell forward over her brow. I smoothed it back. She kept at her work and I kept at my watching. Frankly, I was surprised to feel the old thunder-head gathering inside me. In the mirror, I saw her eyes open, look up toward me. What she saw was that I was looking away from her. Then she unhinged her jaws, like a cobra about to strike.

Now dammit, I had worked hard to develop the left side of my body. Every exercise I did with the right, I also did with the left, and just as many times, too. Oh, I shaved the left side of my face, combed the left side of my head, brushed the teeth of the left side of my mouth, all with my left hand. Ambidexterity had been an old dream of mine, a futile dream perhaps, but not an ignoble one, and in any case less futile than the fashionable dream of androgyny, if you do not mind my saying so. The lamentable fact is that in a crisis I reacted like any other monodexter, all the more so because my wretched left hand was still half-numb. When the alarm signals went off inside me, I instinctively reacted with my right, which no longer held the knife. I cuffed her with the heel of my hand at the same time that I jerked back my midsection. Anything less, and she would have bitten my penis in half. A little more, such as a ventilating of her gullet with the knife, and she would not have caught the tip of my penis between her teeth, which closed with a clack.

She tipped over onto her well-padded bum, and scuttled backward, like a double-jointed crab. I went after her and tripped on the three pairs of pants around my ankles. It is a fortunate thing that my erection had begun to wilt (an instinctive reaction to aggression, which is why men like their women to pretend submissiveness, for pretended submissiveness is about the most you can expect) or it would have shattered, like the plaster banana among the bogus plums and grapes in the bowl on the table in your great aunt's drawing room where you were ordered to sit very quiet. As it was, the belly whopper onto the floor put a permanent kink in my sex life, at least I never noticed any hook to the north and east before then, and I don't care how many women claim that no man has ever felt pain to equal that of childbirth. The only thing equal to my pain was my rage, which kept me going. You could have cut my head off (the one on my neck, I mean) and it would not have slowed me down, not long anyhow.

My accursed and ill-fated left hand let go of the knife when my arm slapped full-length along the floor, so I had to make do by grabbing her foot with my right. Out of the corner of my eye I saw the cats hurtling madly in all directions around the room, and it is funny how you notice a thing like that at a time like this. Stevie reared back her other foot and kicked me in the nose, breaking it. My well-favored and trusted right hand let go. She scuttled out of reach. A cat pounced on my back with a maniacal snarl, fixed its claws into my tender trapezius, and sank its teeth in my neck. Stevie found the knife. I found the cat's tail. We both stood up. She held the knife as though to core out my navel. I took a turn of the cat's tail around my fist, and a joint popped. The cat yowled in my ear, freeze-drying the blood that dribbled from my nose. Stevie feinted at me like a fencer. I swung the cat by its tail, as you would swing a ball and chain. She bobbed her head, as though to slip a punch, so that the head of the cat caught her not in the temple, but on the side of her clean-lined jaw, breaking it. She fell forward on her face and rolled over onto her back, arms flopping out wide to either side.

The cat dangled limply from my hand. I hoisted it by the tail. Something orange hung from its mouth, its brains. I dropped it, as my mother, when once she reached into her washtub for a heavy gray sock she had left to soak, dropped the drowned rat. I sat on the floor, cupped both hands over my battered and bitten groin, and rocked back and forth, yowling —silently, but more abysmally than all the sick cats in all the back alleys of all the razed and contagious cities of the world. Stevie Dickinson was breathing rapidly and noisily, a kind of snuffle-snort. I got up and hobbled over to Samantha's pink sock, which I carefully wound round my poor fallen and bleeding sparrow, at which I could not bear to look. I then pulled up my John's Bargain Store briefs, my Sta-Press pants, my work pants, in that order, for any other order would have required a contortionist. I recovered my knife and gingerly knelt astraddle over her, dripping blood from my nose, and don't think it didn't hurt to spread my knees wide enough to span those oozy hips. She was no longer like a pretty boy, but like a depraved one, with her jaw out of alignment, her mouth slightly open (and empty) as though on the verge of twisting into a sneer. I ripped her shirt apart, the buttons flying, and this was no time to worry whether she knew how to sew them on again. She was not wearing a brassiere, nor had she any need for one.

A line of four moles bisected her fourth and fifth ribs (from the top) at an angle. Single hairs grew out of the first and third moles (from the bottom). I could see how her little heart was going pit-a-pat against the skin stretched between these ribs, as though a demon were knocking against the roof of his prison to be let out. Droplets of perspiration glittered all over her chest, from which a yeasty warmth drifted up. I placed the point of the knife on the second mole (from the bottom), which was between the ribs, but not equidistant between them, for it was closer to the fourth than the fifth (from the top). I revolved the knife until it was parallel, rather than at right angles, to her ribs, getting fussy in my middle age. A cat pussyfooted toward us, then stopped to glare at me. I glared back. It dropped its head, pretended to find something worth sniffing at on the floor, then slunk away. I grasped the handle of the knife with my still weak left hand and rested the heel of my indomitable right on the pommel. I could feel her heart beat through the knife. A drop of blood gathered on the mole, spilled over, and still I hesitated. I looked around the room, my groin and trapezius throbbing. One of the cats must have knocked over the Art Deco screen. Beyond it were a narrow iron cot, a chair, a dresser, all painted white. On the dresser were a bottle of creme de menthe (for which Samantha had a passion) with a white ribbon around its neck, a big heart-shaped box of candy (to which Samantha was indifferent) with a red ribbon around its belly, and in a fancy open silver box, between parted wings of tissue paper, something that at this distance looked like a flimsy, black negligée, which Samantha would have to do without. I leaned forward on the knife.

I felt her heart clench the knife and tug at it. Then I bore down and it went through to the floor. We were nearly touching noses when she opened her eyes. I whipped my head back. She lifted hers, bared her teeth, and hissed. We will never know whether I was hearing things, or whether that hiss was in fact made up of words, the words "fuck you," for example. Her heart tugged on the knife twice more. She shut her eyes and lowered her head. There was another tug, then, after a pause, another, then no more. I reached forward and with a thumb removed a flap of my flesh from behind her incisors. I did not simply throw it away, because I was afraid one of the cats would eat it. I pushed it into a breast pocket of the work shirt. The knife had gone in easier than it came out, much easier. There was no use in my trying to wipe the knife on her shirt, for her shirt was already wetter and redder than the knife. So I wiped it on her pants. The slow tide of her blood washed over the drops from my nose that had spotted her chest, her shirt, the floor. Just before it reached my knees, I pushed off her to my feet. I leaned against the wall, stiff and weary as Pat Nixon's smile, for while a first murder may rev you up, a second runs you down.

I plugged my leaky nostrils with two patches cut from my tee shirt. I washed the drying blood off my beard and scoured the traces of blood off the knife. Then I scoured the sink, a job long overdue. By Stevie Dickinson's narrow iron cot (fit only for a nun, or a priest, not that there's much difference) was an open window. Out of this window I threw the dead cat. Yes, that was a negligée in the box, all right. Sometimes you must resist even the impulse toward poetic justice. Instead of stealing the negligée, to give to Samantha, I stole the fifty-four dollars from the wallet, to keep for myself, and I still lost money on this murder, everything considered. I will not even allude to all the weeks I had been unemployed. I also stole a pack of Lucky Strikes, my brand, for I was nearly out. I stood up the Art Deco screen. With a strip cut from the bottom of my tee shirt I wiped all the hard surfaces I had touched, including the cannister of Ajax, never before used. In this strip I wrapped my knife, which I then placed in the tool box. At the door I stopped to survey the room, and a good thing I did. To the left was a card table, upon which, I surmised, Stevie Dickinson consumed her starches or doused cigarettes in them. Underneath it was her hammer. From the pool of blood by her body to the screen (and presumably beyond) was a line of bloody left footprints. Here's a puzzle for you: how would you remove these clues without leaving new ones?

I ripped off some more tee shirt, all that was left of it below the armpits, and my twisting around like that sent some interesting pains through my crotch. The fetching halter that remained is as much tee shirt as you actually need, anyhow, and it has the advantage of showing off your stomach muscles, assuming you have any. I took off my shoes and socks. On bare tippy-toes, I fetched the hammer (gripping it through the midriff of the shirt) and pitched it underhand onto the loft bed, a perfect strike. Working back to the door, I wiped out my damp toeprints (and a few drops of eye-water, for bending over like that sent some wonderful pains through my fork), leaving a dust-free path for the cops to scratch their heads over.

Working backward from the window by Stevie's cot, upon which a less resolute man would have curled up with his thumb in his mouth, I wiped out my bloody left footprints, my dusty right footprints, and some drops of sweat and tears, for when your nose is broken, your eyes tend to water, even if you have nothing else to cry about. And the cops could purse their lips or furrow their brows or stroke their chins or pull their ears or bite their mustaches over that swath swabbed through the dust all they wanted, for all I cared. They could mangle their faces entirely before I'd do their work for them. To hell with that. Back at the door, I wiped my toes with the least disgusting fold of shirt I could find, so as not to get telltale dust on my socks, not that I seriously thought anybody was about to inspect them. Gripping the knob with a tail of the work shirt, I sock-footed it out, carrying shoes and shirt-rag, nor did I forget the tool box, although it would have been understandable if I had, given all I had been through.

In the john, I tore the piece of shirt into smaller pieces and

flushed them down, with a bon voyage. May they meet somewhere, somehow, with Jude Karnofsky's half-slip and live together happily ever after. Then I rinsed my fingers and flushed.
Then I took off my socks and rinsed my toes and flushed. Then
I put on my socks and hobbled down the stairs. Just inside the
doorway to the street, I put on my shoes, for on the sidewalks
of New York, bloody footprints are hardly unusual enough to
count as clues. No one was about. In the alley, under the mi-
graine-red bulbs, I wiped the make-up off my face with the
surviving bib of tee shirt, which I threw under the mattress, for
if you would just take the trouble to wash your own shirts, you
wouldn't have to worry about those tireless and implacable
pursuers who, right now, are following a trail of laundry marks
to your doorstep. After re-arranging my hair, I flung the de-
fingerprinted comb, mirror, and eyebrow pencil after the bib.
After thinking a bit, I hurled the strip of shirt from around the
knife after bib, comb, mirror, and pencil. Imagine some slow-
witted flatfoot lifting a corner of the mattress for a peek underneath, just to make sure. Imagine some ferret-eyed detective
illegally searching my tool box on a hunch. Imagine their cigar-
smoking chief matching strip to bib, then looking up with a
grin. Imagine me handcuffed and hustled through the jeering
streets in a cart, the guillotine looming eerily in the early morning mist. No thank you. So I risked a few nicks in the perfect
edge of my knife, keen enough to split hairs with, if you've got
nothing better to do. Just don't try it with me.

With the musette bag slung over my undamaged trapezius,
I walked (bowlegged) to Twenty-third Street, and all the street
lights, for some reason, seemed dim and out-of-focus. Outside
of Lüchow's a pair of young swingers decided to race me for a
cab. The man took one look into my face and changed his mind.
I got out at Forty-second Street and Eighth Avenue, where
anything goes. If it came to that, I could always say I had paid
a prostitute to go with me to a parking lot, thus saving the price
of a room. There she had bitten me below while a confederate

beat me above. Such things happen, and not just in New York, as the less sheltered among you can testify. I was looking around for another cab when a black desperado walked up to me. He put a hand into my windbreaker pocket, pulled out a pack of Luckies, helped himself to a cigarette, offered me one, restored the pack, lit us up, exhaled, said: "Slow night."

"I've seen slower," I said.

"You looking to do business with Alberto, forget it," he said. "He's all wired up for sound."

"You just destroyed my faith in human nature," I said.

"Well, you know, he's facing twenty-five-to-life," he said. "That can turn a man around."

"Alberto be lucky to face the day after tomorrow," I said.

"That's what I thought. I'll pass the word around. Meanwhile . . ." he said, starting to walk off, "And you ought to do something for that cold."

I took my time getting off the second cab at One-hundredth Street and Central Park West, making the driver wait and making wait the roly-poly couple who were waving at him from across the street as though he were their last hope. I walked (slowly) through the Park to One-hundred-tenth Street, and that was a rat, not, as I first thought, a black cat, that scurried across my path. I crossed over to Morningside Park, and when at the entrance two skinny pre-adolescents in sneakers looked me over, I stopped, put down the musette bag, and looked them over back, for Stevie Dickinson had put me in a foul mood. I did not like the way she had died (or the way she had lived, either). Under a cairn of rocks, dirt, and clumps of grass, amid the ruined scenery of Columbia University's fatal attempt in 1968 to build a gym, I buried the work suit and fatigue cap. On second thought, I also buried my socks, pushing them down some rodent's hole with a stick. Hugging the shadows, gritting my teeth, I made it home unobserved, so far as I knew, or (at that moment) cared. First I washed my nether wound in Ivory liquid detergent and painted it with iodine. No.

I did not faint, although I may have tottered. Then I wrapped it in gauze, leaving a pee hole, for a Band-Aid would have looked ridiculous. I washed the scratches and bites in my neck and trapezius, and I washed the last traces of blood and make-up from my face, changed my nose plugs of tee shirt for new ones of cotton, changed into my denims, and eased on down the stairs to Bill's place.

I did not know exactly how I was going to explain my broken nose to Bill, but my line might be that if he could get drunk enough to pass out, I could get drunk enough to fall on my face. The crown of his head, like a hairy sun setting, showed over the back of the chair. In spite of everything, I smiled, indulgently, affectionately, paternally, content. While he slept, his mother and I ran around committing felonies in his behalf. Well, that was as it should be. I made for the chair facing Bill's, for I wanted to sit down and spread my legs. Bill was pretty much as I had left him, except for one thing. There was no doubt that he was dead: the ice pick was up to its hilt between the fourth and fifth ribs (from the top).

Let's not talk about how I felt. Let's just say I have never felt worse, and this comes from a man who has almost always felt bad. It was not just that I had gotten Bill drunk, and there-fore defenseless. It is not just that I had left the door unlocked, and therefore no obstacle. It is not even that sure as sin I begat the murder of my best friend when I murdered my best friend's wife. Least of all was it that I had lost my alibi. No, no, by now you cannot possibly think so little of me as to believe that. Say you do, and I'll put an ice pick into my own heart, gladly. The simple fact, friends and fellow-sufferers, is that love is real. I was not grieving for myself, for my own loss, which is the way of most grievers. I was grieving for Bill, for his loss of his life, upon which everything else we are capable of losing depends. I will never forgive God for not existing—I will never forgive him for not building a Heaven from which Bill's spirit could smile and look down on me, indulgently, affectionately, paternally, content. Everything else can be mitigated but death.

No, I did not rant and rave. No, I did not scream and roar in rage. No, I did not pull my hair and rend my cheeks. No, I did not fall in a fit and bite the rug. No, I did not roll in dung and pour dirt on my head—besides there wasn't any handy. I sat in the chair and spread my legs. Leave such ostentations of grief for those shallow people whose emotions are all on the surface. There was the beginning of an apologetic smile on Bill's face. At least I hadn't sneaked my victims' lives away from them while they slept. At least my victims had a chance to fight back. Bill's paisley robe was open a crack, wide enough to expose the area over his heart. Hair curled out of the fly of his preposterous shorts. One garter had slipped down over a skinny calf. A nice job I had done of protecting him. What was Miss Lily going to say? Water streamed from my eyes, for my nose had begun to ache something awful. Oh, I knew what I was supposed to do, all right. A proper avenger, the kind I had striven to be, would have gone to his apartment, fetched his machete, marched implacably to 33 Gramercy Park East, and massacred all the merry-makers inside (except Samantha). Fine. But you need strength enough to get out of your chair first.

After a long time, I dragged myself to the kitchen and wiped fingerprints off everything I remembered touching. Then I did the same in the living room, and it did not bother me that I might be wiping out clues to the killer, for I intended to wipe out the killer next. Then I hauled myself upstairs, where through the endless night I lay on top of the bed shivering, listening for a scream, pleading with the universe that impetuous Toby not pull his hand out of Ursula's and run in to wake his sleepyhead Dad with a giggling leap into his lap. A wolf howled in the distance. Another answered it. Ghouls chuckled outside my window. Flares or some kind of silent firework flashed red. One by one rats swam to the surface in the toilet bowl and climbed out, dripping. A cat with something orange hanging from his mouth jumped onto the foot of my bed and burrowed frantically under the covers. Someone slowly, silently turned the door knob, found the door locked, shook the knob in a rage. Across the alley, ghosts of the Weimar Republic had gathered for a costume ball. You could hear murmurs, clinks of glasses, shrieks of laughter, an orchestra playing "Béseme mucho," over and over and over. The transvestite crooner's plaint was in German, so I could not make out the words, which in any case kept fading away, like the confused and distant din, the shouts and cries from the approaches to the city, where gaunt men in animal skins, their bare legs up to the thighs in snow, overran the last outposts. Their prophetess, wearing white rags that fluttered in the moaning wind, urged them on, howling like a wolf.

I picked up the phone. I was grateful to Samantha for having insisted on a bedroom extension, which at the time I thought a needless extravagance. When you get hit on the trapezius with a hammer, you do not want to move your neck, or anything else, let alone jump out of bed, should you be awakened by phone the next morning, or early afternoon, as the case may be. Gusts of rain beat against the window.

"Boy, that was some party," said Samantha.

"And Darkness and Decay and the Red Death hold illimitable dominion over all," I said.

"Whew, did I get tipsy," she said.

"Rats and cats and bats," I said.

"Everybody was making out like mad," she said.

"Everybody whom? doom, gloomaloom," I said.

"What?" she said. "Lots of famous people you don't know. The Garrulous Gourmet is a real character."

"Tracy?" I said.

"Yes, she was there," she said. "Why do you ask?"

"Casey?" I said.

"Sure," she said.

"Lacey?" I said.

"You mean Stacey," she said. "The three of them were

asleep when I left this morning. They were heaped up every which way with Robin and Kate on this big bed in the "Playroom." It looked eerie cause there's mirrors all around the walls and only this one big red lightbulb in the middle of the ceiling."

"Fiji?" I said.

"Well, yes, and her husband Allerton Guth," she said. "He's a millionaire, you know."

"Yes, you told me," I said. "Erika von Plaack?"

"They had a terriffic argument," she said. "Fiji didn't want to go home."

"Erika von Plaack?" I said.

"It was her party, silly," she said.

"Was she where you could see her every minute?" I said.

"What is this?" she said.

"Was she?" I said.

"Well, it's a big house, you know," she said. "People kept going off to various rooms for more private conversation. Now you tell me what this is all about."

"I thought I saw her off Times Square," I said.

"What were you doing off Times Square?" she said.

"Making out like mad," I said. "Butch?"

"I don't believe you," she said.

"Butch?" I said.

"Really!" she said.

"Butch?" I said.

"If you must know, he was tending bar and serving munchies," she said. "He makes these delicious Oriental canapés out of fish and stuff."

"Stevie Dickinson?" I said.

"First you tell me why you want to know," she said.

"I want to know everything about the people you spend your time with," I said. "I want to know what they do that makes you prefer them to me. Maybe I could develop a taste for Butch's Oriental fish. . . . Stevie Dickinson?"

"Not good enough," she said. "And don't talk dirty."

"The fact is that I want to write a piece on feminism from the victim's point of view," I said. "But I need to know which editor's throat I should shove it down or ass I should ram it up or cunt I should jam it in."

Samantha broke the connection. It took me half a minute to find the cradle and place the receiver in it without turning my head. I waited another half minute, then picked up the phone on the first ring.

"It's with reference to Stevie I called you about," she said. "She couldn't come to the party cause she got tied up working on this big surprise for me, I think. You know I'm moving in with her on Monday? I thought you might like to help me move, since you're always going on about how much you want to see me. You could borrow Bill's station wagon. Maybe we could even have dinner with Stevie afterwards."

"Poor Bill," I said.

"He must miss Jude," she said.

"And that bog-hag Haggerty?" I said.

"She's not a hag," she said. "We had a long talk together, partly about guess who. She wanted to know what you were like, and all. The Garrulous Gourmet came up and offered us five hundred dollars each if we would spend a night with him in Erika's Playroom. He said that with all those mirrors, and 'cause Kathleen and I look a little alike, it would be like making love to a roomful of clones. Kathleen drew her pistol and pretended she was going to arrest him on a charge of contributing to the delinquency of a minor, meaning me. But she's under a cloud with the Police Department. There's this review she's got coming up."

"That woman who went all over catatonic, what's her name?" I said.

"This is the limit!" she said.

"Mourneen Bugaboo, I think her name is," I said.

"Why should I tell you anything when you won't give me a straight answer?" she said.

"Soon, very soon. Trust me," I said. "Now what about Ms. Catatonic?"

"Muriel Bigalow's over at Austin Riggs," she said, "slowly getting better. She has this delusion that she helped someone she calls the Corduroy Kid murder Jude. She says he has three penises and puts them in her all at once."

"Did she say where, no, that's obvious, I mean, how?" I said.

"Erika says her ex-husband always wears this ratty corduroy jacket?" she said. "He's a famous writer, you know. Allerton Guth is paying all the expenses. He's a mil—"

"Another victim, but where's the offender?" I mumbled to myself, so I thought.

"Funny you should say that," she said.

"What's so funny about it?" I said.

"Pete was just saying something about offenders," she said. "Let's see if I can get it straight. He used to say there are no offenders, only offenses: everyone is innocent. That's it. Last night he said, or shouted, that there are no victims, only offenders: everyone is guilty."

"Ah yes, the good Pastor Peter Brevoort, what about him?" I said.

"What about him?" she said.

"He was at the party all evening, I take it?" I said.

"It was the strangest thing," she said. "He came over late, after eleven, all teary and pulling his hair. He kept wailing, sort of, that he was a murderer."

"He did, did he?" I said.

"He said we were all murderers, of other people or of ourselves," she said. "But only the second type finds favor in the eyes of God."

"Never mind that," I said. "Did he say whom he had killed?"

"Erika had a terrible time quieting him down," she said. "He said that after the first murder all the others were inevitable, and I don't know what else. He said we are all Cains or Abels, or rather, all Cains *and* Abels, but that Abel was guilty first."

"Whom did he kill?" I said.

"He said that the Cain in Abel tempted the Abel in Cain to kill him," she said.

"Kill whom?" I said.

"Maybe I got it backwards," she said. "Maybe he said that the Abel in Cain killed the Cain in Abel, or is that the same thing? Whatever. It made my head spin. But the point was, I think, that the victim is guilty, so that, and these are his exact words, the only righteous avenger is a suicide. I don't see the logic, myself."

"There's no logic to see," I said. "Now listen to me carefully. On the basis of what concrete occurrence did Pastor Peter Brevoort conclude he was a murderer?"

"Does it matter?" she said.

"It matters that someone murdered someone, but that Brevoort is still alive," I said.

"Who said anyone was murdered?" she said.

"You can't have a murderer without a murderee," I said.

"All I know is that Erika and Butch talked to him alone for a long time, and then he went home with a kind of exalted look to write his sermon for tomorrow," she said.

"There is a conclusion to be drawn," I said. "A consequence, too."

"Well, you draw it," she said. "I'm too hungover to draw anything. I'm waiting for that straight answer you promised me."

"Yes, I do want to help you move," I said.

"That wasn't the question," she said.

"I'll helb you moob home," I said.

"You got a stuffy nose?" she said.

"I got in another fight yesterday," I said.

"Oh, Victor," she said.

"I got my nose busted," I said.

"Oh, Victor," she said.

"I've been going downhill ever since you left me," I said. "I'm about to hit bottom."

"Pick me up at my office around twelve Monday," she said. "I'll kiss your nose and make it all better again."

"Samantha, come home," I said. "Why can't you live with your doting husband and still have a career? Lots of women do it."

"Be patient," she said. "We'll see."

"I love you, I want you, I need you," I said.

"We'll see," she said, and hung up.

I rolled over onto my face. With my body parallel to the floor from the coccyx up, I stepped out of bed. Then I straightened up, from the waist. Then I nearly fell over from a sudden attack of dizziness. It sounded to me as though Samantha were weakening. The primary material goal of my career as an avenger was on the teetering edge of achievement. Whether or not I achieved my nonmaterial goals, you can decide. And please do not suppose for one second that I mean any disparagement of Samantha by speaking of her as a material goal. Far from it. I walked into the bathroom, balancing my head. It is true that Bill was dead. That battle I had lost, a small matter compared to the fact that Bill had lost his life. I was already beginning to look like a raccoon around the eyes. Well, it was worse than that: with my smashed and swollen snout, my scarred eyebrow, my lumpy lip, my stump tooth, my humped trapezius, I was beginning to look like Douglas Fairbanks Sr. in drag or like Dorian Grey's picture. It is true that Toby had fallen into the clutches of his grandmother, beyond my reach, for you can't go around killing everyone who gets in your way. There was another defeat. I took a long hot shower, and it is a matter of course that what is most sensitive to pleasure is most susceptible to pain. I swabbed on more iodine and wrapped my dead king in mummy cloth to await resurrection in the better world with Samantha to come. In any case, it no longer looked as though I would have to terminate with extreme prejudice the whole editorial staff of *Ms. Chief* in order to get my wife back, although I would have been willing enough, had the need arisen. It also looked as though the killing of Stevie Dickinson had been at the very least premature. Someone else must have been threatening Bill, unless I was up against a conspiracy involving two, three, a half-dozen feminist felons. What's so impossible about that? At least I had removed a threat, how serious there is no way of saying, to Samantha's virtue. A few light twisting exercises sent healing blood into my stiff neck and upper torso, which helped, but not enough so that I could look back over my shoulder. What was standing in the way of my getting a loan so that I could go to journalism school? Your garden variety spendthrift, trying to placate his wife with a mortgaged houseful of micro-wave ovens, mechanical clam-openers, and electronic toothbrushes, can get all the money he wants, just for the asking. I swabbed liniment on my trapezius, and I wished I hadn't forgotten about the bites and scratches. But nature has a way of reminding you of things it is necessary for you to know. Therefore we have pain. Maybe Samantha and I could find jobs together on a magazine. Maybe we could edit our own some day. First I would have to teach her the distinction between "that" and "which." I shaved off my beard, which no one would have noticed anyway, given the condition of the rest of my face. Our magazine would feature hard-hitting investigative reporting. We would become famous for our exposure of fashionable or dangerous quackeries. I put on my denim outfit and my cowboy boots with the new reliable low heels. We would have adventures together, penetrating sinister cults, the intrepid reporter Victor Grant and his resourceful (and beautiful) assistant (and wife). With my tried and true knife I regretfully cut the soles off the desert boots and sent them down the chute for an honorable cremation. There might come a time when I would have to rescue Samantha from mumbling

Satanists in black hoods who were trying to sacrifice her. Out of the suede tops of the desert boots I stitched together a sheath for the knife. Imagine how beautiful Samantha would look tied to a stake, the pure white robe slipping from her shoulder. Out of her red skating suspenders I made a harness to hold the knife (in its sheath) under my left armpit. The Pulitzer Prize is not much of an award, but it might help the sales of our magazine. I put on my denim cowboy hat, for it was raining outside, and my raincoat, which was also my winter top coat, was now too tight to wear over a jacket, even with the lining removed. This murder was going to have a certain purity about it. There was nothing material for me to gain from killing Pastor Peter Brevoort. I had no motive but revenge.

XI

HE First Church of Christ, Androgynous is a restored brownstone, except that the stones are white, or, more precisely, gray. It is on Ninety-third Street, just off Amsterdam Avenue, opposite the Joan of Arc Junior High School, which, I understand, claims an All-City record for the largest number of broken windows in a single year. The windows, broken and whole, were all dark, for this was Saturday afternoon. I splashed up the stoop of the First Church, etc., and tried the door, which was locked. Backing up, I noticed a bulletin board on the wall and to one side of the door. Instead of announcing the title of the upcoming sermon, it said CHURCH CLOSED THIS SUNDAY DUE TO DEATH, which struck me as an odd way of putting it. Under the stoop was another door, leading to the basement. It was not only unlocked, but ajar. I pushed in, shaking rain off my hat, and found myself in a lounge. There was not much light, but I could see a jukebox shaped like a squat Empire State Building, threadbare couches, a pool table, a ping pong table, and a bar ingeniously remade from a vanity such as Carmen Miranda might have used. Beyond the lounge was a furnace room and a storage area. A trunk, the lid of which

squeaked, contained costumes, including a lot of sexy underwear, black strappy stuff.

Spiral stairs ascended to the first floor, on which there was
only one room. Here the flock were driven every Sunday for a
session of woolgathering before their stampede to the lounge.
At the street end was a pulpit, facing an optimistic number of
folding chairs, two hundred or so. Dim light from the rain-
marbled windows shone down, of course, on the pulpit. Between the windows was an object of hammered steel or pewter
or something that looked like this:

I spiralled up and to the right and into a parlor, where the
ghost of a headache was waiting for me. If ancient females had
a distinctive smell, this would be it. Try to imagine an air of
dustiness without the reassuring actuality of dust. The furniture did not please me. I did not like the heavy dark glimmery
wood, and I hated the plush of muddy green or murky maroon.
Nor have I ever cared much for doilies, antimacassars, and
hassocks. Tiffany lamps weigh on my forebrain. You would

have to rummage pretty far back into the stuffiest corners of memory to come up with anything so dismal as those niches crowded with knicknacks, so doleful as that piano top crammed with family photographs, so dreary as the curio cabinet chock full of curios. The figure in the carpet was in this respect like the design on the wallpaper: I could not make it out. To that extent they were both like the pattern in the plush. Perhaps they were faded. Maybe the light was too weak. Or it could be that my eyes were failing, as the ears of an old man with a nagging wife fail. Whatever was capable of having a fringe on it, had one. Yes, I did feel as though I had been in that room before. Yes, I am certain that I had not in fact been there. No, I do not believe in reincarnation. Remember the strain I had been under. How would you like to drop in on your best friend for a quiet chat, only to find an ice pick in his heart?

Beyond the parlor was a kitchen, ultramodern and super-mechanized. Next to the kitchen was a cunning little bathroom: red carpet, bookshelf, polished brass faucets, plants, lace curtains, an enema bag. On the fourth floor, the last, the stairs unwound into a hallway. The doors to the right were shut, locked, in fact, as though I gave a hoot. If the Pastor Peter Brevoort wanted to cuddle his paltry secrets to his breast, why let him go right ahead. To the left, at the end of the hall, a door was open, but not wide. No sound came from the room, nor from the street outside the window at the opposite end of the hall, nor even from me, for I was holding my breath. Either there was an uncurtained window in the room toward which I was stalking a plump and buttery clergyman or there was a light on. Along the way, my keen hunter's eye registered the names on a row of autographed photo-portraits hung at eye level: Sri Ramakrishna, Sri Aurobindo, Judith Malina and Julien Beck, V.A. Ambartsumyan, Marshall McLuhan, Jim Jones, Theodore Roszak, Anton LeVay, Charles Dederick, Mambo Rodriguez, Jumbo Waziri. Has it ever occurred to anyone that Napolean might have kept his hand inside his jacket so that he could hold onto the handle of a knife slung under his armpit? With my left hand I boldly pushed the door wide open.

The curtains were drawn tight. But on the desk was a lamp with a green glass shade. I could make out no more than a piece of cheekbone and the silhouette of Pastor Peter Brevoort's face, for it was above and behind the lamp, in a greenish shadow. He made no move. I glanced down quickly to see if there was an ice pick in his breast. Then he leaned forward into the light, rested his elbows on the desk, and studied me for a moment.

"I've been waiting for you," he said.

"Oh no you haven't," I said.

"Oh yes I have," he said.

"No you haven't," I said.

"Yes I have," he said.

"No you haven't," I said.

"Don't contradict me," he said, wagging a finger. He knit his brows. "I forget what we were arguing about." He put a hand on his forehead and then stroked it down and closed it, so that the thumb rubbed one eye and the fingers the other. "I never got to bed last night, never got to bed."

"I didn't get much sleep either," I said.

"Haven't we met before?" he said. "Your face can't possibly look like that all the time," he said.

"It changes according to the state of my soul," I said.

"Yes, your soul," he said, brooding. "Won't you sit down?" he said with a gracious smile, remembering his manners. He pointed to the chair by his desk. I sat. "You must join me," he said, reaching below and behind to a shelf on the bookcase for a dinky stemmed glass, its capacity about that of a medium-sized cavity. "We wouldn't want you to catch your death, ha, ha. Won't you take off those wet clothes? No? Then don't! What makes you think you have anything worth seeing, anyhow?" He poured us some dark red liqueur. Cheery Herring is I think what it said on the label. "I have a weakness for cordials," he said. "I've had nothing to eat for twenty-four hours, nothing to eat," brooding again.

"Neither have I," I said.

"Seems we have a lot in common," he said. Something must have burst: the white of his right eye was red. "You don't talk much," he said, drumming on the blotter: pinkie, ring finger, middle, pointer. "Not nearly enough." Pause. "My inspiration feeds only on those it inspires." Pause. "You are starving it." Pause. "I need words: my sermon roars, soars, sings to its climax, which is a parable, a fable for our times, a prose poem that flames out, like shining from shook foil. But I can't find the last few burning words, the last burning words." He waited: pinkie, ring, middle, pointer. "You could at least make sympathetic noises," he said.

I did my best.

"I have written all but the last few words of an unforgettable sermon that my congregation will never get a chance to remember me by," he said. "The fold hungers for spiritual nourishment, but the shepherd will not be there to tend them, not be there to tend them." He gave me a sharp look. I made a sympathetic noise. "That is why I have been waiting for you."

"No you haven't," I said.

"A sermon is not a sermon until it is delivered." He drummed. "A sermon is not a sermon until it is heard." He drank. "A preacher is not a preacher until he preaches." He poured himself another. "A congregation is not—"

"I wouldn't mind a wee drop more myself," I said. He poured me another. We drank. He poured two more.

"It is only through the Word that preachers and congregations are consubstantial in Christ," he said. What irritated me most was Brevoort's use of the word "in," which derives, I believe, from St. Paul, another bugger. And if you don't believe me, you can ask that twit Timothy. "Weak vessel though you are," he said, "I have chosen you to be the receptacle, nay the funerary urn, of my sermern, I mean *mourn*. Through it we will become consubstantial, you and I."

"I'm not into consubstantiality," I said. "And sermons give me ants in the pants."

"Not the whole sermon, no calm yourself, not the whole sermon: just the parable," he said.

"I have come here for the express purpose of asking you a very important question," I said.

"Everybody likes a story," he said. "You're in it."

"The question is one of life and death—yours," I said.

"My story asks a question of life and death," he said. "It's about murder," he said.

"It is, is it?" I said.

"Everybody likes a good murder," he said.

"Don't drag it out," I said.

"I seem to remember you as of the tribe of scribblers," he said. "Consubstantially, you and I, we shall engender those last few pregnant words." Pinkie, ring, middle, pointer. "Then I can sleep, then to sleep." More brooding gloom.

"Let's get on with it," I said.

"First a drink," he said. "Spirits for the spirit." We drank. "Did you know that in all the ancient Indo-European languages the word for spirit, ghost, and wind is the same?" He poured two more.

"Begin!" I said.

He picked up the handwritten manuscript before him, but never once as he spoke did he look down at it. "Are you ready?" he said.

"Whenever you are," I said.

"Ahem, hem," he said.

"Roar, soar, sing!" I said.

"You are in a small rectangular room," he said. "The long sides run east and west. You are facing north. The walls are tiled up to about as high as, um, your brawny chest. Above that they are mustard colored. You are sitting at a table of the kind one often finds in school cafeterias: oak frame, inlaid linoleum top.

A woman comes out of the door set in the wall you are facing, to your left. She is middle-aged, stout, severe, short-haired, wearing a skirted suit, perhaps a uniform.

"A dyke," I said.

"An ugly word for what can be a very beautiful thing," he said. "Believe me, I'm an expert in such matters."

"Onward," I said.

"She is leading a boy by the hand," he said. "His clean black hair has been freshly combed, for it is still damp. He is dressed in clothes that I associate with carefully raised boys of the European middle class circa A.D. 1939. Navy blue knit short pants, of one piece with the suspenders, which have a connecting strip in front, so that they won't slide off his little shoulders. A white shirt buttoned up to its round collar. A velvet jacket. His delicate, translucent knees are bare. On his cheeks are those carnation bursts, supernal bloom, raspberry sherbet, that one sees only in the children of the British Isles and Northern Europe: Brittany, Belgium, Holland. He has very intelligent brown eyes. He looks at you trustingly. He gives you a shy smile."

"Get a grip on yourself," I said, for his chest was heaving, his voice breaking, his eyes watering. "Buck up, now."

"Forgive me," he said.

"Here, drink this," I said. We drank. He poured two more.

"The boy sits next to you, on your left," he said. "The matron—let us call her that—goes out. Sitting across the table from you, his chair tipped back, is a man called Stanley. Like you, he has an athletic air about him, muzzled violence. Like you, he is dressed in a manner not quite in fashion: white oxford shirt, striped tie, blue blazer, grey flannel slacks, argyle sox, cordovan shoes. He has a long, strong jaw and deep superorbital ridges. His crisp, rusty hair is cut short. And although he is only in his early thirties, he is balding from the crown down and around. What is that aftershave lotion you are wearing? I like it."

"Sloan's liniment," I said.

"Stanley, looking at you steadily, no expression on his face, leans forward, bringing the two front legs of his chair down with a thump, opens a drawer in the table, and pulls out a forty-five caliber ACP, government issue, just as I now open a drawer to my desk and pull out this dagger," he said.

"Just as I now reach under my armpit and pull out this knife," I said.

"Could you do with another?" he said.

"Please," I said. He poured, left-handed.

"Stanley lays the pistol flat on the table, but keeps a hand loosely on the grip, like this," he said. I followed suit. "He looks at his watch, speaks: 'At 1500 hours you will have an opportunity to utilize this sidearm. First I must brief you on your options.' Where did you get that knife?"

"I made it," I said.

"How clever of you," he said. "Very workmanlike. But this, I am sure you will agree, shows the hand of an artist." He held it up. Everything but the satin-polished blade was hammered steel or pewter or something, or could it actually be silver? The finger guard was long and knobbed on either end. A very pretty Christ slumped pathetically from the guard down and against the top third of the blade, which was at least twelve inches long (leaving eight unencumbered inches to poke holes with). Hyacinthine curls covered the head that dropped poignantly to one side. Together and tucked fetchingly to the other side, were the shapely knees. Wasn't there a *Playboy* centerfold of some bimbo stretched out like this on a pink satin sheet? "But he will never make anything for me again, never make anything again."

"You had gotten as far as Stanley's options," I said.

"This blade is very sharp," he said. "Both point and edge."

"So is this one," I said.

"I sharpened it myself," he said.

"You've got to lean down hard on it," I said.

" 'One of your options is to shoot this boy,' says Stanley.

'Your second option is not to shoot him. You have no others.'
Naturally, you are far from convinced, but you are uneasy. You
do not see how Stanley can compel you to do anything, let alone
shoot a darling little boy. Stanley continues: 'But if you do not
shoot him, thirty other children will die.' "

"I don't like this parable," I said.

"Life is full of things one does not like," he said.

"But this is not life: this is a fiction," I said. "It reflects not
reality, but the mind of the fiction-maker."

"Is not the fiction-maker a piece of reality?" he said. "What
is there to make fiction out of *but* pieces of reality?"

There's a stumper for you.

"Here, drink this," he said. "Buck up, now. Ready? Here
we go: Stanley nods toward his left, your right. For the first time
you see the window, maybe a foot high and four feet wide. It
is obviously a one-way mirror for some nefarious child psy-
chologist to peep through, bruising tender limbs with hard and
horny eyes. 'The subject of this experiment who preceded you
chose not to shoot,' says Stanley. You see tiled walls, a tiled
floor, nozzles, pipes: a shower room. Men in slickers are busy
at something. You can't quite make out. . . . They are hosing
away plaster, broken tiles, and (here you gasp) blood and rags
of flesh. The wall to the left is cratered, gore-splattered. Other
men in slickers and boots are dragging out the mangled bodies
of children. You have no doubt that the bodies are real. No
make-up artist could fake those arms hanging by threads of
tendon, the trailing intestines, the ruddy rubble of organs, those
faces twisted in terror and—"

"Stop! Enough! I can't bear to think of children suffering,"
I said.

"Neither can I," he said. "That is why I have written this
parable."

"No more," I said. "I want no more of this. All right:
granted that fiction can only be made out of pieces of reality.
But the pieces of reality can be so selected and arranged as to

provide, let us say, um, compensatory gratifications. That is what fiction is for: to compensate us for the insufficiencies of reality, the evils of existence."

"Well, well, listen who's talking, the famous reality-monger," he said. "Sounds to me like there was just a bit too much reality for him in my harmless little parable, a clergyman's trick of the trade. Now let me tell you this: it is only when the evil of existence is an ache in your bone marrow, only when you know it as intimately as a lover's caress, only when it is as unquestionably and insinuatingly present to you as your own petty lusts, only when in fear and trembling and in the sickness unto death that you recognize, feel, and embrace the fact that this world is supersaturated with evil, only then does your belief in God find favor in His exacting eyes."

"That was a very well-constructed sentence, all things considered," I said.

"Or else religion is precisely a compensatory fiction," he said.

"It is that in either case," I said.

"No it isn't," he said.

"Yes it is," I said.

"No it isn't," he said.

"Yes it is," I said.

"When are you going to stop interrupting me?" he said. He drummed. "Can I interest you in a drink?" he said, the smiling host again.

"Only if you will join me," I said. He poured. We drank.

"If there is no God, the suffering of children is meaningless," he said.

"Exactly," I said.

"I refuse to accept that," he said.

"Therefore your compensatory fiction of a God," I said.

"Is it nobler in the mind to accept evil or in absurd and heroic defiance to assert its negation?" he said.

"I accept nothing," I said. "And evil is already a negation. The negation of a negation—"

"Accentuates the positive," he said.

"No it doesn't," I said.

"Yes it does," he said.

"No it doesn't," I said.

"Yes it doesn't, he said.

"No it does," I said.

"You cannot bring yourself to look through the window," he said. "But out of the corner of your eye you see that the men in slickers have finished. The matron leads in a double file of children, each holding the hand of his partner. She lines them up, their backs against the pocked and pitted wall, and goes out. Two men dressed like Stanley come in. They are carrying fifty-caliber machine guns. They move to your right, set up the guns on tripods, and sit behind them, facing the children. Then they look toward Stanley and nod. He nods back. He slides the pistol across the table. He speaks: 'You have precisely three minutes.' You cannot bring yourself to look at the boy, but out of the corner of your eye, you see that his eyes are on you. Stanley continues: 'If at exactly 1500 hours you have not terminated this little man, I shall signal to my colleagues with the machine guns.' What do you do?"

"How did I get in this situation?" I said.

"You are always in a situation," he said. "What do you do?"

"I do nothing," I said.

"To do nothing is to do something else," he said. "If you do not shoot the boy, the thirty children will die horribly. Only you can save them. What do you do?"

"I will not shoot that boy," I said.

"Why not," he said. "You have two minutes left."

"There are certain things I will not do, no matter what the consequences," I said.

"No doubt you consider this refusal of yours high-minded-heroic," he said. "But is it not in fact the action, the inaction, of a coward? Suppose the boy makes it easy for you? Suppose he turns away, offering you the back of his head, the fluted nape of his neck?"

"I will not shoot that boy," I said.

"Then the blood of thirty children will be on your conscience," he said.

"It's not me, I mean I, who is going to shoot them," I said. "Let their blood be on Stanley's conscience."

"It will be on yours, and you know it," he said. "What kind of dreams will you have? How can you go on living with the knowledge of what you have done by not doing anything? Only you can save them, and you have one minute to do it in."

"Stanley can save them," I said.

"But he will not," he said. "Therefore it is up to you."

"I will not shoot that boy," I said.

"Are not the lives of thirty children worth more than the life of one?" he said.

"No, yes, I don't know," I said.

"Thirty seconds," he said.

"I take the gun and shoot the two men with machine guns," I said.

"The window is bulletproof," he said. "There is an inexhaustible number of such men to replace them. The children will die."

"I shoot Stanley," I said.

"Stanley considers it part of his job to take that risk," he said. "He has told the machine gunners to take your shooting him as a signal to open fire."

"All right then," I said. "I wait until Stanley gives his signal and the machine gunners open fire. Then I shoot Stanley. If I cannot save the children, I will avenge them."

"Typical," he said. "You men of action are all the same.

Where do you get off thinking you're such an improvement on Stanley?"

"Time has run out," I said.

"I beg you to remember just whose parable this is," he said. "If I want to make time slow down, speed up, stop, or go backwards, who's to prevent me? As of this moment, I have suspended time ten seconds before it was to run out. Bigger miracles than that have been verified by unimpeachable witnesses."

"No they haven't," I said.

"Have you ever seen a man die?" he said dreamily, cheek on fist, fist around dagger, left hand drumming. He waited. He sat up suddenly and pointed the dagger at me. "I mean *you*, big shot. You're such a tough guy, you smart aleck, you quick-draw artist, you homespun Zarathustra, you're in such a big hurry to shoot down an unarmed man, but did you ever give a moment's consideration to how he might feel about it? You, you with your patriarchal complacency, your homophobic constipations, your macho swagger and brag."

"I have seen a man dead," I said. "Quite recently, in fact."

"That's not the same thing," he said.

"I've seen women die," I said.

"I used the word 'man' in a sense that includes women," he said.

"You would," I said.

"I saw a man die," he said, dreamy again. "Quite recently, in fact."

"I thought you might have," I said.

"There is a sympathetic attunement between us, you and I," he said.

"I wouldn't count on it," I said.

"We could have been great friends," he said.

"How did this man die?" I said.

"I pierced his heart," he said.

"With an ice pick?" I said, closing my grip on the knife,

bracing my feet for a lunge, weighing the alternatives of spearing his throat or skewering his heart.

"With words," he said, "with words, words."

"I'd be curious to know just which words those might have been," I said.

"I accused him of murdering Jude Karnofsky," he said. "You recognize the name?"

"You half-basted capon, you suckling, you paunchy steeroid, you pudding parson!" I said. "Have you any idea what an unforgiveable stupidity that was?"

"I have not forgiven myself," he said, very steady.

"Whatever possessed you to—" I said.

"The question is what I thought possessed him," he said. "The answer is *jealousy.*"

"Of whom, for sweet Jesus' sake?" I said.

"I have often noticed that when you atheists need an expletive with some authority to it, you instinctively call on the name of our Lord," he said. "This man knew that I have a weakness for stout, blonde women of a certain age, and for no other kind. He knew that Jude and I were flying to Amsterdam together. He knew that she had left her husband."

"How could he *not* know it," I said.

"He was very drunk," he said.

"I would just as soon not be reminded," I said.

"I did not realize that he had gotten over his jealousy," he said. "What I now see was a childish eagerness to please, I then thought was one of his many deceptions. I saw mere theatrics in his gush about making a new start. I saw an attempt to hoodwink both of us in his promise to spend years of monkish seclusion on a work of art that would bring the world to its knees. He had never grown up, you see." Once again his chest was heaving, his voice breaking, his eyes watering.

"I know, I know," I said, surprised to hear a womanish quaver in my own voice. "It's his mother's fault."

"He did not realize I hadn't gotten over my suspicion,"

he said. "He suddenly held out a package that all along he had been hiding behind his back. It was wrapped in silver paper, tied with a red ribbon, adorned with two white roses. The look on his face was, oh, who can say? a plea for forgiveness, for understanding, for, ah me, for Christian charity, for Christian charity. He began to fumble open his present for me himself. I had refused, you see, to accept it, and may the Lord have mercy on us, for our lives are one long, drawn-out sin."

"Is this another one of your wretched parables?" I said. "You believers, damn it, will you never learn to distinguish between fact and fantasy?"

"I have proof," he said.

"Then let's see it," I said. "There's no way of proving a—"

"Here it is," he said, holding up the dagger.

"I don't see—" I said.

"With a look of desperation on his face, with the look of a man taking his last chance, Karl folded back the tissue paper to show what he had made for me," he said.

"Karl!" I said.

"But I had hardened my heart, hardened my heart," he said. "I repeated my accusation."

"Karl!" I said.

"He asked me with a pitiful smile if I truly thought he was capable of killing someone. Yes, I said, for if a man of God does not tell the truth, who will? If I really believed that, he said, he would kill himself. He hadn't the courage, I said, for this species of blackmail was an old trick of his. He ripped the dagger out of the box and plunged it into his heart."

An involuntary spasm of my whole body made me hiccough.

"What happened next will appeal to your scientific curiosity in the grotesqueries of human behavior," he said. "Before toppling over, he pulled the dagger out of his chest and handed it to me. Needless to say, I shall never forget the expression on his face. It was triumphant in a certitude of vindicated self-esteem."

"This really happened to you and Karl?" I said, "I mean in the flesh, not just in words?"

"Gospel truth," he said.

"I hope you will accept my condolences on the death of your friend," I said.

"Thank you," he said.

"I too am in mourning for the untimely death of a dear friend," I said.

"I beg to offer you my deepest sympathy," he said.

"Thank you," I said.

We sat back in our chairs, our eyes maintaining contact. We exchanged the weak smiles of survivors. He gestured to the bottle. I nodded. He poured. We clinked glasses, drank, sat back again.

"The philosophic ground of my refusal to kill that well behaved lad, clearly a mama's boy, has just now occurred to me," I said.

"Ah yes," he said, "our little parable."

"Every human life is an absolute," I said. "A life cannot be quantified. There is no weighing one against another or one against many. Each one weighs all the weight there is."

"I'm sorry you said that," he said, standing.

I jumped to my feet, knife at the ready.

"Every human life is an absolute," he said. "The inevitable last words of my sermon. And now I can sleep, now to sleep, sleep, sleep. You realize, I assume, that every human life is an absolute only because there is a God."

"No there isn't," I said.

"Yes there is," he said.

"No there isn't," I said.

Yes there is," he said.

"No there isn't," I said.

"There appears to be only one dose left," he said, peering

into the bottle. "You will have to forgive me for not sharing it with you." He emptied the bottle into his glass. "I can assure you that I need it more than you do." He drank. "And now, by a mere reaching forth of my will, I start time up again. Ten seconds to go. There is one final option you and Stanley never thought of. It would have been out of character."

"What's that?" I said.

"This!" he said, and before I could even flinch, the dagger flashed up to one side of his neck and across to the other. He dropped into the chair like a puppet on a cut string. On the rebound he flopped forward, so that his face banged down on the desk and bounced, once. Immediately I heard the splash of blood on the floor. It is quite possible I screamed. Now that I think back on it, I am sure I screamed. I do not remember my spin down the four unwinding flights of stairs and into the basement lounge. I came to myself leaning against the jukebox and looking at the knife in my right hand, the glass in my left. I licked out a last drop of liqueur, for my mouth was dry. I sat on one of the tacky loveseats until the shaking turned into an occasional shiver. Only when I tried to open the door did I realize that my hands were still encumbered. I slid the knife into its holster. I hooked the stand of the glass behind the sweatband of my hat and put the hat back on my head, thus avoiding any telltale pocket-bulge. I probably did not succeed very well in composing my face, for I could feel twitches agitating it, as though to shake off flies. I stepped out, closing the door behind me, careful to leave no fingerprints. Then I walked home through the rain, like a character in Hemingway.

Now why did I write that? Who was I making fun of? Hemingway is the one writer I wish I had known. I could have told him what was wrong with the love scenes in *For Whom the Bell Tolls* (and how to improve them). Besides, that was not exactly rain I was walking through, but something more like a heavy mist. (The rim of the glass rapped on my head like a poltergeist each time I took a step.) Besides, I did not walk straight home. Under the marquee of the Symphony Theater on Ninety-fifth Street and Broadway was a prostitute. I stopped at the curb, swaying on my feet as though drunk, which maybe I was a little. My plan was to doff my hat, bow satirically from the waist, deftly palm the glass, and before straightening up, drop it into the sewer there, which was famous up and down the West Side for an evocative scent of jungle rot. I may not have taste, which is the product of a certain education, but I do have a sense of fitness, which is a by-product of feeling at home in the world, which mostly I do. Pastor Peter Brevoort was a man of the antiseptic North: I left the glass in my hat. "Whachudoo wid Alberto, meng?" said the prostitute.

The light rain or heavy mist, or whatever it was, began to feel, well, refreshing on my twitched-out face. The tap of the glass on my head began to feel half-friendly, like the rap of my mother's thimble, for she never liked me to use her feet as bulwarks for my toy soldiers to shoot across while she was sewing. I pulled up before the Other End, a student hang-out, from which music, talk, and light overflowed to push back the dank. On Friday and Saturday nights the Other End featured live jazz, played for the most part by elderly black survivors of the late swing or early bop eras. What was waiting for me at home that I should be in such a hurry to get there? The student waitress, who wore a cuddly white turtleneck sweater, was prompt with my brandy. The quintet played mostly blues, which (since I have already admitted my lack of taste) I will admit is the only music that moves me. Some of the jangle and jump seeped out of me when the tall, distinguished-looking trumpet player, who reminded me of Roy Wilkins, sang

> I been sitting here, baby,
> The tears rolling down my cheeks.

The three open steak sandwiches I ate didn't hurt either.

Slouched back in my booth, feet propped on the seat opposite, munching, sipping, listening, gliming the girls, sending a round of drinks to the musicians via the good-natured waitress, I felt my mind float off into that free space in which it is possible to think as well as react. That rascally Peter Brevoort. His suicide had been a consummate piece of theater. And it had been an exemplary one in this: like all good theater, it forestalled critical examination of the premises upon which it was based. Until, that is, it had irrevocably worked its effect on you. Between sets, the trumpet player stopped by to thank me for the drink. I asked him if he could manage another. He thought maybe he could. When he was halfway through his second scotch and soda, I held up before his judicious gaze the well-chewed-over core of Brevoort's parable. "Would you kill one man to save thirty others?" I said.

"Maybe," he said. How's that for an answer? Am I a judge of character, or am I? Do I know a sagacious face when I see one, or do I? More discursively, he had said nothing less than that there are no moral certainties in this world.

"It depends," he said. Better and better! Next time you are over your head in the murky depths of an ethical dilemma, reach out for the hand of a man who can play the blues. I challenge you to put into fewer words the fearful and exhilarating truth that all moral issues are contingent.

"It depends on the time, the place, the weather, what I been doing, what my chances are of making a get-away," he said. Bull's eye! He had pierced the heart of the matter. Shall I translate? There are no ethics and therefore no ethical dilemmas anywhere but in concrete material situations occupied by concrete material individuals.

"It depends mostly on how I feel about that man," he said. And there you have it. I nodded my profound thanks as he walked back to the stand, carrying his third scotch and soda, and he could have had thirty. The complete works of Kant, Hegel, and Khalil Gibran would have cost me a lot more, and at the price of less truth. He opened the set with "Bag's Groove," which I had requested, and while those minor thirds, flatted fifths, and diminished sevenths (for I too have taken a course in music appreciation) color your mood, why not syncopate your biorhythms with this question (purely rhetorical): What if Stanley had given you the option of shooting not that lovable little boy, but Stevie Dickinson?

I ordered another brandy and let my eyes slide off the waitress's sweater to the other lively bodies around me, and I still wish someone had paid my way through college while I was young enough to enjoy it. Sure, my father would have paid, but I would have had to ask him first. It pleased me (I exaggerate a little) to think of these Columbia boys and Barnard girls as the children of Pastor Peter Brevoort's parable, now grown up. But it did not please me for long. I suddenly felt queasy. I wanted to touch the waitress, if only to make sure she was not a ghost, never mind any other reasons. For it just then dawned on me that the children in Pastor Peter Brevoort's parable would not have grown up, even if I had acted on his example. Suppose that, instead of shooting the boy, or shooting Stanley, or doing nothing, I had shot myself. The children would have died, but not to me. They would have died to Stanley, to the matron, to any spectator, and most of all, to themselves, but not to me, as they did not die to the good Pastor Peter Brevoort. Suicide is the last resort of an idealist. By an idealist I mean not a person who has ideals, but a person who thinks the world is his idea of it. The suicide of an idealist is an apocalypse, but only to him. What is my point? This: unless you are an idealist, there will be times when your only option is revenge.

What, then, is so admirable about Pastor Peter Brevoort's suicide? Why, then, are you making such invidious comparisons between us? I might just remind you that suicide is every bit as illegal as murder. Pastor Peter Brevoort's suicide did nothing for anybody but himself.

Having justified philosophically my refusal to shoot the boy, I ordered another round of drinks for the musicians so we could drink to his health. Having justified metapsychologically

my refusal to commit suicide, I ordered a cheery herring by way
of nightcap, and for some reason the waitress laughed. Having
forged with subtle links the iron logic of revenge, I slipped
Pastor Peter Brevoort's glass onto the waitress's cluttered tray
when she bent over to put my nightcap on the table; and she
generously remained still while for three heartbeats my cheek
rested against the cordial wool over her breast. It pleases me to
think of that glass as still in circulation, kissed by the lips of
college students. Perhaps I was a milligram severe a few moments ago in saying that Pastor Peter Brevoort's death did nothing for anybody but himself. Certainly I felt less like a consort
of sewer rats than at any time since Stevie Dickinson opened
her door. He died for my sins? You said it, not me. Forgive me
for thinking it is not quite what was on his mind. Sentimental
old fraud that he was, however, if there were a heaven, he
would tip his wings to you in acceptance of the compliment.

A fresh breeze had blown away the mist. In a doorway two
merry hipsters drank from a bottle still in its paper bag; they
hooted, stamped their feet, collapsed from the waist with
laughter. "You didn't hear?" one said to the other. "Man, they
just flushed him away. Whoosh, like that." In the lobby of the
building in which I live is a small table. On this table the
postman leaves packages and bulky magazines when you do
not answer his buzz. I had not this morning answered his buzz
it seems, perhaps because I was unable to distinguish it from the
jangled music of my dreams. The package for me was small and
square. And in my mailbox, which I had not opened for two
days, was a bulky envelope. As you have guessed, there was no
return address on either. The letter had been mailed on
Wednesday, the package on Thursday, but by the same person,
so it seemed. For on package and letter, "Ms. Victoria Grunt"
had been scrawled by the same bold hand.

Upstairs, I got right to work. First I wedged a corner of the
envelope under a gyphon leg of the bathtub. Then I straightened out a coathanger. Then I bent back seven inches of it at

one end, harpoonlike. Then I pliered back an inch of the other end, fishhooklike. Then I carefully slid the seven inches under the top edge of the envelope flap, as you might bait a shepherd's crook with a flounder, though I can't for the life of me see why you would want to. Then I straightened out another hanger and pliered a short hook into one end. This hook I hooked onto the hook of the first hanger. Then I threaded the straight end of the second hanger through the keyhole. Then from behind the door I yanked the second coathanger, which yanked the first, which ripped open the envelope, for I'd sooner slit my throat with an artsy-craftsy dagger than let some homicidal sneak take me with a mere letter bomb. No bomb went off, not outside my head, anyhow; inside the envelope was a cellophane wrapper, of the kind you can find in your corner drugstore hanging on a peg and sealing off from the infected air in which we live and move and have our being a pair of light green rubber gloves. Interesting, no?

I fetched the cunning little embroidery scissors that Samantha had bought for the embroidery she never got around to doing. Then I uncoupled the hangers. Then I bent back the bent-back seven inches that had so efficiently done their work (and in this sentence, as in all the others, I have been more concerned with clarity than euphony). Then I hooked the hangers onto the finger loops of the scissors. Then I pliered the hooks tight onto the loops. If, now, I were to extend my arms, with the straight end of one hanger in my right hand and the straight end of the other hanger in my left hand, I could work the scissors at an approximate distance of two yards from my face, for my arms are very nearly a yard long. You would think I was about to handle a radioactive node or nodule or something, and could you have guaranteed me that I wasn't? Then I placed the package in the middle of the living room floor, and if my worst fears were realized, the people in the apartment below mine were in for a surprise, but I had long ago taught them to live with sudden thumps in the night. Then I gingerly slid one blade of the scissors under the string, right next to the suspiciously big knot, but I know next to nothing about booby traps. At the furthest reach of the hangers from the scissors, I made a barricade of the two cushions (bottom and back) of the easy chair. Then I stretched out on my belly behind the cushions. Then I formed a peep-tunnel between the cushions. Then I slid my arms between the cushions, on either side of the peep-tunnel. Then I grasped the straight ends of the hangers. Then, by remote control, I worked the scissors, my head flat against the floor, for who could tell what shrapnel might find its improbable way through the peep-hole. When you have eyes as good as mine, it is worth taking a little extra trouble to protect them.

I had cramps in my arms and sweat in my eyes before the rest of the string and all of the paper were cut away. What then lay exposed on the living room floor was a blue velvet ring box. From the broom closet I fetched the clamp Samantha had bought for the furniture she had never gotten around to restoring. I clamped it to the bottom of the box, to weigh it down and hold in in place. Then I turned the box so that the hinges faced the cushions. Then I pried one of the hangers off the scissors. On my belly, behind the cushions, I caught the hook of the hanger on the opposite face of the lid. Then I pulled. There was a puff and a pop. I ducked, and if I wanted to look like a Pekinese, banging my nose on the floor like that was a way of doing it, though probably not the best. After my vision cleared, for good as my eyes are, they dim when a pain in my nose becomes excruciating, I crept up to the box. The puff and the pop had been caused by talcum powder and a cap. These had charged a device of the kind you can buy in novelty shops around Times Square, if you don't mind being seen in such places. In the slot that should have held a ring was a zipper tab, such as broke off my pants in Jude Karnofsky's hotel room.

"I see," I said.

XII

ON the balmy spring after-
noon of Sunday, June 9, 1974, I was awakened by the police.
Before I could figure out why total strangers were showing me
their wallets, the two detectives had elbowed their ways in but
without touching me, and I still don't know how they did it. A
patrolman took up a position just inside the door. The first
detective, who looked like Bella Abzug, asked me whether I had
seen or heard anything unusual late Friday or early Saturday.
I decided against giving him a wise answer. Why make myself
conspicuous? Have I ever given you reason to believe that I am
the kind of person who has to get himself noticed, no matter
what the cost? No Sir, I said. I felt at a serious disadvantage, for
one thing, because I was still in my pajamas. For another, I was
stuck to my pajamas by the half-formed scab of my wound,
which stung and itched, not least because I had to pee so bad
that I was sweating urine. While Bella asked what I did for a
living and whether I had been at home from, say, noon Friday
to noon Saturday, the other detective, who looked like Betty
Friedan, ducked into the bedroom. I said that I had been in and
out, so far as I could remember, and that I was a writer. Bella

made a face. Betty came in from the bedroom, caught Bella's eye, and shook his head. What's going on? I said. Mind if we look in there? said Bella, nodding toward the bedroom. Betty peeked into the kitchen. You already did, I said. What's that on the floor? said Bella. Betty came over to look. Talcum powder, I said. They said nothing. Their expressions signified less. Some nights, I said, I take my shoes off in here, while I watch television. Some mornings, therefore, I put my shoes on in here, to save time, I said. I have sweaty feet, I said. What happened to your face, said Betty. You know those push-ups where you clap your hands on the up-swing? I said: well, the other day I didn't get my hands back in place for the down-swing. They looked at each other. What's going on? I said. Guy downstairs got himself killed, said Bella. How, who? I said. Murdered, said Betty. Name of William Austin, said Bella. I must have looked genuinely faint, and I was, though Bill's death was hardly news to me, because they helped me into my easy chair, Bella on one side, Betty on the other. He's got a hard-on, said Betty. You knew him? said Bella. I nodded, obviously too overcome to speak. The patrolman's walkie-talkie suddenly made a row like a goosed duck. Bella and Betty looked over toward him expectantly. He stepped out into the hall, so that he could squawk back to his duck in privacy. He stuck his head back in and jerked it, signifying that his partners should come over. The three of them whispered at the door for a minute. We'll get back to you, said Bella, and they left.

I prepared my toilet, as they say in detective novels written by high-toned British ladies, although I can't remember Milord or Milady ever having to soak the crotch of his (or her) pajamas loose. I was hampered in the performance of my exercise routine by a variety of wounds, but sometimes pain feels good. At least it keeps you awake. Not that it felt particularly good on this occasion, or kept me awake, for prolonged worry is a soporific. Among the worries that put me to sleep in my easy chair were these: I did not know who had murdered Bill, although I

had a pretty good idea. I did not know who had sent me the
cellophane wrapper and the zipper tab, although I had a pretty
good idea, the same one in fact. I did not know whether the
police suspected me of anything. Were the police and the
sender in cahoots? Was there a contract out on me? As for the
sender, did he know anything, or was he (or she, for that matter) guessing? Was he (or she) working alone, or did he (or she,
surely she) have confederates? Who was taking care of Toby,
and how? Would Samantha—I was awakened by the telephone,
and I resolved that the minute things returned to normal I
would rip it out and hurl it headlong down the incinerator
chute, where it could burn for its sins through all eternity.

Samantha's voice was sepulchral. "I want to go home," she
said.

"I'll be right over," I said.

"No you won't," she said. "You'll lock the door and not
open it for anybody."

"If you think—" I said.

"You'll just stay put until I call you tomorrow morning,"
she said. "God, all I need is for you—"

"But we'll both be safer if—" I said.

"For once, will you just do as I say!" she said. "I don't want
to argue. I don't want to talk at all. I don't even want to think.
I haven't finished packing, and Stevie, dammit," and for the first
time I had the ambiguous pleasure of hearing Samantha cry.
"Oh Victor, I'm so frightened."

"There, there," I said. "Once you are safe in my arms
where you belong, nothing—"

"I want to leave the City," she said. "I want you to take
me straight to Pinetop."

"Whatever you say," I said.

"I'll remember you said that," she said. "Maybe this time
we'll get on better."

I rushed to the television set and clicked it on, five minutes
too late for the five minutes of commercials that precede the six

o'clock news. I cursed and hopped from foot to foot while the screen writhed and finally resolved itself into a chastening slice of life on the sidewalks of New York: two bulky men hustling a bedraggled Miss Lily out of 3½ Great Jones Street and into a squad car. The anchorman was talking about something else before it registered on me that Miss Lily's hands had been cuffed behind her. There had been blood on her face. The 6:30 news, presumably, would repeat the whole story. While waiting, I decorated the kitchen table with a display of index cards, spiral notebooks, old shopping lists, and a dozen thick volumes on popular delusions and millenary moonshine. No, this was not an instance of what ethologists call displacement activity. It was, on the contrary, circumstantial evidence in support of my claim to be a writer, should the police return. I regretfully put my knife, slayer of dragons, in a kitchen drawer with lesser cutlery. Its holster I shoved down into the toe of Samantha's skating boot, and it would take an unusual policeman to figure out what it was good for. My stomach moaning for a fresh ham or a brisket of beef or a saddle of mutton, I then sat down to see what new worries the world had coiled up to spring at me.

Ever notice how little of the news is actually news. From a hasty pudding of leftover phrase, refried fact, double-boiled speculation, fantasy, false inference, and blague, I extracted these starveling shreds of raw information: Miss Lily flew in from Virginia early this afternoon. She went straight to Bill's apartment, where she was greeted by the apologetic smile on his murdered face. From under a pillow, she retrieved the forty-four caliber blunderbuss (originally her daddy's) that she must have blackmailed poor Bill into accepting. A snoopy neighbor, whom she nearly knocked over on the staircase, passed the open door to Bill's apartment, came back to investigate, immediately called the police. By this time Miss Lily had jammed the muzzle of her Colt single-action into the ear of a cabdriver. He zigzagged through the city fast as his jaded hack would take him, pretending that he could not find Great Jones Street, hoping that someone would notice his plight, hoping to prevent the murder he saw in Miss Lily's eye. That's what he told the interviewer, anyhow. To prevent his own murder, he finally dropped Miss Lily off at her destination; out of the range of her shooting iron, twenty blocks away, he then called the police. When they arrived, Miss Lily had shot one cat and was trying to shoot another, but the hammer kept falling on spent cartridges. She had blasted away the lock to the door and walked in to find Stevie Dickinson in a pool of congealed blood.

I was nearly dressed—for I had decided to make do with three or four pounds of hot sausages and a smoked whitefish, or better yet, a smoked eel, and one of the things I like about New York is that you don't have to go hungry on a Sunday night—when the phone rang, for a change. It was Brunhilda, who asked if I needed company. Well, I did, in a way, and it would have been soothing to hear Brunhilda free associate about her family. But I was in no condition to benefit from her professional services, and she might not have understood if I refused them. So I told a white lie, which I expect you to forgive, as I forgive in advance all the lies you will tell about me. I said I already had company. I said further that my wife was coming home the next day. She understood, she said; she would not call me any more. She would wait for me to call her. All mature people, she said, understand that a real man occasionally needs another woman, that an occasional other woman makes a good man a better husband. What was her work, after all, but that of serving as the other woman? It was not in her nature to hold grudges. What right had she to be possessive? It was just that she was feeling so blue. Another distant relative, a crook named Alberto, had disappeared, and her mother had just called to say that her son had punched Sister Teresa, a good and pious woman, if a little bit strict, but Madre de Dios, what could you expect, the way children were nowadays, someone had to beat right and wrong into them, but Jorge was not really a bad boy, only a fatherless boy, if I could understand what that meant, and as for herself—I interrupted to say that I had to get back to my company, and I was beginning to hate all kinds of bells, for someone was at the door. She understood, she said, she only hoped I did, and she hung up. Well, all right, there *are* times when men exploit women, but I deny that feminists were the first to notice it or that they have correctly ascribed the causes. And what about all the times that women exploit men? Or are you of the considered opinion that Aristotle Onassis got his money's worth?

Imagine with what surprise it was I opened the door to find Bang standing there, a guitar case in one hand, a bulging paper sack in the other, a duffel bag beside him. The lower half of his face was purple, except for the little pink polka-dot Band-Aids.

"Trick or treat," he said.

"Guess you better come in," I said, toting his duffel. "This is a respectable neighborhood."

"Ivan would have come himself," he said. "But he's laid up."

"With whom?" I said.

"Seems that sow had a dirty mouth," he said. "I never did meet up with one that knew enough to brush its teeth. I must have sewed the germs right in. But don't worry. Your father ain't going to lose his foot. Leastways, I don't think so." While saying this, he opened the guitar case, removed something heavy wrapped in an oily chamois skin from under the guitar, unwrapped it, screwed the barrel of the shotgun into its receiver, loaded it, stood it against the wall. "That ought to do the trick," he said. "Now here's the treat."

He handed me the bulging paper sack. Inside were four hero sandwiches, two of pastrami with cole slaw, one of roast beef with Russian dressing, one of five kinds of cold cuts and three kinds of cheese with lettuce, tomatoes, mustard, mayonnaise, oil and vinegar; a container of Greek olives; a container of garlic-rich new pickles; twelve cans of Ballantine Ale. "Always was partial to Ballantine Ale," he said. "I had them put on double portions of meat. One thing about the Adirondack back country, you don't see much pastrami."

I placed a pastrami sandwich, half a roast beef, and half a combination on a platter for Bang and the same on a platter for me. "I see where you got another maniac running loose down here," he said, accepting the platter, sitting. "Rough place, New York," he said, laying the shotgun on the floor beside him. "When's the last time you ate?" said Bang, and it hurt my nose to stretch my jaws like that, but I paid no mind, for when one has to choose between the lesser evil of pain and the greater evil of hunger, one eats.

The phone could have rung itself into laryngitis, for all I cared, but Bang picked it up. "For you," he said, "some smoothie, says his name is Parker." That solicitous stooge wondered whether in this dark time he might so far intrude upon my grief as to have a few words with me in his capacity as Miss Lily's attorney.

"Sure," I said, "the more the merrier." I put the phone down and picked it up immediately, because I thought it had rung, but it was the doorbell.

Bang waved me back and went over, shotgun in one hand, the last corner of his last sandwich in the other, and shouted, "Who's there," but not clearly, for his mouth was full.

"Friend to this ground and liegeman to the Dane," said a voice.

Bang opened the door a crack and said, "What's the password?"

"Long live the king," said the voice.

I threw open the door. Chi Chi was holding two boxes of the kind you carry pizza in and a bag that had the look of containing beer. "I once played Francisco in high school," he said.

"Bang," I said, "this is Chi Chi Quatrone."

"Honored," said Bang.

"Chi Chi," I said, "this is Bang Olson."

"The honor's all mine, I assure you," said Chi. He was wearing a black team jacket with white trim and white leather sleeves. On the back, in raised white letters, were the words,

MASON TENDERS

Local 29.

He handed the pizza to me and the beer to Bang.

"The riff-raff who deliver ready-mix cement are about to call a strike," he said. He zipped open his jacket and pulled an automatic out of his belt. "There's two things Fawn don't like," he said, withdrawing a clip from his jacket pocket. "She don't like me to hang around the house from nine to five on week days. And she don't like me to hang around anywheres else from five to nine. Sunday nights I can hang around where I want, within reason, long as she doesn't have to hear about it." He slapped the clip smartly into the magazine. "The Sicilian pizza's got pepperoni on it. The Neapolitan's got anchovies." So I was going to get my hot sausage and preserved fish, after all.

"Do I see a Colt Gold Cup MK IV Series 70 with Bo-Mar sights, Swenson safety and Pachmeyer grips?" said Bang.

"You do," said Chi-Chi. "And do I see a Remington 1100 Magnum 12 Autoloader in a southpaw model with a Bishop myrtlewood rollover trap buttstock?"

They looked at each other's guns while I served pizza and beer. The doorbell rang. Chi Chi went to one side of the door and Bang to the other. "Come in," I said.

"Bang, Chi," I said, "these are Messrs. Parker, Carter, and Barker." The last was carrying a shopping bag.

"I thought maybe it was Larry, Moe, and Shemp," said Chi Chi. Carter looked disgusted.

"Do I smell lobster in shrimp sauce?" said Bang. "Or do I smell shredded beef home style?"

"Never did like to eat alone," said Barker.

"Might we speak in private?" Parker said to me.

Barker removed a bottle of Yukon Jack Bourbon from the shopping bag.

"Is that a goiter under your arm?" said Chi Chi. Carter looked bored.

"We can speak in here," I said, leading Parker toward the bedroom. As we walked in, I heard Bang saying, "Do I see a Smith & Wesson 357 Combat Magnum Model 19 with Behlert mumble?"

"I am here at the request of Miss Lily," said Parker. "A remarkable woman."

"How is she?" I said.

"Her release was not easily arranged, of that I can assure you," he said. "But my firm is not without influence in high places."

"What does she want from me?" I said.

"Only four days ago Mr. Austin asked me to modify certain provisions of his will," he said. "One of these provisions now states that in the event of Mr. Austin's demise you become Toby's legal guardian. He more than once made me swear I had so worded this provision that it would stand up in a court of law, no matter who contested it. I made allowances for Mr. Austin's grief; clearly, he was not himself. I declined this invitation to take offense. He had your authorization?"

"Sure," I said. I had no intention of showing my feelings to Parker, or to anyone else, except you. Just to give your sympathetic imagination a rare work-out, try to imagine Bill's state of mind when he asked Parker to change his will. No doubt he wanted to live more than at any time in the previous ten or fifteen years. No doubt he feared death more than at any time since his adolescence, when you expect every minute to be punished for the abominable longings you only gradually come to cherish. But he had no intention of showing his feelings, even to me.

"Among your responsibilities," said Parker, "will be the administration of a considerable trust fund."

"Where is Toby now?" I said.

"Mrs. Lindquist arrived with Toby a few moments after

the police," he said. "She is very upset, of course, but claims not
to be surprised. It appears that she had a premonition. A malign
fate, she feels, keeps thwarting her attempts to find happiness.
These sentiments were imparted to me in her husband's apartment, from which I called you. My understanding is that Mrs.
Lindquist asked Mr. Lindquist to take her back. He refused. In
fact, he ordered her to leave the premises. She has no place to
go but back to her father's farm near Middleburg, where, in her
words, she is treated like an indentured servant. In return for
certain material favors that I was able to promise her on Miss
Lily's word, she has agreed to take along Toby, who, by the
way, flourishes on country living. Carter is waiting to drive
them to Middleburg in Mr. Austin's station wagon. Miss Lily
felt it best that Toby stay with Mrs. Lindquist until the perpetrator of these foul murders has been apprehended or until we
are otherwise sure that neither your life nor Toby's is in danger.
Miss Lily felt that as a matter of courtesy I should inform you."

"Is that so?" I said. "From now on, as a matter of law,
anything she plans to do to, for, or with Toby requires my
permission first."

"It is about her plans for Toby's future that Miss Lily
wishes to speak with you," he said. "She expects you to call her
promptly at 10:00 A.M. tomorrow, by which time the police will
have finished with Mr. Austin's apartment. Inspector La
Paloma, I am glad to report, has been made to understand the
narrow limits of his authority."

"Does Toby know of his father's death?" I said.

"We considered calling his therapist," he said. "We spoke
to Martine, who refused. Miss Lily finally decided that in the
light of Mr. Austin's will—and we both reproached ourselves
for not having seen this straight away—the privilege was
yours."

"You say Toby was happy on this farm?"

"Mrs. Lindquist assures me that she had never seen him
happier," he said. "In an aside, she led me to believe that her

father is unduly satisfied with himself on all scores, except one: in spite of efforts that produced six daughters, he was unable to beget a son."

"All right," I said. "For a couple of days. Until I finish mopping up. There is no need for anyboy to tell Toby anything, not yet. Maybe he'll just, ah, sort of, well, guess."

"One last point," he said. "Miss Lily ordered Barker to stick with you 'like dog shit on the door mat.'"

After showing Parker and Carter out, I went into the kitchen. Someone had piled my pads and papers on the drainboard, where they were blotting up water. Bang, Chi Chi, and Barker were leaning their 650 pounds on the dainty glass-and-wrought-iron breakfast table for two Samantha had bought on sale from Sloan's. "Gentlemen," I said, smearing hot mustard on a sparerib, "I have just become a father. It's a boy."

"This calls for a celebration," said Bang.

"I know this place . . ." said Chi-Chi.

"In the midst of death, we stand for life," said Barker.

What the hell, I said to myself: an experienced professional ought to know how to work around a wound like mine.

It took some sneaking about, but I managed to get my knife and holster in place without anyone seeing me. We drove to Sunnyside in Bang's pickup, Chi Chi and Barker riding shotgun in the box. If they noticed that Bella and Betty were following at a safe distance in an unmarked car, they never mentioned the fact, if fact it was. The evening was dark, though warm, and in any case the damned rearview mirrors were all at the wrong angles. It is true that the street was deserted behind us when we turned into a parking lot off Stillman Avenue. Mrs. Seeling, said Chi Chi, did not want a telltale clutter of cars parked around the front of her whorehouse. I disliked her looks (which were those of Angela Lansbury in *The Manchurian Candidate*) right from the moment she opened the door for Chi Chi, but no one else seemed to mind them. "Nice to see you, Chi Chi," she said, letting her eyes rest on each of us in turn, most heavily on Bang, who was doing a slow fox-trot on the lawn, cheek to cheek with his guitar case. "I had no idea the Green Bay Packers were in town," she said.

The property, like its proprietress, had the air of a past association with quality. The fine lines of the fancy plaster work were obscured, blunted, buried, in ages of paint. The wainscoting of the billiard room, in which Barker showed three quiet men and four oo-ing prostitutes how to run twenty-seven balls in a row, was dented and scratched. The stained glass windows of the gaming room, in which Chi Chi showed three kibitzing men and four commiserating prostitutes how to feed twenty-seven quarters into a one-armed bandit, were repaired with plastic. The grand piano in the parlor, on which Bang showed three club-footed men and four long-suffering prostitutes how the left hand puts the woogie in the boogie, was out of tune. The carved oak bar at which poor resourceless Victor showed three impatient men and four unresponsive prostitutes how he could dilate the pupils of his eyes, was sticky with caking shellac. It did not seem to me that this was the time or place or occasion for a one-handed, left-handed push-up, but my social instincts are weak from lack of nourishment. You be the judge.

Chi Chi went upstairs first. His companion was young, energetic, gap-toothed, frank, fat, and firm. Bang was half a foot shorter than his black-haired, freckle-faced consort. She lead him upstairs by the hand. Barker's escort had obviously been trying for some time to look like the phthisic daughter of an exiled Russian prince. She held his arm on their way to the stairs as though dinner had been announced and the Czar was waiting. She assumed an attitude both regal and oblivious when Barker disengaged to pull me aside. "The treat's on me," he whispered. Miss Lily, he assured me, was not a woman to cavil about expenses incurred in the line of duty. Charity ("You can call me Charlie") was notable chiefly for her perfect calves and her profound sleepiness. She dozed against my shoulder, while, for a joke, I carried her up the ornate staircase, as though she were a bride. Half the way up, this staircase took a hairpin turn. At the turn was a landing. On the landing was a window. In our room, and it pleased me to note that the sheets were clean, I explained that I was temporarily incapacitated, did she mind? The thing was, I just couldn't fall asleep without a woman beside me. "Where've you been all my life?" she said, and plunged into unconsciousness before I had my right boot off, for it is my whim to remove my left boot first.

I made it to the window on the landing at the turn of the staircase without being observed. I crawled over the sill, hung from the case, and dropped three feet onto grass. Picture, if you will, a row of houses. Behind these, a row of gardens, in one of which I now stood. Behind the gardens, a walk. Beyond the walk, another row of gardens, and beyond them, another row of houses. From letters to the editor of the *Daily News* I gather that people who live in such places look down at Manhattanites. On what grounds, I wonder. I strode boldly down the walk to its end, as though I had a right, and then stepped out onto the sidewalk, without a glance either way. Three brisk blocks away was the Bliss Street subway station, where I caught the Number 7 to Grand Central. Within forty minutes I was looking up at the tails of curtains breathing in and out the bay window of 33 Gramercy Park East, from which no lights showed.

No one was about that I could see; no one was spying from a window, so far as I could tell; no gimlet eyes that I could feel were boring into the back of my neck. I backed up, then highstepped forward like a high jumper, pushed off the ground with my left foot, pushed off the brass plate with my right, caught the ledge with a hand and a forearm, pressed myself up, rolled over the sill and onto a thick Persian rug, all in one motion, like a young Burt Lancaster, who otherwise I do not resemble, though I used to wish I did. All quiet on the first floor, which was split down the middle by a hall. Under a forty-watt night light, next to the staircase, which ascended in a series of hairpin turns, was a sheet of plywood on two saw horses. Gloomy paintings of old stuffed shirts looked down on it. The cause of their frowns, apparently, was a heap of sketches in Fiji's neo-Nouveau manner. These, I took it, were plans for the grand renovation, in the very worst taste. If I had to choose, I would take stalagmites and bat guano every time over a lot of tinfoil and tatami mats, never mind the zebra skins and stunted conifers. There was plenty of gorgeous old wooden furniture in the rooms on the second floor, but no people.

I was looking into the pier-glass on the third floor when I began to hear faint, whispery sounds that at first I thought were coming from inside my head. They were insinuating, intimate, familiar; they made my heart race and my wrists throb; but I still could not picture what caused them. Nor could I decide whether my eyes were full of blood or whether there was a dim red line along the bottom of a door down the hall. Certainly I had glanced that way before without seeing it. I heard a moan or maybe I made one. The knob turned silently in my hand. The door swung open toward me silently, and if anyone had been hiding behind it, I would have made her quietus, for my bare bodkin was at the ready. But no one was.

These facts registered simultaneously on my already over-taxed sensorium (or so it seemed, for whether you can perceive more than one thing at a time or whether you can only perceive one thing after the other, in rapid succession, I cannot say, for although my reading in the psychology of perception is scant, it is also more extensive than is good for me): 1. The globe was transparent, but red. 2. It was larger than a medicine ball. 3. It was on the ceiling less than a third of the way into the room. 4. It was decorated with black figures in silhouette who were doing things to each other. 5. The reddened figures in the round on my right were doing some of the same things.

Supine on the largest bed I had ever seen was a woman, no possible doubt about that. A forearm covered her eyes. Her ambrosial thighs were spread, but I could not see her calves, for they hung down over the farthest rim of the bed. Her hair blazed out from her face, like a black sun. Its running highlights were violet and deep purple. Her skin was pink and luminous, as though the light came from inside her. The hand by her cheek slowly opened, then quickly closed; the other hand clawed the white satin quilt. A head of long straight blonde hair, parted down the middle, was feeding at her crotch. The slim, trim, limber body attached to this head was bent over from the hips, so as to form a right angle with the legs. These were encased in black, patent-leather boots. The boots must have been very tight, for the rounds of thigh above them plumped out a good half inch beyond the poor delicate flesh crushed within them. Her skin was lavender, for this too was unmistakeably a woman. Ruby-red beads of sweat stood out on the upper slope of her haunch. They spread, touched, fused, broke, ran. I could not see the lower slopes of her haunch, but I could see that it was parted down the middle by Butch, who stood behind her, his eyes closed, his face tilted toward the ceiling. His skin was orange maroon, and mottled. I am not easily unnerved—you have sufficient evidence of that in the pages before you—but I was unnerved by the length of Butch's slow, steady strokes. Could he have been wearing an extension of some sort?

In and out went Butch, in and out, and up and down went the blonde head, like a cat lapping milk, up and down, without pause or hitch, without quickening or slackening, as though they had been going at it for days and could go at it for days more without exhaustion or climax. If you wanted proof of my superhuman self-control, you have it in the fact that I did not rush in and chop them all to pieces. Never before I had felt such rage, and never since. There was a roaring in my ears. My face and neck puffed up to twice their size. All that stayed me was an uncertainty about the black-haired woman, who moaned and turned her head to one side, but without removing her forearm. Suddenly I realized that there were movements around the periphery of my field of vision, that they had been flickering at the edges of my eyes all along. I jerked my gaze left, then right. In the mirrors around the room, ghostly pale-pink reflections went in and out and up and down. My plum-colored face hung in the doorway. I turned back to the bed, where Erika von Plaack was slowly lifting her burning face from between a pair of ambrosial thighs.

Her eyes were bloodshot and blank. A swollen, crooked vein ran down from under her hair to the left side of her nose. Her features were thick, stiff, masklike, as though the blood had clotted under her skin. Her bruisy lips were parted to reveal the long, glistening teeth. Her chin was slick with moisture—none of which prevented me from wanting to kiss her or to bite off her lips, either one would do. She was staring in my direction, but I could not tell whether she saw me, or anything else. Slowly she lowered her head. In spite of my undiminished rage, I mumbled "Pardon me," backed out the door, and closed it, and sometimes I wonder what gets into me. All right then, just what would you have done?

It is a measure of my agitation that instead of sneaking out the shadow-cloaked window, I blundered out the front door, right under a wrought-iron lamp affixed to the lintel. How long it took me to get back to Mrs. Seeling's parlour, where my bodyguards were playing poker, I shall never know. I do not remember the off-color jokes they made about my alleged staying power. Nor do I remember the drive home or how it was decided that Bang and I would sleep in the bed, Chi Chi on the easy chair, and Barker on the couch. Bang woke me at 9:00 A.M., after what seemed like maybe eight minutes' sleep. The others were already dressed.

"I'll go out for some breakfast," said Chi Chi.

"I'll pay for it," said Barker.

"I'll cook it," said Bang.

"In that case, I'll eat it," I said.

"What's your pleasures?" said Chi Chi.

"I grew fond of calves' brains and scrambled eggs when I was out Montana-way," said Bang.

"You wouldn't know how to make steak and kidney pie, would you?" said Barker.

"Now if I could find some blood pudding . . ." said Chi Chi.

"Any of you guys ever try smoked eel," I said.

"I'll get started on some biscuits," said Bang.

Downstairs, Carter, who was rumpled and sulky, led me into Bill's study. Miss Lily was seated behind the desk, staring at stacks of index cards. Where she got the natty widow's weeds on such short notice is her secret, but then she always wore black anyhow. Through her veil I could see four red furrows dug in her right cheek, from the ear to the corner of the mouth, and three on the left cheek. Otherwise, her face was subnaturally white. She was still as the figure of a notorious felon in a wax museum. Then she turned her head to me as though rigor mortis were setting in.

"I had it in mind to come after you next," she said. I sat down across the desk from her.

"My understanding is that you had run out of ammunition," I said.

"You cannot imagine how much I detest cats," she said. "The filthy brutes had been feeding on her blood. Their bloody pawprints were all over the place."

"What did I do that you had it in mind to come after me?" I said.

"It's what you didn't do," she said.

"But I *did* do it," I said.

"You were not standing by my son's side when his enemies came unto him like thieves in the night," she said.

"I was out following your instructions," I said.

"I gave no instructions," she said.

"They sounded like instructions to me," I said.

"That was your mistake," she said.

"Yours too," I said. "Bill died because of it, *them* rather."

"This is no time for recriminations," she said. "It is a time for us who are living to show that we know how to honor our dead; time for me to avenge my only son's death and for you to take charge of his only son's life. Go with him to your father's estate in the Adirondacks, and stay there. I don't want either of you in the way. I'll have enough on my mind without having to look after the two of you. In return, I promise not to contest my son's will."

"That is a contest you would lose," I said.

"It is a contest you cannot begin to afford," she said.

"My father could," I said.

"There are things you can afford even less than the money," she said, "although you should not underestimate its usefulness. Parker already has considerable evidence arguing your unworthiness of the honor of raising my grandson. You are, for example, unemployed, destitute, intemperate, wifeless, and a frequenter of whores. Should Parker need more to go on, there are in my possession tape recordings of certain telephone conversations."

"But you gave me your word that there weren't any duplicates!" I said.

"I lied," she said.

"You're a remarkable woman," I said.

"You don't know the half of it," she said.

"What you don't know is that I also have a tape recording," I said.

"Go on," she said.

"Last time we talked I was all wired up for sound," I said, I consider it blatant sexism to assert that lying is exclusively a woman's prerogative.

"My admiration for you increases daily," she said. And would you believe it?—her features softened a touch.

"As of this afternoon I shall no longer be wifeless or a frequenter of whores," I said. "It is Samantha's wish that we remove to Pinetop. Toby, of course, will come with us. My father's assistant, who is visiting me, will drive them. I'll follow in a day or so, after I've terminated one little piece of business."

"If your plans for Toby were already the same as mine, why in thunder were you being so contrary?" she said.

"I was making a point," I said.

"You know I can't stand symbolic gestures," she said.

"There aren't any other kind," I said, standing up.

"Here are the keys to William's station wagon. It's yours. Use it, you hear? And these are yours," she said, pointing to the index cards, sounding at last a little weary. "It was my son's whim to name you his literary executor. Am I to understand that literature is one among your many accomplishments?"

"You don't know the half of it," I said.

Bang, Chi Chi, and Barker were elbow to elbow around the kitchen table, eating breakfast. They made room for me, although there was not much room to be made. On a shelf above the table, where Samantha and I used to have our clock radio, was a pocket-sized transistor radio with a voice like that of Alvin the Chipmunk.

"I liberated it from Whalen's," said Chi Chi.

"I would have paid for it," said Barker.

"We're fresh out of eels," said Bang, taking a platter of steak, eggs, biscuits, and fried peppers out of the oven and setting it before me.

"Can't go wrong with steak," said Barker.

"I've had this craving for meat," said Chi Chi.

"Your wife doesn't love you anymore?" said Bang.

"That's just it," said Chi Chi. "She keeps on cooking all these things that are good for me."

"I know what you mean," said Barker. "My wife and I would probably still be living together if it wasn't for her waldorf salads. But she meant well."

" 'All vegetables and no meat makes the blood thin and the waist neat,' she says," said Chi Chi.

"Ask her if she's ever seen a fat lion," I said.

"Consider the hippopotamus," said Bang.

There wasn't what you could call a pokey eater among us. Barker brought down his empty cup and sighed. "Well, I guess Miss Lily will be wanting me," he said. We followed him into the living room, where he put on his well-made jacket over the Smith and Wesson 357 Combat Magnum, nodded once to each of the rest of us, and went out.

"Well, I guess those turkeys have chickened out on the strike," said Chi Chi. He put his team jacket on over his Colt Gold Cup MKIV, nodded once at Bang and once at me, and went out, picking his teeth.

"Well, I guess I better get back to my chores," said Bang, unscrewing the barrel of his Remington 1100 Magnum 12 Autoloader.

"Well, I guess I can take care of myself," I said.

"You got a lot on your mind," he said. "That's why you didn't take in what they were saying on the radio. It's all they been talking about. They found the guy who did it, this here Holy Joe, name of Brevoort. Nobody's coming right out and saying it, but it's gotta be, he killed Karnofsky, cause she wouldn't boff him, sad to say. You oughta hear how this Chink Fiji comes down on him. Then he killed your pal, 'cause he found out about it. Killed Dickinson, cause he spotted her when she spotted him coming out of this house. The word is she was snooping around to see if she could pin the first murder on your pal. This other Chink, Franklyn Luala, ain't got nothing good to say about her. Then Brevoort killed his boyfriend, this here Karl Wiener, and who knows why?—maybe cause by then he couldn't get out of the habit. Killed himself, who cares why, maybe to keep in practice. What he used on the boyfriend and himself was this dagger the boyfriend was known to have made for him. The police also found some cockamamie confession he was writing. Most of it was blotted out with blood, but what was left seems to be ravings about the mass murder of innocents."

"This is how the police figure it?" I said.

"This is how I figure the police figure it, going by how they tell it on the radio," he said. "Why, you figure it different? You want me to stick around?"

"I'll manage," I said. "The fact is, I was just wondering whether you would take my wife with you."

"I nearly forgot," he said. "She called, said to tell you she changed her mind, didn't say about what. She'll get back to you tomorrow."

"You ever beat any of your women, Bang?" I said.

"Yeah, but I got rules," he said. "I never beat them for my own pleasure, only when they need it." He shouldered his duffel. He pointed toward the easy chair. "Chi Chi found that package, guess it's for you, on the table downstairs." He opened the door. "Ivan says he wants you home. He wants you right now. And he don't want no excuses," and out he went.

The package was addressed to Ms. Victoria Grunt. The box inside the wrapper was about the size of the box in which ages and ages ago (ten days, to be exact) I received an ice pick in the mail. I ripped it open. Then I dropped it, because there was a live salamander inside. With the salamander was a nametag that said "Morris Blankman, Wade County Community College," and I'll bet you can't remember where you first saw it. I couldn't, not for a half minute, or a quarter. I flushed the salamander down the john.

The rest of the day was uneventful, for I did not go out until after dark—unless you consider washing the dishes an event. It is not in my character to leave dirty dishes lying around, even if there is a chance I will never see them again, or anything else. I don't know how many times I have tried to impress upon you that a personality is made up of everything within its reach. You are what you interact with and how you do it. That is why these confessions are so full of fascinating detail. That is why I have not disdained to portray with minute fidelity the clothes, occupations, residences, family relations, friendships, and food that define me and the people who have nearly driven me crazy. I do not live in a void, nor am I one. I'll leave it to you to decide what I am full of. (But only if you promise not to say the first thing that comes to mind, just for the sake of the joke. We are beyond that now, you and I.)

I did not listen to the radio. What would have been the use? No matter what new piece of face-saving hoodwinkery the police came up with, the fact would remain that Erika von Plaack was still alive. The fact would remain that Bill's death was not avenged, nor could I leave the job to Miss Lily, or even to the police, not at this stage. By obligation and by right, the first crack at Prankster von Plaack was mine, the line forms on your left. Enough is enough, you say? If you were me you would grab Toby and beat it to Pinetop? Well, you are not me, and if I were you, I would not be so quick to congratulate myself on the differences between us. If you would take the trouble to count on both hands, you would realize that seven people, so far, had died because of the offenses committed against me by the editorial staff of *Ms. Chief.* Their ghosts could only be laid to rest by the removal of the editor-in-chief offender. I had no intention of cringing out my days with attendant revenants chirping in my ears that they had died in vain. Only I could silence them, and silence them I would, or go to chirping school myself. If you had asked me, that is what I would have told you. And I really do not see what is so amusing about my claim that in the coming showdown with Erika von Plaack I would be acting not just for Bill Austin, not just for Gilbert and Rosita Nieves, but for Jude Karnofsky, Stevie Dickinson, Peter Brevoort, and Karl Wiener as well. You can become reconciled with death if the cause is great and the survivors do not betray it.

Oh, I meant to live, don't fool yourself about that. Pastor Peter Brevoort was the other guy, remember? But I had no fear of dying, or worse, of getting caught. That was the remarkable thing, my composure. I was as free from anxiety as I ever get, free from hope, doubt, or regret, free of push or drag from the past and shove or lure from the future. There was nothing I wanted, except what was to be, inexorably. I was simply ready. This time, you see, my vengeance would be free of impurity. This time there would be no last-minute wavering. Jude Karnofsky had embarrassed me; Stevie Dickinson had disgusted me; Peter Brevoort I had not killed at all, in spite of your eagerness to blame me, and you might try to keep the gross facts straight, never mind the nuances. This time my opponent was worthy and waiting for me. O, 'tis most sweet when in one line two crafts directly meet. This time no baser natures would come between the pass and fell incensed points of mighty opposites. This time my vengeance would finally be like a work of art, gratuitous, impersonal, disinterested, intending only itself, only its own formal perfection. I had nothing to gain from it but self-expression and, if I didn't cheat, self-justification.

No, I had not forgotten Samantha, nor had I given up on her, but she just did not figure. Sure it had crossed my mind that the death of Erika von Plaack would mean the death of *Ms. Chief,* that the death of *Ms. Chief* would mean that Samantha had no place to go but home. Her fall into my arms, however, would be a side-effect, an accident, as if while singing in the bathtub you were to hit a note that shattered the antique vial in which your great-grandmother had hidden her pearls. That's what I told myself, to the extent I talked to myself at all during the quiet hours I spent stretched out on my bed, loose, relaxed, dozing, watching the rowdy images that capered before my mind as though I were not even there, never mind inspecting them with the musing cool of a sated connoisseur.

At four o'clock I ate lunch, a light one, on the chance of a stomach wound, for experience had taught me that murder is sometimes dangerous to the murderer. At six o'clock I did some loosening-up exercises, to loosen up. The hot shower on my trapezius hurt enough to make it feel good. I shaved off my mustache, for I was through with disguises. My naked face did not look as I had expected it to look, or as it had ever looked before. I looked younger, for one thing. I looked, let us say, as the man I had become would look if he had shed seven years, rather than as the man I was had looked seven years before his wife left him. By 8:30 I was driving Bill's station wagon (now mine) to Mrs. Seeling's house, and if no one was following me, why did the same pair of headlights keep peering into my eyes from the rearview mirror? The street behind me, however, was deserted when I turned into the parking lot off Stillman Avenue. By 9:00 I was buying a drink for Charity ("My demon lover!" is how she greeted me). By 9:30 she was asleep, after having made me promise to wake her before 6:00 A.M., so she could get home in time to feed and dress her two daughters before driving them to school. By 10:30 I was rolling through the whispering curtains in the bay window of 33 Gramercy Park East and onto the thick Persian rug.

XIII

MY rubber heels made no noise on the Persian rug. It was when I opened the door to the hall that the noise came, an explosion. Flash, crack, a puff of smoke, a smell of gunpowder, and I reached for my heart, which stopped—but not because of a wound. Dangling by a string from the hall side of the knob was a shredded Party-Popper, as I believe the wretched things are called. Unless she had some-one's thighs clapped around her ears, Erika von Plaack now knew that I had come, and what for, but I also knew she knew, though she knew that too. My predatory prey was no longer downstairs, but she had left her spoor. On top of the heap of Fiji's sketches was a card, decorated with cupids and flowers. It was the kind of card that might come with a basket of fruit. Typed upon it was this sentiment:

> Here is Belladonna, the Lady with rocks,
> The Lady of situations,
> With a stacked pack of cards. Yours is blank,
> Man, hypocrite lecteur—my semblable—ma soeur.
> —Madame Sosostirs

I thought the pun on *blank, Man* was strained, and I did not know what a *soeur* was (for, if you will remember, I fulfilled the language requirement at the School of General Studies with German, not with French); neither could I figure out why she called me a hypocritical lecturer; but I had no trouble working out who the poisonous Lady with rocks was. I started silently up the stairs, my knife drawn.

As I put my foot down on the eighth step, a sudden braying fluttering shriek made me run down to the landing and halfway to the door, riffling Fiji's sketches with my backdraft. The noise had combined the worst features of a donkey's haw and a Bronx cheer, many times amplified. Under the deep pile runner on the eighth step was a Whoopie Cushion, a contraption like a hot water bottle fitted with a noise valve. I continued up the stairway carefully, dilating my pupils to catch what little light there was, on the look-out for suspicious bulges in the runner. Maybe that is why I never noticed the tripwire until it cut into the tender skin of my neck, about the same time as a flash of white light blinded me. I slashed around in front of me with the knife until I could see again, but no one took unfair advantage of my defenseless condition. The camera with a spent bulb was wedged at an angle between two banister posts, but there was no film in it. I knew without looking that my quarry would not be hiding behind the heavy old wooden furniture in the rooms on the second floor. That was too much like something a normal person would do.

There were no booby traps on the second flight of stairs, and no one ambushed me on the third floor landing. By squinting, by looking sideways, I could make out the dim red line along the bottom of the Playroom door. I stole toward it. I nodded to myself as I passed the pier glass, then stopped short, back-stepped. On a shelf at the bottom of the glass was a blue velvet ring box. I picked it up, hesitated, looked around, opened it. A snake jumped out and bit me on the nose. I dropped the box. The snake lay still on the floor. I poked it with the knife and perforated the black paper wrapped around a spring, into one end of which a plastic cobra's head was stuck. I turned the box over. In the slot that should have held a ring was the broken-off piece of my left incisor. I stole up to the Playroom door. Then I stole back to the pier glass and retrieved my knife, which I had placed on the shelf when I pocketed my tooth. While I was at it, I squeezed the snake back into the box and put the box back on the shelf. I stole up to the Playroom door. I braced myself, knife at the ready, and gripped the knob. Then I yanked the door open. A plastic pail full of confetti fell on my head. I did not blink, duck, flinch, or otherwise move a muscle, not when the pail hit me, not when the confetti fluttered down, not when something hard poked me under a shoulder blade, not when a voice right behind me said, "The Corduroy Kid, I presume."

"At your service," I said.

"Come into my parlor," she said, nudging me toward a door across the hall. "And you can keep up your bright sword, for the dew will rust it."

I sheathed my knife. "A pretty line," I said. "Who did you lift it from?"

"The androgynous Bard of Avon," she said. The room into which she herded me was not your everyday parlor, or anything else. Sets of custom-bound volumes filled the floor-to-ceiling bookcases. On the walls between the bookcases were heads of animals with prominent teeth, or horns. In the corners were little statues of nymphs and sprites, and if they weren't made of sugar, they should have been. Looking at them for five minutes straight would give you a toothache. In a showcase under one window was a collection of creepy African masks. In a showcase under the other window was a collection of frilly old dolls with vacant smiles and imbecile eyes. Erika von Plaack marched me up to an easy chair covered with red leather, such as I had long dreamed of owning.

"Stay put," she said. Then, from a distance: "About face,

plotz, keep your hands on the arm rests," and that's what I did. She was standing behind a desk about the size of a snooker table and wearing a warm-up outfit that matched her slate blue eyes. She sat and put her feet up on the desk at an angle, presumably so that she could shoot at me without damaging her boots. These were of soft thick brown leather and with rolled-over tops, the kind you associate with D'Artagnan. On the wall behind her hung a painting of a young man in a flight jacket, World War II vintage. He had pale hair, pale eyes, a straight nose, thin lips, and an air of idealistic ferocity—another blond beast. Right under the painting were a pair of crossed spear-heads, each about two feet long. She twirled the pistol on a finger, placed it on the desk, and spun it halfway across the polished top toward me. I had last seen that nastily little stain-less steel automatic in a drawer in a night table next to the bed on which Jude Karnofsky died. Erika von Plaack leaned back, clasped her hands behind her head, and smiled brilliantly, showing too much teeth.

"You can take a fling at rushing me, if you'd like," she said. "But I give you fair warning that I've got quick hands and a dead eye. I once shot a javelina in the snout at this range. The slug travelled up its nasal cavity and into the brain."

"What's a javelina?" I said.

"A kind of pig," she said.

"That's not much of a gun," I said, as though I knew anything about it. "You've got a fifty-fifty chance of missing, if I bob and weave. And even if you hit me, I've got a fifty-fifty chance of getting my knife into you."

"Numbers make my head swim," she said. "What kind of odds does that add up to, overall?"

"Three-to-one against your coming out of it with an intact liver," I said.

"All right, I'll play," she said. "Your move."

Nuts to that. Having an eye out for risks is not the same thing as being a compulsive gambler.

"Good," she said, showing all her teeth again, and I must say that the lips framing them were perfect, although I realize, of course, how much tastes differ. "I've been hoping we could have a little talk before I killed you."

"What made you decide it was me you wanted to kill?" I said.

"Do you really want to know?" she said. "We've got more important things to talk about."

"I'd appreciate it," I said.

"Well now, let's see," she said. "This and that decided me. Lots of little thises and thats. Everybody kept coming to me with bits and pieces that no one else was in a position to fit together—which is how I wanted it. From the beginning I meant to save you for myself."

"I'm flattered," I said.

"You should be, wise guy," she said. "I had plenty of competition, and we have yet to decide what you're worth, if anything. Maybe if you're not worth killing, I'll sentence you to Muriel Bigalow for life. It would only be poetic justice, you know. You turned her head until she didn't know whether she was coming or going, and the poor dear's not ever likely to get it back on straight. She went stiff as a board again when she heard about Stevie's death."

"I never knew her any other way," I said.

"Then there's my houseboy, who is probably chasing around after you right now," she said. "You ought to kiss my feet in gratitude that he hasn't caught up to you yet."

"Okay," I said.

"He'd take you apart with no nevermind who else was around," she said. "He had begun to love little Tobias like a son, and a damned good father he'd make."

"And all the time I thought he was queer," I said.

"What's that got to do with it?" she said.

"How old would he have let Toby get before he stopped loving him like a son?" I said.

"You *are* a pip-squeak," she said, shaking her head. "At least you needn't worry about him disturbing us, because I told him I wanted the house to myself until dawn."

"I suppose you think I ought to kiss your ass for that," I said. "That's okay with me too."

"And Stevie would have tumbled to you sooner or later," she said. "She saw a guy in corduroy at the convention watching Jude and then nearly ran into a guy who looked something like him outside Jude's husband's pad. Like all blow-hards and blow-tops, she was easily flustered. She didn't think to go back and check the nameplates, or she would have been reminded that her rival for the divine Samantha lived there; but I hadn't ever forgotten. Then Stevie got herself in such a state when your turtle dove agreed to nest with her that she couldn't think of anything else. Ah love, it's grand, but dangerous too. It's an affliction I've managed to avoid since my father died."

"You have my sympathy," I said.

"Save it," she said. "Who needs it?" She sighed. "Listen: if you've got nothing better to offer than bargain-basement bromides, I might as well shoot you now. I can get all of those I want from your dear, dim Samantha. Her deepest instincts, by the way, which lie about a quarter-inch beneath her pretty skin, will always be those of a conventional little hausfrau. She still maintains what amounts to a proprietory interest in you—did you know that?"

"I'm glad to hear it," I said.

She put her hands down, into her lap, and stared at a window, which like the other, was shrouded in drapes. "Still, it's mainly because her account of you was so at odds with what you've been doing that I wanted our little talk," she said.

"What did she say?" I said.

"I kept turning it over and over in my mind," she said. She turned her face to me. "It was important for me to know." She put her feet down. "The question was whether or not you were a genuine case of self-transformation." She leaned forward on the desk. "I wanted to know, for my own sake. I wanted to know whether it could be done. So far the prince has always turned into a frog, rather than the other way around—and that goes for the princess too." She caught up with herself, smiled slowly, broadly, leaned back. "I don't want you to get the wrong idea. As for self-discovery, self-awareness, self-realization, self-authentication, all that's a canard—a duck, to you. Cigarette?"

She opened a tin box of custom-built smokes, threw me one, took one for herself, stuffed it into her long silver holder. "I can never remember to keep matches about me," she said, patting the pockets of her warm-up jacket. "And I always lose lighters."

Taking a chance, I walked over and lit her cigarette. "Thanks," she said, never glancing at the pistol, keeping her eyes on mine. I went back to the chair. She put her feet up on the desk again.

She inhaled deeply, then let the smoke flow out over her lip and into her nostrils. "Where were we?" she said. "Oh yes: a detective friend told me about the corduroy under Jude's fingernails—and you can thank the patron saint of clowns that this friend didn't get to you first, or you'd be rehearsing your snotty repartee six feet under. Can you tell me," and here she blew a smoke ring, "how it is that a stumblebum like you manages to land on his feet all the time?"

"Luck was with me, and promises to stay with me," I said. "By luck I mean the tendency of things. The way of the world. Nature."

"Aha!" she said. "Now we're getting somewhere. You realize, don't you, that all human greatness is achieved against nature, *à rebours?*"

"I realize that a queer is bound to think so, or at least pretend to," I said.

"Queer!" she said. "Queer, what do you mean *queer?* Just who the hell are you calling a queer?"

"You're a queer," I said.

Without dropping her legs, and the woman was amazingly limber (and fast), she bent forward like some Yoga nut, snatched up the pistol, and pointed it at my already damaged nose, her elbow propped on the desk, one hand bracing the other. I concentrated on her trigger finger, waiting for it to contract, wondering whether I could move my head to the side (like a Balinese dancer) fast enough to duck the bullet.

"You've got some explaining to do, Buster," she said. "And you better be damn careful what you say."

"I stumblebummed in on you last night," I said. It is not easy to sound abject with dignity, but that was my intent.

She did not move for a long time, maybe twenty seconds. Then she lifted her head from the line of sight. "I see," she said. She let her gun hand droop toward the desk. "Don't you believe in knocking?" She let go of the gun and sat back. "Just what do you think you saw last night?"

"I saw you making like a queer," I said.

She stiffened, held her breath, then let it out, slowly. "Why do I bother?" she said. She studied my face in a way that reminded me of Miss Lily. "What you saw last night was a woman trying to take her mind off the death of her closest relative and best friend, the one person who knew or cared enough to nurse a teen-age girl through periodic fits of suicidal depression—and he no more than a teen-ager himself, and no stranger to fits of suicidal depression either."

"You still were doing it the way a queer does it," I said, not entirely pleased with the sound of my voice. Darwin never mentioned what evolutionary purpose was served by the female instinct for putting a male in the wrong.

"I am not a queer!" she said in a shout. When she slammed her hand on the desk I thought for a second that she had shot me.

I did a little shouting myself. "What would *you* call it? Go ahead, shoot me: at least I won't have to listen to doubletalk about bisexuality. You want to know what a bisexual is? A bisexual is a homosexual who goes down under the prevailing heterosexual weather. A bisexual is a disectual, two halves each wishing it was the other."

"I am not a homosexual" (slam) "and I am not a bisexual" (slam, slam), she said.

"What are you then?" I said.

"A supersexual," she said.

I was so dumbfounded that I forgot to sneer.

She lit a fresh cigarette from her stub, but neglected to offer me one. "Little girls who love their fathers never grow up to become lesbians," she said, and with her cigarette she pointed wearily at the trumped-up Ace hanging over her. She stuffed her cigarette into the holder and then suddenly thrust out her arm to aim the smoking tip at my nose. "And are you going to sit there and tell me that when you were all Portnoy and pimples you never let the local queer give you a blow-job?"

As a matter of fact, I had not, but only because the other guys never asked me along when they went to look at his dirty movies. "Whoever got the blow-job," I said, "I was not the one who gave it. Whether or not you cross that border makes all the difference there is. It's like death on the other side—you can never come back."

"No lapdog like you will ever understand what it cost me to cross that border," she said.

"Then why do it?" I said.

"To see if I could," she said. "To derange my senses. To create a new nervous system. To further my project of self-mastery, self-conquest, self-transformation. To become a complete person, a complete feminist. To strike a blow for human freedom. To assert the human in us over the animal. To express my contempt for mere biology. You want more? I crossed that border because I refuse to be bound. Because I can't resist a risk. Because it was the most difficult thing I could think of doing among those things not impossible of achievement. Because I wanted to prove that human sexuality is a will, not a fate. Because I want my epitaph to be not that I submitted to my destiny, but that I shaped it. Because I wanted to show that a woman could put into practice all these slogans preached by men. Because I knew that if I could go down on a woman, I could do anything. Go ahead, you can laugh if you want."

"Can you stand on the edge of a cliff without having to fight an urge to jump?" I said, moving in for the kill.

"No," she said.

"One part of you wants to jump," I said. "Another part resists. Which is more heroic: to overcome the urge, or the resistance to it? Which is more cowardly: to submit to the resistance, or to the urge?"

"I did not submit to any urge, you can bet your cowboy boots on that," she said.

"There had to be an urge, or there would have been no resistance, and therefore nothing to overcome," I said.

She studied my face. "Let's try a little experiment," she said. "Sit back, relax, that's right, close your eyes, that's the boy. Now: imagine taking some guys' joint in your mouth. Close your eyes, I said. And I mean really imagine it—the colors, the texture, the smell, the taste, the drop of moisture—"

"Stop!" I said. "I can't do it, no more than I can imagine my own extinction. The mind goes blank."

"You don't say," she said. "Pray tell me, then, which would take more courage—more self-mastery, a more heroic will—: to overcome the resistance, or the urge? To go down or not to go down?"

"In my case there was no urge," I said.

"There had to be an urge, or there would have been no resistance," she said.

"For God's sake, will you let me have a cigarette?" I said.

"In a minute," she said. "I'm waiting for your answer."

"It's different for a woman," I said.

"Bah," she said.

"All right," I said. "Let's agree that you overcome the public compulsion to heterosexuality. You did it so that you could submit to a private impulse toward lesbianism."

"Oh, I see," she said. "You mean something like the process through which a Milquetoast becomes a mass murderer. Now I get it. You mean something like the inward struggle through which the champion of womanly women becomes a lady-killer. So *that's* it: an unleashing of the dog beneath the skin. Here, Fido, catch," and she sent a cigarette end over end through the twenty feet of space between us, until it came down to hit me on the snout.

"You're an interesting person," I said. Inadequate—I know: but the best I could manage.

I tried to match her cheeky smile, but I do not think I succeeded. The attempt reminded her of something, however. "Yes, I saw you last night, you with your face hanging out like a purple balloon. Your mouth was open. A tooth was broken. That clinched it. There: now you know how I decided you were the Corduroy kid, alias Ms. Victoria Grunt. Satisfied?"

"It was good of you to answer so fully," I said.

"Don't be such a smart-ass," she said. "It so happens that I'm in the mood to talk." She blew another smoke ring. "You know, it's as though we were husband and wife, with you home tired from a hard day of loafing at the office. Except, by Jesus, you'll damn well listen to every word I say, or I'll shoot you."

"Here I thought we were going to talk about me," I said. "And then you won't let me get a word in edgewise."

She got up, stretched, walked around to the front of the desk, rested her back against it, studied me. Then she came to a decision. She walked over, leaned her hands on mine, where they lay on the armrests, bent forward until our noses nearly touched, spoke in a low voice. "Haven't you grasped the fact that there is no need for either of us to hold anything back? Don't you see what a rare opportunity we have, you and I? We can bare out souls to each other without fear of consequences.

Before this night is over, one of us will carry the other's secrets to the grave."

"All right," I said. "I'll play."

And so began the most interesting and intimate conversation I have ever had, or ever will have, except when I play it over again (and again and again) in my head, unless we are to consider these memoirs a conversation. It was not long before we were both out of our seats, pacing the floor at all angles to each other, waving our arms for emphasis or in exasperation, dropping ashes on the rug. There were times we stood chin-to-chin, her sharpened fingernail poking holes in my chest, as, for example, when she pointed out that in the whole line-up of Watergate sneak-thieves there was not a single woman, except for Rose Mary Woods, who, typically, was just taking the heat for her boss. This was in response to my remark that the superior virtue of women was an illusion, that they would be as corrupt and competitive as men, if given a chance, that if the world were put in their hands, they would fumble it too. There were times we walked in rapid circles around the open center of the room, my hands in my pockets, she tugging me along by a grip on my arm, gesturing with her free hand. Was it fair? she said—and if I knew what was good for me I'd give her a straight answer—was it fair that one-half of humanity was denied an opportunity for adventure? Once I grabbed her slim, firm arms and shook her. Was it fair? I said, was it fair that a man will love a woman for herself alone, namely her body, but that a woman always loves a man for something else? Foo, she said. For his wealth? I said, for his energy, his intelligence, his social position? Suppose it's true, she said. What's to blame? Answer me that. Estrogen, I said. Testosterone.

She got me to tell her all about myself, more than I have told you, and what business of yours is it anyway, more than I knew there was to tell. I told her how when I had just backed a few years into my teens I ran away from home and became a dishwasher; how a kindly short-order cook taught me his craft; how I assumed he had never married simply because he was shy and backward with women, until he offered me a room in his mother's house rent-free, and I discovered how forward he could become, once I was where he wanted me. I told her of other humiliations with older men and younger women during the years I worked in a series of greasy spoons; how I read the wrong books every night in the Forty-second Street library; how finally I passed the High School Equivalency Test; how I saved every penny I didn't need to keep my 130 pounds stumblebumbling along; how I planned to go to college, become a journalist, expose chicanery in high places. I told her how I enrolled in the School of General Studies and worked myself up from stock clerk to manager of the Columbia Bookstore; how I met Samantha, whose first words to me, one day after a class, were "Say, could you lend me ten bucks?"; how her acceptance of my proposal was clear proof to the world and to myself that I was not a worm. Erika von Plaack understood everything. That much I was sure of, from her gestures, her questions, her exclamations. Whether she sympathized or not is another matter. She clapped me on the back, as a man does, when she told me that of all evils, self-pity was the worst.

She was fascinated by my training regimen, especially my accomplishments in self-hypnosis. We held hands, like kids playing London Bridge, so she could feel me put a fever in my right hand, a chill in my left. She looked into my eyes while I dilated my pupils. She sat on my stomach while I lay stretched between desk and desk-chair, my heels resting on one, my neck on the other. She asked if this meant I could maintain an erection all night long. Damn near, I said, not quite truthfully. She applauded when I did a left-handed one-handed push-up, and she admitted that such feats of purely physical strength were beyond her. So far she had admitted very little else about herself. (She wanted to talk; of that I was sure; but she also wanted to be coaxed; of that I was convinced, for in spite of everything, she was a woman; of that there was no doubt. Or is it possible, dear friends, that even Erika von Plaack was bashful?) But when I said there was no such thing as purely physical strength, that all strength was strength of character, she asked me if I had ever read André Gide. Wasn't he a queer? I said. Her face froze over. But when she saw mine, she started to smile. When I started to smile in return, she deftly back-handed me in the groin. I bent over. She kicked me in the behind. I straightened up. She left-hooked me in the stomach. I bent over. She goosed me. I straightened up. She tickled my ribs. I bent over. She leaped onto my back and grabbed my ears. Giddy-up, she said.

I straightened slowly, in stages, so that she could hoist herself onto my shoulders. As we posted around the room, like a poltergeisted totem pole, she talked. She told me how when she had just recoiled a few years into her teens, she was inspired by a character of Gide's, an adventurer, a rogue, a picaro, an unconscious androgyne named Lafcadio. She told me how, like Lafcadio, she devised pitiless rules of conduct for herself, set herself harrowing tasks; how she would stab herself in the thigh for any infraction or failure, and she had the scars to prove it. Show me, I said. She reached down, put one hand over my mouth, the other over my eyes. Reach forward, she said; pull out a book, any book, open it anywhere, turn it upside down. I did so. At a normal rate of speed, her breath tickling my ear, she said these words:

> Experience, already reduced to a swarm of impressions, is ringed around for each of us by that thick wall of person-ality through which no real voice has ever pierced on its way to us, or from us to that which we can only conjec-ture to be without.

Now look, she said, removing her hands. I turned the book right side up. She had read the first complete sentence on the page, word perfect.

Take another book, any book, she said; hold it up, over there, in front of the mirror. I did so. Rapidly, slightly out of breath, she read, "Man doth not yield himself to the angels, not unto death utterly, save only through the weakness of his feeble will." Over there, she said, steering me with her knees and a tug on my ear. As I cantered by the desk, she bent over, like Attila spitting a burgermeister, and picked up two marker pens. She steered me to the painting of her father. Whoa, she said. With her arms stretched, she wrote with both hands at the same time. On the wall to the left of the painting, she wrote, *Non amo te. Sabidi; nec possum dicare quare.* On the wall to the right of the painting, she wrote *Das Ewig Weibliche Zieht uns hinan.* Then she wrote again with both hands simultaneously, but this time she wrote on the wall to the left of the painting what she had before written on the right, and vice versa; and this time she wrote upside down, in perfectly formed letters. Can you do that? she said. I started to say What for? but she was already talking. The floodgates were open.

She told me how until she was eleven, when her father died (for which she would never forgive him), she was Daddy's queen and huntress, chaste and fair. See that doll? she said; it arrived on the day she was born, sent from a South Pacific Island, where her father was stationed near the end of World War II. And that doll, no, that one, was sent from Korea two hours before her father soared off into the wild blue yonder on his last fatal mission. Between wars, he took her with him wherever he went on business (for the von Plaacks were merchants and importers), or if for some reason she had to stay behind, he sent her a doll. A number of the dolls had interesting pedigrees, which she told me. Her grandfather tried heroically to continue her father's program for her education, which was designed to turn her into a kind of universal genius, but Grandpa had been a rake-hell for too long to change. He found it impossible to tear his attention away from hunting and women for more than three days at a time. She went on safaris with him, and she stayed with him at fashionable resorts while he hunted loose ladies of international notoriety. Her aunt,

Peter Brevoort's mother, a divorcée, was one of them. Grandpa had been given that mask, the one in the middle, by a tribe whose soccer team he sponsored, and that was only one day before a dying impala put a horn through the head of the most entertaining old gentleman she had ever known. She patted the bust of a mild-eyed grass-eater with scimitar horns.

Poor Momma, she said. Sometimes her mother looked at her as though trying to remember who she was. To the end her mother remained faithful to her calling (her father had been a minister), which was the rehabilitation of nineteenth-century statuary. She felt that a fickle drift of fashion had unjustly devalued the stuff (and with it an ancestor of hers, who manufactured oodles of it). She dithered her way up and down Europe, dragging precocious Erika along, looking for pieces to display in her otherwise deserted gallery. Sometimes they travelled with her mother's sister, Peter Brevoort's full-bodied and flamboyant mother. While Erika's mother visited decaying mansions and overgrown gardens, while Peter's mother visited well-appointed playboys, the children stayed behind at some pension or spa, getting into mischief, putting Limburger cheeses behind the dining room radiators or gin into the carafes of sulfur-water, playing Russian roulette with a debauched Egyptian princeling, who lost. All this time, Erika read and read and read, up to twelve hours a day, but seldom spent more than two months together at any school. She must have read half the books in her great-grandfather's very decent library, for he had been a merchant of the old school, a pressed flower of high bourgeois culture, a composer of occasional verse, in Latin. Then, as the sixties were drawing to a close, when Erika was already a quarter-century old, her mother died, leaving her daughter in sole possession of a considerable fortune. But she didn't know what to do with it, or with herself.

She dismounted, gave my neck a pat ("Good old Rosinante," she said), walked behind the desk, lit two cigarettes, and handed me one. She leaned against the wall, under *Das*

Ewig-Weibliche, etc. I was pleased to discover that her thigh had massaged away the ache in my trapezius. She spoke quickly now, as though time were running short. What were her options? she said. The family business was out. It was not her style to splash in someone else's bathwater. She already had all the money she needed, and why would anyone go into business, if not to make money? Power? She had no desire to control people; she wanted to lead them, but only by example. She wanted, that is, not so much to lead, as to be followed. Politics were out, because she was too particular about whose hand she would shake. Law, all the usual professions, were out, because (for starters) she had never been ground through any diploma-mill. Anything that required mathematics was out, because no one had taught her any since her father died. There were worthy causes around for her to take up, but she distrusted people who gave themselves to causes not their own. Their motives were unclean. Music was out, because she had a tin ear. Painting was out, because she could not paint. She had tried to write, but she did not have the patience or obsessions that made for great writing. Of the other kind there was already enough. (Journalism was not writing.) Besides, she wanted to grip the world directly, through action, rather than indirectly, through words. Exploration was out, because there was nothing left to explore. She might have become an athlete. In fact, she had already won fencing matches in four countries. But athletics were for the young, and what she was after was a life, not an episode. Acting? Modelling? She would rather become a prostitute outright. Halfway measures were not in the family tradition.

How about marriage? I said. To whom? she said. Well, it was not the kind of question you could answer right off the bat. Suppose she did get married, she said. What then? Grease the career of some aspiring boob with her charm? with her money? Sponsor charity balls? Preside at a salon? Waste away in conspicuous consumption? Collect painters? Breed dogs? Show horses? Tyrannize the servants? Take it out on the children?

Blunt her purpose, dull her edge, in cutting her husband down to size? Run away to join some nest of ninnies in a commune? I saw her point, I said. But what a mistress she would have made, I said—an adornment and an instigation for dashing, dangerous men, such as racing-car drivers, revolutionaries with prices on their heads, Existentialists with lung cancer. I had a one-track mind, she said. Well, she had thought of that. She had even tried it. But after a while you feel tarnished. And such men lose their dash overnight. Besides, from the beginning she had decided against shining in reflected light; she wanted to do such things that dashing, dangerous men would come to her. Not likely, I said, not once she had become the Queen Bee of American Feminism. Was I kidding? she said. I had just proved again, as though proof were needed, that the one constant in a transitory world of fading illusions is the stupidity of men. Could anyone be so obtuse as not to see that feminism is also a form of flirtation? Among other things, it was a last resort of women who could not get men to notice them otherwise. I admitted that the idea had never occurred to me.

We were walking slowly around the room now, she a half-step in advance, my hand on her shoulder. No, she said, there was only one profession, and that was closed to her. There was only one career for which she was fit, as a plug is for its socket. Only one career that would have been a worthy test for her discipline, her daring, her designs on the world, her capacity for grace under pressure. And that profession was closed to her for the most arbitrary of reasons—her sex. What she was cut out to be was a soldier. She turned to look at me, but I was careful to nod sympathetically. She did not mean a WAC or a WAVE, she said, typists in uniform; she meant someone who shot and was shot at. She had even gotten in touch with mercenaries, but they wouldn't take her, although they offered to take her money. She stopped and spun around to face me. Now did I see why women became feminists?

Women's Liberation came along just when she needed it.

And she had better not hear me refer to it as Women's *Lib!* It was not that feminism removes obstacles, uncovers opportunities—it is itself the opportunity. All true feminists do nothing but feminism, whatever their jobs. You do not become a true believer as a means to something else. That is why the movement, like all revitalization movements, attracts so many misfits, so much of the human flotsam floating about. It lifts from their bent and sinking shoulders the burden of deciding how to live. Erika von Plaack saw her role right away. Her role was to give it style, to give it humor, generosity, yes, go ahead and laugh, to give it nobility. She was just the woman to substitute the playful growl for the plaintive whine, the expansive gesture for the cringe and yowl. Did I know the Greek word *megalopsychia?* It is sometimes translated as "aristocratic pride," but its literal meaning is "great-souledness." Aristotle called it the highest of the practical virtues. Heroic self-possession would be her contribution to feminism. She wanted women to follow her lead, and then men to follow women. She had no intention of haggling with men over rights. Her plan was to shame them out of their hoggishness and conceit. Her calling was to liberate women until their lives were a reproach to everything petty, small, mean, and miserly—namely men.

That was five years ago. Today she was America's most conspicuous feminist. Did I know that a firm had asked for rights to market a doll in her image? They wanted to call it "The Pacifier," complete with boots and whip. She sighed. We had unwound ourselves down into the red leather chair. She sat on my lap. My chin rested on her head. I could feel her words vibrate through my skull. She blew a smoke ring, then blew another through it, then a third through the second. Something had gone wrong, she said. No one had changed. Letting it all hang out is nowhere near what she had meant by self-transformation. For all her followers, she had only one disciple, the grim and gorgeous Kathleen—who mistook a kind of impetuous ferocity in revenge for heroic virtu.

Erika von Plaack understood very well the attractions of revenge. Hadn't Jude's murder yanked her, as by the hair, out of a chronic low-grade depression? Revenge, too, was an opportunity, a career, a revitalization cult—but for isolatoes. No doubt I knew what she meant. For a few days she had sailed on a crest of resurgent energies, which broke on the first issue of *Ms. Chief.* She suddenly felt beached, but had no idea why. In her bewilderment she studied her reflection in the magazine. She took stock. She saw that in her relations to other feminists she had become a common scold; in her relations to men she had become a prankster, a practical joker, a mere mischief-maker. But these were only the symptoms of an inner resistance. Behind the resistance she could just make out the specter of a question come back to haunt her. It was the immaterial weight of this question that had been depressing her. The question, an old one, is not the kind you ask if you want to accomplish something great; she had buried it when she embraced feminism. But now it had risen from the pits of her mind to possess her entirely. Suppose every consistant feminist goal were achieved. Suppose women achieved complete social, political, and economic equality. Suppose they achieved what was infinitely more difficult, complete equality in the consciousnesses of all men and women. Suppose all sexist ideologies and superstitions were banished forever. *Would one single thing of importance be different?* The answer to that question shriveled her entrails.

"You shouldn't let it get to you," I said. "All human effort is futile."

Apparently I had said the wrong thing again. She slapped her hands on the armrests, pulled herself to her feet, and walked toward the desk. "About time we got down to it," she said. She unhooked one of the spearheads crossed under the portrait. "I spent all afternoon sharpening it," she said. "You've got to use two hands and bear down, if you want a good job." There were maybe eighteen inches of blade and six inches of shank, a nifty little two-edged sword. "Draw, Podner," she said.

I stood up and drew my knife. "It's a shame," I said. "I don't like to kill good-looking women. There's not enough of them to go around. But you shouldn't have put an ice pick into my best friend, not while he was asleep."

"You measure everyone by yourself," she said, taking off a boot. "I haven't killed anybody. Not yet."

"Erika," I said. "I thought we weren't going to hold anything back."

"Oh, 'Erika,' is it?" she said. She took off her other boot and slammed the two of them down on the table. "Since we're so cozy, how come you're accusing me of murdering a man unarmed and in his bathrobe?

"Who killed him, then?" I said.

"How should I know?" she said. For some reason it gave me a shock to see that her feet were bare. She had not been wearing socks under her boots. "And who cares?" she said. Her feet were high-arched, brawny, and compact. I liked them. "I thought you did it," she said. I liked in particular that they did not splay or flatten when she put her weight on them. "What's one more corpse to a desperado like you?" she said.

"Ever do any ice skating?" I said

"What did you have to kill Pete for?" she said. "Jude was a dope, and Stevie was a beast. But Pete, Pete was . . . a good guy."

"I believed you," I said. "Now you've got to believe me. I did not kill Pastor Peter Brevoort."

"Then who did?" she said. Her face was twisted by a half-smile of appeasement, guilt, and fear: a child who sees the blow coming.

"He killed himself," I said.

"Shit." she said.

"I was there," I said. "I would have stopped him if I could."

"Shit. Shit. Shit," she said. Then she took a deep breath and straightened her shoulders. And there was the brilliant smile again. She turned to the portrait, kissed the flat of her blade, and raised it to her father. *"Morituri te salutamus,"* she said.

We walked toward each other, to the open center of the room.

"Who was that woman I saw you with last night?" I said.

"That was no woman—now, wouldn't you like to know," she said.

We touched the tips of our blades.

It was then that I noticed that Erika von Plaack was left-handed. My strategy came to me in a flash. I would circle to the left, like Muhammed Ali. She would have to reach for me past her own body, I reasoned, while I wore her down with jab-stabs to her right arm and side. Except that she had already slashed my jacket across, breastpocket high. Before I could blink, she had slashed across my jacket again, sidepocket low. Before I could wonder if my innards were hanging out, she slashed up, at an angle, with the motion of a fisherman rearing back to cast a fly, and I felt my pants sag, for she had cut through my belt, not to mention pants, shirt, and jacket. My body revised my strategy for me. As it started to bolt, she slashed off a shoulder pad. As I pivoted sharply on my right foot and shot off my left, I felt the wind of her blade as she vented my jacket from collar to hem.

She chased me once around the desk. On the second turn I threw a boot at her. She chopped through it, at the instep. In one frantic motion I ripped the portrait off the wall and flung it. She split it down the middle and was striding through the pieces before they hit the ground. I back-pedalled, pulling books off the shelves and hurling them at her. She hacked them to either side, backhand and forehand, as though fighting her way through a flock of killer pigeons. Chunks of books, whole covers and pages, strips of leather and paper filled the air. I ducked in back of a showcase. Her cutlass whistled behind me, nipping a leg of my pants and amputating a leg of the showcase, which tilted, fell, and shattered, spilling dolls and broken glass.

I scuttled behind the other showcase. Before I could heave it over on her, the spearhead crashed down through the glass top, where a micro-second before my hand had been. The tip of her blade lodged in the eye socket of a mask with a long, doleful face. As with a jerk of her wrist, she shook the mask off, I lunged for her midsection. But I never reached it. With a clang her blade came down hard across the back of my knife, which dropped from my fingers. I spun away, looking for a window to jump out of. "You forgot something," she said. She was backing off, pointing to my knife with the spearhead, struggling to keep a straight face, or at least pretending she was. As I approached and stooped to pick up the knife, I saw that her toes were cut and bleeding. "I don't suppose you'd like to talk some more?" I said. But she was already cutting figure-eights in the air, her spearhead noisy as a bullroarer. "I thought not," I said.

She backed me into a corner. I reached behind me for the statuette of a pubescent Diana and thrust it at her face. With a backhand slash she decapitated it. With a forehand she cracked it in half. I threw the rest of it at her feet. She jumped straight up. I lunged for her navel. She caught my wrist. She stabbed for my neck. I caught her wrist. We stood face to face, our arms crossed between us, her right hand around my right wrist, my left hand around her left wrist, neither of us able to let go, both of us pushing toward the other and pushing away the other at the same time, a fierce grin on her face. A middling-strong man, however, is stronger than an unusually strong woman. She was forced to give way, step by grudging step, across the room, until her back was against the wall, under the bust of a tusky warthog.

I thought of stomping on her toes, but refrained, for chivalry is catching. Instead I bunched up and pushed, slowly, steadily, mindlessly, until I saw the point of my knife dimple her jacket, then nudge through it, just far enough to draw blood. My arm recoiled, as from an electric shock. I was aghast (or something) at what I had done, as though it was all right to try, but not to succeed. "Erika," I said, for some reason shouting. "Listen. Blood has been shed. Honor requires nothing more." She was grinning with gritted teeth. She raised a knee, as though to let me have it in the fork. But she didn't. She planted her foot against the wall and pushed off it mightily and with a twist, at an angle to my right. At the same time she tugged my knife hand toward my left. And at the same time she hooked with her spear hand toward the side of my neck. I understood immediately what she was trying to do. She was trying to use my strength against me. If I had been thrusting with my knife, it would have passed harmlessly by her. If I had been pushing against her spear hand, I would have hastened its progress toward my neck. But I was not pushing or thrusting. I had simply locked my muscles, when I made my pitch for a truce. I hardly moved at all, therefore. But she moved far too much. She had impaled herself on my knife, a good six inches' worth.

She dropped her right hand. I released her left, as she sagged, and caught her by the armpits. She assumed the unmistakable attitude of a woman who expects to be kissed. Let me tell you, Ladies and Gentlemen, that was some kiss. I had pretty well disappeared into it when a terrific pain in my neck pulled me back. Another half inch frontward, and Erika von Plaack would have severed my carotid. Naturally, I opened my eyes. Her eyes were already open. The spearhead thumped on the rug. One thing you never want to do, my friends, is look into someone's eyes while the intelligence seeps out of them, for good.

I laid her out on the desk and crossed her hands on her breast. One eye was open and the other was half-closed, as though she were winking, so I pressed her eyelids down. But the same eye winked half open again. I put the spearhead in the crook of her left elbow and the Korean doll in the crook of her right. What is done is done, past undoing; I was in no mood to deal with Butch; so I hurried. I picked up the ribbons and rags

of my jacket and wiped off fingerprints. In a well-stocked medicine cabinet, I found a Band-Aid large enough to cover the
wound on my neck. In Butch's well-stocked closet, I found a
denim suit, the real thing, not almost-matching jeans and coat,
and it fit me to a T. He did not have a red-and-white striped
rugby-style shirt, but he did have a blue-and-red striped body
shirt. I tied one of his ascots over the Band-Aid. On the way
out, I picked up the camera, the Whoopie Cushion, and the
Party Popper. I threw them into an umbrella-holder cut from
an elephant's foot. The police could make what they would out
of the plastic pail and confetti, the ring box, and the snake. I
strolled out the door with the air of someone on his way to
work, hat down over my eyes. No one was about, that I could
see, except for the Gramercy Park gardener, getting an early
start. But he had his back turned to me.

I walked ten blocks north and east, discarding my damaged
clothes on the way. Then I caught a cab to the Bliss Street
subway station in Sunnyside. I walked to the whorehouse,
climbed in the window, woke up Charity. The time was 5:45.
"Sure I can't do anything for you?" she said. "No one can do
anything for me," I said. It was not until I was driving crosstown through Central Park that I thought to check what was
in my rearview mirror. There was a cab fifty yards behind me
and a black sedan fifty yards behind the cab. I had to settle for
a space in front of the Grotto Church of Our Dame, over on
Morningside Drive. A parking ticket was the least of my worries. I never could figure out why there's a law against parking
in front of churches anyhow. And for a neighborhood full of
educated people, there's an awful lot of churches around Columbia. As I turned onto my block I saw a black sedan double-
parked across from my doorway.

As I approached the doorway, Butch stepped out. With a
blood-curdling yell he leaped into the air and aimed a kick at
my nose. I moved my head to the side, like a Balinese dancer.
His foot whizzed by my ear. As he tried to retract it, the heel

of his sandal caught on my swollen trapezius. Butch came down, therefore, not on his other foot, but on the back of his head. "I saw that," said Bella's voice, and a car door slammed. I knelt beside Butch, to see how he was (rather than to finish him off). A piece of the suspender holding up my knife sheath parted, for Erika von Plaack had slashed most of the way through it. The sheath turned upside down, for the pommel was heavy, and the knife dropped out, onto a wing of Butch's jacket, by his waist. A wing of Butch's other jacket, the one I was wearing, hid the evidence from Bella and Betty, who were nearly upon us. Butch opened his eyes, turned his head to the side, vomited, turned his head back, said, "You're next," closed his eyes. "I heard that," said Betty. Bella picked up the knife by its finger guard. "What have we here?" he said.

Afterwords

THE leaves have burned them-
selves out. The first dusting of snow has fallen and melted
away. The New York Giants are losing again. Nixon's abdica-
tion is no longer news, but Patricia Hearst is still at large. We
are all looking forward to the big game hunting season, which
opens next week. There has already been an early bow season,
an early black powder season, and an early bear season, during
which Bang brought home a three-hundred-and-fifty pounder.
Last week we slaughtered the first of the hogs. My father says
that if we can "harvest" just two deer, we will not have to buy
any meat all winter.

The loss of a toe has not slowed him down. His limp is
quite distinguished. Every afternoon, before cocktails, he puts
on a tweed jacket over a plaid shirt, and, leaning on a black
cherry cane that Arne Olson made for him, takes Miss Lily for
a stroll. She has been coming up for visits of a week or so all
summer and fall, supposedly to be with Toby. There has been
talk of my father building her a chalet next spring on the four
hundred acres of woodland she bought a few miles south of
here. Thus we end, as we began, with Venus up to her old tricks

again. There is a possibility, I mean, that some day Miss Lily will become my stepmother. There is nothing I can do about it. I've spent twenty-five years wishing for a mother, but not this one. She knows, of course, who killed Erika von Plaack.

It was generous of my father to vacate the Master Bedroom, so that Samantha and I could have it. She and the other women have been busy preserving meat and produce. There is a good deal of quiet laughter, at the expense of men I suspect, as they sit together, canning, salting, drying, smoking meat; slicing jerky, pounding pemmican, pressing cider, shredding cabbage. Samantha is becoming expert in many of the domestic crafts, about which she often writes in her weekly column for women in the *Tannerton Times*. She now understands the distinction between "that" and "which," but refuses to observe it. She has become something of a local figure. A number of people, including the incumbent, have been urging her to run for the job of Vandernut Stage Town Supervisor next fall.

Our relations have changed. She now takes me for granted. Things are settled between us. She has lost her old restlessness and irritability, her impatience with me. Ever since adolescence, I have yearned for some beautiful woman to treat me as a sex object, but I never thought it would be my own wife. As usual, the fact turns out to be different from the fantasy. It's demoralizing is what it is. Sometimes I look up to catch her studying me. Maybe it is just that I look different to her, now she is pregnant with our child, due May 31, as we figure it. Samantha is blooming.

She still gets news from Robin, Tracy, Casey, and Macy, but not so often as at first.

Kathleen Haggerty resigned from the Force, rather than face a full-fledged departmental investigation into the deaths of Gilbert and Rosita Nieves.

Allerton Guth is suing Fiji for divorce. Detectives he hired took pictures of her in bed with another woman. He spends some time nearly every day at Austin Riggs with Muriel

Bigalow. She went all over catatonic again when last month some fool of an attendant told her of Erika von Plaack's death.

Butch is still in a coma. It is unlikely that he will ever be able to stand trial for the murder of Erika von Plaack. There is a question as to whether he had nothing to do with the other murders, everything to do with them, or something to do with them, along with Pastor Peter Brevoort. Samantha and Miss Lily have not granted interviews to people writing books or articles on the case. Neither have I. Inspector La Paloma has implied that only the vigilance of Bella and Betty saved me from becoming the next victim.

Spokespersons for Gay Liberation and for Women's Liberation deny with equal heat that there is a murderous rivalry between them. Chi Chi says that this rumor was planted by the police, who otherwise have professional reasons for preferring to let sleeping dogs lie, meaning Butch. Chi Chi and Fawn visited us around Labor Day, during a strike. They hit it off well with my father, who likes people who like to keep busy, which they are. He offered them a cabin and a promise of steady work. Fawn is willing; she wants to have children. She was tense and stand-offish at first, but Samantha did a good job of thawing and drawing her out. Chi Chi told me privately that he is afraid of going stir-crazy. We all expect him to come around, however. If I can stand it, he can.

Bang knows. There were pictures in the newspapers of the murder weapon, on which traces of Erika von Plaack's blood were found. He has not said anything, of course. But I have come to realize that he knows a lot more about most things than he ever lets on. He got the windmill built, with the help of Jack Longhenry and Hank Littlejohn, young Charlie (with the bad ear), Floyd (at the junk yard), and the latter's son. But he hasn't got it functioning. The inner workings of a windmill are more delicate and complex than any of us realized.

He is very good to Toby, who loves his Uncle Bang. Toby will probably always have a slight stutter. He no longer has an invisible dog named Luke, but a visible one named Blondie, a golden retriever pup. I have a pup myself, a shepherd-husky named Mischief, who follows me everywhere. He is the color of woodsmoke in a snowstorm. Just this last month Toby has begun to call me Dads and Samantha Moms and my father Gramps—to distinguish us, I suppose, from his dead Dad, his dead Mom, his everlasting Grandma. At bedtime I tell him stories of Upsidedownland, where the wolves are meek and the lambs are maneaters. In the morning I wait with him for the yellow bus that takes him to kindergarten. Bang's daughters and Kristal spoil him shamelessly, unlike Samantha.

Patch, the tall, thin cop with the birthmark, finally broke up the Millville-Smuggleton Law Ornament Gang. He also broke the jaw of its leader, the fourteen-year-old son of an alderman. Patch was dispatched. Without letting me in on it, Samantha pressured the Chief into hiring a female replacement. It was time that Tannerton had a policeperson, and Samantha just happened to know of someone who just happened to be available, who was more than qualified, who was anxious, for some reason, to live in the vicinity. One night, while Samantha was writing at her rolltop desk in the "Bedroom" (now her study) that was once furnished with my childhood memories, I drove over to the Stop and Go Inn, where Bang sometimes plays his guitar. Sitting at a table with him was a black-haired beauty, petal-white skin. As we shook hands, Kathleen Haggerty closed one eye, deliberately, broadly, and I believe, threateningly. On her lips was the premonition of a smile. She knows, or guesses maybe. She killed Bill, or maybe not. I won't know for sure until she tries to kill me. The first move will have to be hers. I'm through with preventative murder.

Jude Karnofsky, you never intended to submit Toby to a sex-change operation; you were only the occasion of Samantha's departure, not the cause. I was the cause. Forgive me.

Gilbert Nieves, you would not have been killed by Kathleen Haggerty, if I had not killed Jude Karnofsky. Forgive me.

Rosita Nieves, you would not have been killed by Kathleen Haggerty, as it is sure you were, if I had not killed Jude Karnofsky. Forgive me.

Stevie Dickinson, you may or may not have intended to murder Bill Austin. In any case, forgive me for murdering you, even though you asked for it.

Bill Austin, you would not have been killed—yes, it must have been by Kathleen Haggerty—if I had not killed Jude Karnofsky. I know you have forgiven me already. Haven't you?

Karl Weiner, you would not have killed yourself, not then anyhow, if Peter Brevoort had not accused you of killing Jude Karnofsky, if I had not killed Jude Karnofsky.

Peter Brevoort, you would not have killed yourself, not then anyhow, if Karl Weiner had not killed himself, if I had not killed Jude Karnofsky. I'm sorry, Pete.

Erika von Plaack. Erika von Plaack. O Erika, Erika, what fatality drove us to make war, not love! If my child is a girl, we will name her Erika.

I am not blooming exactly, but I am doing all right. I have changed physically during the last five months, as I have changed otherwise, during the last four, while writing these confessions. (I hardly recognize my own voice, as it sounds through the early pages. I can't say I entirely like it, either.) My wounds have become mere scars. Heavy outdoor work, lifting weights with Bang, sawing wood with my father, have all thickened my chest and shoulders. They have also reduced my agility. I would now find it hard-going to heave myself through the bay window of 33 Gramercy Park East (which is occupied at present by Peter Brevoort's mother). Butch's denim jacket no longer fits me. People tell me that I look more like my father every day. Everybody who works for him knows that sooner or later they will be dependent on my good will. They act accordingly. There is nothing I can do about it. The townspeople, I notice, treat me much as they treat Bang—very carefully.

I have periods of restlessness, naturally, of unassigned

longings. For a few days, when I had just begun writing, I seriously considered running away from home, going underground, tracking down Bernadine Dohrn, Jane Alpert, Kathy Boudin, Cathlyn Wilkerson, Susan Saxe, Katherine Power, Patricia Swinton, and the rest. Middle-aged men are prone to such fantasies. Sometimes they act on them. But I have not allowed myself to forget that I am a son, a husband, a father, an heir, a man with responsibilities, with a position in the world. My biggest responsibility is to my own past desires, for I have gotten what I thought I wanted, almost. No, my time for adventure has passed forever. Besides, there are no more Erika von Plaacks in the world.

For the past six weeks, with the help of my father and Bertil (Bang's brother), I have been supervising a job three miles north of here. A blustery Norwegian, his athletic daughter, and her sheepish husband are converting a lodge and six hundred acres into a winter resort. The lodge, which had been locked up for forty years, belonged to a glove manufacturer who went bust during the Depression. My father contracted to clear and enlarge the pond for ice skating, to open trails for crosscountry skiing, and to build a dozen cabins, each with a Lily-Belle Prefabricated Sauna. I like these Norwegians, who are not out to get rich, but only to make expenses. (They have already talked Samantha into giving skating lessons next year.) To my surprise, I have become pretty good at telling people what to do without offending them, a new talent for me. The work is tiring enough so that I sleep most nights, but it's a waste of my college education. I never think of becoming a journalist any more.

Every evening, at about this time, at dusk, the blustery Norwegian's athletic daughter jogs out of the woods on the other side of the brook. She jogs over the footbridge, across the field, and onto the new patio, where the others have gathered for cocktails and to watch the sun go down. She joins them for a glass of *saft,* a soft drink Kristal makes out of berries. Then she jogs home, along the road. I always watch for her through the window beside my desk, here on the third floor of the north tower, where I sit and write while the others socialize. At first I worked on the book Bill meant me to write, *An Anatomy of Fitness*. And I will write it yet, for my life has become a system of obligations. But before the end of June I had put it aside to pour out these memoirs, and I want you to remember that all the jokes at my expense in them were made by me. She ought to be along any minute now.

There she is. She is out of the woods. She crosses the footbridge, into the last of the sunlight, and her yellow hair bursts into flame. She ascends the field, moving effortlessly in her royal blue sweatsuit, thin face cleaving the wind.